continued . . .

"Author Ace Atkins paints a vivid picture of the decadence and debauchery . . . A thrilling dark ride into the sleaze and brutality of a town in the grip of corruption and crime. [Atkins] does a masterful job of building tension, right down to the final shootout."   —*St. Petersburg (FL) Times*

"The book whips along at a fast clip . . . Atkins' ear for good-ol'-boy dialogue is pitch-perfect, though most of what they say can't be printed here. This is a profane, violent book, filled with people who talk and fight dirty . . . It's an entertaining read, with an evocative style and a distinct sense of place. And it's all the more fascinating for being authentic."   —*The Atlanta Journal-Constitution*

"The tension is taut, the pace brisk, and the dialogue ample and aptly noir. Atkins, though he fictionalizes the account, has done his research and gotten the facts right, doing a commendable job to retell one of the more disturbing, yet interesting, episodes of Alabama history. With *Wicked City*, Ace Atkins also serves up one fine crime thriller. He's been compared to James Ellroy and James Lee Burke, two modern masters of the genre, giving you some idea of his chops."   —*Mobile (AL) Press-Register*

"The novel transports the reader to the Phenix City of a half-century ago: a rat's nest of brothels, gambling dens, clip joints, drug dealers, moonshine whiskey, rigged elections, intimidation, and murder."   —The Associated Press

"A riveting story about how the triumph of evil is forestalled when good men do something . . . Atkins is clearly in love with his colorful characters—on both sides of the moral divide—and makes them wonderfully believable."
                    —*Kirkus Reviews*

"A gripping, superb crime story; all the more remarkable because it really did happen."   —*Library Journal*

White Shadow

"A great crime novel ... Ace Atkins has done a superb job of re-creating old Tampa, a place whose underworld was as dangerous and debauched as Chicago's in its prime."
—Carl Hiaasen

"Ace Atkins makes 1950s Florida as cool and hip as tomorrow in this outstanding novel. It's a stunning achievement and sure to be a book of the year."
—Lee Child

"A sweeping page-turner anchored in a beautifully wrought time and place."
—Laura Lippman

"Mesmerizing ... Wonderful detail of character and history ... A tour de force from one of the best crime writers at work today." —Michael Connelly

"It's atmospheric stuff, spit out in staccato bursts like a rewrite man pounding a Remington on deadline." —*Pittsburgh Post-Gazette*

"A delicious slice of noir ... The dark, twisted plot of *White Shadow* and its complex, often surprising characters make it a fine example of hard-boiled crime fiction, but for anyone who remembers Tampa before the days of chain everything and metastasizing development, it's a fabulous piece of time travel ... *White Shadow* will give you an extra serving of thrills."
—*St. Petersburg (FL) Times*

"How these characters and stories converge to make a history of their own is the heart of a book that is obviously a labor of love ... If you don't end this book wrapped up in their lives like tobacco in an old-time Tampa cigar, you have missed the glory in the tale." —*Rocky Mountain News*

"*White Shadow* is a big, poetic, and muscular novel, as sleek and tough as the stylish characters that inhabit its pages." —George Pelecanos

TITLES BY ACE ATKINS

WICKED CITY

ACE ATKINS

BERKLEY BOOKS, NEW YORK

THE BERKLEY PUBLISHING GROUP
Published by the Penguin Group
Penguin Group (USA) Inc.
375 Hudson Street, New York, New York 10014, USA
Penguin Group (Canada), 90 Eglinton Avenue East, Suite 700, Toronto, Ontario M4P 2Y3, Canada
(a division of Pearson Penguin Canada Inc.)
Penguin Books Ltd., 80 Strand, London WC2R 0RL, England
Penguin Group Ireland, 25 St. Stephen's Green, Dublin 2, Ireland (a division of Penguin Books Ltd.)
Penguin Group (Australia), 250 Camberwell Road, Camberwell, Victoria 3124, Australia
(a division of Pearson Australia Group Pty. Ltd.)
Penguin Books India Pvt. Ltd., 11 Community Centre, Panchsheel Park, New Delhi—110 017, India
Penguin Group (NZ), 67 Apollo Drive, Rosedale, North Shore 0632, New Zealand
(a division of Pearson New Zealand Ltd.)
Penguin Books (South Africa) (Pty.) Ltd., 24 Sturdee Avenue, Rosebank, Johannesburg 2196,
South Africa

Penguin Books Ltd., Registered Offices: 80 Strand, London WC2R 0RL, England

PRINTING HISTORY
G. P. Putnam's Sons hardcover edition / April 2008
Berkley trade paperback edition / April 2009

Berkley Books trade paperback ISBN: 978-0-425-22707-7

The Library of Congress has catalogued the G. P. Putnam's Sons hardcover edition as follows:

Atkins, Ace.
    Wicked city / Ace Atkins.
        p.   cm.
    ISBN 978-0-399-15457-7
    1. Alabama—Fiction.   I. Title.
    PS3601.T487W53   2008   2007032774
    813'.6—dc22

PRINTED IN THE UNITED STATES OF AMERICA

10   9   8   7   6   5   4   3   2

FOR BILLY

You could climb a tall tree, spit in any direction, and where the wind wafted the splutter, there you would find organized crime, corruption, sex and human depravity.

—Edwin Strickland and Gene Wortsman,
Phenix City: The Wickedest City in America, 1955

Woe unto the fighter that goes into battle with the thought of keeping his features regular and his hair parted neatly in the center. He is a sucker for the rough, tough, one-track-minded youngster who carries mayhem in each foot and murder in his heart.

—*Scientific Boxing by a Fistic Expert,* 1936

Many of the large events in this novel are true. However, some characters have been drawn as composites to share space alongside historical figures, and in several instances time has been compressed for brevity. That said, no author could ever exaggerate the sin, sleaze, and moral decay of Phenix City, Alabama, in the fifties or the courage of the people who stood up to fight it.

WELCOME TO PHENIX CITY, *Alabama, population 23,305. Located across the Chattahoochee River from Columbus, Georgia, we offer all the basic amenities of small-town Southern life. There's Cobb's Barber Shop, where kindly gray-headed gentlemen discuss local politics and current affairs between the buzz of the clippers and local radio ag reports. And we have the friendly Elite Café, where Mr. Ross Gibson will cook you up the best plate of eggs and grits with red-eye gravy you ever tasted. We have a small but bustling downtown filled with Seymour's Ready-to-Wear Shop, Bentley's Grocery, the Phenix City Pharmacy, and the wonderful Palace Theater, where on Saturdays a kid can get in for fifty cents and watch the latest B westerns or the new adventures of Francis the Talking Mule. Phenix City also boasts Idle Hour Amusement Park—you can take a miniature train from downtown into the hills and roller-skate, bowl, and swim. There is even a little zoo there with bears and lions and monkeys. All of this mixed with dozens of churches, Christian and civic clubs, and one of the best hospitals in east Alabama make Phenix City an ideal place for the family.*

Not to mention the world-famous nightclubs, clip joints, and brothels. Phenix City is probably known best for its whores.

*We have only the bawdiest of burlesque down on Fourteenth Street.
Many of the acts come in straight from Nevada or Tijuana, showing off
women who can smoke cigarettes and cigars from their privates and dish out
cut-rate favors in back rooms. Perhaps that's the reason we are the chosen
nightspot for GIs in from Fort Benning and the overworked businessman
visiting Atlanta or Columbus.*

*Folks come from all the United States for our games of chance, too. But
don't expect a winner; here in Phenix City every pair of dice is loaded and
every stack of cards marked. And complaints? Yes, sir, we deal with complaints with speed in this Southern town. Usually, unfriendly words from
outsiders are met with the point of a pistol or the blade of a knife slicing
across your throat before being dumped through a trapdoor directly into the
swirling waters of the Chattahoochee.*

*But don't let that worry you. Most of the joints—the Hillbilly Club, the
Atomic Bomb Café, the Bamboo—are more than gambling halls. Almost
all are equipped with back rooms with skinny metal beds, a pillow or two,
and stained mattresses. You could take your pick from the B-girls and the
whores and dancers out on Fourteenth Street and out on Opelika Road,
where the motor courts and trailer parks all work on an hourly rental.*

Any deviant can find the most bizarre of sexual acts to his liking.

*And all whores must register with the chief deputy of Russell County—
Bert Fuller—where their teeth and bodies are inspected and noted before
being tattooed and sent out to please the customer.*

*Of course, any stories about Phenix City have the occasional negative
words by newspapermen and the like. Look magazine called us "The
Wickedest City in America," and, during the war, it was noted that General
George S. Patton thought the entire town should be bulldozed on account
he was losing too many soldiers.*

*But where else would grotesque black-and-white pornographic movies
be shot or babies of whores put up for sale to the highest bidder?*

Phenix City may be a small town, but it's a giant in Alabama when it comes to the state's economics and politics.

Just ask newly elected governor Big Jim Folsom. There he is, smiling into the camera at a fund-raiser with Chief Deputy Bert Fuller and our county solicitor Arch Ferrell, a man who hasn't prosecuted a single clip joint operator, moonshiner, or whoremaster in his tenure.

Look at the smiles on those boys' faces. That's the look of power.

Maybe because just a few weeks back about a dozen cars left from Phenix City, all loaded down with briefcases full of cash. They drove from Auburn to Slapout, Alabama, distributing Phenix City's might to local officials and sheriffs, and, by God, they pulled out for ole Big Jim.

So who are They?

This is the redneck mafia, the Syndicate, the Phenix City Machine, a group of gamblers, pimps, thieves, and dope dealers big enough to fill a football stadium. There's the old guard, the duo who built this town, Jimmie Matthews and Hoyt Shepherd. And then there's Miss Fannie Belle, the red-headed devil who feels as comfortable calling a murder as getting a manicure and her hair done. And we could jump from Johnnie Benefield to Godwin Davis to Clyde Yarborough, a man whose face resembled fleshy pudding from dozens of skin grafts.

Sometimes it's a chore to find out who works for who and exactly who to trust. The night Mr. Patterson was killed, the list of suspects was about as big as the city itself, because, after all, Mr. Patterson won the state attorney general run-off on a platform of a Man Against Crime.

What followed his murder was a movie, a Randolph Scott western, played out not with horses and Winchesters but with Chevys and Fords and .38s and switchblades, until the city was dismantled, stacked in vacant fields, and left to burn in smoldering trash heaps for the entire state to see.

The fires burned all that fall, filling your eyes and nose and clothes with that acrid smell.

We never rebuilt.

How could we?

I'll always remember that bonfire smoke in '54, when it all came tumbling down to the bugles of Guard troops. The burnings seemed to last for months, destroying the guts of the Machine, huge trailing snakes of blackness high up into the fall sky. I remember thinking to myself: This is a hell of a place to raise a family.

THE SPRING OF 1954 had slipped into summer with little notice. My routine hadn't changed much; there was always the jog down Crawford Road at daybreak and then back to the little brick house I shared with my wife and two kids. As my wife, Joyce, would start coffee, I'd finish with a few rounds against the heavy bag hung on chains in an old shed and then maybe jump some rope or hook my feet under a pipe and do sit-ups until my stomach ached. That morning, a Friday, June eighteenth, my daughter, Anne, walked outside, still in her pajamas, and asked if she could work out with me, and I smiled, out of breath, my bald head slick with sweat, and reached into the shed for an apple crate. Anne, just eleven, with the same slight space in her teeth as me and the same fair skin and hair, stood on top of the shaky wood and began to work the leather of the speed bag with her tiny fists.

I stood back and smiled.

It wasn't unusual for the neighborhood boys to ride their bikes over and watch with amazement as my little girl would work the bag with a right and left, keeping that steady, unmistakable rhythm I'd known from Kid Weisz's gym during the Depression, when a hot cup of coffee and a donut was a feast.

Soon, Joyce called us inside and fussed at me for letting Anne run outside in her pj's, the cuffs dusty with rich red mud, but she laughed as Anne continued mock punches, and Thomas woke up, only six, working a fist only to pull the sleep from his eyes. We sat down to a plate of ham and eggs and biscuits and grits and we said a prayer to our Lord and Savior and ate, Joyce refilling my cup when I returned to the kitchen from the bedroom, already dressed in my Texaco coveralls, ready for a day's work at Slocumb's—the filling station I co-owned with Joyce's dad.

"Thomas is chewing with his mouth open," Anne said.

Thomas smiled and chewed even wider with his eyes crossed.

"You want more coffee, Lamar?" Joyce asked.

"Yes, ma'am."

"I put your shoes outside, you had grease and mud all over them," she said. "And would you mind, please, emptying out the ashtrays when you're finished?"

"What would I do without you?"

"Nothing," Joyce said and winked, and soon I was off, with a lunch pail rounded and red like a construction worker's, and I followed a worn, smooth trail back behind our house and by the speed and heavy bags and through a thicket of brush, over the step of one, two, three flat stones in a little creek and then down a short stretch of smooth path and I was out behind Slocumb's, unlocking the back door and cutting on the lights and opening up the front door for Arthur, a negro who pumped gas and cleaned windshields and had been my friend for some time.

Arthur didn't say much, just turned over the OPEN sign as I made some coffee and loaded up the cash drawer in the register. I turned on the radio and began to hum along with some old swing stuff, music that brought back memories of being newly married at the start of the war, and Joyce and I taking everything we owned down to Eglin Airfield in Florida, where I worked as an airplane mechanic until '46. My memories were still fresh of how the test planes could roll and crash and burn and I'd be left to pull out the bodies from the wreckage and try to make sense with what had gone wrong.

"You making the coffee?" Arthur asked. He was dressed in similar green Texaco coveralls.

"That's what it looks like."

"Hmm."

"What do you mean, hmm?"

"I just wish Joyce would've been here is all. You ain't one for cooking."

"Coffee ain't cooking."

"And grits ain't groceries," Arthur said. He walked outside, ignoring the slurping pot, and stood by the big pumps waiting for their first customers to come rolling on in.

I whistled along to Harry James's trumpet on the radio and, even as the first customer rolled under the tin overhang, kept on with the old tune "I've Heard That Song Before."

The car was a two-tone tan-and-white Oldsmobile Rocket 88, and I knew the car before the engine even died and the man walked around and checked out the day just coming on from down east along the river, the morning shadows growing long and thin, almost disappearing into the harder light.

He was a tall, thin man with white hair and round spectacles. As he had stood, he used the door frame and placed the rubber tip of a wooden cane on the ground, smiling and limping his way to me with the steady *clog, clog, clog* of his heavy, specially fitted shoe.

"Mr. Patterson," I said and shook his hand. "You headed somewhere?"

"Montgomery," Patterson said, smoothing the lapels of his suit and shifting off the leg that he'd nearly lost in the First World War in the cold no-man's-land of St. Etienne. "Promised a friend that I'd be at a hearing."

I started to pump his gas. Usually Arthur did the pumping, unless we got really busy or there was someone special I wanted to talk to.

The light seemed to shift and grow in only seconds and covered Mr. Patterson's soft, old features in a nice gold light. He smiled at me, as I checked the tires, and looked down Crawford Road toward the business district of Phenix City—an area where he worked but despised—and then back down the road toward the west and the capital of Montgomery, where he'd be headed next year to become the next attorney general of this state.

"I don't know if I've told you this," Patterson said, "but I sure appreciate all the support of you and all the boys. I couldn't have done this without you."

For the last two years, I'd been a member of an anti-vice group—the Russell County Betterment Association—that Mr. Patterson had helped found.

"I think you would have done fine."

"I'll need you even more in the coming months, Lamar."

"How's that?"

"Things will get worse before they get better."

I smiled. "Don't think they could get much worse," I said and hung up the nozzle and noted the price. I asked Patterson to open his hood and I checked the oil.

"How's this engine treatin' you? I bet she really can open up on the highway."

Patterson stood behind me and said in a low voice, almost a whisper: "They're coming for me, Lamar. I think I have a one-in-ten chance of ever taking office."

I stood, feeling ice along my neck, and wiped the dipstick on a dirty rag. The oil was clean and full, and I replaced the stick and closed the hood with a tight snap. Mr. Patterson gave a small, wan smile.

I shook my head. "Don't talk that way. We got 'em."

"A cheater never lets you win."

Patterson clasped my hand and then reached into his pocket for a couple of dollars before getting back into the Rocket 88, climbing the hill, and then turning out of sight toward the west.

EARLIER THAT DAY, BILLY STOKES HEADED DOWN TO FOUR-teenth Street to turn in a sack of dimes and quarters after selling a mess of Bug tickets to some poor blacks down by the railroad. The Bug was a lottery they'd been running in town since forever, and during the summer when he was out of school he got paid five dollars by his daddy to make the Friday run. Most every house in Niggertown bought the tickets, just like some kind of religious event. Old women even bought dream books to turn what they'd seen in their heads into lucky numbers. Billy sure needed that five dollars; he'd promised to take a girl he'd just met to a picture show down at the Palace Theater.

He'd spent his last dollar on a Bug ticket himself, hoping his numbers would come out in the morning paper from numbers on the New York Stock Exchange.

Billy hadn't seen his daddy, Reuben, since Wednesday, which wasn't that unusual because, sometimes, he'd take off for days and return either red-eyed and sore and grumpy or dressed in a new suit with ruby cuff links and spreading out money on the table of their old house that he knew would be gone by week's end.

He pushed his red Schwinn down the slope of Fourteenth Street, looking down to the old muddy river and between the cavern of clip joints and honky-tonks that had just started to heat up on an early

Friday night. It was twilight, and the neon signs started to flicker, advertising exotic women and games of chance. THE SILVER SLIPPER. THE GOLDEN RULE. There was laughter and bawdy saxophone music, and the soft green and red and blue neon seemed almost magical on that summer night as he passed GIs drinking straight from bottles of Jack Daniel's and friendly, plump whores who would smile at him or pat him on the head as he passed by, either because they thought it was funny to see a kid down here or because they knew Billy was Reuben Stokes's boy.

Down toward the river, Billy left his bike outside the giant, twirling yellow neon for CLUB LASSO, Reuben's joint, and walked into the narrow café, over the beaten honeycomb-tile floors and through small little groupings of tables and chairs. On a stage toward the back by the toilets there was a girl dressed in a cowboy outfit shaking her big titties to a lone saxophone player who played the theme to *Red River*.

Reuben was behind the bar dressed in an ugly tropical shirt and talking on the telephone—more like calling someone a jackass on the phone—between drinking a beer and smoking a cigarette, and when he saw Billy he nodded and crooked a finger toward the bar and his son sat down and stared into the bar mirror over his dad's shoulder. Billy saw just a skinny kid in a rangy white T-shirt and silly green military hat that once belonged to his old man during the war. He was so skinny and his teeth so big that he looked away.

Reuben reached into the cooler and pulled out a cold Coca-Cola, and Billy sat up there and drank while the saxophone music ended and the girl stepped from the soft red light by the toilets and slipped into a Chinese robe.

"Hey, I've been busy," Reuben asked, "you still got food?"

"I could use five dollars."

"What for?"

"We need some milk and cereal. I also wanted to go to a picture show."

"You love those picture shows, don't you? You know, you really should go see *The Robe*," Reuben said. "It's a picture about Jesus Christ."

"I'm going to see *Hondo*. John Wayne's in it."

"That the one in 3-D?"

"Yes, sir."

"Well, finish up that Coca-Cola and get gone."

"Yes, sir."

Some of Reuben's negro dealers sat at empty tables waiting for folks to play blackjack and roulette and craps. And they looked funny and slick in their ill-fitted tuxedos while they shuffled cards and worked a pair of dice with fast, quick hands—with palms oddly pink to Billy—that loaded every flick and throw.

One of the men wore a pair of dark sunglasses as he fanned out a hand of cards. Reuben had once let Billy try on a similar pair, and he could see hidden red patterns on the back of each card in a red light.

The stripper sidled up next to the boy as he looked around Club Lasso. She was kind of attractive but a little soft-faced, with a round white belly under her cowhide bra. She placed a hand on his knee and asked him his name.

"His name's Billy," Reuben said. "And he's too young for you, Birmingham. Get back on stage."

The boy turned back to Reuben, who was smoking, and Reuben smiled at his son, cigarette clamped square in his teeth. But his eyes grew unfocused as he stared into an empty place on the opposite wall. He smiled again before heading back to the bathroom.

Billy sat there for a while and watched Miss Birmingham strip down to her panties and shake her fat titties while winking, and he borrowed a couple nickels from Reuben's stickman—a teenage negro named Charley Frank Bass—and played a few slots, winning a few bucks.

But he still needed the five and walked back to the toilets and knocked. He heard water running and opened the door.

Reuben stood with one foot up on the commode, his trouser leg rolled up to his knee, showing a leather rig above his left calf. His blue knee sock had been rolled down to the ankle, and in his left hand he had a pistol cylinder open from the frame where he fed bullets with his fingers.

Billy smiled at him.

But he gave the boy such a hard look back that Billy shut the door and left Club Lasso with only his winnings.

ALBERT PATTERSON RETURNED FROM MONTGOMERY LATE that night, too late to watch his youngest boy, Jack, in the high school play, where Jack played Lord Bothwell in *The Pipes of Dunbar.* Jack had been pretty excited that week talking about how Lord Bothwell symbolized justice in a time of bloodshed and that the girl who played his wife Mary, Queen of Scots, was a real looker. And Patterson had asked his son which one was it, did he like the story better or the girl? And Jack said he wasn't sure, but he knew he wasn't excited about wearing those damn black tights they'd given him.

Patterson told his boy to forget about the tights, even Errol Flynn wore them, and that he'd try to make it back for the show. But Patterson had been sucked into attending an ethics hearing and then had to check with the secretary of state's office on the final vote canvass. And although the press had already named him the winner, it sure felt good knowing he had the official results in hand.

As he came back to Phenix City, he parked in that familiar narrow alley across from the Elite Café. Using his cane, he slowly made his way to the post office to check his box, feeling every damn step the six bullets that remained in his leg from a machine gunner in that no-man's-land outside St. Etienne. And he thought back on that time during the First World War, learning to walk again and living in that hospital in Atlanta in a narrow bed and having little else to do but watch a pear tree bear fruit outside his window for two seasons.

It was hot and dark at the top of the staircase of the Coulter Building when he pushed open the frosted-glass door of the office of Patterson & Patterson, a partnership with his oldest boy, John.

He set down his keys and grabbed some thank-you letters that his personal secretary, Lucille, had left with him. He flicked on the old banker's light on his desk, staying there for God knows how long signing his name and then rummaging through the bills that had left him eleven thousand in debt since entering the race.

His office walls were bare except for two framed diplomas and several short wooden bookshelves holding volumes of law. But the plaster still bore black scorch marks where the Machine had tried to burn him out two years ago.

Soon he heard a short rap on the door, and his old buddy, Leland Jones, walked in and asked him if he'd like to join him and his wife for supper. Patterson said he sure appreciated that, but he'd had a milkshake with an egg and a hamburger at a drive-in before he left Montgomery.

"Why'd you put an egg in it?"

"Mmm-hmm."

"Why'd you put an egg in it?"

"What?"

"Pat, you ain't paying a damn bit of attention to me."

Patterson crumpled up another envelope and tossed it over his shoulder, his eyes slowly meeting Jones's. "'Course I have."

"The hell you say."

"What is it?"

"You got to eat."

"I'm fine," Patterson said. His eyes returned to the desk, that narrow space of white light on the letters.

"Something eating you, Pat?"

Patterson shook his head.

"What do you think about the hearings?"

"I'll let you know Monday."

"What's Monday?"

"When I testify against those bastards."

"So you're going to do it."

Patterson nodded.

"You found something on them, didn't you?"

Patterson nodded again.

Jones asked Patterson to dinner one more time, saying his wife was waiting in the car, and Patterson told him no again, saying he had more paperwork to do. But it wasn't but ten minutes later that he signed the last signature of thanks, fixed the last stamp on the last bill, grabbed his hat and cane, and cut off his lamp.

A ceiling fan rocked and squeaked above him. The air conditioner hummed and dripped. He locked up and used the handrail to clog his way down the narrow staircase with that specially fitted shoe bumping all the way down to Fifth Avenue.

On the street, the nearby honky-tonks and cathouses were in full swing early on a Friday night, and you could hear the saxophone music and the yells and loud talk of the GIs from Fort Benning and smell the cigarettes and vomit and urine. On Fourteenth Street, the neon cast a pinkish hue down the road and almost up on the steps of the Russell County Courthouse.

It was a hot night, as are most summer nights in Alabama, but it hadn't rained in weeks, and the asphalt and concrete seemed to absorb the sun and radiate with the heat, making the wind seem like a fan off a stove. His Rocket 88 waited in a slot in the narrow alley between the Elite and the Coulter Building. Patterson rounded the corner, his right hand in his right pocket reaching for the keys, the sounds of Phenix City like a carnival midway in the distance, when he saw the shadows, the shapes of the men, heading into the alley.

Patterson opened his car door, sat down in the driver's seat, and pulled his leg in after him. The men called out to him in the darkness and he turned.

Three shots were heard cracking in echo through the little downtown.

Moments later, Albert L. Patterson walked from the alley, staggering and shuffling without a cane for the first time in more than thirty years, with a couple teens pointing at him from across the street, snickering and saying that man was drunk as hell.

And Patterson walked more, a struggling, dignified shuffle step and another, robotic and forced as a drunk trying to convince himself of being sober, his face blank and unseeing, with steps growing shorter and shorter, until he fell to his knees, out of juice, batteries drained, and then pitched forward on the heated concrete.

He fell to his face, shattering his glasses, a hot, wet stain spreading under him, and soon heard a boy's question: "Who did this to you? Who shot you, Mr. Patterson?"

But instead of a helping hand, Patterson saw the branch of a pear tree and the buzzing of bees jumping from bloom to bloom. He tried to explain this to the voices he heard, but instead of words blood flowed from his mouth.

IDLE HOUR PARK WAS QUITE A PLACE IN THE SUMMERTIME after school let out. You could take a boat ride down at Moon Lake or swim in this big pool—nicknamed the Polio Hole—and there was an arcade and a bowling alley and a roller-skating rink. Idle Hour even had a two-bit zoo, where they had a skinny, mangy lion and a half-dead bear that slept almost all day on a concrete slab unless you nailed him on the head with a pebble. They had a big iron cage full of monkeys that chattered and swung from old tires, and on the real hot days they'd jump and yell, and the males would get close to the bars and would look you in the eye while they masturbated like they were trying to pull the damn thing off.

But at fourteen, Billy had grown bored with the zoo and preferred watching girls out on the bandstand along with his buddy Mario. The boys didn't have to say much, they'd just see a girl walk by in a nice summer dress and one of them would look to the other and raise his eyebrows. If she was really cute, Mario would pretend he'd just burned his hand on a stove. And if she beat that, Billy would act like someone had punched him in the stomach and roll to the ground.

They did this for a long time that night, until the conversation shifted pretty quickly to monsters from Mars, and Mario said there was absolutely scientific proof that other planets held horrors the government didn't want the public to know about. Billy said that was a goddamn fool thing to say, but Mario held his ground until a cute little blonde with an upturned nose and tanned legs walked by and then it was his time to get punched in the stomach and roll to the ground.

When he returned to the bench where they sat, Billy said: "That don't make no sense."

"Sure it does," Mario said. "I saw it on *Tales of Tomorrow*. We just bought us a TV. You can watch it if you like."

"How does your mom afford all that stuff?"

"She's a nurse. She makes a lot of money."

And the silence just kind of hung there, because both of them knew Mario's mother worked under the stage name Betsy Ann and that, on several occasions, Billy had lingered outside the Bama Club on Dillingham just to see a naked black-and-white photo of her, not in overalls or sloppy men's shirts the way she looked in the apartment she shared with a redneck mill worker named George but made up like a Hollywood star in cowboy boots and a leather belt and stars pasted across her boobs.

"You wanna go back to the zoo?" Mario asked.

"I'm all right."

"I don't think she's gonna show."

"To hell with you."

Billy still had a few dimes left, and, alone, he walked into the sweet air-conditioning of the roller rink and punched in some of his favorites on the jukebox. More Hit Parade. He tried out some Eddie Fisher and Tony Bennett, and "Come On-A My House" by Rosemary Clooney.

That's when he heard her call his name.

Lorelei.

Billy smiled, his face turning red, and his voice shook as he said hello.

"Where you been?" she asked.

"Nowhere."

She was cute in her boy's western shirt, high-water blue jeans, and saddle oxford shoes. She wore her black hair up in a ponytail; her bangs had grown longer since he'd last seen her and shadowed a good bit of her blue eyes. She didn't have makeup on or anything like that.

"I wasn't waitin' around or nothin'."

"I had to go home and change," she said. "I'd been at the pool and had to put on something dry."

And, man, that was a hell of a thing to say to a teenage boy, because the thought of Lorelei in a wet bathing suit—something Billy could imagine a great deal and had—was perhaps just too much for him to take. Her pale skin had a red, healthy flush to it, and she smelled like sunshine.

"What's wrong with you?" she asked.

"Nothin'."

"Well, your face is turning funny colors."

"No, it's not."

The corny organ music came from over in the skating rink, and they heard people clapping in time with it.

"You want a shake?"

"I just had one."

"I'll buy," she said.

"Sure."

He'd met Lorelei just a few weeks before school had let out, over on the Upper Bridge from Columbus, and helped her carry a sack of groceries home. Billy figured her for the daughter of a mill worker—a Linthead, is what they called them—and they ended up talking till it grew dark out back of the Riverview Apartments, nothing but government housing, smoking cigarettes on a swing set. He'd never felt more comfortable with a girl in his entire life and finally got up enough nerve to ask her to a picture show at the Broadway.

"I went to that house where you were staying last week," he said.

"We don't live in the Riverview no more."

"Where do you live?"

"My folks' over in Bibb City," she said. "Got some good mill jobs."

"How 'bout you?"

"I'm over there some, too," she said.

"You gonna go back to school?"

"Not now," she said, rolling her eyes and pulling the straw from the shake. She sucked out the frozen bit of shake and tucked it back into the glass. "It's summertime, dummy. It's all as cool as a breeze. You ain't supposed to do nothin' now but swim and skate and not worry about a thing."

Billy looked at her and rolled up the white T-shirt over his skinny bicep and wished he'd had a pack of cigarettes to tuck inside.

"What movie we going to see?" she asked.

"*Hondo,*" he said.

"What's it about?"

"Apaches."

"I like Apaches," she said.

IT WASN'T LONG UNTIL BILLY AND THE GIRL SAT IN THE cool air-conditioning of the Palace Theater watching *Hondo,* Wayne playing a cavalry rider protecting a woman and her son from some Apaches. There was never any question if Wayne would get the woman or if he wouldn't whip some Apache ass. They were no match for Wayne armed with a rifle he could work with one hand. It was a good picture, and Billy's head was still kind of in it as they milled through the crowd down by the Elite, the girl at his side, watching the world through the 3-D glasses he refused to take off.

Billy figured the crowd had to be on account of some cockamamie street brawl between a couple of GIs or some poor slob of a woman with her lip busted and some man crying and telling her he was sorry nearby. Growing up on the river, he'd seen it all before. But then he saw all the squad cars and the ambulance, and as he stepped out on the street a PC cop told him to get back on the curb just in time for the ambulance to pop into gear and slowly drive to Homer C. Cobb Memorial.

The girl watched as it passed and put her hand to her mouth.

They followed the street right into the thickest tangled bunch of the crowd, elbowing their way through as only kids can do; the headlights and red lamps on the squad cars making old Fifth Avenue seem like Hollywood Boulevard.

A mess of Boy Scouts in their dress green outfits stood on the corner pointing at the motions of Chief Deputy Bert Fuller of the Russell County Sheriff's Office.

Fuller squatted onto his fat haunches, his eyes following a thick mess of dried blood on the warm concrete by the windows of Seymour's Ready-to-Wear Shop, rubbed his face, and motioned to a couple deputies.

Fuller wasn't a tall man, but what he lacked in height he made up with girth. He walked through the town slow and deliberate in those tailored western clothes with snap buttons that some said he'd bought while stationed in Texas. Billy had never seen him without a hand-tooled gun rig—holding gold-plated pistols—and a Stetson hat.

He watched Fuller follow smaller drops that led back toward the Elite.

Fuller slipped his Stetson back on the back of his head and called out: "Would someone get me some cardboard to cover this fucking thing up?"

Many times Billy had seen Fuller at the Palace or the Strand or the Victory Drive-In, settled into his seat watching the cowboys on the big screen. He'd prop up his boots and munch on a sack of popcorn with that small, cruel mouth and peer at the screen with his beady brown eyes.

He looked straight at Billy, as if he'd been caught peeping into someone's window. "Where's your daddy at? Go on and pull at his pant leg about what you seen."

Then Fuller's gaze fell upon the girl with her pegged jeans and boy's shirt and hair twisted into a ponytail and tied with a red bandanna. Fuller wet his lips and smiled, as if he was about to speak, his eyes wandering over her body and face as he stood there with all that activity around him, just breathing her in.

When Billy turned back, the girl—Lorelei—had disappeared.

BEFORE I MARRIED JOYCE and settled down in Phenix, I'd come to Columbus, Georgia, at the end of the Depression to make my way as a prizefighter. I was only a teenager, just old enough to leave the corn and cotton farm I'd grown up on outside Troy, Alabama, where I'd heard about Kid Weisz from boxing magazines. I knew he'd trained some of the top fellas like Corn Griffin, who was supposed to be heavyweight champ before getting upset by Jim Braddock in '34. And I'd showed up at his sweaty hothouse brick gym with little more than a duffel bag, an old jump rope, and some dog-eared paperbacks with titles like *Scientific Boxing by a Fistic Expert* and *The Sweet Science*.

I was skinny and rangy, and my feet got tangled up about every time I sparred. But I lived in that gym every day and listened to old Weisz and his strange, loopy philosophies I still hear in my head about every morning in the shaving mirror: *The world is largely made up of gropers, kid, little people who are always being pushed around by the natural bullies of society. But you got to remember that the gropers of this world are the real people. And that the bullies of the world are only the elements that make up the froth of society. They foam so freely that they necessarily come to the top more easily. But it's the solid, substantial members of human society who remain below and grope to the top only on real, basic ability.*

And he'd stop and look at me with that one clear eye, that cloudy one staring off dead in the distance, his ears jugged and cauliflowered, and pull me from what I was doing, on the speed bag or the heavy, and grab me by the thick of the forearm, so I could smell his coffee-tinged breath: *Murphy, the gropers are those who want to learn. They are always grasping the means to find out ways of improving their lot.*

When I came to the gym, I didn't even own my own pair of gloves. I worked in the off-hours for my gear and training at the candy factory on the river and would emerge late at night smelling like burnt sugar and grease. I made my living with my fists in pickup bouts for the enjoyment of two-bit hustlers over the river in Phenix City—the same rings where they fought roosters and dogs—and soon in the legitimate ring, taking the Atlanta Golden Gloves in 1938. From there, I never thought it would end, boxing my way from New York to New Orleans and even down to Mexico City.

I bought new tailored suits and carried gobs of cash in a silver money clip, even being able to afford a nice little convertible that was a hell of a thing in the country on a spring day.

But then I met Joyce, and when we danced one night on my new nimble feet at a bandstand down on Moon Lake, the fighting didn't seem as important. She worked as a beautician in Phenix City, was about the prettiest thing I'd ever seen. And unlike most of the girls you meet on the road who were with you until the booze and prize money ran out, she could've cared less about me being a fighter. In fact she hated it, and about the time the Japs bombed Pearl Harbor she asked me to please quit getting myself beat on, just like that, never acknowledging that the other fella was taking most of the beating.

Before Mr. Patterson was shot, I remember the rust-flecked mirror over the station commode becoming the boxing mirror—the place where all fighters must examine their every move and weakness—and I saw a man that had grown soft and old. At forty, I didn't care for that feeling a bit.

I'd always been a groper.

WHEN THE PHONE RANG, I WAS HALF ASLEEP IN AN EASY chair, an empty bowl of peach ice cream in my lap, and watching television over the heads of my two children who lay on the floor, inches away from the screen. We'd just watched a show called *Topper* about a ghost couple and their ghost Saint Bernard who haunted an uptight banker. The kids liked it a lot anytime the ghost dog got into the banker's booze, but now had grown a little bored and sleepy with *Schlitz Playhouse of Stars*, and that's when I'd begun to doze after a long day of pumping gas and fixing engines.

Joyce walked into the room, drying her hands on a dish towel, and took a deep breath. Her face was white as she pointed me back to the kitchen.

I put down my spoon and followed. "Hugh Britton called. Mr. Patterson has been shot. They've taken him to the hospital."

"My gun is in the nightstand."

"I know where your gun is."

"Keep it close."

"I'll lock the doors."

The hospital was just up the hill from our little brick house, and I ran all the way through the fine, heated summer night. The little windows of the postwar cottages on the gentle slope glowed with soft light, and in the tiny square yards children played and grimy men drank beer and worked on cars. Women sat on stoops and smoked cigarettes

in hair curlers, and I ran by them all up a curved drive, past all the cars
and a few ambulances, and into the dull, attic heat of the hospital
lobby.

I found John Patterson speaking to two doctors with a large gathering of newsmen and photographers. They popped off flashes from
their boxed Rolleiflex cameras, John's face sweating and dull eyes
vacant in the quick strobes of light. They asked him questions about
his father and the rackets and the reputed Phenix City Machine and he
didn't answer them, unblinking in the quick strobes, until I grabbed
his elbow and steered him into a hallway, where he just stared down
the long vacuum of tile and linoleum and nurses and doctors in antiseptic white.

John hadn't been back from the service long, a World War II combat veteran who'd served from Africa to Austria with France in
between. He'd been briefly recalled to Korea but ended up with some
legal work in Germany before returning home to partner with his
father. He was a stocky guy with a heavy brow, the kind of man who'd
rather be in a boat fishing than be involved in anything political. But
John was a loyal man, loyal to his friends and his family, and I knew
he'd spent the better part of the year dropping his practice to crisscross
the state to campaign for his father.

They took him into a room in the emergency ward, never telling
him a damn thing, where he found his father on a gurney, hidden
under a white sheet. Sheriff Matthews was there with Chief Deputy
Bert Fuller and the county solicitor, Arch Ferrell, and when John
walked into the room you could only hear the *click, click, click* of his
shoes across the floor and the stiff pop of the sheet as he pulled it away
and looked down at his father.

Sheriff Matthews sucked a tooth. Bert Fuller leaned against the wall
and fanned himself with his cowboy hat. And Arch Ferrell rubbed his
face, his finger trembling across his jaw.

Mr. Patterson lay there dressed in a brown suit with a bloody white shirt and blue tie. His mouth was open, teeth shot away, and blood spotted upon his face, his eyes open and staring into nothing particular, glazed and empty.

"I don't want a goddamn hand on him," John said. "I'm sending for Dr. Rehling in Opelika. He'll do the autopsy. No one is to touch him."

Matthews, Fuller, and Ferrell didn't say a word. Fuller just looked to me and then back to John, fanning his face some more and then slipping his hat back on his head. I watched as John took a breath and then reached into his father's pockets, taking his wallet and keys, and removed a wristwatch loudly clicking off the seconds.

I followed John out into the hall. He tucked his father's belongings into his own pockets.

"Murphy, will you stay?"

I nodded, and he walked back to the lobby.

Soon Arch Ferrell came outside and he looked at me, dressed in my Texaco coveralls: "We'll do everything we can."

"Who's gonna run this?"

"Sheriff Matthews and me, of course."

A slight sheen shone across Arch's forehead and upper lip. His breath smelled of cheap whiskey and cigarettes. Arch was the city's war hero—one of the first into Normandy and one of the last out of Germany—and was known to tear up at the Foreign Legion post when they played the "Star-Spangled Banner."

Arch took a long breath. He knew me only from the service station and looked at the grease on my nails and across my uniform as he smoothed out the tie on his chest. He was shorter than me, with pointed features and large ears. The hair on the side of his head had been buzzed tight, the top curly and uncombed.

"I've got to get back to the scene," he said. "The coroner will be here soon."

"We're waiting for the state."

"This doesn't involve the state. Mr. Patterson was one of our own and we will handle it here in town."

"Nope," I said. "No one goes in that room until the state examiner gets here."

Arch shook his head with great disgust. "You RBA people won't rest until you turn this whole thing into a goddamn clusterfuck."

His right hand flexed and clinched. I didn't say anything, just watched his face turn a bright crimson as he held his breath. "Y'all just want to be heroes," Arch said. "But I think it's a little too late for that."

He turned and walked away.

I stayed there for hours, as everyone in town and every newsman in the state turned up at Homer C. Cobb Memorial. The flashbulbs were endless; twice, I had to stop newspapermen from entering the room with Mr. Patterson's body.

Hugh Britton, who installed carpet by day but did counterintelligence for the RBA at night, stayed with me, not uttering a word, until the state medical examiner arrived. Later, we sat outside by the fountain, smoking cigarettes.

That's when I saw John Patterson, wandering in and out of the cars parked along the hill. I found him, sweated through a casual yellow shirt, and he looked up to me from the hot asphalt as if seeing a man he'd never met.

"You okay?"

"I can't find my car."

He steadied himself against the hood of a red DeSoto Deluxe, finding purchase on the hood ornament, a likeness of DeSoto himself.

A Russell County sheriff's car slowed, Bert Fuller leaning out the driver's window and asking, "You need a ride?"

John nodded, stepping through Fuller's headlights and climbing in the passenger's seat. Fuller looked at me standing there and gave a slight grin before turning back to John and saying, "If I find the son-ofabitch, I'll bring him right to you. You got my word on that, partner."

Fuller checked the tilt of his cowboy hat in the rearview before knocking the car in gear and moving out slow and steady down the hill.

THE FIRST LIGHT ON THE RIVER WASHED OVER THE CRIME scene and over the tired faces of men standing in that narrow shot of alley taking pictures and measuring Mr. Patterson's last steps and answering newsmen's questions and talking and talking. I hadn't been home since the hospital, and I waited with Hugh Britton outside the ropes they'd set off to keep the gawkers back. John Patterson was there, talking to investigators who'd come down from Montgomery, and we were left with little to do in that early gray light but stand back and drink coffee and shake our heads and wait for John to tell us what to do next. Some Phenix City deputies waded through knee-deep kudzu at the far end of the alley, poking sticks into the green leaves and kicking around with their feet. Another man in a black suit finished up looking through Mr. Patterson's car and then called out to a deputy, who opened up the rope and motioned for a wrecker to come on in and take the Olds away.

Cameras clicked and clicked, with an undeniable headline of DEATH CAR, the pocked glass on the driver's window evident as the wrecker turned onto Fifth and into the weak light.

"Where they taking it?" Britton asked.

"Only one way to find out."

I walked down the middle of the street—there was almost no traffic—and watched as the car turned slow down Fourteenth and then took a hard turn back behind the courthouse to the county jail.

By that time, Britton had caught up with me. He was a wiry, little gray-headed man, and he was out of breath standing by my side as I pointed behind the courthouse.

We walked around the edge of the big brick courthouse and looked down into the little cove surrounded by razor wire. There, the wrecker had stopped, and trusties in denim uniforms worked to unlatch the car as it was slowly lowered onto its fat whitewalls.

After the wrecker drove out of the gates, three of those trusties approached the Rocket 88 with big galvanized buckets and brushes. Britton pointed toward the edge of the jail, and we saw Bert Fuller pointing and yelling words to the men we couldn't hear.

Britton pulled a little notebook from his shirt pocket and jotted down some details, no doubt to go into the endless files he'd been keeping for the RBA since we started three years ago.

Two of the trusties were black and one was fat and white. They opened the car door and crawled inside and worked their buckets and brushes all over the leather and floors. One of the men duckwalked to a nearby drain and tossed out some soapy water that was a bright pink. He repeated this a half dozen times till the interior carpet had been cleaned and he tossed the last bucket down into the drainpipe that would twist and run downhill out to the Chattahoochee.

Britton looked to me and then back to the men. He noted the time on his wristwatch and wrote it down.

We walked back together to Fifth Avenue and toward the Coulter Building. The summer sun was full up now and painted the blacktop and sidewalks. The mannequins inside Seymour's Ready-to-Wear Shop, now slatted in early sun rays, coyly turned and smiled, showing off their stiff summer dresses, patent leather pumps, and costume jewelry.

Hugh Britton tucked a toothpick into his mouth and set one of his hands in his trouser pockets. He took off his glasses, blew his breath on the lenses, and cleaned them with a white handkerchief. Satisfied, he slipped them back on his face.

"I don't like this a bit."

I nodded.

"Having Fuller in charge of this show is like making a chimp the circus ringmaster."

"You think these state boys will be much better?"

Britton shook his head and smiled, and we both knew that only two years before a special group of investigators—fronted by a state man named Joe Smelley—had come down to investigate the illegal activities of our town. Not only did Smelley deny he saw a set of dice roll or a single whore on a street corner, he wrote a damn letter of accommodation to Governor Persons praising Bert Fuller as one of the state's outstanding lawmen.

The state investigators stood across Fifth Avenue, almost identical in their short-sleeved dress shirts and ties, pleated trousers, and lace-up shoes. They held notebooks, pens tucked in the pockets of their shirts, and smiled and shook hands with the local boys in uniform. We watched it all from the other side of the street as hands were shook and backs were slapped. The investigator, Smelley, noticed us and leaned into Sheriff Matthews, who quickly caught Britton's eye, whispered something to Smelley, laughed, and then spit on the sidewalk.

"The footprint," said a voice. John Patterson stood behind us. "It's gone. Last night they had enough to pour a mold, but when they pulled up the board someone had covered it up. I need help."

"Anything," I said.

"Y'all find out what you can," John said. "I'm gonna try and get us some federal help."

"I'll ride with you," Britton said. He stuck the toothpick back into his mouth and stood up on his toes like a banty rooster. He opened his mouth to speak and then closed it. He shook his head.

John rested his hand on the old man's shoulder. His father had been one of Britton's closest friends.

"Your father knew it," Britton said. "He knew they were coming for him. I told him a thousand times to carry a gun. But Pat said it wouldn't matter. Said they'd shoot him like some kind of coward and he was right."

"If you find who did this," John said, "I want you to bring them to me. They didn't even give my father a chance."

MUCH TO REUBEN'S AGGRAVATION, FOURTEENTH STREET stayed empty that Saturday night. The National Guard had been called to town by Governor Persons to keep order, and although they did little but drive the streets in jeeps and hold roadblocks it was enough for the Machine to keep their business behind closed doors while guardsmen checked driver's licenses and IDs of everyone who drove over the river. Baby-faced, buzz-cut boys in khaki from all over Alabama walked the beat down by the two bridges with rifles slung over their backs, guns on their hips, staring up at the neon signs and advertisements for busty ladies along plateglass windows.

Still, the beer flowed from brass taps and the jukeboxes played sad and rough-and-tumble country songs. But the B-girls sat alone at the long bars and cafés and the stick men took nothing but smoke breaks out on the streets and the bartenders had nothing but time to talk to the one or two customers who would walk in the doors to discuss the latest of what they were calling an Occupation.

That first night, Reuben made a quick stop-off at the Atomic Bomb Café and asked Clyde Yarborough for Budweiser in the bottle and a pack of Camels. He felt bad about running off Billy last night. But he didn't have time to play daddy when there was work to be done. His boy would someday understand that.

In the center of the room stood a tall bombshell that Yarborough had bought from an Army/Navy store and had someone paint a nude woman with enormous breasts on the casing. Instead of nipples, the woman wore the symbols for nuclear fallout. A fiery mushroom cloud for hair.

Yarborough pulled the beer from an old Coca-Cola cooler and shuffled off a pack from a bin by the cash register. He looked at Reuben, tilting his head like a dog, most of his face and jaw eaten away by cancer.

Most of the time he wore a bandanna over his mouth to cover the loose flesh and toothless opening of what had been a mouth. But tonight the skin grafts and holes and mush face glared back at him like a rotting jack-o'-lantern.

Reuben tapped the cigarette pack against his palm and broke out one. It remained unlit and fresh in his mouth as he leaned against the bar and shook his head. Clyde Yarborough, six foot three and still as strong as an ape, garbled something unintelligible and shuffled off.

Grime and dirt clung to the black-and-white linoleum floors and fingerprints and smudges filled the mirrors along the back of the long bar. A simple jukebox sat between the men's and women's bathrooms toward the back, and Reuben walked over and used a key to check the bin.

Not even enough to empty. He used a few of the coins to play some Hank Williams, his old friend who used to drink with him in this very bar before that long, last ride.

He looked down the long, empty bar and toasted Yarborough, and hearing the music cutting on the jukebox, "I'm So Lonesome I Could Cry," his rubbery face contorted into what may have very well been a smile and he snorted in what could've been a laugh.

Reuben smoked and drank and, when he put down the beer, tapped his fingers against the beaten bar, in all the coolness of the room and the dull, dim light of the neon beer signs.

About nine, he was piss-drunk and drinking each new beer with a side of Jack Daniel's, thinking about arriving in Bora-Bora in that troop ship and being greeted at the landing craft by a half dozen crazed GIs who ended up ass-raping a fresh-faced boy from Iowa who'd never even fired a shot in combat.

"Did I ever tell you about those goddamn monkeys in the Philippines?"

Yarborough sliced through some lemons, a big mug of a soft gray gruel that he drank for food by his side. The big man shook his head.

"They had monkeys all over the place. That's what this place needs. A goddamn monkey. Lose the A-bomb, I'll take a goddamn monkey any old time."

Yarborough's white puckered face didn't move, and his eyes and hands turned back to the lemons.

About that time, the front door opened and in walked Bert Fuller, dressed in his full khaki outfit and wearing his Texas gun rig and his Stetson hat. He sidled up next to Reuben and asked Clyde for a shot of anything strong and just looked at the endless lines of booze behind the bar, his face flushing the color of a beet.

"What you say, Bert?"

"What you smiling at, asshole?"

Reuben stubbed out his cigarette and stood from the chair.

"Ain't you heard? We've been overrun with little green men."

Reuben sat back down and looked at the bar. Fuller toasted himself in the mirror and sucked down the whiskey.

"Doesn't matter," Reuben said. "It's all talk and posturing. They been shutting down this place since the Civil War. Phenix City will close, they'll bust up some slots and empty out some moonshine and then two months later it'll open back up."

"Not this time."

"You want to make a bet?"

Yarborough refilled Fuller's glass and Fuller fired back the shot in his throat and wiped his mouth and it was all done quick and practiced as in every B western that Reuben had ever seen.

Yarborough garbled out something, and his eyes, the only part of his face that revealed something human, flashed to Reuben.

"He asked if you want another."

"I reckon not."

"Where you headed?"

"I don't know," Fuller said. "I had a half dozen whores run off on me today. I heard a bunch of them were working out at some trailer park out in Columbus."

"You gonna drive 'em back?"

"I'm gonna least get my cut of the gash they're dishin' out."

"Thatta boy."

"You think all this is funny, don't you?"

"Like I said, it's just a big dog and pony show. Just keep your head down and take your licks and it will be over. Sit down and drink with me. Don't fight it. It won't be long till the GIs will be so thick in here that you can't stand."

Reuben nodded to Yarborough, and Yarborough uncorked the whiskey bottle again, filling three glasses, the sticky sweet alcohol spilling across the bar and shining with red light.

He clicked glasses with the two men in front of him. "To the end of the Occupation," Reuben said.

Fuller snorted. Yarborough grumbled and poured the whiskey into the hole in his face.

"So where were you last night?"

"Where am I every Friday night?"

"I got to ask," Fuller said. "A lawman has to look to everybody."

Reuben squinted one eye at him, trying to hold him in focus, and then turned back to his drink.

"I tell you one thing," Bert Fuller said. "I'm not gonna lie down and let them RBA people run me down in the newspapers and corn-hole my ass. I want them to think about every fucking lie they tell about me."

Reuben looked down at his empty drink and then laid down some money.

"And the worst of them all is that that goddamn bald-headed son-ofabitch who runs the Texaco station. Murphy. You know that bastard, don't you?"

"For a long time."

"You his friend?"

"We used to box together before the war."

"I think it's time he just disappeared from the scene. *Comprende,* partner?"

Fuller affixed his Stetson in the mirror and readjusted the rig on his fat belly and walked out as Hank sang on about a mournful wooden Indian named *Kaw-liga*.

PEOPLE HAD ALWAYS CALLED Phenix City wicked. Or Sin City. For those of us who lived and worked outside the rackets, we tried our best to ignore it. But it was hard when most of the vice boasted services in neon down by the river, on the way to the only two bridges out of town. But we had schools and a hospital paid for in dirty money, and sometimes big-time poker chips would end up in the collection plates on Sunday. My son and daughter went to school and church with sons and daughters of bootleggers, pimps, and whores. Bert Fuller was a deacon, and Hoyt Shepherd, who most called the town's kingpin, sometimes sang in the Christmas pageant and liked to play the part of the innkeeper who turned away Mary and Joseph.

It was just an engrained part of our local economy, and the vice had gone on so long, it was very much like a strand of barbed wire that cuts a tree but is later absorbed, becoming part of its growth.

Until that June, I guess I didn't even know how deeply that wire cut. But there were things I learned, the darkest of moral depravity that went far beyond slot machines and illegal liquor that I still can't wash from my mind.

The night after the shooting, for the first time in months, it rained. Big, thick thunderheads blew in from the west and pounded the dry Phenix City asphalt, running off the bottles and cigarette butts and trash into narrow rivulets and into the Chattahoochee. You could smell the wet asphalt and concrete, the rich red clay, and scraggly pines on the hills. The windows in my Ford station wagon fogged as Hugh Britton and I crossed the roadblock at the Lower Bridge to Columbus, the river frothing and boiling over the Rock Cut Dam to the north.

"Did you notice anything unusual about Bert Fuller this morning?" I asked.

"Something's always unusual about Fuller."

"You notice his rig?"

"I've seen it. Asshole thinks he's Randolph Scott."

"He wore it this morning, but those pearl-handled revolvers were gone," I said.

Britton looked at me, the windshield wipers spastically working over the window.

"Now, have you ever known him not to wear those guns?"

"No, sir," he said.

At a corner filling station just off Broadway, I made a phone call, and then we ate some toast and drank coffee over at Choppy's Diner for half an hour before getting back in the station wagon and heading toward Fort Benning on Victory Drive. On Victory, there were dry cleaners and pawnshops and liquor stores and churches of redemption. Little trailer parks and workingman's diners and drive-ins that pulled you in with neon arrows. The rain hardened and fell in long, endless sheets, and I heard little else but the drumming on the cab, until I spotted the big flashing marquee for the Victory Drive-In and another long, sweeping neon arrow that pointed past an empty box office and through an open chain-link gate. There was supposed to be a Creature Double Feature tonight and a special showing of *The Robe* on Sunday.

But the customers had already gotten a weather refund and had pulled out of the lot.

The screen was big and concrete and seemed like an ancient monolith in the endless gravel lot pinging with rain. I slowed by the bleachers covered by a corrugated tin roof and parked close to the lighted overhang, and we made a run for it.

Soaked, Britton wiped the drops from his pressed slacks and shook his straw summer hat. "Damn it."

Moments later, a rusted Ford pickup stopped short of us and a little man came running for the overhang, a newspaper held over his head. No one shook hands, and the little man, now out of breath, nervously wrenched off his glasses and wiped them on the front of his blue coveralls. When he sat them back on his face, he looked like a bug.

"Anyone follow?" he asked.

"No," Britton said. "We're fine, Quinnie."

"You sure?" Quinnie asked.

"Sure we're sure," Britton said. "We did what you said. Now, what'd you know?"

Quinnie Kelley was a little man, not much more than five feet, and wore enormous Coke-bottle glasses and a short little fedora. He still had on some dirty blue coveralls from his work as the courthouse janitor. As he looked out into the rain and watched little rivulets forming and tilting toward a long, narrow ditch, he wiped the rain from his neck and put his hands on his waist.

"Heard some talk 'round the place," Quinnie said. "Not much, but some."

"Who?" I asked.

"I don't know who. Some peoples is sayin' that Mr. Shepherd called in a killer from Chicago. And others say Miss Fannie Belle. I cain't be sure. You heard the name Thomas Capps?"

"You said you saw something?" I asked. Everyone knew about

Thomas Capps. He was a thug and a killer, but not dumb enough to shoot Mr. Patterson on Fifth Avenue on a Friday night.

"I don't want this known. You hearin' me? I got a family. I got kids. But when I was locking up last night, I heard them shots and seen this man run across Fourteenth and back behind the jail."

"Who?"

Quinnie froze. "I didn't say who. I don't know nothin' about *who*. I'm just sayin' I seen a man."

"What did he look like?" I asked.

"If you say I saw somethin', I'll deny it. And I didn't see his face. He was runnin' back in the shadows and I didn't have on my glasses."

Hugh Britton looked to me and then back at Quinnie.

"That's all you got?" Britton said. "Well, good God Almighty. You call up Lamar at supper and have us driving through roadblocks and the rain for somethin' that you ain't even gonna admit to? And then you tell us that it may be Hoyt Shepherd or Fannie Belle who had him killed. Well, thanks, Quinnie. That's some fine work."

"Hold the damn phone," Quinnie said, balancing up on his toes. "I know a man and I ain't sayin' his name because that sure as hell is a one-way ticket to the river. But I'll tell what he told me. He heard someone, an officer of the court, say he wanted Mr. Patterson dead. This man said Mr. Patterson wouldn't live if he won that election."

We looked at him as he shifted from foot to foot.

Quinnie Kelley shook his head and looked out in the rain, the neon sign, the long sweep of the Victory Drive-In arrow. "I'd keep my eye on Mr. Arch Ferrell, if I were you. That's the meanest son of a gun in Phenix City. But you didn't hear a word from me. Not a dang word."

EARLIER THAT DAY, ARCH FERRELL CHUGGED DOWN THREE glasses of bourbon and smoked eight cigarettes before hustling down the courthouse stairs to meet the outgoing attorney general, Silas Coma Garrett, on Fourteenth Street. Garrett arrived in Phenix City in a long police escort, leaning over his driver to honk the Cadillac's horn while he waved to cops and constituents, broad smiles and thumbs up, as if the goddamn carnival had come back to town. As soon as they stopped, Garrett emerged from the passenger's side in his white suit, tipping his matching white Stetson hat to the crowd.

Arch had to shield his eyes out in the bright light, the American flag popping crisply on the courthouse pole.

Arch straightened his tie, smoothed down his suit jacket, and popped a couple of sticks of Doublemint gum in his mouth. By the time he reached Garrett, he again showed remorse and sadness, to the click and whir of the newsmen's film, and hung onto his mentor's hand for a few beats longer than was customary, pulling him up onto the curb with him.

Garrett wore a concerned, if not confused, smile and clutched a leather satchel while touring the crime scene. The attorney general was well aware of the cameras, too, and would often hold an emotion or hand gesture just to make sure his visit was captured for immortality.

He was a tall, strapping man, and gave a reassuring wink to Arch as Arch continued to light one cigarette after another. Garrett slapped Arch on his back several times, and that big hand felt like that of a father letting a boy know he could relax and that he'd done good. After a while, Arch felt like he could breathe again.

Soon, the men found their way back to Arch's office, and all the assistants and investigators waited in the hall, all except Chief Deputy Bert Fuller, who was the last inside, closing the door with a click and finding a place to sit by the radiator.

Fuller switched a toothpick to the other side of his mouth and looked down at the ground and then took to staring at each man, who talked in low, steady tones, tones of people in mourning. His eyes went from Arch to Garrett like watching a fucking tennis match.

"Arch, we need to step back for a moment," Garrett said, resting his shoes up on the desk and folding his big, oversized hands in his lap. "When is the last time you slept? You know I spent the morning at the country club. I swam, ate lunch, had some family time. You can't let your job swallow you whole. I needed to be clearheaded before I drove over here. You understand that, don't you? A mind that's cluttered can turn to an awful case of the nerves."

Arch's upper lip was sweating, a cigarette bobbed and twitched in his mouth. He watched Garrett, but while he watched he poured another few fingers of bourbon into a short, stumpy glass, the kind you'd find by the sink of a roadside motel.

He drank it down.

"That's it, boy," Garrett said. "That's it."

"The governor has turned my town into a circus."

Arch stood up and began to pace the office, fingering up the blinds to see newsmen filling up the city streets. Outside, more newsmen and photographers waited, one of them with a whirring newsreel camera perched on the stock of a shotgun, and Arch flinched at the sight.

He paced more and ran his hands through the hair at his temples. He could feel the blood rush through his ears and pound the veins in his head. "They blame me for this. They blame me for all of this. Did you hear what Governor Persons said? He said all of the debauchery and gambling has to stop and mentioned me by name, as if he didn't know a goddamn pair of dice had ever rolled in Phenix City. Well, goddamn him to hell."

Arch hauled off and drop-kicked his trashcan across the room and it landed with a hard clatter and a crash, and two framed diplomas fell from the wall. A black-and-white picture of Arch, a captain standing by the Rhine with his boys holding up captured Lugers and bullet-riddled helmets, loosened from a nail and hung crooked on the cracked plaster wall.

Thirty minutes later, Garrett decided to call in all the favorite news-boys into the grand jury meeting room, where he sat thoughtfully at the head of the table, the windows open, letting in hot breezes and the sounds of bullhorns and sirens. He waited for another siren to pass, face drawn and solemn, thoughtful as hell, watching his hands till he spoke. He'd left his white Stetson on the rack outside and wore a pair of large, round gold glasses that made Arch think of a cartoon owl.

Someone leaned back into their seat and the wood clicked and groaned as Garrett nodded to Bert Fuller, who closed the door to give them all some privacy. Arch wanted a drink very badly and wished he'd filled a coffee cup with bourbon.

Fuller, still in his Texas hat and western shirt, leaned against a wall, just a cowpoke against a fence. His arms were crossed.

"I want to make it plain I have complete confidence in these elected officials," Garrett said. "Sheriff Matthews. And Mr. Ferrell. Who I believe is the best damn solicitor in the state. These men are already working on three different theories on the murder."

One of the reporters, a worthless sonofabitch from Birmingham named Ed Strickland, didn't miss a beat: "Does one of these theories factor in the vote fraud case concerning Mr. Patterson's election as attorney general?"

Jesus H. Christ.

"Since I will be testifying in that particular case, I don't think there is any reason to ask me for comment."

"What about the accusation that you and Mr. Ferrell personally added six hundred votes in the Russell County tally to his opponent? It's been said that Mr. Patterson knew of other cases like this across the state."

Arch mopped his face with a handkerchief. He could excuse himself for a moment, fill the coffee mug, and step back into the meeting.

"Considering the situation, I don't think we need to visit a mess of political slander."

"Are you working on any leads?" asked another newspaperman.

Si Garrett nodded and nodded, his face drawn like an old hound. He brushed some dirt off his crisp white suit and stood, peeking through the slatted blinds and then back to the small group of men in the room.

Arch took a long breath. Si's goddamn pauses working on his last nerve. If he would just be quiet, he could sneak off for that drink.

"We've had such little time. In fact, I only just learned that this horrendous act occurred at the exact moment Mr. Ferrell and I were on the telephone discussing the recent *Brown versus Board of Education* decision. I never dreamed something so horrible was happening at that very moment."

Arch nodded along with Garrett, feeling good about him again, but as he did he noticed a few of the newspapermen looking at each other. They looked to have grown uncomfortable in their hard chairs in the closed-off room.

ON SUNDAY NIGHT, GARRETT DROVE ARCH OVER THE RIVER to his deluxe suite at the Ralston while troops continued hammering signs on telephone poles announcing that Fourteenth and Dillingham streets were off limits to Army personnel. Arch watched them all, slunk down in the backseat of the big black Cadillac, as Garrett talked to his driver about this wonderful place where they were all going for steaks and cocktails tonight called the CoCo Supper Club. As long as they could sneak him some liquor, all was right in the world.

"Take me home," Arch said. "Please."

"Nonsense," Garrett said. "I invited half the newsmen in town to come have Sunday dinner with us. We got to get the good feelings back again. We got to let them know that you are doing everything in your power as solicitor to make sense of this horrible situation."

"I didn't create this place. It was here long before me."

"Since the Civil War."

Arch tipped a bottle of Canadian whiskey to his lips, switching from the good bourbon he'd brought from his home out in the country. "You're goddamn right. If I tried to stop the gambling, they'd run me out of town on a greased pole."

Garrett turned full around in the front passenger's seat and smiled as if he'd just had a spot of great news. "Did I tell you last year I had to be institutionalized?"

"What?"

Arch just looked at him, the view of Phenix City fading from the windows around him, one of the Guard troops saluting the car. He narrowed his eyes and waited for a punch line that didn't come.

Not long after, they were seated at the CoCo Supper Club, a hell of a little restaurant just off the runway from the Columbus Airport where you could eat fried Gulf shrimp and lobster and the best T-bone in the city while you watched planes take off and land. Garrett sat at the head of the table and ordered cocktails for everyone but himself, instead asking the waitress—a pretty little girl who called all the men doll— for an entire bottle of sparkling water with a bucket of ice and a glass. The men ate and laughed, the newsmen telling jokes and Garrett roping them back into points about the murder investigation, telling them all that they were working on those three theories and letting that bit pass just as he saw the food coming out of the kitchen and then hushing as they all settled into the shrimp and T-bones and bourbon and Gibsons with tiny onions.

Arch just looked at his food, feeling outside himself, and sometimes Garrett would ask him something and Arch would just look up expectantly, looking for another place, another situation from the one he now found himself in, and he drank. He drank at least a half dozen bourbons until he began to rattle on, mainly to himself, about Arch

Ferrell—using the third person—being a good man. "Arch Ferrell never did anything illegal in his life."

And this caused some looks from some of the newsmen and some wry smiles and poked ribs, but they all kept eating under the constant, weighted stare of Si Garrett's owl glasses. *To hell with 'em all.*

Sometime during the meal, Arch looked up, sure he'd been asked a question but not sure of the question, and simply said: "Si Garrett is the best friend I got. He's one of the greatest men in Alabama."

And with that, Garrett motioned to the little waitress, and Arch heard him whisper into her ear: "Please bring Mr. Ferrell another. But make this one a triple."

"Sure thing, doll."

Later on, the steaks were polished off, just bloody bones on the plates, the fat and grease congealed into a purplish pink mixture where some of the newsmen had squashed the cigarettes they continued smoking. Arch smoked, too, but he stared beyond the newsmen and out beyond the grand dining room of the CoCo Supper Club and the empty bandstand. For a long while, he watched the planes and the flashing of red lights on the tarmac, but then he noticed the long ash on his cigarette and realized he hadn't taken a puff.

He studied the cigarette, blinked, and then leaned in close to Garrett's ear.

"I know all about that talk," Arch said. "I've heard it since Pat was killed. I'm tough and mean, nobody knows that better than me. I'm not a religious fella, never have been, but this thing is making me wish that I were. But no matter what anybody says, I didn't kill Patterson. I just couldn't kill a human being."

He nodded to the group, stubbed out his cigarette, and then took down all the bourbon in one gulp. Some of the men kept gnawing on the bones, freeing those last pieces of gristle. Arch nodded again, satisfied with an answer to a question no one asked, his eyes closing and then opening, his head bobbing down and then jerking back up awake.

And then he stood and wished everyone good-night before placing his hands on the table, taking a deep breath, and vomiting all over the white linen.

"I WAS GOING TO LEAVE THIS DIRTY GODDAMN TOWN," John Patterson said to me, searching through another row of files in the endless wood file cabinets in his father's law office. After a Sunday morning service, he worked row by row, pulling out anything that could be of help, or anything too personal, and setting manila folders into cardboard boxes. He stopped, resting his arm on top of a cabinet. "I don't want to be a vigilante or savior now. Hell, I never understood my father. His political ambitions. Why he stayed here. He could've made better money in about any other town in Alabama."

I didn't say anything. I just waited for another box of files to take down to a truck I borrowed. The window air conditioner had been cut off by mistake, and I fanned my face with a ball cap.

"The only reason I wanted to be a lawyer was to make enough money to retire early. Go fishing. Enjoy life. Not this mess."

"Nothin' wrong with that."

"You are damn right," John said. "Listen, Murphy, I want you to store this at your house, all of this. I don't want that bastard Si Garrett going anywhere near my father's papers."

I reached for another loaded box on Albert Patterson's desk.

John had rolled up his dress sleeves to his elbows and his hairy forearms glistened with sweat, not a bit of comfort coming from an old Emerson table fan.

He kept flipping through files, his fingers moving each one, another drawn and then slipped back, more yet for the growing boxes we had started to stack.

"You and Britton turn up anything?"

"A little," I said. "Heard something about our old friend Thomas Capps."

"Dynamite?"

"Hell of a name," I said.

"He'd never kill my father."

"He blew up Hugh Bentley's house," I said, talking about the attempted murder two years ago of our little anti-vice group's president. His two sons and wife miraculously survived.

"You know those men from Montgomery accused Bentley of blowing up his own house to get sympathy."

We worked for an hour in the heated second floor of the Coulter Building, the old plaster-walled law office feeling like the loft of a barn or an attic. Every few minutes, I'd take a box down to the back of the truck. Armed guards and local hick police watched the still Sunday streets, but no one asked what we were doing.

Everyone seemed to be afraid to look John Patterson in the eye.

Just before John locked up, we heard heavy footsteps on the wooden stairs and up on the landing. Deputy Sheriff Bert Fuller walked inside the office, mopping his face with a red bandanna, with Joe Smelley from the state police right behind. Fuller wore a suit, and Smelley wore wrinkled pants and a short-sleeved dress shirt soaked through the armpits.

Smelley didn't say anything, only walked to one of the boxes and immediately helped himself, searching through the files.

John's jaw clenched and his eyes flashed from Fuller to me.

"Well, howdy, palooka," Fuller said to me. "Ain't you got some gas to pump?"

"I'd rather be here with you, Bert," I said. "You make us all feel so safe."

"You better watch your step," Fuller said. "I don't care what you used to be. I'll beat you silly."

John stepped in front of him.

"We came by for a talk," Fuller said.

"You can set a time with my secretary."

Fuller snorted. He looked over to Smelley, who'd picked a file from the box and glanced through it. Smelley looked to Fuller and snorted back.

"Funny you should mention your secretary."

John's breathing was loud and rapid. I unconsciously staggered my feet, fingers opening and closing into a fist.

"What's her name? Vicki?"

John breathed, temple throbbing, and Bert Fuller popped some chewing gum, waiting for a response. The short, grubby fingers of Joe Smelley flipped through Albert Love Patterson's personal papers.

"I came up here as a favor to you, John," Fuller said. He took a seat on Albert Patterson's antique desk and placed his Stetson on his knee. "I know you sure would hate for the newspapermen to start poking around this thing. And your wife, Mary Jo. Good God. That would set the tongues a-waggin'. So why don't we just sit and talk about things as men. We all know men like pussy, and it don't mean you're not a Christian if you set out for a little poke once in a while. Hell, I seen your secretary and I wouldn't mind having a taste myself."

"Shut your filthy, foul mouth and get your fat ass off my father's desk."

Fuller snorted again and breathed and waited a few beats. And then stood and looked back on the desk, as if mocking the idea he could have soiled the wood. He grabbed his hat and placed it back on his head, knocking it off his brow with two fingers. Resting his hands on his gun belt, he nodded and popped his gum. "Joe?"

Smelley placed the file on the desk next to the box he'd sifted through. He stood and started to pace. I lifted my back foot and shifted, watching the three men in an orchestra of heated movement. Dogs circling around each other.

"I knew your daddy real well, John. He was a fine man. I know you know he was a fine man. I don't think there is any delicate way to say this, but it's my job to ask these questions."

"I have not even put my father in the ground."

"I know," Smelley said, holding up a hand. "I know. But, still, this is my job, and I want you to understand and respect that. Okay? Listen, there has been some talk around town that maybe your daddy was staying up late with that secretary of yours, too. We know her husband was overseas, and we know how young ladies can get real lonely looking for a daddy to cozy up to. Well, we just thought there isn't a lot that could set daddy against son, except one thing."

"Don't say another goddamn word," John said.

Fuller popped his gum again. "Hell, I'll say it. We think you and ole Pat was hitting that same pussy and you might've gotten riled, is all. We got to ask these questions."

John leapt for Fuller's throat, but I'd seen the moment, muscles coiled, and I reached around my friend's waist and pulled him back. Patterson jabbed his elbows back and yelled and bared his teeth, but I held on tight.

Fuller rested his hand on his gun and shook his head with feigned sadness. He shrugged, spit his gum in the wastebasket, and motioned for Smelley to come on. He shook his head for the weakness he'd seen in the office. I wanted to let Patterson go so badly, to let him unleash all that rage, but I knew Fuller wanted to shoot, had maybe come there to shoot, and there had been enough blood for the week.

We sat in the office for a long time, until it grew dark. We didn't talk. I just wanted to hold him there until he had relaxed a bit. Later, we finished up hauling the last of the boxes, and when I walked up into the hot, dark office, just about nine, I found John Patterson sitting at his father's desk. There was a small scrap of paper before him.

John wiped his wet face with a white handkerchief and coughed.

I started to turn around.

"It's all right," he said.

I nodded.

"Guess he thought this was important," he said. "'All that is necessary for the triumph of evil is that good men do nothing.' Edmund Burke."

He looked up at me and nodded, seeming to make a decision that had been weighing on him for a while.

"What is it?" I asked.

"I'm taking my father's place."

"I figured you'd stay."

"Not here," John said. "Not this office. I want to be attorney general. I'm adding my name in place of my father's."

HE'D LOST HER.

But all Sunday, Billy searched. He rode a red Schwinn Reuben had given him for Christmas from the top of Summerville Hill down to the river and through the poor little neighborhoods of Phenix City and government housing where they'd spent those first hours together. They knew the girl, although no one seemed to recall her name the way the boy did, but, on most accounts, she'd gone back to Columbus, most saying Bibb City, and by nightfall he walked his bicycle over the bridge, past the police and troops, and followed the Chattahoochee north to the mill town just outside the city limits. He rode and glided under the cooling shadows, the gold light softening over the river and on the brick mill that seemed to stretch for almost a mile, hammering and pulsing inside like a live thing. And he was given hard looks by hard people who sat on their porches in their identical white mill houses and bony women would stare at him and spit and children playing touch football on their lawns would stop in midplay because they all knew he wasn't one of them, the way a pack of animals can sniff something in the wind. But he paid them no mind and rode past the commissary and the post office and the trading post and the mill bars that were closed down on Sunday. There was a church picnic and a preacher who waved to the boy. The man had a mouth filled with gold teeth and smiled before placing a big slice of chocolate cake in his mouth and licking his fingers.

Billy soon came upon an old woman who sat in a plastic lawn chair by a crooked oak and he coasted and stopped. She sipped from a pitcher of Kool-Aid, next to a platter of deviled eggs on a TV tray covered with buzzing bottle flies. When he spoke to her, the old woman jumped, not because she was afraid but because her eyes were clouded, filmed over in a milky blue, and she listened to the boy's questions about a black-headed girl named Lorelei, and the woman asked about "her people" but the boy knew no names.

He pedaled more, in and out of roads and little cul-de-sacs, and soon it was dark and he was lost, all the little houses and streets all the same. Every house a perfect little white box kept up to mill standards.

He asked a group of teenage boys about her, because surely they would know her. How would boys of that age not know a girl like Lorelei? He found them with their three heads ducked under the hood of a Nash that had to have been built before the war, and they turned when he called out: "Y'all know a girl named Lorelei?"

The boy in the middle had oil-stained hands and fingers, thick-jawed with a baby-fat face. "What kind of name is that?" he asked.

"You know her?"

He looked to his buddies, with the same fifty-cent haircuts, and he shrugged. A skinny, pimple-faced boy asked him, "Where you from?"

But Billy was gone and in and out of the mill town roads, his white T-shirt soggy wet and his legs exhausted, each time stopping to ask, having to gather his breath. He slowed again on top of a hill that over-looked the brown, jagged river and the endless mill bigger than a dozen airplane hangars stacked end to end and heading halfway out into the river.

He lifted up his T-shirt and wiped his face, and he knew it would probably be coming up around ten or so. He didn't have a watch. But when you had a father like Reuben, there never was much accounting for yourself.

In the darkness down at the gentle curve of the road stood a big magnolia tree with fat arms covering a small bare lawn with dirt so trampled it seemed to be made of talcum powder. Little fireflies clicked off and on, and Billy just caught his breath and ran his hand over his sweating face, squinting into the shadows, seeing the shadow of a girl with long black hair and long white legs and arms. Her skin the color of milk.

He walked his bike and followed the curve and without thinking he called out to her and the figure turned, with his heart still beating into his throat. The figure moved into the porch light and it wasn't a young girl at all but a pinched-faced old woman who smoked a cigarette in a flowered housecoat.

She looked at him and then quickly walked inside, and Billy almost turned right into the greased boy who'd worked on the car.

"You didn't answer me," said the skinny, pimple-faced teen. He ran his fingers under his nose and sniffed. He pushed at Billy's shoulder.

Billy just kept walking, trying to go around, but something stopped him, and as he turned back they held the bicycle by the seat. He pulled, but then the pimple-faced boy was in front of him, twisting the bars of the bike like a steer and trying to pull him off.

"Cut it out."

"Where you from?"

"Phenix City."

"The shithole of this earth."

He pushed him with one hand and Billy quit trying to push back. The other teen had yellow eyes and rotted teeth. He reached out and grabbed Billy's shirt and ripped it from the neck.

"Do you know Lorelei?"

"Who is she? Your sister?"

And before Billy could say another word, the pimple-faced teen shot out a fist and busted Billy's lip. Billy fought back, blind to it, because the one thing that he had heard over and over from Reuben was to never take a single ounce of shit from a living soul because, if you did, the shit would bury you. He fought with his eyes closed, windmilling, but his hands were held back, and the teen punched him hard in the eye and in the stomach, all the air rushing from him, and he was on his face, trying to catch his breath, when he heard the puttering sound of a broken muffler and looked up into the twin headlights, shining like eyes, the engine gunning, the car lurching forward.

He rolled just before it reached him.

The car bumped over his bicycle, the teens calling him a little pussy as they hit the gas around another turn, part of the bicycle caught beneath and sparking in the darkness, their laughter and yells following them down the street.

UNDER THE TIN ROOF of Slocumb's Service Station, noted above with a sign reading COURTEOUS and a big red button for Coca-Cola, I watched the cars speed by Crawford Road with their big-eyed head-lights glowing white in the weak gray light. It had been a sluggish, heated morning between rain and sunshine when the air almost wants to break, thunder in the distance. Fat-bodied Fords and Chevys and Hudsons and Nashes would stop in every few minutes and Arthur and I would wander out of the garage to check their oil, clean their wind-shields of mosquitoes and lovebugs, and fill them up with the all-new, high-test Petrox.

And soon they'd again join the snaking line up and out over the bridge and out of Alabama or deeper on to Birmingham or Mont-gomery. Arthur liked to talk to folks, excited to know where they were headed, maybe secretly wanting to escape Phenix, too. He'd smile and speak in that careful, deferential safe ground for negroes, but always laugh and joke with me as a friend, not a boss.

I wore an Army slicker over my green Texaco coveralls and a matching ball cap with the red star logo. In between customers, I checked the shelves for Vienna sausages and saltines and searched the cooler for Coca-Cola and Dr Pepper. There were cases filled with candy and bubble gum and cartons of cigarettes and chewing tobacco; Borden's ice cream was hand-dipped from a freezer by the register.

It was almost lunch when a sky blue Buick coupe wheeled in.

Reuben Stokes walked into Slocumb's, announced with the tingle of a bell over the door, and I looked up. Reuben's hair had been freshly cut and combed tight in the back and sides with a high poof on top; he wore a royal blue leisure coat with long, vertical white stripes and pleated white pants. He smiled like a confident circus performer.

"You're not gonna rob me, are you?"

"How much you got?" Reuben asked.

"Couple hundred."

"Maybe I will."

Outside, a skinny man in a pink cowboy shirt and a fat man with a head the size of a watermelon got out of the Buick, stretched, and talked with Arthur. I recognized the man in the pink shirt as Johnnie Benefield, a local clip joint operator and safecracker. He was bone thin, with big teeth and a face that resembled a skull, black eyes, and a few strands of black hair combed over his bald pate.

The fat man, whom I didn't know, wore big overalls and a dirty white undershirt. His face was pink and jowly and looked like he hadn't shaved for days.

"Me and Johnnie headin' over to the Fish Camp. You want to join us?"

I smiled because it wasn't a serious offer. Anyone in town knew an invitation to Cliff's Fish Camp wasn't about dinner. Sure, they served fried catfish and hush puppies with slaw. But their main attraction was a stable of whores that Cliff kept up in glorified stalls out back and you could take your pick for dessert while you waited for your meal.

"Who's the other fella?"

"Moon? We just givin' him a ride."

Over Reuben's shoulder, I watched the fat man walk to the edge of the gravel lot and begin to unhitch the straps of his overalls. He hefted himself out and then began to urinate in the weeds.

"You can tell him we have restrooms here."

"Moon wouldn't know how to use 'em any more than a mule."

Reuben stuck a cigarette into the corner of his mouth, his breath smelling of sharp whiskey.

"Johnnie workin' for you now?"

"Some. Been with a few different folks since Big Nigger got himself killed."

For some reason people had taken to calling Johnnie's old partner "Big Nigger" before he'd been killed in a shoot-out last year. The man had been as white as me.

"I can always use a good man who knows engines."

"Shoot."

"It's gonna last. Y'all can't even open back up."

"You saying Phenix City's going straight?"

"I'm just saying people around here are fed up."

The man finished urinating, pulled back the straps on his overalls, and wiped his palms on the bib.

"You sound like this crazy man who walks up and down the streets at night. Have you seen him? He wears a blue robe and holds up a sign painted with Bible verses. He says this is all the end times and that we stand in the center of Sodom. You ain't headed that way, are you?"

"I didn't say it's the end times. I just said it's going to be different."

"Pat wasn't Jesus Christ."

"Didn't say he was."

Outside, Arthur cleaned off Reuben's windshield and ran a gauge on each of his fat whitewall tires. When the car was filled, he walked in and told me it had been three dollars and forty-five cents.

I made change and shoved it across the counter, closing the register with a sharp snick. Reuben crushed the bills into his wallet and left a crisp fifty on the counter. I took it and followed Reuben back out, the light growing dark.

"I'm sorry about Pat," Reuben said, holding open the door of the Buick. "I really am."

"You know anything about that?"

He was about to turn, but the question amused him and he smiled at me with a big cigarette clamped between his teeth.

"Do you remember our last bout, before the war?" he asked. "A five-rounder, wasn't it? You always wondered about it."

"Not really."

"You miss that? Waking up and going over to see ole Kid Weisz at that rathole of a gym, working out till you couldn't even stand or lift your arms? You know I felt like I was invincible, like I could bust through a brick wall."

"Haven't felt like that for a while."

"Haven't felt like that since the war."

"I'm sorry about that."

"Shit, I ain't lookin' for pity, Lamar. That wasn't nobody's fault. That was just the world on fire."

I tucked the fifty into his leisure coat's pocket.

He grinned at me. "Your head has always been like a rock."

I stood in the doorway and watched him leave. More thunder grumbled in the distance, but it didn't feel like serious thunder and I paid it little mind.

The fat man, Moon, and Johnnie Benefield waited in the car. Johnnie hunched into the center of the car, turning the radio's dial. The fat man stared straight ahead, immobile in the backseat, a simple, solid smile on his face.

Reuben walked back, leaving the car door halfway open. "There's no need to be a hero right now," he said.

I smoked down the cigarette and flicked a tip of ash into the gravel.

"Just go home, Lamar. Watch your family."

"A threat's not really your style."

"It's not a threat," he said. "You understand?"

I nodded at the words and watched as the car drove off, my stomach feeling weak and cold.

WE BURIED ALBERT PATTERSON OUTSIDE A SMALL CHAPEL in Tallapoosa County on a hot, airless June day after an endless stream of handshakes and condolences and sermons and prayers. After, a train of cars followed the long highway back east where the women of Phenix City filled the Patterson home with fried chicken and deviled eggs and macaroni and cheese and cool Jell-O molds and chilled lemon and chocolate pies. Most of the men still wore their black suits, the doors opening and shutting and battling the summer heat, while people mourned by exchanging loose talk about the killing, giving hugs, or exchanging funny stories about how stubborn ole Pat could be or how rotten this town had grown.

I grabbed a plate of cold fried chicken and some baked beans and found a little chair out on the small front porch with my wife and kids.

I still wore a black armband as one of the pallbearers.

"You doing okay?" Joyce asked.

"Fine and dandy."

She had a soft summer glow on her face and a light dusting of freckles across her nose. A hot wind brushed the brown hair, which she'd recently cut short to match the new Parisian styles, over her dark eyes.

I smiled at her. She winked at me.

"Reuben came by the filling station the other day."

"What did he want?"

"He tried to warn me off. Tried to give me fifty dollars."

"Fifty dollars? You should've taken it."

"You don't mean that."

"Sure I do."

"He's connected to this thing. They all are, whether their hands are dirty or not."

"Did you ask him about it?"

I nodded.

"You two were such good friends. When I married you, I thought Reuben was part of the deal."

"You never liked him."

"The thing you hate about Reuben is that you have to smile when you see him. He has that way about him that just makes you laugh."

"I don't think it's intentional."

"I think it is."

"You know, when we used to spar, he'd play and josh around for the first couple rounds. Always smiling and laughing, tapping out the jabs, while the Kid would yell at us for half-assing it. And then he'd come on, drop that head and lay into you with a cross that would leave you with stars. That's Reuben, all laughs till he decides to knock your lights out. He's been up to something, I know it."

"When is Reuben not up to something?"

"Did I tell you he was with Johnnie Benefield?"

She shook her head and looked away. "He never learns."

We stayed till late and helped the Pattersons clean up, the night growing cool and dark, Anne and Thomas joining a cluster of kids in the backyard, running and chasing lightning bugs in little shadowed pools under oaks and magnolias. The kids held fat pickle jars with holes poked in the lid with forks so the bugs could breathe.

Joyce stayed in the kitchen with some other women cleaning dishes, while I helped Hugh Britton stack some folding chairs they'd borrowed from the Methodist church back into his station wagon.

I'd barely seen John Patterson all night, but when I came back into the house to grab Joyce and the kids John called me into a back room. He'd dropped his jacket somewhere and loosened his black tie. He looked out in the hall and then quietly shut the door.

An old mantle clock whirred away in his parents' bedroom by a loose grouping of sepia photos in silver frames. The room smelled soft and ancient, like an old woman's powder box. Albert Patterson's cane hung on the back of the door.

"Hoyt Shepherd called."

"Now, that's class."

"He wants to see me."

"When?"

"Now."

"Tonight? You got to be pulling my leg."

"Would you ride with me?"

"Sure. You want me to get Hugh?"

"Maybe you can get him to take your wife and kids home," John said. "You mind driving? Not really feeling up to it."

I nodded and then watched as he opened the top drawer of his father's bureau and pulled out an Army-issue .45 he'd probably carried in North Africa and Sicily. He checked the magazine. "Let's go."

HOYT SHEPHERD CAME TO PHENIX CITY DURING THE DE-pression to make it in the mills built alongside the Chattahoochee. But instead he found out his talent lay elsewhere and joined up with a British-born hustler and cardsharp named Jimmie Matthews. Soon, the two learned they could make more money playing poker with soldiers at Fort Benning than they ever could working looms or in the hellfire heat of the foundries or delivering laundry, like Matthews had done. Hoyt Shepherd never even graduated high school, but he'd

always had a peculiar—some said genius—way with numbers and figures and was the man to ask when playing the odds. He and Jimmie
soon took over the Bug racket—the town's numbers game—and by
the time the big war was in full swing, they were knee-deep in whores
and cash and hoped to hell the good times would never end.

But it had been a decade since D-day, and the rackets game couldn't
be played as wide open as the old days. Once again playing out the
odds, he and Jimmie had sold off their interests on Fourteenth and
Dillingham a few years back and parlayed their twenty-year hustle
into some good real estate and a factory that made marked cards and
loaded dice for saloons and casinos from Atlantic City to Havana.

John and I drove out on Opelika Highway, heading toward the Lee
County line, where I turned onto a backcountry road that dipped up
over a hill and followed a loose downward curve into a little private
valley. The narrow road softly turned again, causing the car to glide
and flow on its own, and we could see the massive brick ranch house
set among long, wide wooden fences corralling Black Angus and a few
quarter horses that pricked their ears as the car neared.

At the iron gate, I slowed, and a man carrying a hunting rifle tapped
on the driver's-side glass. I rolled down the window and told him who
we were, and the man looked into the front seat and checked the back.
He asked us to step out of the car and we did.

He patted both of us down, taking the .45 off John and checking the
trunk.

Finally, he unlatched the gates and swung them wide to a long
gravel road.

The house glowed bright, as perfect as a doll's house, and we
weren't halfway up the concrete walk, landscaped neatly with a row of
crepe myrtles and sweet-smelling gardenias, when Hoyt Shepherd
shuffled outside.

He was shoeless in black trousers and a big Cuban-style shirt and he smiled and waved and walked toward John, offering him a big, meaty hand, a soft smile on his lips.

John looked to me and then back to Hoyt. Not knowing what else to do, he just shook his hand. But I could see it pained him, and he tore away as soon as making contact and Hoyt invited us inside.

Hoyt didn't shake my hand. Only looked to me and grunted.

He asked us if we wanted a cocktail and we both declined, and he walked us through the house, past a big old stone fireplace with a big deer head over it holding an antique rifle and through all the modern, boxy furniture and out back to a kidney-shaped pool. A little record player on a drink cart played a rhumba.

Jimmie Matthews sat at a table under an umbrella, only a soft blue glow coming from the pool, and the light made Matthews's face look strange and pale as he nodded to us and also offered his hand to both of us.

We sat in a loose grouping of lounge chairs, and Hoyt relit a dying cigar while I pulled a pack of cigarettes from my shirt pocket. Ripples of light from the water scattered across them.

"Ain't you the fella from the fillin' station?" Hoyt asked.

"That's me."

"I know your wife's daddy. He sure is a pistol."

Matthews was dressed in a blue pin-striped suit, white shirt, and no tie. He waited, his legs crossed and posture erect.

Hoyt got the stogie going and pulled an ashtray close. He smiled and grunted. That man really liked to grunt.

"Now, John," Hoyt said. "I want you to know right off that I didn't have a thing to do with what happened. I didn't want another day to pass 'fore I said that to you."

John nodded. The filter of the pool made whirring sounds in the silence. Matthews just looked into the face of John Patterson, meeting his eyes, and nodded along with Hoyt's words.

Hoyt had grown fatter since I'd seen him last, and his nose had started to swell in that big Irish way. He lifted up a Scotch filled with melting ice and took a sip and alternated it with the cigar. He'd always reminded me of W. C. Fields with a Southern accent.

"Can't I please get y'all somethin'? I know it's been a heck of a day. But I've heard what all the newsmen have been saying about me and all those stories about me and Jimmie and the Bug and the nightclubs and all that ancient history. I never suspected you'd pay attention to it."

John looked up at him, his jaw tight. "Why wouldn't I?"

"Well," Hoyt said, and grinned and then closed his mouth. His face flushed red. "Well, I mean, you know how things were between me and your daddy." Hoyt turned to me. "Hey, you. You mind goin' somewhere else while we talk?"

"I do," I said.

"He stays," John said.

Hoyt just nodded. He pulled a wet napkin from under his drink and ran it over his face and fattened neck.

"I know you did everything in your power to make sure that my father lost the election and the runoff," John said. "I know you bought off every vote you could in Russell County and sent your men all across Alabama to do the same. How many tens of thousands of dirty money did you put out there?"

"And we both know that Monday he was set to tell the grand jury in Birmingham about every dirty penny," I said. "He had folks who could prove it."

"Boy, why don't you go and scrape the grease from your finger-nails?"

I smiled at Hoyt. "And to think I got all dressed up to impress you."

Hoyt grunted. He smiled at me. It was like watching a bulldog pant.

The back of the ranch house was mostly windows, and, inside, Hoyt's wife, Josephine, glided through the family room in a pink satin robe with feathered ruffles. She was blond and built like a brick house, a damn-near twin for Betty Grable, and when she appeared outside and came toward us it was brisk and upright on three-inch high heels that I soon noticed were made from a cheetah print.

A little dog yapped after her, a poodle trimmed in the traditional way and dyed a bright pink. (I knew she also liked to dye the dog blue on occasion.) "Can I offer you men a cocktail? We have some fresh cocktail shrimp."

John didn't even acknowledge her, still studying his eyes on Hoyt Shepherd and Matthews, and they exchanged glances.

"I don't think these boys are stayin', Josie."

I thanked Hoyt's wife and she smiled and winked politely and moved away, her shapely backside switching and swaying like a pendulum.

"You believe that woman married me for my looks?" Hoyt asked, watching her walk, and laughed till he coughed. He swigged down some more Scotch.

"Are we finished?" John asked.

"Just listen," Hoyt said and reached out and touched John's hand. "I may be a real sonofabitch and sometimes what many people may call a fool. And maybe I didn't want your daddy becoming attorney general. I mean, can you blame me?"

"Yes," John said.

I remained quiet and finished out a cigarette and crushed it under the heel of my shoe. I leaned forward, listening, watching the pool, watching Hoyt and silent Jimmie.

Jimmie looked to me and nodded with recognition.

"I'm not a stupid man," Hoyt Shepherd said. "I know that the killing of your father wouldn't do a thing but topple down my world. The man who did this just stopped business in Phenix City cold. What do we have now? No GIs in bars. Girls off the streets. National

Guardsmen on every corner. That's not something I ever wanted to see in my town."

John watched him. Hoyt offered his hand, again.

Not caught off guard, he just looked at it. Out in the valley, the cattle grew nervous and groaned and called out, sounding almost like screams, and I could hear their heavy feet shuffling and brushing against each other, frustrated under the moon.

I started a new cigarette.

"Last night, that nutcase Si Garrett and his trained monkey, Arch Ferrell, hauled me into the courthouse at three o'clock in the morning," Hoyt said. "Ferrell was as drunk as a skunk, and Garrett talked so fast I couldn't even understand most of what he said. But most of what he said, Jimmie, correct me if I'm wrong on this—"

Jimmie nodded.

"They like both of us for this," he said. "Garrett called us the crime lords of the den of iniquity. And I'll be goddamned if I didn't have to look up what that meant in the dictionary when I got home. And, men, it wasn't good."

"What do you want us to do about it?" John said, standing.

I joined him.

"Just keep an open mind," Hoyt said. "I hear you're aiming for your dad's spot."

John nodded. "I am."

"I understand," he said. "I wish you luck."

"You don't mean that, Hoyt."

The air smelled of chlorine and the gardenias and cow shit.

Hoyt smiled and kind of laughed, his face clouded in his exhaling breath. "Guess I don't."

"I haven't been back in Phenix City long, but I know to watch where I step."

"That's not what this was about," Hoyt said. "I just wanted you to know this isn't my deal. I have no part in this. I didn't leave my neck out for no misdemeanor vote fraud. We're all hurting. Did you know the same night your daddy was killed, someone broke into my other house and blew a safe bigger 'an a truck? They 'bout cleaned me out."

"What does that have to do with my father?"

"Everything," Hoyt said. "You can't trust a crook no more. There was a time when a man's word meant something. This town has gone to hell."

John simply nodded. He then looked over at Jimmie and said, "Good night."

Jimmie gave a soft smile and both older men remained seated.

"You boys listen to me," Hoyt said. "I will cut out my heart and place it here on the table if Bert Fuller and Johnnie Benefield didn't have something to do with your daddy. Benefield is the most cold-hearted, sadistic sonofabitch I've ever known."

THEY FOLLOWED A LONG PATH INTO THE WOODS, PUSHING along a fat man in handcuffs, Fuller knocking him in the back of the head with a revolver when he'd slow down. The man wore pressed pants, no shirt, and a tie, his shirt torn away after they'd run his car off the road. Reuben walked between Fuller and Benefield, who wore a brown western suit with gold stitching.

There was a path, but it hadn't been trod since hunting season, and Fuller swatted away branches that slapped back and hit Reuben in the face and eyes as he struggled along half drunk on Jack Daniel's. He still carried the open bottle from Club Lasso, where he'd gotten the call, and quickly met the men in the woods.

Benefield had worked PC for years and had taken on jobs in Atlantic City and in Tampa for some Italian boys down there. He was a natural-born killer, loved the job, and had killed so many in Phenix

City that Reuben had lost count. Benefield and Fuller were as thick as thieves, and, under Fuller's protection, Benefield could do about whatever he wanted. The man's eyes were black and soulless, and when Benefield smiled Reuben felt an icy prickle run along his back.

They wandered up a hill and through a rusted stretch of barbed wire that had been cut away by hunters. Most of the trees were young, planted on cleared land. In the glow of the fat flashlight Fuller carried, he saw a mammoth oak that seemed lost in the immature forest. The trunk as large around as an automobile, prehistoric and crooked. The men were drawn to it.

Reuben set down the bottle and stared up at the big tree and waited. Fuller pushed the fat man to the trunk of a nearby pine and lashed him to it. Benefield kicked up mounds of pine straw around the man's legs, covering him up to his shins.

The shirtless man was breathing hard, his back and shoulders covered in acne. Fuller pulled a little notebook from the man's back pocket and slapped him across the face with it.

The man's head turned and he was slow to look back at the men before him. Reuben lit a match against a thumbnail and stared at the man.

Fuller took in an audible lungful of air and walked over to Reuben and held out his hand. Reuben handed him the bottle and Fuller took a drink. He walked back to the man and then stared up at the night sky, thinking, contemplating.

Benefield caught the edge of a cigarette from Reuben's match.

"Why'd you put them lies in the newspaper?" Fuller asked.

"I didn't write any lies."

"I said admit it, goddamn you. You cain't come to a man's town and put them things in print. People think that garbage is the truth."

The man looked away. Fuller reared back and struck the man in the face.

"You wrote in that rag of yours that I was—" Fuller looked to Bene-field, who reached into his pocket for a piece of folded-up newsprint. Fuller took it and read: " 'The town bully. A common criminal who is a disgrace to the badge.' Isn't that your name at the top there?"

Fuller hit him again. Benefield took back the piece of paper, folded it dramatically, and placed it back into his pocket.

"I stand by it," the reporter said. His mouth bled.

"Say it to my face," Fuller said. "You goddamn Communist."

Fuller slapped him and the blow turned the man's head quick to the side.

"I'm not Communist."

"What would you call it when you come to a town and piss on the head of the law?"

Johnnie Benefield kicked up some more pine needles and checked the knot binding the man to the tree. He stared up through the branches of the forest at the summer sky and took a breath. The man spit out blood from his mouth.

Reuben took a long pull of the whiskey and then poured another out on the pine needles. Fuller adjusted the rig on his fat stomach and pitched his Stetson back with his thumb.

"How 'bout it, boy?" Benefield asked. "You gonna come to Jesus?"

"Excuse me?"

"Come to Jesus," Benefield said, answering, and plucked the ciga-rette from his mouth and touched it to a book of matches. He smiled to the man, looking him dead in the eyes, as the match caught to the other matches and the entire book began to burn.

The portly, shirtless man started to cry.

Almost casually, Benefield pitched the book into the dry rust-colored needles at the man's feet. The fire kicked up instantly, the needles start-ing to churn smoke and then crackle with flame. The man screamed and flailed and tried to pull loose from the lasso around his waist.

The fire caught in a ring about the reporter.

"I'll do it."

"Do what?" Fuller asked.

"Whatever you want."

Reuben stood next to Fuller.

"Cut him loose," Reuben said.

"Not yet," Fuller said. "Say what you did."

"I wrote lies."

"Is that an apology, Reuben?"

"Oh, hell."

"Are you, or are you not a card-carrying member of the Communist Party?"

The man was crying, wrenching his feet from the flames and crooking them from the burning earth, curling his toes for just an inch of space from the heat. His eyes looked as if they were about to burst from the sockets as he strained against the ropes.

"I am," the man yelled. "I am a Communist."

Benefield doubled over from laughter, his teeth like a rotten picket fence, as he searched for some dry branches.

Reuben spit and pulled out a fat bone-handled pocketknife from his pants. With one hand, he pushed at Fuller and went for the rope, but Fuller caught his hand and easily twisted the knife from his grip.

"Do you feel what hell is like?" Benefield asked, grinning. "Get used to it, boy. Hellfire, yes, sir."

The reporter pleaded. He cried. He said he loved Mother Russia.

Benefield just added more pine needles to the smoking, curling mass.

There was a scream, a long, howling animal scream, the smell of burning flesh, and the piercing sound made even Fuller turn his head. He nodded with strong approval and threw the knife down at Reuben like you would slop to swine.

"Get him down from there."

When the man was free, he turned and bolted from the tree like a loose cat. Just as he was about out of sight, jumping a warped run of barbed wire on cedar posts, Benefield leveled a .44 and fired off a hard, booming shot punctuated with a rebel yell.

The shot missed, and Benefield laughed, the pine needles smoked and burned out into a perfect blackened circle. "That boy shit his drawers. Did you smell it? Did you smell it?"

THE NEXT MORNING, ARCH FERRELL AND SI GARRETT waited outside the short driveway leading to a little brick house in Cullman. Si Garrett leaned back in the driver's seat, having given his man the morning off, and Arch slept one off in the back of the Oldsmobile, just coming awake. Garrett listened to the first morning news out of Montgomery, nothing but more and more reports about the killing of Patterson and his funeral and John's announcement he was taking his slain father's slot, and, as Arch sat up, he watched a man emerge from the simple white house with a mug of coffee. The man walked down the drive, careful not to spill the contents, and Garrett opened his door.

He handed Garrett the coffee.

Garrett turned down the radio.

"Mr. Folsom said to set up an appointment for later."

"We already tried that."

The man squatted, craned his neck toward the house, only one light on showing some movement behind a curtain. "He said he can't miss his walk. You know how he is about that walk. And after that, he's due in Montgomery."

"We just need a second of his time."

"I'm sorry, Mr. Garrett," the man said, looking into the backseat at

Arch with a wry smile, the cocky sonofabitch, and turning to walk away. "Enjoy the coffee."

Garrett cut the radio back on, watching the house with the single light on, tapping the steering wheel. More news about the killing and an interview with John Patterson coming on, piercing Arch's head. Garrett turned it up after a commercial for Dobbs Buick in Alex City and ads for Vienna sausages and Bama jellies. *The very men responsible for the condition of Phenix City are the ones running this investigation. The only true way we will see justice in this case is with the involvement of federal authorities. This whole thing is rotten all the way up to the capital.*

Garrett tuned the radio to a hillbilly station playing an Ernest Tubb number called "Walkin' the Floor Over You."

From the backseat, Arch stared at his reflection in the rearview mirror. His hair was scattered wild, rat nose twitching and big ears pricked, as he ran a hand over an unshaven face, opened his eyes, and then closed them. He breathed in and coughed and opened the side door and vomited into a drainage ditch.

After some snorting and gagging, he sat up again and asked Garrett if he had some chewing gum. Garrett handed back some Black Jack gum, and the song changed and this time it was Alabama's own Hank Williams—that's the way the announcer said it—and Hank sang "Move It On Over."

Arch started to sweat in his wrinkled dress shirt. He looked to Garrett, playing with the brim of his white Stetson that matched his suit, and then up at the simple brick house of the governor-elect, James E. Folsom, alias Big Jim.

"You ever think radio waves can get mixed up in your head?" Garrett asked him. "Sometimes I hear songs and I think they're written just for me."

Arch plucked a few more sticks of gum in his mouth. "I feel like death warmed over. Last thing I remember is that catfish house outside Opelika."

"I wanted you to sleep it off. Get your mind off the worry. Worry will eat a man's soul."

"Think Big Jim will see us?"

Garrett didn't answer.

"Si?"

"I'm not moving an inch till he does," he said. "He owes us."

Moments later, the door opened and out walked the big six-foot-eight, two-hundred-and-fifty-pound sonofabitch in khaki pants, plaid shirt, walking boots, and with a walking cane. Before Garrett could reach the door handle, Big Jim was striding down the road, reminding Arch of storybooks about Paul Bunyan, and Garrett cranked the car and followed loosely, just nosing along, and pretty soon they were beside the governor-elect.

"'Morning, Big Jim."

Big Jim looked fresh, his hair slicked back, square jaw out, blue eyes clear and directed ahead on the narrow country road lined with oak and pecan trees. Cicadas started to click and whir high up in the trees.

"I thought Drinkard told y'all to find me later."

"He did."

"Well."

"Can't wait, Jim."

The walking continued, Garrett moving alongside him in the Olds, Arch leaning between the front seats, feeling like a kid at a picture show. Garrett kept moving, the car idling and him smiling, trying to keep it affable and slow.

"We got real problems."

"I'll say."

"They want me back in Birmingham next week," he said. "They want me to testify on those votes before the grand jury."

"Don't see how that concerns me. I don't take office till next year."

"Just figured you could make some calls."

Big Jim looked at Garrett and then over at Arch, who gave a self-conscious smile and a half-assed wave. The strides lengthened, but Garrett continued. Sonofabitch.

"You helped us out with Patterson," he said. "You talked to him for us."

"And where did that get us?" he said. "He was going to testify against you boys on Monday anyway. But I guess y'all know that already. Did you really think you could add seven hundred goddamn votes with no one noticing?"

"We're only accused of six hundred," Garrett said and leaned back in the driver's seat, steering with two fingers, a boy on a country road following an insulted girl.

"Arch and the boys in Phenix City came through for you on this election," he said. "You know that money gave you a big boost."

"It did," Big Jim said, eyes still staring straight ahead, not even winded, walking with the stick up in his hand like a drum major.

"I just need you to call the dogs back."

"It's too late, Si."

"It's not too late. Goddamn Governor Persons is going to try to make this his big political send-off because he doesn't care what bridges he burns. He's gonna leave you a pile of flaming dog shit for you to clean up when you take office."

"Too late," Big Jim said. "I'm making an announcement later today that I'm supporting the Patterson boy."

Si Garrett threw on his brakes and the big, clunky Olds skidded to a stop. He got out of the car and slammed the door behind him. Big Jim Folsom stopped and peered down at the much smaller man.

"You . . . you . . . this is going to break me. You know that? Do you understand what you are doing to my head?"

"You're a sick man, Si. Get some help. But Phenix City is over. The sooner we all understand that, the better."

"But throwing in with John Patterson. How could you do that? He's not qualified or well-bred. He doesn't have the qualifications."

"Of someone like who? You, Si?"

Garrett stood on the side of the road, hands on his hips and shaking his head. He stayed there for several minutes, as Arch watched the sun rise high over a big, endless pasture bordered by a broken cedar fence and rusted barbed wire. Big Jim grew smaller and smaller down the long, winding road.

REUBEN AND JOHNNIE PLAYED POKER ON THE BIG PORCH of Fannie Belle's whorehouse, a broken-down old mansion hidden way out in the county. They'd been drinking most of the morning, after shoveling down some grits and eggs a little colored girl had made for them, and now smoked cigarettes, a half bottle of Jack at their boots, as the heat broke up high through the weeds and little pine trees down the dirt road.

"Where's Fannie?" Reuben asked.

"Asleep."

"That woman is gonna screw you blind."

Johnnie smiled, leaned into the table, and squinted at Reuben as if he couldn't quite make out his face.

"Is it true she's got sixteen husbands?"

"Oh, come on, now. It's only a dozen or so."

"She makes them fall in love with her and then she sends them overseas, collecting their checks like a good ole Army wife. I seen her sitting in the bar, writing all those horny letters to those boys, telling them all the illegal things they can do to her."

Johnnie smiled. "Hell of a scam."

"You know you're gonna get yourself killed when one of those boys comes back to PC and sees you mounting their trophy to the wall."

"Aw, hell."

Reuben tossed another few chips into the pot. And behind them they heard the screen door creak open and slam closed. Fannie walked outside, naked except for a light green man's shirt loosely buttoned. She played with her stiff red hair that Johnnie had mussed up pretty damn good and then reached for a cigarette from him. As she did, Reuben got a nice view of her right tittie.

"'Mornin', boys."

"Fannie," Reuben said.

She was a green-eyed devil with fair skin and red lips, an upturned nose that some might say was pug but others might say pert. But she'd made her way with her chest, and even that early in the morning she made a big show out of taking in that first lungful of smoke, smiling in a lazy, careless way like she was still in a dream.

The door creaked again, slammed shut, leaving only her perfume and smoke on the wind.

"Be careful," Reuben said.

"You be careful."

"I ain't never careful," Reuben said.

"I'm sayin' be careful 'cause you're playin' with my money."

"The hell you say."

"Where is it?"

Reuben fanned the cards in his hand and leaned back in the metal porch chair. He took a deep breath and shook his head. "Thought we agreed on that."

"Things gonna die down real soon."

"Didn't say they wouldn't."

"You know every time you tell a lie, Reuben, the left corner of your mouth turns up. I heard fighters got tells like that, too. Like before they 'bout to nail you with a sucker punch, a good fighter will know it."

"That's true."

"So when you gonna skip town?"

Reuben looked over the fan of cards. On the backs were photographs of naked women with big old titties. He blew out some smoke and rested the butt of the cigarette against his temple.

"A man can ask."

"Johnnie, did your mother love you?"

"Sure," Johnnie said. "Why wouldn't she?"

"No reason."

"You know, if Hoyt figures us for robbin' him—"

"No reason, if both us keep our goddamn mouth shut," Reuben said. "We'll make the cut when we can. Till then, it's tucked away."

"Well, looky here," Johnnie said, tossing down a pair of kings. "It's Hoyt and Jimmie."

Reuben laid down his cards. Two pair.

"Aces and eights."

Johnnie looked up from his cards and into Reuben's eyes. "You know what they call that hand, don't you?"

I FINISHED ADDING sweet feed for my Tennessee walkers and capped off their water tank from a nearby well pump. I liked afternoons like this most, when I could break away from the filling station and drive out a few miles into the country to my little piece of land and work with Rocky and Joe Louis. I didn't get to ride as much as I used to, but I'd often take Anne out on the weekends. She'd taken a keen interest in brushing the horses and taking them for rides along the winding trails that had been beaten smooth by the animals' hooves. But I was alone today and cleaned out the stalls, replaced the hay, and checked their shoes and teeth. While the horses ate, I ran some saddle soap over their tack and talked to them in a smooth calming voice, and then sang to them a bit of "My Wild Irish Rose" and even "Danny Boy." Songs that I'd heard on the radio between the westerns and comedy shows I'd known as a child in Troy and, because I had the red hair and the Irish name, always thought they'd been important.

I'd just hung up a bridle and some rusted shoes on the nails in the barn when I heard a car approaching from the long dirt road out back. When I looked out the narrow door, I saw Hugh Britton.

I met him at the metal gate and let him inside. Britton wore a black suit in the summer heat, careful where he stepped in his dress shoes. He looked like he was headed to church and I knew that meant business. He never looked quite right when wearing a suit on his old bones.

I walked back toward the barn, where we could stand in the shade under the rusted tin roof.

"Si Garrett's gone," Britton said.

"What do you mean?"

"Got on a plane in Montgomery last night and headed for Texas. No one knows for sure. Some say he checked into some kinda nuthouse for his nerves."

"Is he coming back?"

He shook his head. "Doesn't look like it. Left the investigation in charge of a man named Sykes."

"Does John know him?"

He shook his head again.

"At least we still have the Guard," I said.

"Bunch of babysitters," Britton said, running a handkerchief across his sweaty neck. "They can't get a lick done without the damn governor allowing them to bust up a single dice game. They are worthless, and, hell, no one believes they'll stay. And this new fella, Sykes? He's cut from the same cloth as Si Garrett. I guarantee as much."

"Any new word from Mr. X?"

The mysterious Mr. X had been Britton's inside source for some time. Mr. X was constantly sending typed letters on the rackets' latest movements and underhanded deals. Lately, he'd been sending us small black records of phone conversations with Hoyt Shepherd. Most of them had happened years ago, but they'd proved pretty useful when it came to figuring the Machine's business.

"He just sent me a new record. He was real scared about this one.

Had me go to the Columbus bus station and fetch a locker key from a phone booth. Said this one might get him killed."

"Who was on it?"

"Our esteemed governor, talking about campaign contributions from Hoyt and Jimmie."

"You want to go to the newspaper boys with this one?"

"I think I want to keep this one in my back pocket," Britton said, giving a sharp smile. "But there is one thing."

I brushed the dirt off the front of my work pants.

"A woman in my church told me about this man," he said. "He was on Fifth Avenue when Mr. Patterson was killed."

THE MAN LIVED LESS THAN TWO MILES AWAY FROM MY land in a little cottage on Sandfort Road. I drove, following the twisting road cutting through the red bluffs of the Chattahoochee, and finally found the address and the small gravel drive. But when we knocked on the door, we were met with the sliver of a face behind the chain asking what the hell we wanted. Britton told the man we were with the Russell County Betterment Association and said he'd like to talk to him about Mr. Patterson. He didn't mention the name of the woman from the church.

The man stood there for a few moments.

"I don't know why you'd want to talk to me."

"Were you on Fifth Avenue when Mr. Patterson was shot?" I asked.

There was silence and then: "No. You are mistaken."

"Some people saw you there," Britton said, in his smooth country drawl. "Said you had dinner at the Elite."

"They were mistaken."

"You weren't there?" Britton asked.

"I said they were mistaken. Now leave me be."

"Sir, if you're afraid," Britton said, "you don't need to be. The National Guard troops are on every street corner. We could get you help."

Fingers reached into the crack, like small pink worms, and unlatched the chain lock. The door swung open and we walked inside. The room was empty save for two chairs and a suitcase.

"Going somewhere?" I asked.

"Far from here, if people don't quit running their goddamn mouths."

"We can help you, sir," Britton said, putting his hands in his pockets and shifting back on his heels. "Unless we speak out, they'll go free and the city will fall right back into that hellhole."

"Speak out?" the man asked as he walked toward Britton and stopped. He was pudgy and wearing a dirty white T-shirt. "My wife and daughter are gone. I put them on a bus two days after the killing. It wouldn't stop. The phone wouldn't stop ringing. I had to take the phone off the hook and sit up for two days straight drinking coffee with a shotgun on my lap, sitting out there on that porch, my heart up my throat every time a car passed on by slow or I saw the police. Do you understand? This is none of my concern."

"Yes, sir," I said. "Things are different now."

The man laughed, it was a harsh little laugh out his nose, like he hadn't intended it. "Last time I checked, the same sonsabitches still hold badges."

"What exactly did you see?" Britton asked, keeping his tone even and slow. He looked to me and then back. "Sir?"

"Please leave."

I watched the man, saw the arms hug himself, the sweating brow, the pacing, eyes reddened and twitching. I looked to Hugh Britton and then touched the older man's shoulder: "Come on."

ARCH FERRELL SAT AT THE EDGE OF HIS FOREST IN A METAL lawn chair watching the sun set and drinking bourbon from the bottle. His fingers had grown yellow from the nicotine of the endless cigarettes, and he wore the same suit of clothes he'd had on for two days, his own smell sickening him. When the phone rang inside his house it was a distant thing and he paid it no mind as the sun crisply broke through the perfectly laid acres of pines that his daddy had planted before the war. Simple and straight, a lush curtain of rust-colored needles on the ground.

His wife, Madeline, seven months pregnant and waddling, came out and called to him from the ranch house they owned in Seale, ten miles from Phenix City. He heard her but didn't, and for a while just kept concentrating on the light, the shifting of shadows pouring like ink from the trunks on the blanket of needles.

She called to him again, and he felt for the arms of the chair, pulling himself up. For a moment, he blinked, thinking he spotted a German soldier in the depths of his acreage. He saw nothing but heard the explosive thud of artillery and the *snick-snick-snick* of machine-gun fire. The Germans seemed to be buzzing through the trees and he squinted into the neat rows, the bottle falling and rolling at his feet, even as he turned toward Madeline's voice and they all dissipated, the little shadowed Germans, into the full-on sunset.

The walk was endless, and he made himself count the steps, maybe a hundred feet, and she pulled the black phone out on a long cord and handed it to him by their backyard grill and he answered, hearing his voice more in his head than outside his body.

"Arch?"

"Si?"

"Listen, I want you to hear me and hear me good."

"I'll certainly try."

"I'm gone."

"What do you mean 'gone'?"

"I just left the courthouse and I've fully packed. I have a car waiting on me."

"Where?"

"Where no one on earth can find me, I assure you of that."

"You're not going to testify," Arch said. The words came out slurred and long.

"I did," Garrett said. "For ten hours straight. They have me and they have you."

"Come again?" Arch asked, stepping backward on the patio, nearly tripping, and holding himself level only by the strength of the phone cord in his hand.

"Reid made a statement. He gave all of it. They had some kind of jew detective named Goldstein check out his stories. The grand jury knows about us at the Molton Hotel and changing those vote tallies. You hear me? Reid told it all."

"Goddamn all to hell."

"Don't panic. I'll be in touch."

"Where? What do I do?"

"I'll be in touch. I gave my briefcase over to my secretary and the papers on Patterson to my chief investigator. Everyone knows we were on the phone together, buddy. You can't argue with the facts."

"Si? You said you could handle this. You said you could stop any investigation. Si?"

The phone clicked and clicked, and an operator came on the line asking if Arch needed assistance and he told the woman yes, to please go fuck herself, and the woman gave a little yelp. Arch walked back to the chair and the bottle and the ramrod-straight rows of pines. Acres and acres.

Madeline was there, stomach about to pop, and a gentle, assuring smile on her face. He walked to her and she pulled Arch in. He smelled her neck that was all good things, flowers and biscuits, and wrapped his arms around her, crying low and hard, the night coming on, filling the trees in an endless lake of shadows.

"I need to know," she said.

He hugged her, burying his head into her neck, just holding her. They stayed there until she nudged him; he'd drifted off and was on the chair again. She stood behind, and he could feel the weight of their unborn child pressing against his neck.

"I need to know."

He coughed and leaned forward, finding the bottle that had rolled under the metal chair. He uncorked it and took a drink, cleansing his mouth with the taste.

"No," he said, throat cracked and raw. "I wasn't anywhere near Albert Patterson. I was on the phone to Si. But now Si has up and lost his mind again. A coward, a fearful coward."

Madeline rubbed the top of Arch's head and placed the cool back of her hand against his forehead as if checking for a fever. "I knew it," she said. "I just knew it."

Arch watched a wall of shadow at the edge of the forest, hoping to hear the clatter of gunshot and artillery that was always present. He wanted to walk in and join them, hoping that the two worlds and time could somehow be joined. But instead he just caught the riffle of the wind picking up and blowing through the pines, sounding to him of a gentle breeze against bulrushes.

HOYT SHEPHERD PARKED HIS BRAND-NEW LIGHT GREEN Cadillac Eldorado in a safe spot away from the others but well in sight of the massive barn out in the county where they held the fights. There was some worry that there would be any fights at all, on account of the killing and all those goddamn Guard troops. But leave it to good ole PC ingenuity to find a barn big enough for the ring and stretch the canvas tight and set up church pews for seats. Judging from the cars, it looked like at least two hundred folks had found the place and left the Guard in the dark. Shepherd waited for Jimmie to follow and he dogcussed him as he passed for his slowness, and then wiped the solid-gold Cadillac insignia on the hood with a little white handkerchief. Matthews ignored him, and up at the barn paid the black boy at the door a tenspot. As they passed, the boy asked Hoyt when he was coming back to the steak house.

And then Hoyt recognized him as Charley Frank Bass and clasped his hand and hugged him and told Jimmie that Charley Frank could make a mess of liver and gravy that would make you want to slap your mamma. He asked him about his brother and mamma and the black kid told him.

They strolled on in, and Hoyt shook more hands and patted some boys on the back and they wandered around the smooth dirt floor all lit up with spotlights someone had stolen out of the Baptist church along with the pews. And there were country men who sold shots of corn liquor for fifty cents and some boys from downtown selling bottles of beer in troughs filled with ice.

Hoyt bought a shot of corn liquor, and he and Jimmie found a place close to the ring. The seats were taken, but when they walked close the man organizing the whole thing—Frog Jones—kept two steps ahead and shooed out the men who had already sat down.

The fight was already on, in the second round, and two tough ole nigger boys from Columbus were getting after each other like there was fire in their britches. They were rawboned and muscular, one in blue shorts and the other wearing white. And they worked around the ring, stomping and dancing, like colored fighters will do, and then they'd tear into each other. The boy with the blue shorts had a two-mile reach and the sonofabitch landed a solid hook right before the bell that sent the other fighter reeling backward, his eye swollen to the size of an egg.

By the fifth—announced by a fat-tittied whore wearing nothing but black panties and high-heeled shoes and holding up the ring card—Hoyt had found someone who'd brought in some boiled peanuts and he'd sent Jimmie to go get him another bit of corn whiskey and Jimmie didn't say a word about it, as silent as a fucking sphinx. After he left, the fighters turned on each other, people calling out: "Fight 'em, nigger. Fuck 'em or fight 'em."

Hoyt stood up as the crowd yelled when the blue fighter backed the other boy into a corner and commenced to whipping the holy tar out of him. His head slapped back and forth, the fighter barely able to raise the gloves to protect his face, as the blows went from a jab to a cross to a jab to a cross, and then as an exclamation a final hook walloped the boy down to the ground and the crowd went wild.

About that time, he felt someone take a seat next to him and he figured it was Jimmie and reached out his hand for the jelly jar full of hooch. But when he looked down, it was Fannie Belle sitting in Jimmie's chair, and Hoyt's smile dropped.

Fannie wore a tight red dress with her freckled tits hanging out. Bright gold rings on her long white fingers and a diamond-encrusted cross on her neck. She said she was in her twenties, but Hoyt guessed she'd been on God's green earth at least thirty-five years. She had an upturned nose, a slight pug to it, and wide, painted-on eyebrows. You wouldn't look twice at her face, but you'd give her body a good inspection.

She crossed her muscular legs and placed a hand on Hoyt's knee.

"Do you mind?"

"Thought I'd say hello."

"You're sittin' in Jimmie's spot."

Hoyt watched the little black man in the ring, the referee, pull the fighter to the side and look at his face and shake his head but then change his mind, as the crowd began to throw bottles into the ring, striking him and the fighter in the head. The referee reeled back, holding his bloodied temple, and the fighter staggered to the center of the ring. His trunks were now pink from the blood, and both eyes had closed so tight that Hoyt didn't know how he could see.

"Jesus H. Christ Almighty." Hoyt turned his eyes away.

"How's tricks, Big Daddy?"

Hoyt looked to her.

"I like that shirt. You get that in Cuba?"

"Talk English, Fannie. What the fuck do you want?"

Fannie Belle uncrossed her legs, straightening out the dress from her ample—but not fat—ass, and turned to Hoyt, moving close to his ear like a lover, and whispered: "This thing is only gonna end in one way. And you boys can sit around with your dicks in your hands or we can hit this mess straight ahead."

"You plan on attacking the National Guard?" Hoyt said, and raised an eyebrow. "You know they have tanks?"

"I have a plan, Big Daddy."

"Shit, it's over. Quit tossin' your pussy around. This was a beaut while it lasted, but you're out of your goddamn mind if you think you can do a thing about it."

"If Patterson's boy takes over, he's gunning straight for us."

"Well, get ready, because unless there is an actual Republican contender in Dixie he has the job. If I were you, I'd think about changing my address."

Hoyt watched the woman's eyes narrow. Her face was a flawless mask of coated white makeup as she played with the rings on her fingers.

"Be a hell of a thing if a couple of them cocky newsmen got killed," Fannie said. "Or a few prissy-ass RBA boys. Sometimes you got to cut the nuts off a dog that gets too bold."

"It's over."

Fannie Belle smiled, her teeth big and white and capped, a dab of lipstick across them that Hoyt thought for a second was blood. She stared at Hoyt a good thirty seconds and Hoyt stared right back.

"I heard you were a hell of a lay back when you worked the B-girl trade."

"I could've fucked you cross-eyed, Hoyt."

Hoyt laughed and popped open the shell of a boiled peanut. He grunted and smiled.

Jimmie sat back down moments later and handed his friend the jar of moonshine. He dabbed off some of the moonshine that wet his new seersucker suit and then wrinkled up his nose and turned to Hoyt: "Does something smell like rotten eggs around here?"

"Yeah," Hoyt said. "That bitch wears evil like a perfume."

THEY CAME FOR ME THAT NIGHT. I NEVER LEARNED WHO, but around four I found Thomas pulling on my arm and telling me that Santa Claus had come early. I pushed myself up from the bed as he repeated the news, and I listened, finally hearing what he'd heard, feet shifting and moving on the roof. It was still dark, and the crickets made music with the frogs in the creek.

Joyce switched on the bedside lamp, and I was already reaching into my closet for the Winchester I'd borrowed from my father-in-law. I cracked it open, checking the breech for shells, and snapped it back together with a sharp click.

I tried to steady my breath, blood racing through me, and nearly jumped five feet when Anne turned the corner from her bedroom. She was half awake and almost screamed when she saw the gun in my hand.

"It's okay. It's okay. There's some kind of animal on the roof."

"Are you going to kill it?"

I shook my head and steered her back to Joyce and Thomas. "I'll be right back," I said, forcing a smile. "It's okay. Just a raccoon."

It was hard to breathe, gunstock slick in my hands, as I walked to the kitchen door in pajama bottoms and a T-shirt, hearing nothing but the air-conditioning unit humming away and dripping outside on the concrete platform.

I unlocked the door and pushed my way outside. The light a purplish black, the air conditioner even louder outside, the warm summer heat being sucked into my lungs as I walked backward in the yard and looked up to the chimney.

I saw the inky figure of a man.

I crept back.

He turned and looked to me, his face nothing but a shadow.

Without thinking, I pulled the trigger tighter and the shotgun hammered into my shoulder. I heard feet skidding and then a hard thud, and I raced around the side of the house, my face slick with sweat, blood flushing through my ears, and crossed the front of the house just in time to see the car door close to an old Pontiac with both brake lights busted. Two men in the front seats.

The Pontiac skidded out from my house, something flying loose and free from an open window.

I heard the laughter of the men as they turned quick down toward Crawford Road and disappeared.

I walked toward the road and stared down at a dead black puppy with a soft white chest. Its neck had been broken, but its eyes were open and glassy, staring out with hope.

As the sun broke over the backyard creek, I buried the animal, listening to every sound from the house, praying to God that my children wouldn't wake up and see the dirt and blood on my hands.

"I DON'T KNOW ANY YOUNG GIRL WHO ANSWERS TO THAT name."

"She lived here," Billy said. "In the projects."

"Where?"

"Never mind."

"What does this girl look like?"

He stood across from the woman who hung laundry on wires stretched between two T-shaped metal posts. She'd placed a radio on the window, and it reported a storm coming in from Montgomery and then broke into some old-fashioned gospel music.

"She's about my height," Billy said. "Maybe a little shorter."

He made a motion with the flat of his hand.

The clothes on the line, the beaten, worn denim and gingham print and large, old-woman drawers, picked up in a bright spot of wind and began to flutter like flags. He wiped his nose. The woman kept the wooden pins in her mouth, her silver hair breaking through the black like wire.

"Her hair's black and her skin is real white. She cuts her hair across like this." Billy worked his middle and index finger over his eyes like a pair of scissors.

"She have blue eyes?"

"Yes, ma'am."

"Real blue? Kinda light?"

"Yes, ma'am."

"And what is she calling herself?"

"Lorelei."

The woman nodded and nodded, placing more old fat-woman

drawers on the line and a coverall suit and two threadbare dresses. She looked off to the west, shielding her eyes from the momentary white-hot streaks of sunshine breaking through the gray.

Some children played with a football in the narrow shot between the rows of cheap brick housing. They screamed and yelled. One of the boys called the other a damn cheater.

"I know the girl."

His face broke into a smile. "Can you tell me where to find her?"

"I just heard where she worked, is all."

The woman told him and he was off before she could ask or say more, and Billy followed Fourteenth Street up through a cavern of brick storefronts: the Riverside Café, Davis's Pawn Shop, the Oyster Bar, Manhattan Café, Silver Dollar, Yarborough's Café, Blue Bonnet, Boone's, Haytag, the Coffee Pot, and the Golden Rule. The doors open and the joints empty, listless men standing outside and watching a boy running uphill from the river, weaving through the guardsmen strolling along with rifles strung across their backs.

On a quick turn, he made his way past Central High and more service stations and motor courts and cinder-block barbecue joints, and soon onto the road to Opelika, nearly stepping in front of an Army jeep that crossed his path, but he was moving now, breathing and pumping his legs, and finally slowing into a smooth curve and down past Kemp's Drive-In and into a pocket of more joints and motels, and finally stopping just as the first spit of rain dampened the blacktop.

Rain dented the dust of the crushed-gravel lot of the old motel that he'd known immediately when the old woman said the place looked like the Alamo.

Only they didn't call the old place the Alamo, even though it had probably been there since before they invented cars. The neon sign read CASA GRANDE. Rates hourly, nightly, weekly.

It started to rain harder, as if the whole bottom of the sky had dropped out, the sky darkening almost to night, and Billy found shelter under a crooked, long roof, leaning against the old stucco wall and catching his breath.

The walls of the Casa Grande were stucco, and the roofs of the main building, the one that looked like the Alamo, and the little cabins behind it were made of red tile. The place seemed like some kind of half-remembered dream to Billy, and as he walked down the rows of the little cabins, getting wet but not minding it, he tried to recall what picture show that this place seemed out of. He thought maybe the *Lone Ranger,* one of the serials, or maybe a Lash LaRue, but none of it seemed to make a lot of sense, as he found shelter again, all the doors closed, rain pounding hard on the roof. Only dim little pockets of lights from their front porches and that buzzing glow from the Casa Grande sign broke through the storm.

He sank to his haunches and pulled off one of his sneakers, draining the water from it. He unlaced the other shoe and then wrung out his socks. Billy sat there for a long while, scared that maybe the manager would come out and try to run him off, but when he looked into the little sign-in area there wasn't a soul around.

Billy sat back down and waited, and it seemed an hour before the blue Buick rolled into the motor court and killed the lights. Not on sight, just from the sound, he knew it was his daddy's car. And Reuben wasn't the man who would whip him for getting lost for a while. In fact, he kind of half expected his kid to find something to do besides lay around the house at night. But Billy knew Reuben had come for him, maybe because of the rain, but maybe because someone had seen him running this way and maybe Reuben had been drinking. Really, the drinking was what caused the whipping, not the sin of not coming home.

But when the car opened, it wasn't his father. It was Johnnie Benefield, with his thin, greasy hair and skull head and protruding teeth, wearing a loud pink cowboy shirt and carrying a bottle in a sack. He knocked on the second cabin from the road and a little light flicked on the tiny porch.

The door opened and out walked a girl, who pressed close to skinny ole Johnnie, raising up like a child on her tiptoes and locking her hands around his neck.

Billy's breath caught in his throat, the rain falling harder.

He was soaked, walking through the rain without a thought, a car leaving the motor court sweeping its lights across his eyes, blinding him, and then readjusting as he walked to the little cabin. He wiped the light and water from his face, shoes soaking again and crunching on the gravel. The back of the Casa Grande loomed above the boy like a Hollywood set as he found the window, just one, with some dead shrubs planted underneath, stunted and brown.

He stood just a foot away and saw nothing, the sound of rain muffling all else. He watched the thin shadow of a man, and then the pink shirt fell away and he saw a small white hand on each side of Johnnie Benefield's lower back with painted red nails almost like bloody talons.

And then the scene flipped, both figures framed in the window, and Billy tilted his head the way a dog does when hearing a high-pitched sound and none of what he saw seemed to register. There was a girl, with white skin, milk-colored, and that raven black hair. But it was older, all of it, the outfit, the hair. She wore it done and teased, her lips painted the same bloodred as her nails. Her eyes covered in thick, heavy eye shadow.

The only thing the same was how she smoked when she broke away from Johnnie, pulling a cigarette, teasing and delicate, from his big teeth and tucking it into her lips.

She smiled and cocked a coy finger at him as she sat on the edge of the bed, him walking over, opening her knees, and her reaching roughly for his western belt and unbuckling him.

The room was dark, maybe a small glow coming from the open door of the motel bath or maybe a table lamp. But it was enough to see, with Billy there in the darkness, the dim glow coming from the boxed window like a television set, standing there, the players blind to the audience. The rain coming down even faster now, blinding him, but he didn't even care.

Johnnie Benefield was nude, back covered in spots of black hair and pimples. His back facing Billy, the little girl was on her knees, and Johnnie worked her head against him with his bony hands, head tilted back and wide teeth grinning.

He pushed her away, and she wobbled to her feet. Johnnie moved out of frame and then reappeared with a Jack Daniel's bottle that he turned up and placed on the nightstand. With fumbling hands, he pulled her to him, her standing on the bed on her knees, and he pulled her from a black lace top and pushed her back with the solid flat of his hand to remove her matching dress. She lay there, head turned to Billy but not seeing anything but blackness and rain, in her underthings, which were quickly pulled away without much notice, her head still turned, mouth open, and eyes dead to the black panel.

Billy walked toward the window, rain dotting and sluicing down the glass, and put his hand on the frame. He breathed through his nose, eyes filled with more water mixing with the rain, the dull sound of breath and heartbeats in his ears feeling like his head was about to break open and his chest would explode.

Billy's loose, aimless, and useless hand hung loose at his side.

Johnnie Benefield was on top of her now, Billy's hand upon the glass, watching Lorelei's eyes watching nothing. Her eyes reminded him of when he'd found his grandfather dead on the outhouse stoop when he was a child and how the old man seemed to be staring but the eyes didn't have anything in them. It made him think that something truly lived in the body and left at the time of death, just like all those stories he'd heard in church or from Reuben when he got real drunk.

His hand held a connection on the glass, mouthing nothing in the rain, idiot words, speaking in a low, busted murmur.

Johnnie's skinny body thrusted and pumped like a piston, up and down, up and down, his skinny white ass shaking in the low light, the slab of the girl's perfect milk flesh beneath him.

Billy wondered if it hurt badly.

But Billy tilted his head again, moving his hand away from the glass of the Casa Grande motor court, because he saw nothing in her. She was just watching nothing, the monster pumping up and down and up and down and all of it, until he stopped and shuddered. And the girl worked her way from under him and stood there completely nude in that flood of bathroom light. Her makeup and hair a mess, but her body thin and long and perfect. It was the first time Billy had seen a woman. He'd seen girls by accident or swimming, but he knew now she was a woman from the way she'd stood and cocked her hip, lighting a cigarette and pulling in a deep drag, as if wanting the smoke to cleanse her.

She tilted her head back and knotted her long black hair behind her back.

She spotted something in the glass and turned her head and walked forward as Billy walked backward, the rain slowing to a steady pattering, his feet making noisy crunches from his sneakers.

And he walked as she peered outward, and he turned and broke into a straight-out run as far as he could go. Billy had no direction in mind.

BILLY DIDN'T GO HOME. Idle Hour Park never closed that summer, and on Friday night, four nights after he'd seen Lorelei at the Casa Grande, the kids from Phenix City and Columbus had the grounds all to themselves, free of the GIs that picked up prostitutes and disappeared for five minutes at a time or bought little bottles of booze from toothless hicks in from the country. Billy was the Pinball Kid, winning four dollars that night from two juniors at Central High, and then trying to take on his pal Mario but deciding instead to take the winnings and buy them both a Coca-Cola and hot dog, dinner for the night. They found a bench to sit and eat, two old men at fourteen, and watched some buzz-cut football players, maybe from Auburn, tossing peanut shells to some mangy monkeys. One of the boys spit on one of the monkeys when it got close to the bars and laughed like hell, and the monkey wiped away the insult with its tiny little hands, smoothing the spittle down into what was left of its fur.

After eating, the boys roller-skated for almost an hour, until their heads swam with the endless laps and they turned in their skates and Mario left. Billy stayed, having not been home for nearly four days, sleeping at friends' houses and out in an abandoned cabin not far from the park. Pocket money kept him fed with full, hot days at the park and cool nights down on Moon Lake. He often thought Reuben would come get him, but he never did, and he'd grown fine with that, he thought, smoking and looking out on Moon Lake as most of the kids had trickled away from the park. The calliope music piped in on the loudspeakers now silent, with only negroes picking up the wrappers and bottles the kids left. It was then that he felt her, before seeing her, and turned around.

Billy just stood and flicked the cigarette into the weeds, already reaching for the pack rolled up tough in his T-shirt sleeve, waiting for something. He heard the sound of a motor gunning and frogs chirping along the muddy banks.

"You had no business coming there."

He waited.

"I saw you. You watched me, standing there in the rain. Why did you do that? You had no right."

Billy turned from her and followed the curve of Moon Lake, the chirping frogs almost deafening, rounding the corner past the rental boats and floats and down by a loose grouping of clapboard cottages. He felt a rock whiz by his ear and turned and saw Lorelei on her knees, crying and reaching for more stones. He didn't move, and she stopped a cupped hand of pebbles and her arm in midthrow.

The stones missed him and fell with a dull thud into the lake, and she dropped her arm and walked near. Behind her, the lights strung over the pool and bandstand cut off, and they were left in complete shadow. He could hear her breathing, she once again a child in T-shirt and jeans and a ponytail, and there was a cracking feeling in his stomach as he watched the disappointment in her face, holding steady but angry and crying.

"That's not me. Don't you understand that? Don't you believe me? Why won't you say nothing? Why don't you hit me? Hit me, or are you just going to run? That's right, run away and hide, you coward. Can't you see me anymore? That's not me. That's an act, a kid playing around. Dress-up. I don't have no choice in that. It was a path made for me and I have to travel on it. But it won't last. It's a trial. It's a trial. Don't you see?"

She came to him, and he listened to her breathing and he breathed, his skin sticky in the summer air, and he looked into her face and hated himself for wanting to touch her face and cheekbones and pull her close. But he watched her and shook his head and felt uneasy, as if he would vomit, and he put his fingers to his lips thinking that he might, but he caught himself and rocked back, uneasy on his feet and on the banks of the lake.

"You are a stupid boy. I never asked you to be my savior or my friend. You followed me." She reached for his hand, and he left it there dead to her fingers, and she held on to him so hard his knuckles popped. "Do you want to understand it? Or do you want to stand there and blame me and call me a whore a thousand times in your mind, not knowing a damn thing but how to be a child and blame people for things you see? You don't see anything. You are blind, Billy Stokes. I see myself. I know what I am. Do you want to understand it? Do you want to understand how I am that awful, disgusting girl and am also me?" She pounded her chest with her fist. "Do you want to? Or do you want to just know always that you are in love with a filthy whore?"

Billy slipped his fingers from her hand and continued along the banks of Moon Lake. The surface was flat and black and endless.

IN THOSE FIRST FEW WEEKS, I DIDN'T SLEEP MUCH. I drank a lot of black coffee and sat up most nights on a hard metal porch chair, a Winchester 12-gauge at my feet. Joyce usually woke me with sounds coming from the kitchen, the rattle of pans and such, and with more black coffee and bacon and eggs. And when she left for work at the little beauty shop we'd built behind our house, serving up the best in permanents and dyes for the ladies, she was unaware that Hugh Britton was parked right down the road reading the funny papers and keeping an eye out for most of the morning. Sometimes he'd be there when I'd walk home, sweated down to his old bones, and I'd check the mail in front of the little brick house and he'd wave from his open window and drive away.

I was studying a *Ledger* cartoon, with three Phenix City officials as the see no evil, hear no evil, speak no evil monkeys perched atop a box marked VICE, PROSTITUTION, MURDER, when I heard a knock at the door. Anne ran ahead of me and I yelled for her to step back, and she looked at me, hurt from the harsh sound of my voice.

"I got it," I said. "It's okay."

Two men stood at the door. One huge man wore a khaki Guard uniform and the other a navy suit and hand-painted tie. The man in the suit asked if I was Lamar Murphy and I nodded.

"Bernard Sykes," said the man in the crisp navy suit. He introduced the guardsman as Major Black.

I shook both their hands and invited them inside. Sykes walked in, but Black said he'd prefer to wait by the jeep.

We sat down at our dinette, and I offered him some coffee.

"I'm fine. Thank you."

Bernard Sykes was a little younger than me, a little taller, with a ski-slope nose and neatly combed brown hair. His suit was linen, recently pressed, and he wore a gold watch, cuff links, and some kind of class ring. The gem was red, so I figured he went to the University of Alabama.

He started out talking about the heat, how it was going to get up into the nineties, and then I responded with something about hoping for more rain. As we talked like farmers, Sykes opened up a plastic briefcase and pulled out a yellow legal pad and began to twirl a pen.

I excused myself and poured more coffee.

"I guess you know why I'm here."

"To talk about the weather?"

"John Patterson is in Washington."

"Flew up yesterday," I said. "It was in the papers."

Sykes looked down at the blank sheet of paper and then back at me across the dinette. My wife had hung some skillets on the wall, and we had one of those small cuckoo clocks that sounded eight just as he was about to speak.

I smiled and shrugged.

"Mr. Patterson has made statements publicly about us being baby-sitters."

"John's frustrated."

Sykes looked up. "When no one in town even admits they've heard the name Albert Patterson, there are bound to be problems."

"You might want to start disarming the town first."

He looked at me.

"Until you strip those gangsters of their pieces, no one in their right mind is going to talk to you."

Sykes nodded. "We'd have to place the entire city under martial law, and I don't believe that's been done since Reconstruction. Governor Persons wants alternatives."

I nodded and shrugged. I lit a cigarette and sipped a bit of my coffee. From the kitchen window, I saw two elderly women walking through our backyard with shower caps on their head. Joyce helped them up onto the steps of her little white-clapboard beauty shop and greeted them with a smile.

"Did you know old women like their hair to be blue?"

"You men are going to have to trust somebody," Sykes said.

"That would be nice."

Sykes put down his pen. He took a deep breath and picked it up again, drumming the point on the blank paper. "Just pass this on. I do not work for Silas Garrett. He's not a part of this."

"And what about Arch Ferrell and Sheriff Matthews?"

I watched him. Sykes drew something on the blank pad.

"You don't need to concern yourself with Mr. Ferrell," Sykes said.

"You want to tell me a little more, doc?"

"Let's just say that the attorney general's office is in complete control of this investigation."

"What about the town? Are you going to just leave it the way you found it?"

"No, sir."

"When are you going to really shut it down?"

"We haven't found anything yet," he said. "That's the problem."

I took another sip of black coffee, emptying the rest, and then washed out the cup, leaving it to dry on a wooden rack. Out in my little shaded backyard, my children played cowboys and Indians in the dirt. Thomas had a pair of those silver six-shooters with caps and blasted and blasted from behind a tree.

"Is it that hard?" I asked.

"What's that?"

"Finding what you're looking for," I said, grabbing my Texaco ball cap from the counter. "Let's go. I'll show you the way."

FIFTEEN MINUTES LATER, MAJOR BLACK BOUNDED THE jeep along a backcountry road, not too far from Seale, and pulled over where I pointed. The road was dirt and endless and covered in a canopy of oak and pecan branches. And soon they were behind me, me leading the way down a little fire road maybe a half mile into the woods, where we came across another dirt road and followed it for a while until I held up a hand and pointed into a clearing. Sykes followed along, swatting branches away from his face, his suit jacket in the car, his suit pants rolled to above his ankles, wingtips covered in red dust. He'd sweated clean through his dress shirt, but Black didn't show an ounce of perspiration as he squatted down behind a long row of privet bush and waited.

I motioned over to a large barn that had once been painted. The doors had been locked with a long two-by-four and then sealed with a chain and lock. Nearby, two black men in dirty undershirts sat on the hood of a shiny red Buick. One played with a pistol while the other cleaned his nails with a pocketknife. The man with a pocketknife wore a pistol sticking out of his trousers.

"How do you know what's in there?" Sykes said, whispering.

"You want to ask them?" I said.

Black looked at me and then back at Sykes, who was wiping his brow with his painted tie.

"So this is it?" Black said. It was the most he'd spoken since we'd met. The man stood six foot five and must've weighed two-fifty. Standing near him was like being under an oak.

I shook my head. "One of a dozen or more," I said. "They've got slots and horse-racing machines and tables tucked away in most of the county."

Sykes nodded, his Hollywood hair covered in briars. He picked one out and tossed it to the ground.

We followed the dirt road back and then trailed along the fire road back to the jeep. The cicadas this summer buzzed away like screams in the trees, the heat covering our bodies like a thick wool coat.

"I'd be glad to give the governor the same tour," I said.

Sykes reached for his suit jacket over the back of the seat and slipped back into it. "You really think he'd be surprised?"

ARCH FERRELL LEFT HIS WIFE'S PONTIAC STATION WAGON
at a filling station across the road from the Citizens Bank Building and
walked back down Dillingham, back toward the river, keeping a straw
hat down in his eyes and not making eye contact with the Guard troops
he passed. He walked by the 260 and 261 clubs, the Original Barbecue.
From across the road, he could see the weathered and beaten words on
the side of a brick building advertising a slave market held on Saturdays that no one had thought to paint over since the Civil War.

Most of the buildings down on this stretch of Phenix City were just
old wood-frame clip joints and Bug houses. Some of the joints on this
side of town allowed blacks, and Arch passed the men in their out-of-
date zoot suits and two-tone nigger shoes and felt dirty just being in
their presence when they'd give him a rotten smile and stare. He knew,
just fucking knew, that they now recognized him as no better than
they were.

Dillingham dipped down at the bridge. Hung onto the riverbank,
stuck on the lower level of a storefront, was the Bridge Grocery. He
ducked inside the door just as soon as he could. His eyes had to adjust
to the light, red bulbs screwed into sockets, making his vision feel like
that of an animal. He heard men talking and walked past the horse-
racing arcade games and the green felt tables stacked in heaps in the
center of the concrete floor. He entered a back room, passing over a
creaking wooden floor that almost hung right out over the water,
under the level of the bridge. His eyes searched for the part of the floor
he'd heard about that could spring loose like that of a stage, rolling a
drunk or beaten man out onto the banks, tumbling and rolling and
falling out into the Chattahoochee.

Godwin Davis was a portly little man, not even coming up to Arch's
chest. He was bald and fat and had a constant cigar plugged into the

side of his mouth. The man had an odor about him, too, of nicotine sweats and vinegar, breath as fetid as moldy cheese.

Arch looked at his own feet, the slotted floor, and stepped around broken poker chips and shards of glass, sandwich wrappers, and empty beer bottles. He was pretty sure the grocery, which hadn't sold a can of beans since before the war, hadn't been open since the troops arrived.

Davis grunted something to him, an affirmation maybe, and nodded him into a back room with brighter light, this coming from another red bulb over a little table, where Miss Fannie Belle sat smoking a thin brown cigar and leaning back in a seat. She smiled up at Arch, and Arch looked to Davis, never thinking in a million years that these two could be fifty yards away without trying to kill each other. But allies were tough to find these days, and Arch understood you took what you could get.

"Counselor," she said. Her red hair had been twisted up into a bun, and she wore big false eyelashes that looked like spider legs. In front of her were a couple rows of cards where he'd interrupted her game of solitaire. On the back of the facedown cards were naked fat women like something from Victorian times. Fannie's shirt was low-cut, and he could make out a front latch on her pointed black bra.

Godwin Davis clamped the damp cigar in his jaw and closed the door behind him, leaving the two in privacy.

"Telephones make me nervous," Arch said. He sat and lit a cigarette, his hands shaking as he held the match to the end.

"Nervous as a cat," Fannie said and smiled. She had a thin scar on her lower right jaw and an oblong scar in the center of her forehead that stayed white against fair, sun-flushed skin. She wore a pink, fitted shirt—like one made for a little boy—and skinny black britches of some sort that matched that pointed black bra.

"I hear a click. A double click at home. They're listening to me. You know that sound? When you ring off, but they're still there and don't know you're still there? I'd watch your phones, too. Don't trust anyone."

"Didn't see you at the fights," Fannie said, starting up her game of solitaire again and flipping over cards with a quick snap of fingers with long red nails. "That's a first. You know, I used to date a fighter. They called him the Canvas Cannibal. Ain't that a riot?"

She looked up over the cards with her slow, lazy eyes and drowsy smile, but Arch didn't smile back. The smile only made him more nervous.

"I want order restored, Fannie," he said, blowing smoke up into the ceiling. He alternated softly pounding his fist and tapping the table with his fingers. "I want my town back under control. I want men in Montgomery to quit fucking with this town like a political poker chip."

Fannie smiled more, and he couldn't goddamn well tell if she was agreeing with him or the cards. But then he knew it was the cards as she picked them all up—finished with the game—and shuffled the naked ladies into a neat pile.

Arch gritted his teeth and slouched back into the chair, his arm hanging loose at his sides.

"You're the only one who understands," Arch said. "You hear me? You've sunk too much into Phenix. You know we got to have order. You think Hoyt and Jimmie care anymore? They're too old. They don't understand what all this means or are just too stupid to care. Listen to me. This is a battle. A fucking battle." Arch leaned over the small square table and made an invisible line with his index finger. "Lines have been drawn, but now these RBA men and Pat's son are hiding under the governor's skirt. They don't want to come out and fight fair."

Fannie shook her head and shrugged. She plucked at her pink top with the tips of her taloned fingers. "Boy, it's hot."

"Are you listening?"

She stopped plucking and placed the cards back into the pack. She looked over the table at Arch and said: "Next year, they'll be just a memory."

"I don't have till fucking next year," Arch said, pointing at Fannie with the end of his cigarette. "They're gunning for me. This crazy Guard general and this man Sykes. They want to make a statement. They will remove me from office and they want me for Pat's murder. They need someone and they want me. They're gonna fuck this scapegoat silly."

Elbows in all four corners of the table had worn the green top white. Fannie ran her hand over the smooth spots, keeping the little brown cigar in the corner of her mouth. She pulled it out, examined the tip, and then tucked it back into her molars like a man.

"Tell me this," she said. "Where were you?"

"When?"

"When Patterson was killed."

"You know where I was."

"Hell, I know. Talking to Silas Garrett on the telephone at the exact fucking minute the trigger was pulled. Damn convenient, Arch."

"I wouldn't doubt Si Garrett's word if I were you." Arch's hand found a spot on the table, his smooth, worn place, and rubbed it, working his fingers in and out of the bleached color, studying the design like an ancient map. "He's a fine man. What about you, Fannie?"

Fannie pulled the cigar from her red lips and just stared at him, reeking of perfume.

"People say someone hired a button man from out of state. Chicago. Las Vegas. Or Miami. Don't you have a place down in Miami?"

She leaned back into the creaking chair, studied Arch's face, and set her feet on top of the table. She unbuttoned a single button and used the material of her shirt to fan herself, giving Arch a better view of the black lace.

Arch wiped his brow and returned the stare. Fannie Belle laughed. The red light was giving him a headache, making him feel like they were underwater.

"People are talking," Arch said. "People are lying. These men, these men who don't know and understand Phenix City, are listening. They don't care about what's true. People look at me different. They stare. Niggers on the street look at me like I'm some kind of joke. They used to get off the goddamn sidewalk and let me pass."

Her cigar smoke floated up and burned into the low light of the single bulb. She shook her head and looked at Arch. "Since when do you care what niggers think?"

Arch stood and began to pace. He had sweated deep into his dress shirt and his back felt wet. "Did I tell you my wife is seven months pregnant? We need control."

"You don't need to tell me what we need," she said. "Everyone is squirming and squealing like a nest of rats."

She stopped his pacing cold with a quick motion of her left hand holding him between his legs. Arch looked at her and blinked several times as if trying to right his vision.

"Hoyt and Jimmie have grown fat and lazy and are useless in this war," Arch said. "I've heard they've thrown in the towel and gone with Pat's son."

"War?" she said, still holding him at his crotch. "Goddamn. All the Guard can do is walk the streets and pose for pictures. Have you seen one clip joint shut down? Get yourself together, Arch, and go take a fucking bath. I'm handling this now."

"You need help."

She kneaded him with one hand and pulled the cigar from her

mouth with the other. She held him tight in her grip, and, as she smoked, Arch tilted his head, amazed at the way she could take care of two things with such little effort.

"I've got help."

"Fuller ain't enough," Arch said.

She unzipped his fly and reached in and touched him through his drawers. Arch closed his eyes. But just as quickly, she let go and pulled the cigar from her mouth and crushed it into the ashtray. She stood and put her hand on Arch's shoulder.

The cigar smoldered in the cut glass.

"I'm not talkin' about Fuller," Fannie said, a smile slicing up to her pointed ears in the red light. "I'm talking about sending a mess of messages Western Union. You understand, don't you? I know you do, Arch. Because you're a goddamn American hero."

BERT FULLER PUNCHED ON HIS HEADLIGHTS WHEN THEY hit Crawford Road, and they drove away from Phenix City and out toward Seale and into the country. Reuben reclined in the patrol car's seat while Fuller made some calls on his radio to the sheriff's office and then hung up the microphone.

"Where we headed?" Reuben asked, arm hanging out the window. The wind seemed hotter than the air when they were parked.

"Cliff's."

"I don't want to go to Cliff's."

"I wasn't asking you."

They passed groupings of ragged shanties on eroded pieces of land and long stretches of cotton just planted. A few of the farmers had roadside stands that were closed up for the night but still advertised with hand-painted signs for corn, field peas, squash, and boiled peanuts, even though corn and peas wouldn't be in for some time.

Reuben reached under his seat for the bottle of the homemade liquor Fuller had brought along and, after taking a long pull, passed it on to the assistant sheriff. Fuller smacked his lips and said: "That could peel the paint on a barn door."

"Or make you blind."

"Pussy will make you blind, too."

"I'm worn out."

"Naw, you ain't," Fuller said, slowing and turning down an unmarked dirt road and under a tunnel of pecans growing along a slatted fence. They passed a burned-out car and another stretch of plowed-under land and then took another turn, the headlights cutting through the darkness on a moonless night like going into a long, endless cave.

"You know what ole Hank used to say about the moon."

"What's that?"

"Said the moon was hiding on account of its sadness. How'd that man think of that?"

"He was a drunk."

"He was one of the best friends I ever had and the best goddamn singer that ever came out of the state of Alabama," Reuben said when Fuller stopped the car and turned off the ignition, the words coming out louder in the quiet than he'd intended than over the motor.

"When did you meet him?"

"After the war, when I got home. He'd just been fired off WSFA and needed someone to drive him. Keep him sober for singin' at all them roadhouses."

"And they hired you."

"His mamma did."

"Well, his mamma didn't have sense at all."

"He could write songs from picking the words out of the air."

They followed a path to an old unpainted house situated next to a small two-acre pond. Reuben turned up the liquor, damn near finishing the bottle, and watched as the moon reappeared from outside a cloud just like Hank had always said. A broken-slatted pier walked out into the water maybe six feet.

"I want you to listen to me," Bert Fuller said. Tonight, he'd dressed in blue jeans and his usual boots with a white snap-button shirt and matching hat. If he didn't know better, Bert Fuller sure looked like one of the good guys. And Reuben smiled at the thought.

"What are you laughing at?"

A bass flopped to catch a bug in the pond. Reuben turned to look at it.

"Listen," Fuller said. "Cliff's done got him this Mexican gal that you won't believe. I know you was always sayin' how you like those little Filipino women. The Mexes ain't a hell of a lot different. All that talk about their pussies smellin' like tacos is a bunch of trash. This gal has golden skin and big old brown eyes, titties the size of watermelons. Man, I just could bury my pecker between them."

"What's that mean to me?"

"It means I'll let you have her after I fuck her. But I ain't goin' after you."

"Bert." Reuben laid his hand on Fuller's shoulder. It was embroidered with lassos and bucking horses. "You sure are good to me."

Reuben followed him inside Cliff's Fish Camp, and in the elongated, camp-style room was a roundup of most the Machine, minus Shepherd and Matthews and a few others. Most of them were bit-part players who'd come out of the hills to run 'shine or come from Nevada or Atlantic City to deal cards or work on slots. There were the locals, too. Godwin Davis and Red Cook, the Youngblood brothers, Slim Howard, Papa Clark, Jap Sneed, and Frog Jones. And at the end of the table was the Queen herself, Fannie Belle, and she pulled Fuller in close.

Since Shepherd and Matthews had gone into semi-retirement, Fannie had snatched up most of the PC action, including some business down in the Florida Panhandle. She'd partnered with Cliff Entrekin in the fish camp and worked the needle-and-pill racket with some buck-toothed flunkies who worked out of back alleys and barns. Some say she got a big cut of the sale of whore's babies, too, with Dr. Floyd. But to Reuben, she'd always be that tired, big-titty, redheaded B-girl who used to work at his club, writing letters to her twenty husbands who sent her checks monthly.

He had to admit she had a hell of a scam, getting some horny Army boy to marry her and then getting the dumb, pussy-struck sonofabitch to head overseas. Reuben used to call Fannie the Queen of Hearts.

Fannie laughed some more with Fuller, her teeth bright and big, and Fuller probably telling some dirty joke he read in the back of a comic book. Then her face retreated into a half smile and she wrapped an arm around his fattened stomach, whispering into his ear, and Reuben wondered what the hell you had to whisper about in this world.

Fuller stepped back from the whispering and nodded. The top of Fannie's red hair caught in the light like a red flame. They both stood and motioned for Reuben to follow them.

A strand of bare bulbs had been strung over the camp tables, and the men and whores talked as if this was a big old family function with half-eaten plates of catfish and hush puppies before them. Ole Moon sat in a corner, away from the whores in their kimonos and housecoats, working on probably his fifth plate, wiping the grease from the whole bone fish across his overalls.

Outside, Fannie walked them over to a beaten-up old Nash and popped the trunk. She reached inside for a flashlight by the wheel well and pulled back a knitted blanket. She shined a beam onto two wooden boxes.

Fuller opened one and gave a short little laugh.

"So easy even you two jackoffs could do it," Fannie said.

"Good God Almighty," Reuben said. "What's this shit for?"

"I don't want to fuck up a perfectly good manicure."

"You always were particular with your hands," Reuben said.

Fannie clawed at Reuben's face, but he quickly sidestepped and told her to calm her ass down. She walked back into the night on wobbly high heels, and both the men stood there looking down at the two boxes.

Fuller gave a low whistle and walked back into the fish camp. Reuben peeked back inside the box, looked at all those sticks of dynamite, shook his head, and closed the trunk.

He sat down on the edge of a slatted porch and stayed there for a while and watched the loopy motion of bats gobbling up the night insects. He lit a cigarette and thought about what he'd just seen and how he always found himself taking the high dive into a tub of shit.

When he turned, he saw a woman had joined him. She told him in a broken accent he was a handsome man.

"Sometimes it's just a burden, darling."

She smiled, a little cleft in her chin about right for his thumb, and he decided to turn and kiss her. Most people minded kissing whores, but Reuben had never had any trouble with it.

She reached between his legs and felt for him. Reuben didn't seem to mind or notice, still watching the loopy flights of the bats in the purple evening.

"No?" she asked. Her eyes were brown and big as half-dollars.

He turned to her, her black-and-red kimono half open and showing part of an ample brown breast.

"You wouldn't happen to be from old Mexico?"

She nodded.

Reuben grinned, turned, and looked through the door, not seeing Fuller but Frog Jones, with his trademark fatty throat, clog-dancing on top of a picnic table, a bottle of beer in his hand.

"Well, come on, then," Reuben said. "What the hell we waiting for?"

THE NEXT MORNING, Arch Ferrell woke as if he'd died. He sat up in bed, feeling his heart had just again started to beat, and tried to breathe. As he sat awake, the shadowed men stood before him, craning their necks, studying him as one would an insect, faceless, one poking a shadow rifle close to his feet. Arch pulled his toes back toward himself, only getting in some air as the men joined up together and marched into his shallow closet, single file and as one. Arch got to his feet and felt for the closed doors and opened them, running his hands over his sport coats and ties and pressed pleated trousers all arranged together in neat rows. By now, Madeline had turned on the bedside lamp and stared at him, wiggling with some difficulty in her pregnancy to sit against the headboard.

"Arch?"

"Did you see them?"

"Arch?"

He looked back at her, with labored breath, clutching his chest and still seeing the rounded shape of the Storm Trooper helmets. He pointed to his wife and opened his mouth, but nothing came out, and he walked into the bathroom and shut the door, running water so she could not hear the sound of him vomiting up a bottle of gin.

Twenty minutes later, he'd shaved and showered, his face and scalp feeling as if they could peel from his skull, as he fought to keep his car on the road and headed out of Seale and to the courthouse before first light.

He was the first in the Russell County Courthouse, as he'd always been in better days, and walked with dull, empty, cavernous footsteps to his office and unlocked his desk drawer, finding a revolver. He studied it for a moment in the darkness, only a thin stretch of fluorescent light from the hall, and then tucked it away.

In the bottom drawer, he found what he wanted. A flag folded in neat corners. And he clutched that flag to his chest, walking down the steps, at once feeling almost six feet tall, winding his way to the cool, damp lawn, listening to the sounds of the crickets and early-morning birds in the darkness.

He walked to the flagpole and hooked up the Stars and Stripes he'd carried with him from the depths of France to Germany and hoisted it high in the hot, windless air of the summer and stood and watched its flaccid droop, standing near the monument to the dead Confederate soldiers, some who fought the last battle of the Civil War on this very bluff, and he saluted until tears ran down his cheeks.

A little later, he grabbed coffee at the Elite and took it with him out the door, feeling the furtive stares of the truckers and contractors following him. He soon found refuge behind the pebbled glass of A. FERRELL COUNTY SOLICITOR and drank coffee and tried again to reach Si Garrett's family. He spoke to a Democratic chairman named Frank Long for at least two minutes, but Frank had to go, and Arch tried some other important people he knew who were either not in or already in conference. So he lit a cigarette, no secretary in the anteroom, and no morning briefings with his staff. He just smoked in silence without the lights, staring up at the cracked ceiling and trying, just for a moment, to piece together his mind.

But there was a knock at the door, and he stood and quashed out the cigarette and found two guardsmen dressed in khakis with .45s clipped to their canvas belts asking if he was Archer Ferrell.

"Can't you read the fucking door, you goddamn morons?"

They said they had orders for him to come to the city jail, where a warrant was issued.

"For what?"

"Sir, I hate to inform you that you've been indicted for vote fraud by the grand jury in Birmingham."

"Well, if that doesn't fuck all. One minute."

"Sir?"

"I said, one goddamn minute."

He slammed the pebbled-glass door in their faces and returned to the black phone on his desk, calling up the operator and calling direct for James E. Folsom, Big Jim. But Big Jim wasn't in, according to that liar of a wife. And so he tried again for Si Garrett and only got the secretary again, who didn't answer his question, only asked him if he'd read the papers.

He slammed down the phone so hard that it cracked.

He stood and paced. He lit a cigarette and looked back at the desk. He reached in the desk for a bottle of Jack Daniel's that always waited in his bottom left drawer and as the guards began to grow furious and call out to him with pussy-sounding "sir"s he drained nearly three-quarters of the bottle and called out to them, "One fucking minute."

He called Madeline. He was firm. He was angry.

He was sorry.

He cried.

And then the door opened and the guardsmen appeared with

several of their friends and they didn't say a word, only came at him from both sides of the big mahogany desk that had been in his family for nearly a century, and each one grabbed a forearm, yanking him to his feet.

Arch Ferrell reached out with a desperate hand for the black phone and grabbed the receiver and clocked the one with the bad teeth right in the ear, and then he hopped over his desk and ran, scooting down the hallway, his heart pounding in his ears, seeing shadows with helmets behind all the pebbled-glass doors of every office he passed. He finally turned, not remembering how to find the stairs, and ran right into the men, who braced him and grabbed him by the arms.

They marched Arch right out of the courthouse, and in a sloppy, half-lidded, lazy way he tried to remain high with dignity. His tie hung loose off his neck, his dress shirt pulled from his pants, trouser knees skidded and black.

And then as they approached the flag, he dug his heels in the ground, stopping the men, pulling a hand free and saluting to the "Communist States of America," and then yelled, "Three cheers for Bert Fuller."

Then he burst out laughing, half forgetting the punch line, before they loaded him into the back of the jeep and bolted him to the floor.

"HAPPY BIRTHDAY," SHE SAID.

Billy sat up from the bunk's mattress, yawned, and reached out for the covered plate Lorelei handed him.

"I couldn't find any candles. You want me to light a match to stick in the frosting?"

"Where'd you get this?"

"The Elite."

"You know it ain't my birthday."

"Says who? Birthdays always make you feel better."

The boy smiled and shook his head.

"Do you feel older?"

"On account it's not my birthday?"

"Yes."

She sat at his feet while he peeled off the tinfoil and began to eat the chocolate cake with his fingers. They'd been together two days straight, never leaving Moon Lake, breaking into the little clapboard cabin on the opposite shore when it started to rain the other night.

She'd gone into town when they got hungry and brought back fried chicken and hamburgers from the park and small green bottles of Coca-Cola. Yesterday, she brought back a sack of comic books and magazines from the Phenix City Pharmacy, and Billy had spent the day on the bunk reading *Superman* and *True Crime* and *Front Page Detective*.

"Don't you want to go outside?"

"Not really," Billy said.

"You still feeling sick?"

"No."

"We can't stay here forever. Someone's gonna kick us out."

He shrugged and left half the cake for her. She refused, and then took it and ate the last bite, before resting her head on his lap.

The cabin was just a big bare room with two cots with rolled-up mattresses and a little kitchen with a skinny stove and sink. If you wanted to use the bathroom, you had to go to the community showers down near the boats.

Billy leaned back into the mattress, the springs squeaking as Lorelei joined him and lay on her back. She lit a cigarette, and they both stared at the ceiling, and he could feel the blood rushing into his chest and into his pecker when she moved against him. Her raven hair smelled like the roses on his granddaddy's casket that had stunk up the front parlor of their house even after the old man was put in the ground.

"People are probably looking for me," she said.

"What people?"

"Who do you think?"

Last night was the first time they'd kissed. When everyone had left the park and the lights had clicked off at the dock and along the shore, the moon slipping behind the clouds, they both undressed and swam quietly out into the lake. They swam away from each other, not leaving from the safety of the bank, and floated on their backs, him seeing her chest and other parts, and when he'd swim close she'd drift away with a laugh. The water was as warm as a bath, the light silvery on the pine needles, and when they finally found their stiff clothes and dressed, Billy turning away as she darted from the water to the shore, they kissed.

"Will your dad be worried for you?" she asked.

"Naw," he said. "When my daddy gets drunk, he says he won me in a poker game and that the only reason my bitch of a mother left without me was on account I didn't belong to her or nobody."

"Is that true?"

"Hell, I don't know. Reuben once told me he'd known a mule in the Army who could talk and sing."

"Who's your dad?"

"Reuben Stokes."

He looked over at Lorelei for recognition, but she was still looking at the ceiling, and when she felt the focus upon her she crooked her arms around his neck and kissed him again.

"Reuben was in the Philippines during the war and got captured," Billy said. "They were taking him and everyone on the island on a long march, and Reuben waited till the guards looked the other way and rolled into a ditch full of piss and shit. When the damn Japs passed him, they figured he was dead. He said he even left his eyes open and stuck out his tongue all funny. He hightailed it after they left, and fought up in the mountains till the troops came back."

"My daddy was too old for the war."

"Is he still alive?"

"I don't know."

"What about your mamma?"

She didn't say anything and he kissed her some more, and his small chest felt like it would just explode. And then she told him everything.

SHE WAS ONLY THIRTEEN WHEN THE LONG BLACK CADIL-lac pulled off to the side of the highway and she saw the fat man taking a leak into the mosquito ditch. She was long-legged and scabby-kneed, with black hair that grew down past her rump, hair that women in church whispered was pure vanity. As the man finished, she kept picking corn to fill a wire basket, and then ran a red bandanna over her neck and across her face before tying back her hair. He looked to be rich, not only with the car but by the way he stood and looked down off the road at all those poor people having to work on a hot summer day. He shook his head and knocked back a little from a silver flask that reflected hard in her eyes. It must've been about a minute later that he whistled for her in the way that a man whistles for a beaten dog.

She came.

And she hated herself for that, and would hate herself all the way from the summer of '50 onward, but she was a country girl with not a thought in her head. The only world that she knew was a clapboard shack fashioned from scavenged wood and twisted metal from wrecked automobiles and the half acre that her daddy rented out from their neighbor. A rotten-toothed, soulless man who cheated and lied more than the pharaohs of Egypt.

She walked to the rich man, her head down, and he took a step toward her, pulling her from the red dirt road and onto the shoulder where he stood. He wore a checked gray suit with a red tie and a straw cowboy hat. He smiled at her, looking down at her face, as he brought it up with a light finger and smiled for a long time.

She didn't smile back on account of the big space between her teeth.

"How old you, girl?"

"Thirteen, sir."

"Well, you look to be sixteen from where I'm standin'," he said. "Turn around."

And she did, as stupid and blind as a trained dog waiting for a rancid piece of meat, and he looked at her long legs and scabby knees in that dress made out of old gingham and flour sacks. The man pulled her hair back and twisted her head from side to side.

She pulled away and looked into the corn for her father, but he was gone somewhere into the woods. Or was it town?

"You want to take a ride?"

"No, sir."

He reached into his gray coat, and she could see he'd been sweating the way big men do, soaking their fat stomachs and under their arms, and she saw the flash of two golden pistols, as gold as pirate's treasure, and he saw the smile, too, and handed her a card.

"Can you read?"

She shook her head.

"'Course not."

She looked at him.

"You bring yourself to the big city," he said. "You hear me? What's your name, girl?"

And she told him, but she'd soon forget that name because it was so country that it made men laugh, and he laughed, too. It would be a couple years before she'd start calling herself Lorelei, after a nickname they'd given her at the Rabbit Farm.

"You come lookin' for me," he said. "Anybody in Phenix City will know where to find me. Bert Fuller. I'll make sure you get some work."

She nodded and, despite herself, felt her lips spread against that space in her buckteeth, and he kind of winced at her and said, "Don't smile so much."

She dropped her head.

"Come on, come on," he said. "No need to be frownin', with a face and legs like that. I bet them country boys chase you plenty, huh?"

"Naw."

"Naw?" he said, laughing. "You are as country as corn bread. You in those sacks and bare feet. You ever feel what it's like to wear a real pair of shoes? Look at that mud caked between your toes. You're too good for this, little girl. You hitch a ride, you take a bus whenever you want, but you come see me."

"Yes, sir."

"Sir?" he said. "Honey, hush."

She looked at him again, as if her chin had been lifted again, only feeling that he wanted to see her eyes without even the slightest touch. His face was broad and fat, pink-skinned and fleshy. His hair was buzzed above the ears, up to the cowboy hat, like men in the service. He winked at her, knocked back some more from his flask, and passed it to her.

She shook her head.

"It ain't the demon's blood like they tell you," he said. "It's just bourbon."

And she looked down the endless red-dirt road for another car coming or her father or any sign of life by the clapboard house made from wrecked cars and trash. But there was only the wind and the unbearably hot sun, and as she took a drink the bourbon was hotter than the air and made her face turn hot and glow. But she kept drinking, not knowing it wasn't like water, and the muddy-colored stuff ran down her chin and on her dress, and it smelled like the way her daddy smelled on Saturday nights, only without the cigarettes.

Bert Fuller took back his flask, wiped her chin with a scarred knuckle, and opened the door to the big, long Cadillac.

"See that star on the card?" he asked. "That means I'm the assistant sheriff. That means I'm real important. You understand?"

And then he pulled away, giving her a preacher's wave before disappearing into a cloud of dust and becoming a black ink spot on the horizon that burned away into the molten sun.

Two months later, she found a ride.

She'd never been to a city before, and she'd saved pennies to buy shoes and borrowed a cotton dress from her best friend at church, May, who'd also given her a dollar she'd been saving since she was twelve. With the dollar, the new shoes, and the old dress, she hopped out from the Chevy pickup truck loaded with hay and chickens and turned and looked at all the buildings and people milling about. It was Friday afternoon, and there looked to be plenty of men from the Army around and she felt safe with that, finding one boy and showing him Deputy Bert Fuller's card—now so crunched and wrinkled it was soft in her hand—and the Army boy just shook his head, chewing gum with a cocky smile, and winked at her.

The wink made her pull the dress tight against her chest, and she kept walking toward the lights, past bars with signs reading GIRLS, GIRLS, GIRLS *and* QUICK MONEY, *and she got a few whistles and catcalls, and pretty soon she was sweating with all the noise of the music and the ringing of slot machines and the sight of things she'd never seen—like a big black-haired woman dancing on a stage with tassels on her titties, whipping them around in circles. Pretty soon, she was down by the bridge and could see the big, wide Chattahoochee, and it was the most beautiful thing she'd ever seen, and the city beyond it, over the river, just shined with light so bright that it hurt her eyes.*

More Army boys passed her, and one bumped into her, slapping her little rump with the flat of his hand, and she hugged herself, because the dress was thin and the wind had kicked up on the bridge.

She walked back into the city, asking a girl in a dark corner if she'd heard of Mr. Fuller, and the woman looked at her, smoking a cigarette, almost looking through her, and said: "No."

But there was something about the no that made her keep walking, and she soon left the neon lights and bars and music and service boys and followed the train tracks. There were train tracks near her house, and she figured if she kept walking maybe she'd make it back home before morning and maybe her father would not take her to the smokehouse and beat her with the horsewhip.

The houses were rickety and old, with broken wood porches where negroes sat and drank whiskey and smoked cigarettes and called out to her or just laughed and pointed. She could only see the rocky track. Then she heard a train and wandered off the railroad and right into the path of a car that skidded to a stop and honked its horn. She'd fallen to her butt and stared into white, hot headlights and searched into them before there was the sound of a siren and red lights and the voice of a man.

"You lookin' for me, doll?"

They kept her in jail all night. It wasn't till the next morning that Deputy Bert Fuller watched while a guard unlocked the door of her cell and let him inside. He stood smiling at her with a steaming cup of coffee in his hand while she waited on the bunk with her nervous legs kicking back and forth. He opened the front pocket of his uniform and offered her a stick of gum. She shook her head and looked down at the dirty concrete floor and the corroded drain.

"Oh, come on, baby," he said. "It don't have to be like that."

She looked up.

"You just can't walk the streets like this is Podunk, Alabama," he said. "This here is Phenix City. You got to have somewhere to go."

Her eyes met his.

"You got somewhere to go?"

"I thought I did."

"How's that?"

She shrugged.

"You got somewhere to stay?"

"Naw."

"Money?"

"Naw."

"Little girl, I do believe you are in a pickle," he said. He made a tsk-tsk *sound with his tongue and slurped his hot coffee, and it must have burned his tongue because he kicked back his head and some of it stained the front of his shirt.*

He came back an hour later with an old man, a much older man but just as fat and fleshy as Deputy Bert Fuller. The man wore a pin-striped suit and had thinning hair that he'd dyed red and oiled tight to his freckled skull. He smelled like burnt onions and old fish, and he walked to the girl on the bunk and held up her face and, when she turned away, plunked his fingers deep into her mouth, jabbing around for her teeth.

"Strip," he said.

She looked at Bert Fuller, and Fuller just smiled, a tan uniform hugging his pear-shaped body, those golden six-shooters at his sides. He shrugged.

She twisted her head from side to side. "No."

"Strip, you country thing," the old, smelly man said and yanked her to her feet and tore the borrowed dress from her body and with dirty fingernails clawed at her cotton underthings until it was all in a heap by the floor and she was left crawling like a pig in a trough down by the corroded drain, trying to pull the rags together and cover her embarrassingly developed breasts.

"She'll do," the old man said.

"Okay," Fuller said. "Here's the deal, girlie. You can either stay here and wait a week to see the judge about what you were doing out there, selling yourself like some kind of Jez-bel, or you can come with me, ride into

Columbus, and we can get rid of those pieces of cloth you call clothes and go shopping at Kirven's, and let me feed you a steak dinner at Black Angus. You'll need some perfume, too."

From the floor, she looked up at him.

"I didn't do nothin' wrong."

"'Course you did," Fuller said. "In Phenix City, whorin' is a crime. Ain't it, Mr. Red?"

He just smiled a rotten row of teeth.

The girl began to cry.

"Mr. Red, I do believe a decision has been made."

The man opened up a wooden box while Fuller ran an electric cord into the hall and a little needle attached to a blue vial began to pump and buzz. "Hold 'er down, Bert. Shit, she looks to be a wildcat to me."

And Fuller let out some air, rolled up his sleeves, and pinned the girl's arms to the concrete floor with his fat hands until she screamed, as the old man squatted with creaking knees, opened up her bottom lip, and began to write inside her mouth.

WHEN SHE STOPPED, SHE ROLLED DOWN HER BOTTOM LIP and showed him the mark 618 tattooed in blue ink. And when she tried to tell Billy about other things, things that happened later, he'd stop her, feeling sick deep within his stomach.

"Why don't we just leave here?" Billy said. "Run away?"

"We don't have no money."

"I can get money."

She pulled away from him and rolled on her side, facing the wall.

He put his hand on her shoulder and started to talk about moving out to Hollywood, where they could work in the picture business or pick oranges or sell ice cream at the beach. He got so excited about all the plans, he could already feel the Greyhound ticket in his hand and almost didn't notice she was crying. Billy moved his hand from her shoulder and just listened.

The calliope music was going strong up at Idle Hour, and they could hear the kids laughing and screaming and splashing up by the pool. The shades were drawn, but he could feel the heat from the window and knew the sun was shining.

"I'll go outside," Billy said and ran a finger along the window and looked at the black dust. "I'm really feeling better."

"Sometimes I just wish this whole rotten town would burn to the ground."

He rolled off the bed and found his shoes. He looked out the window up on the hill and saw a young boy about his age crawling up a tall ladder, the contraption looking loose and rickety like something fashioned from an Erector set. The boy got to the top and walked to the end of the diving board before giving the thumbs-up to his buddies below and launching into a perfect cannonball.

He let his shoes fall to the floor with a thud, lying back into the bed, back and butt finding the safe, soft curves of Lorelei. He felt the rise and fall of her chest, her raven hair on his neck and over his eyes, and, before long, Billy fell into a perfect sleep.

BILLY WOKE from an afternoon nap with a hot, bright light in his eyes, as if looking directly into the sun. He swatted at the light, blinked, felt a big hand grip his wrist, and stared straight up into the jowly face of Bert Fuller. Fuller yanked him out of bed and threw him to the floor and then he reached into the bed for Lorelei, who was dressed only in the boy's white undershirt and her underwear. He wrenched her wrist, pulling her from the mattress, and twisted her arm behind her, forcing her nose to the floor, where he kicked her in the side like a dog. The flashlight fell from his hands in his fury of kicks and punches and the light went scattering in circles on the wooden floor. Billy reached for the scattering light, but, as he moved, Fuller let go of the girl and went for him, kicking the boy in the head and sending him reeling, tumbling up and then backward, knocking him against the wall.

Fuller kept a hand on the butt of his revolver and reached down with his pudgy fingers for Lorelei's thick black hair, and he pulled her like a caveman across the cabin floor, kicking away a small card table that held their dinner from the night before and sending Coke bottles rolling in the drum of the little room.

Fuller moved his left hand from the gun and punched at the screen door, while Billy lay on his back, bleeding. Billy moved to his knees and then found his feet, wobbling, and then ran for Fuller. But Fuller paid no mind when he sent pounding fists against the back of his shaved head, knocking off the Stetson.

The white hat rolled to the floor like a half-dollar.

He turned and looked at the boy, standing there with his fists at awkward angles near the steps to the cabin, Lorelei's head crooked into Fuller's arm, face turning red as she tried to breathe. He smiled and laughed at Billy, a big goddamn joke, and reached down and retrieved his western hat. All around Moon Lake sat families on blankets and in boats and eating Fourth of July cold fried chicken and ice-cold watermelon from the backs of cars and trucks.

"Does Reuben know you consort with whores?"

The boy's vision faded for a moment, and Bert Fuller appeared to him in wavy lines like an apparition but with a strong, solid voice that laughed.

"You got your dick wet. Now, go back inside before I stomp the shit out of you. Don't make a scene."

He took Lorelei as if leading a calf, half walking and half pulling, to where he'd parked his car along the banks of Moon Lake.

"Come on, you filthy little cunt," he said. "Back to work."

I SAT WITH MY FAMILY NEAR THE BOATHOUSE ON A RED-and-white tablecloth Joyce had packed along with deviled eggs, fried chicken, pimento cheese, potato salad, cut tomatoes, and a gallon of sweet tea. I wore a cool short-sleeved shirt and straw hat that day and pretended I was asleep, the hat over my eyes, as I heard my children trying to wake me up. I started to snore, Thomas poking me with a piece of grass in the ear, and then Anne pulling at my foot, trying to remove my shoe, before I roused and made sounds like a bear trying to catch them. Anne ran off, and Thomas grabbed another deviled egg, licking out the inside and leaving the egg white.

Joyce poured some more sweet tea and sat down next to me, and we sat there, looking out at the boats on Moon Lake and at the little bandstand where we'd met in '38. We'd danced there until the band stopped playing, and I kept moving with her, in my own romantic, ridiculous way, taking her for more light turns across the dance floor with my nimble boxer's feet. I reminded her of my good feet as often as I could.

"Anne wants a dog."

"Then let's get a dog."

"I don't want a dog."

"Then don't get her a dog."

"Do you always have to be so damn agreeable?"

I smiled at her and kissed her on the forehead. "No, Pieface. I'll work on becoming a real pain in the ass."

"Won't take much," she said and pinched my arm. "Pieface? I wish you'd quit calling me that."

I kissed her again. "Okay, Pieface."

Thomas walked up and stood before us, smiling. He handed me three empty egg halves and worked on a fourth.

"Thanks, boy. I sure do appreciate it."

"You're welcome," he said, adding the last, and laughed.

On the small shore of the lake, I saw Anne talking to another young girl who was about her age. She stood tall like an adult, with hands on her hips. I knew the boys would be coming around soon and that was okay with me because I knew she'd gotten pretty damn good on the speed bag. And for an eleven-year-old, she had a killer jab.

"Who is that Anne's talking to?"

Joyce squinted down to the shore, the darkness finally setting on, lights clicking on at the old bandstand. "That's the Ferrells' girl."

"Are they friends?"

"I guess so. They've been going to school together from the start."

"You know they officially removed Arch as county solicitor yesterday?"

"I saw that."

I lay down on my back. "When are these damn fireworks going to start?"

Down toward the Idle Hour parking lot, I heard a woman scream and a car door slam.

BILLY FOLLOWED. HE WAS SHIRTLESS IN BLUE JEANS AND no shoes, face a bloody mess. He breathed, a hot ticking in his ears, as he watched Fuller open the back of his squad car and point inside. He saw Lorelei pull away from Fuller and shake her head, and he saw Fuller's hand spring back and slap her across the mouth. Billy jogged toward them, yelling obscenities and picking up rocks to throw at Fuller. He ran through the crowd huddled near the shore of the lake and pushed and moved, some heads turning to Fuller, who reached for the back of Lorelei and pushed her to the car door. She clutched her hands on the door frame and pushed back, digging in her heels and refusing to get inside. Billy yelled for her and hoped others would hear and stop Fuller. But Fuller looked across at the crowd, maybe fifty people forming a circle around them, and told them all to mind their own fucking business, this was police work. Billy saw the backs turn, almost orchestrated on cue and trained, as Fuller knocked Lorelei across the ear and dumped her purse out on the sidewalk and gathered up the last two dollars in change they had.

When Fuller felt the coins in his hand, he punched her hard in the stomach and she deflated, crushed to the ground and trying to suck in air like a dying fish.

Billy pushed and ran up the slope to the parking lot, his feet cut on the stones and crushed glass but not even knowing pain, only feeling the wetness of blood between his toes. And he slowed and walked toward Fuller, his heart beating hard and steady like an Indian war drum, and he gritted his teeth and brushed the girlish tears from his eyes and yelled to Fuller that he was a fat, pig-eyed sack of shit.

Fuller smirked, red-faced. "Just because you got your dipstick working doesn't mean you're a man. But if that's what you want, that's what you'll get."

Fuller reached for his revolver and, as Billy stepped back, turned the barrel away and raised the butt like a club, pulling back to wallop the boy.

But the butt got only halfway.

BILLY PROTECTED HIS HEAD AND WAITED FOR THE BLOW that didn't come. He peered up to see me catching the gun in the palm of my hand and wrenching it from Bert Fuller. Fuller grinned back at me and spit some tobacco on the asphalt.

"You want to hand that back, palooka?"

I smiled back at him and then turned and pitched the gun over the crowd and into the lake. Kids and teenagers stood up on the hill of Idle Hour and looked into the parking lot. Most of the adults still turned away.

"Shouldn't have done that."

I looked over at Billy, the blood on his face and skinny chest and arms. Fuller shook his head.

"You know my guns come in a pair."

"Just let 'em go, Bert."

"Maybe that's just what I was aimin' to do before you came up and involved yourself once again in a police matter. For your information, this isn't some nice little old gal. This is a common whore who was sucking this boy's peter for a quarter out in the woods. We can't have something like that with decent people about."

"Decent people," I repeated. "What's wrong, you didn't get your cut?"

"Take it back."

I looked down, hands on my hips, and shook my head. "No, I don't think I will."

Fuller put his hand on his remaining gun and walked toward me. "Maybe you were waiting in line to get your damn cock sucked, too."

I saw women hustling their children away. A young boy not much older than my own son stared at the scene, his jaw hanging loose. And there it was, better than television, and in live Technicolor: a bloodied girl in panties and ripped shirt, an angry boy with a bloody face, and Deputy Bert Fuller, standing and spitting, hand on his gun, ready to make his order and sense of it all.

The girl moved to her knees and found purchase against the car, one hand covering the ripped place on the thin shirt, her legs scraped bloody. Her cotton underwear had turned a damp yellow from where she'd urinated while being dragged and beaten.

"You are the worst kind of coward," I said. "I know your secret. You hide behind the gun."

Fuller nodded with the words and then went for the belt and unlatched it, the leather and gun falling to the asphalt.

"Come on."

"Let them go. I don't want to fight."

"They're coming with me. And so are you, after I whip your ass."

The crowd became a ring, the asphalt the canvas, and my vision shifted from the kids and townspeople, and even the two men in khaki uniforms who stood just on top of the hill but didn't move.

I put my hands out, showing my palms, and shook my head and turned my back.

And that's when Fuller rushed and tackled me to the ground and pounded into my kidneys with his fat fists. But I was up and standing, with Fuller grasping for his feet and then taking huge, muscled punches toward me that I sidestepped without losing a breath. And more wild punches did not even make a bit of breeze near my ears, as I moved and bobbed and weaved with an instinct that came to me as natural as walking, although I hadn't practiced the science for more than fifteen years.

I found my feet and balance and kept my fist raised to my jaw, although Fuller never connected a single punch, finally growing out of breath and red-faced. He jumped on me again and pummeled with his fists, but I wrenched from Fuller's grasp and moved backward, the ring disappearing now, seeing the faces and people yelling and cheering, and Fuller's uniform coming undone, his deputy's star clapping to the ground from his wrinkled, sweaty shirt, the hat laying crown down on the ground. And I moved more, working him into a slow circle, keeping him slow and ragged and awkward and clumsy, as cheers and yells came from more faces perched on the hill. Backs that had turned before now turned and watched us, and I took a breath, feeling all of them behind me and not wanting to, knowing the ease of what I was about to do was not even a task. I sidestepped Fuller and moved him about, setting him in a perfect stance, posing him as a sculptor works his model, and then with Fuller leaned back, hands dropped by his potbelly, I worked three quick punches. *One, two, three.* Again. *One, two, three.* Kid Weisz screaming in my ears.

The two, the cross, connected with the head, spewing a plug of tobacco from Fuller's mouth, and the three, the hook, connected with sinew and bone of the ribs and I felt the crack and compression up through my knuckles. Fuller lost his balance, his eyes wide in surprise as his body failed him, and he teetered backward, falling toward Moon Lake and onto his back, rolling and rolling down a hill of stone and scree, coming to rest in a defeated heap as, up on the hill, people pointed at him as they would a circus oddity. I knew what would bother Fuller most was the laughter, the laughter coming from grown men and women, not just the awkward, bloody humor of it all, but like a great rush of wind coming through in gigantic release.

I felt hands on my back and words in my ears. But I walked through them and reached down for the girl, unbuttoning my shirt and handing it to her. I stood there in my undershirt and turned to Reuben's boy, asking him if he needed a ride home. But he didn't answer. He just nodded over and over, too shaken to talk, and grabbed Lorelei's hand and disappeared into the crowd.

When I returned to the blanket, Joyce held Thomas up in her arms and to her chest and she paced. Anne looked to me and then back to her mother. I looked to my wife and she just shook her head. "They wanted to go see the show," she said. "But I kept them here. Right here on this damn blanket."

"What was it?" Anne asked.

I got down on my knee and pretended to pull a quarter from her ear.

"I haven't fallen for that one for five years, Dad."

I shrugged, hearing the sounds of sirens in the distance.

Two men approached from the lakeshore and walked toward us. One was Jack Black, the big soldier who reminded me of a professional wrestler.

Joyce handed me some ice wrapped in a towel and I placed it over my knuckles.

"I could've sworn I saw you watching up on the hill, Major Black."

Black crossed his arms over his massive chest and smiled: "You must be mistaken. We're just here to restore order."

"What do you call that?" I said. "Pretty stupid, huh?"

"I'd call it a hell of a start, chief."

ARCH LIT HIS NINETEENTH CIGARETTE OF THE NIGHT, BOR-rowing a second pack from one of Bernard Sykes's young prosecutors, who hovered in the room like it was a stag party, and sank back into the uncomfortable chair, answering more questions. A negro man in whites brought another pot of coffee up to the suite of the Ralston Hotel, and Arch drank another cup and answered the questions with a firm yes or no, trying not to elaborate any more than was necessary. Sykes paced the room. They'd been there all day and night, and Arch had lost track of the time hours and hours ago, and the little man at the desk would peck away on his little machine, taking down every word they said.

"Can I please go? This doesn't have a thing to do with that grand jury mess."

"As I've said to you, Mr. Ferrell, you will be taken to Birmingham in the morning to answer to your charges of vote fraud. But I'm afraid this is all the same mess."

"That's a lie and could be considered slander."

"How's your headache?"

"I'm fine."

"Do you need more coffee?"

"No, I don't need any more goddamn coffee. And my drinking is my own goddamn business. There was no call to have those boys come in and bust in on me like I was a common criminal."

"Would you please continue about the morning of June eigh-teenth?"

Arch's head fell into his hand and he squeezed his temples with his fingers. "Like I've said, I got up and took my daughter's puppy out. Do you want to know how many times it shit?"

"If you think it would help," Sykes said.

"Twice. I'll collect the evidence for you."

"Then what?"

"I ate breakfast. Bacon and eggs. Grits, too. Then I walked my property. I thought about maybe doing some yard work. My garden needed to be cultivated and weeded."

"Don't you work on Fridays?"

"No, I had the day off. I hadn't had much sleep. Maybe three hours all week."

"Why didn't you sleep?"

"You wouldn't sleep either if you had crusading idiots out there calling you the brains behind the Phenix City Machine."

"Are you?"

"As I told the press, I think that's giving my brains too much credit."

"Did you work in your garden?"

"No, I wasn't feeling well. This man came over who wanted to buy some timber. His name's Perdue. Don't ask me his first name 'cause I don't recall. He owns a sawmill somewhere around here, and I put my boots on and walked my land showing him what could be thinned."

"What about the rest of the day?"

"I returned home and, I don't know, just read the paper. I fell asleep in my chair."

"Why did you go back to the courthouse, sir?"

"I went back because I had a mess of paperwork. I needed a day off. But, hell, when you're the solicitor you work all the goddamn time. Can I please get some more cigarettes in here?"

Sykes nodded to another attorney and the attorney set a pack of Camels before Arch. Arch looked up at the boy, who smiled, and Arch gave him an eat-shit grin, popping the cigarette into his mouth. After a few moments of Arch sitting there looking at Sykes, Sykes leaned in with a Zippo and lit the cigarette.

"Hell, I got it," Arch said, and Sykes pulled the hard flame away with half the cigarette gone.

"What time did you arrive at your office?"

"About eight. Maybe a little after. I can only guess. Jesus Christ, I never figured on this."

"What work did you do?"

"First, I went to the post office across the street to get my mail, and then I unlocked the courthouse. I walked upstairs and bought a Coke. I read through my mail and drank the Coke. I tried to call your fucking boss, Si Garrett."

"I've heard you state that you spoke to Mr. Garrett. Is that not true?"

"Would you please shut the hell up and let me finish my goddamn story?"

Sykes breathed in deep and looked up to a couple other prosecutors. He took another breath. "Please continue."

"His wife said he was in Birmingham. So I called the operator and told her to check around for the attorney general at the better hotels in town. She finally called back around nine and connected me to the Redmont."

"How long did you talk to Mr. Garrett?"

"Twenty minutes or so."

"What did you talk about?"

"I don't believe that information is pertinent to this investigation."

"Did anyone see you come and go from the courthouse?"

"I don't know."

"When did you leave the courthouse?"

"Shortly after hanging up the phone. All telephone tolls will verify the call. And then I collected paperwork and drove home."

"Is this when you learned of Mr. Patterson's death?"

"Yes."

"Did you see Mr. Patterson on June the eighteenth at any time?"

"No."

"Would you tell me how you learned of his death?"

"I stopped off right by my house for a beer at Huckaby's grocery. I was so tired from the week and the lies in the newspaper that I asked for a second, and I had just punched the top on the can when this boy from down the road ran in the store yelling that Mr. Patterson had been shot. Then Mr. Huckaby's wife ran in the store and said she'd seen it on the television."

Sykes watched Arch's face, but Arch didn't flinch as he reached for another cigarette from the pack. Sykes leaned in with the lighter, faster this time, and caught the cigarette.

"I drove on home, told my wife, and tried to reach Sheriff Matthews and Governor Persons. But all lines were busy. Then Mr. Garrett called and wanted to know what was going on in Phenix City, and, I had to be honest, I wasn't quite sure."

Sykes didn't say a word.

"And that's when I returned to the courthouse and saw the whole scene down by the Elite, and I walked down there and saw the blood and learned the horrible news." Arch leaned back and watched the smoke coming from his mouth and through his fingers and up toward the ceiling, scattering in a ceiling fan. He looked toward Sykes, but his eyes were on the suite's window, watching nothing. "The whole thing was just awful. Mr. Patterson's blood on the sidewalk where children could see it, and the first thing I thought about was his family. How do you tell a good family that their husband and daddy is dead?"

Sykes reached into his briefcase and pulled out a small notepad, flipping through several pages. He finally looked up with his eyes and said, "This little ledger was in Si Garrett's briefcase. Does this look like your handwriting?"

REUBEN WALKED BACK through the kitchen screen door carrying a sack of groceries, a carton of Lucky Strikes, and a bottle of Miller beer. His eyes were bloodshot, and his skin glowed with a pasty whiteness, slick from the alcohol, as he slipped by Billy and landed everything on the old wooden counter. Billy had some trinkets he'd found out by the creek laid out on the table, some arrowheads, pieces of old china, a rusted horse bridle, and when the beer landed they all rattled on the planks.

"Where the hell you been?" he asked.

"I've been here."

"Since when?"

"Since two days ago."

"Where were you before that?"

Billy shrugged. "With Mario."

"You know that kid's Italian."

"I do."

He nodded and leaned back against the stove. He reached for a box of kitchen matches and lit a cigarette. "Mario, huh?" He squinted those droopy, sad eyes at Billy and said: "I heard you'd shacked up with some whore."

The words sank like a knife in the gut, and Billy stood and scraped the trinkets he'd collected back into a Hav-a-Tampa cigar box filled with more arrowheads, old bullets, and cracked pieces of china. Last year, he'd found an old bayonet from the Civil War out by the well.

"I don't want you going around her again. Bert Fuller is one mean sonofabitch. He'd just soon kill you as look at you."

Billy walked by him and went to his room, locking the door. He had an old baseball mitt under his bed, and as he sat down on his bunk he fired the ball into the sweet pocket over and over until he heard Reuben try the handle. Then Reuben started to bang hard and tell him to open up or he was going to whip his ass, which Billy knew was a goddamn lie.

He stood and unlatched the door and sat back down on the metal bed. The wallpaper was pink and flowered, and drooped and peeled from the summer heat. He looked at his father and waved a fly away from his face.

"Who's the girl?"

He didn't say anything.

Billy could smell his breath. It was sharp and smelled like gin and cigarettes, and as he took another sip of beer he tousled his son's hair—like he did when he didn't want to talk but only to let him know he was still a kid—and left his room with the door wide open.

Billy stayed there for a while, dropping the mitt and examining the arrowheads and rusted old bits. He studied their grooves and points and thought about them being buried down in the mud for so damn long, and wondered what else was hidden by the creek.

He fell asleep like that until the shadows crept up on the walls and it became a late-summer night and he could hear the whistles and cracks from the back field. At first, he thought Reuben was firing his gun, or someone had come for him. He thought a lot about Johnnie Benefield coming over, and knew that if he saw him he'd want to kill that bastard. Billy thought of the ways. With a rusty knife and with a gun. He thought a lot about knocking Johnnie in the head and old crotch with a Louisville Slugger.

But as he pulled away the sad, yellowed curtains of their old house, he spotted Reuben deep in a cornfield that he hadn't planted since his father died. He sat on his ass, a hunched figure like a sullen statue, and Billy walked outside, catching some fresh air from the boxed heat.

There was a sizzle and some sparks and a loud whistle and boom. He saw Reuben smoke and stumble from where he sat and affix another bottle rocket into the empty Miller beer.

"Where you get those?" Billy asked behind him.

"Some lady give 'em to me."

He stood behind his father, looking at his back, the two-tone blue-and-black shirt and wide stance of his legs and cowboy boots. His hair was oiled and pomaded like boys in high school, and although Billy couldn't see his face he watched as smoke leaked up above Reuben's head. Then Reuben reached over and touched his cigarette to another bottle rocket.

One started to fizz and smoke without ever leaving the beer bottle, and Reuben laughed and tripped on one knee before pushing Billy a good three feet away as it hissed and burned out. A dud.

"Well, goddamn."

"I didn't mean nothin' about being gone," Billy said.

"That's all right," he said. "I ain't gonna beat you or nothin'. I ever lay one hand on you? Hell, no, I haven't. I've had enough goddamn beatings from my daddy for ten generations. I ever tell you about this strop he had called the licorice stick?"

"Yes, sir." Billy had seen the rotting, hard piece of leather hanging from a rusted nail in the smokehouse. He'd never understood why his father kept it there like some kind of trophy.

"I think the sonofabitch enjoyed it. Use to take me and my brother to the shed out yonder."

"What'd you get at the store?"

"Be careful with those whores," he said, ignoring the question and getting to his feet, dusting the dirt off his legs. "You know when I was your age, I was so horny I would've screwed a snake."

Billy didn't say anything.

"Pussy is good, son," Reuben said. "But it can just about eat a man alive."

His father reached into his pocket and pulled out a thick Case folding knife and handed it to him. "This was your granddaddy's. Stick that in your cigar box."

Billy opened the blade, the unoiled metal hard to pry with a thumbnail but finally coming loose and gleaming back the reflection of his eyes.

Reuben stayed there in the field for a while, and Billy walked back past the empty laundry line and dead peach trees and a rusting, tireless car. And he checked in the grocery bag, placing the bacon and eggs in the icebox and turning on their radio to listen to the late-night radio show out of Birmingham that played "Louisiana Hayride," featuring Hank Snow and some kid from Memphis named Elvis.

Before he went to bed, the boy looked back out the kitchen window for Reuben but instead saw a massive, crackling fire from one of the old sheds. It was his grandfather's smokehouse, and the fire inside had grown so hot the red paint crackled and flaked like a snake's scales. He sprinted down and found Reuben, who didn't seem fazed at all. He just stood there drinking, two-tone shirt open, with his face and chest shiny from the summertime fire.

He stepped back and wiped his face, black smudges crossed under his eyes and his chin. He laughed at himself.

Billy's hands and voice shook as he screamed at him, telling him it was gonna burn down if they didn't get some water. But he was invisible to his father.

"I always hated that fucking place," Reuben said and threw his beer bottle at the building.

And he tripped and wandered back to the house, grabbed the keys to his baby blue Buick, and sped off into the Alabama night.

THAT SAME NIGHT, JOHN PATTERSON AND I CLOSED DOWN the Elite Café. We drank coffee down to the dregs and ate lemon icebox pie, having met right after dinner with our families. We smoked cigarettes and talked little except when joined by the cook, Ross Gibson, who'd just scraped off the grill and shut down. Gibson was an old, wiry man with gray hair in his ears and a grease-splattered apron and white T-shirt. He smoked a lot, tired after a long day's work, and took a cup of coffee while I asked him about the night Albert Patterson had been shot in the alley beside the kitchen.

"I saw just one man," Gibson said. "I went outside to get some air and I seen that one fella in the tan suit at the back of the alley."

"And you didn't recognize him?"

"No, sir."

"You never saw him before?" I asked.

"No, sir."

"What kind of tan suit? A uniform?"

"Naw, just a suit. You know. A Sunday suit."

"How long until you heard the shots?"

"Couple minutes."

"Would you recognize the man's picture?"

"No, sir."

"How come?"

"I didn't get a good look at his face."

"Was he a white man?"

"I couldn't say."

Gibson excused himself, and John Patterson pulled a notebook from his suit jacket and made a notation. He started to take another bite of pie but instead mashed the crust with his fork and pushed away the plate with a grunt. He just stared into space for a while and breathed.

"You know your mother gave Anne a kitten," I said, just reaching for something in the silence. He leaned into the table and watched his hands. "Would you tell her thank you for us?"

Patterson nodded. "That old cat is always having kittens."

"How's your mother?"

Patterson shrugged and blew out a long breath. Ross Gibson walked to the front of the Elite and clicked off the neon OPEN sign.

"You know, there was a long black car parked just across the street," Gibson said. "Now, that fella sittin' at the wheel had to have seen somethin'."

"You know the make?" I asked.

"It was dark."

I laid down a couple dollars under the smoldering ashtray, and we left through the front door, passing by the long, vacuous stretch of alley in between the Elite and the Coulter Building.

The alley was quiet and warm, almost absorbing the sounds from the passing cars and our dress shoes. I stopped as Patterson walked into the alley. I didn't feel it was my place, and knew there was little for John to do but to play back the killing of his father over and over like a broken projector.

A long mural advertising Coca-Cola had been painted on the side of the café. The sky above was broad and open and black, a ceiling lightly shining from a soft moon.

I stayed on the sidewalk and watched as Patterson found the spot where his father was shot and kneeled. He touched the warm asphalt and stood, turning his head slowly in each direction.

A patrol car roamed slow on Fifth and shone a spotlight down into the alley—we were frozen in its swath. The black-and-white looked as if it hadn't been washed in ages, and craggy faces peered out from where windshield wipers had cleared away red dust.

Patterson looked into the light, blinded. I waved the men on. But the car stayed, the two cops conversed, and then it finally moved on down Fifth.

"Did you know about that car Gibson mentioned?" he asked.

"Lots of folks saw it. I think it was one of those long cars they made before the war. No one seems to know the make. Britton and I've been checking around, but we're not getting too far."

John and I walked together in the stretch of alley behind the Coulter Building—a long embankment filled with mulberry trees and scrub oak and long, twisted stretches of kudzu. We moved up and around the post office, just across the street from the county courthouse, and Patterson took off his jacket and held it in the crook of his arm.

He placed his right hand in his pocket. Even at night, the summer heat was tremendous.

"I make bad decisions when I'm mad."

"Don't doubt yourself."

"Attorney general? I don't have any business holding office."

"And Si Garrett does?"

At Fourteenth Street, Patterson looked past the Confederate monument and up to the second floor; all the lights were dimmed. He then twisted his head back to the alley and bit into his cheek.

He nodded to himself.

"You're sure, aren't you?" I asked.

"I don't have a doubt in my mind that Arch Ferrell is shielding the man who killed my father. He helped plan it and probably stood at that window in the courthouse, watching this very alley, probably took a drink after he knew it was done, and then rang off a long-distance connection with the attorney general for this state."

I nodded. I opened and closed the fingers of my swelling hand.

"But knowing doesn't give us much," John said. "Fuller must've been invisible on a Friday night in Phenix City. Didn't anyone see that sonofabitch run from that alley and back to his sheriff's office or into a getaway car? He has this entire town scared shitless. They saw him. That cook saw him. I know there are others, but we can't do a thing but sit and wait. I just hope the pressure works on that man's rotten soul."

ARCH FERRELL TOOK A SEAT AT BERT FULLER'S BEDSIDE AND waited for a chunky woman with blond hair to leave the room. The woman kept baby talking to Fuller as she finished shaving the left side of his face with a straight razor. She cooed and rubbed the fresh red skin—half his face still covered in lather—while he stared at the ceiling and spoke to Arch.

"You can speak freely," Fuller said.

"I'd rather wait," Arch said.

"You need a shave. Come on, let Georgia take care of you."

"I'm fine."

"Arch, you look terrible. Look like you haven't bathed in a week."

"I said I don't want a fuckin' shave. Now, get your snatch out of here and let's talk."

The woman's head snapped back as if Arch had slapped her and she dabbed off the last bit of shaving cream from Fuller's face and briskly walked out of the room.

"Arch, there was no need for that."

"Did you break your goddamn head, too?"

"No."

Arch leaned in and whispered, "I need to know what you did with that gun."

"It's taken care of."

"What did you do with it?"

"It's gone. Ain't nobody gonna find it."

Arch nodded and leaned back into his seat. He looked around Fuller's huge garage apartment and four racks of guns by the front door. Western movie posters were tacked to the walls, along with wanted posters and mug shots, maps of Russell County and Columbus. A framed picture of Fuller with Big Jim Folsom and another with Lash LaRue.

"I have news," Arch said.

Fuller raised up with a groan and placed another pillow behind his back.

"Si is coming back. He plans on resuming his duties as attorney general."

"What about . . . you know," Fuller said and made a circular motion with his index finger around his ear.

"He said he's well. I spoke to his brother about an hour back."

Fuller nodded. "I pray for him."

Arch snorted. "You pulling my leg?"

"No, sir," Fuller said. "I pray for his soul. I pray for you, too, Arch."

"Jesus H. Christ, you've gone off your rocker."

"I think those rocks set me straight. When I came to, I saw every-thing so much clearer. It was like being at the movies when the picture ain't in focus and someone up in the booth sets it right. That's the way I feel. I didn't tell anyone about it till I told Georgia on Sunday. And she had me talk to the preacher. He brought me up front and placed his hands upon my head. All I can say is that I felt a change in me. I don't see things like I used to. I've been washed in the blood of the lamb."

"Goddamn."

"Not in here."

"What?"

"Don't speak like that in my home."

"You live in a garage, Bert."

"I pray for you."

"I don't need prayer. I need you to pull your head out of your ass. I need for the goddamn Guard to leave town. Hell, I need a goddamn drink."

"Georgia?" Fuller called out. And the woman came to him, giving a sour, skeptical look at Arch before sitting in a small chair by Bert Fuller's side. "Get your Bible, darling. Mr. Ferrell is in some pain."

"There is nothing wrong with me. You've lost your mind."

"Mr. Arch," Fuller said. "I've never been better in my life. Would you pray with us?"

Arch shook his head, and, as he reached the door, he heard Fuller and his whore girlfriend singing the first verses of "The Old Rugged Cross."

IT WAS MIDNIGHT, AND JOHNNIE BENEFIELD RAN HIS HUD-son to the redline, taking hard turns on country roads for the hell of it, kicking up dust and grit and spinning tires. You couldn't see far ahead, clouds covered up the moon that night and out in the country, the headlights sliced across the countryside like knives.

"That's twin H-power under the hood, buddy. That 308 can press the sonofabitch to 170 horses. This little Hornet can fuckin' fly. Listen to that buzz. Listen to that."

Reuben sat in the front seat with his two-tone cowboy boot on the dash, nursing along a bottle of Jack Daniel's, as he liked to do most nights. Moon sat in the backseat, a sullen child taking up most of the bench.

The fat man ate an ice-cream cone, working his leviathan tongue around the pink mass and slurping on the milk dripping down his hands, wiping his chin on his fatty arms.

Johnnie looked back in the rearview, taking the turns now with one hand on the wheel. "Jesus Christ, Moon. I believe you'd eat till you bust at the seams."

Reuben took a hit of Jack. He passed it back to Moon, who washed down a big bite of ice cream with the whiskey. He handed it back, and Reuben wiped the mouth with the flat of his hand.

"I ever tell you about the night Big Nigger died?" Johnnie asked. "See, me and him was supposed to crack this safe in Newnan. It was a big job, one of those walk-in Wells Fargo numbers. We got word that this sonofabitch kept all his money in the back of his hardware store. We figured maybe a hundred grand in cash and guns and jewelry and all. But before we could get to it, a couple niggers robbed it on Halloween night. I mean *real* niggers, not Big Nigger. I don't know how they knew, but they knew, and we think it may have been one of the stickmen at the Bamboo who told. Anyway, Big Nigger was mad as hell. We had the job all lined up. I could've cracked that sonofabitch in five minutes with a stethoscope and a drill. But those goddamn thieves went to it with crowbars and blowtorches. I shit you not. I heard the safe was rigged with tear gas, and one of those boys got it in the eyes real good. I would've paid to seen that."

Reuben jostled a bit as Johnnie fishtailed out onto the paved road and went up and down some small hills on the outskirts of Phenix. He took another hit of Jack. He could smell Moon's animal stench behind him, and that and the goddamn jitters made him want to puke.

"So ole Jim, Big Nigger, went over to where those boys lived and hopped on one and started choking the ever-living shit out of one of 'em, but he didn't know the other was there hiding in the kitchen and, when he stood up, the sonofabitch jumped up behind him and blew the back of his head off."

Reuben nodded, lulled by the long ribbon of blacktop.

"We took both those boys out to the river, shot them just like ole James was shot and kicked 'em right into the river."

Reuben nodded again.

"Say, what's the matter with you?" he asked.

"This ain't my idea."

Johnnie laughed and drove with one hand while he punched the lighter on the Hudson's dash. "No, it ain't your idea, but you'll sure as shit spend the money we're about to get paid. Just sit tight and I'll do all the work. We ain't paid to think."

"What if we get stopped?"

"Quit pissin' your britches. Everything is copacetic."

He turned down Summerville Road, and they coasted and twisted down the hill past a couple white-clapboard churches and little cottages strung along the road. Most of the lights were out, and they didn't see a single jeep or roadblock. They soon turned into a little neighborhood on Twenty-eighth Street, and Johnnie took the big engine down to a little purr and killed the lights as they wound their way around the little ranch houses and cottages. Little postage-stamp pieces of lawns with nice mailboxes and short little driveways. Folks who worked in Columbus but lived in Phenix City because it was cheaper.

Soon Johnnie stopped and killed the big jet engine. The windows were down, and Reuben wiped his face with his hand. Moon had worked the ice-cream cone down to a nub and chomped in the backseat until Reuben looked back at him and he stopped.

The air smelled of the pink-and-red box roses planted outside the little houses and gardenias, all heated and freshly watered. They sat there until there was a light flecking on the windshield, the short patter of rain, and then more rain, and Johnnie sat there and smiled and smiled. And Reuben asked: "What's so goddamn great?"

"This is good. This is better."

"Will it still go in the rain?"

"It would work at the bottom of a fucking lake."

Johnnie looked down at his wristwatch and wound the stem. Reuben took a deep, long breath and followed Johnnie out of the car. He popped the trunk and pulled out some paint cans packed with dynamite sticks and mud. They called them slug bombs.

He tossed Moon the keys and Moon moved up to the front seat, squeezing behind the steering wheel. He looked like a rat trying to escape into a small hole.

"We shouldn't have taken your car," Reuben said. "I coulda stole us something."

"My car is the fastest car in the state of Alabama and ain't no way nobody can catch us. My God, it's got a jet engine, Reuben."

Another car slowed at the end of Twenty-eighth Street and soon coasted to a stop behind them. Reuben's heart was up in his throat as he shielded his eyes with his hand and watched as two large shadows stepped into the headlights.

It was the Youngblood brothers. Glenn and Ernest.

"Jesus," Reuben said. "You didn't say nothin' 'bout this."

Glenn, a big, buck-toothed boy with a wide squirrel's nest of a pompadour, pulled the Jack from his hands and took a drink. He passed it to his slightly shorter, slightly fatter brother, who did the same, and passed it back to Reuben. The brothers worked a couple clubs out on Opelika Highway, the Hillbilly and the Bamboo, with B-girls and whores. They made some money on the side as muscle for Miss Fannie Belle, and two years ago had made the papers for beating some RBA members bloody on election day right in front of news cameras.

The RBA boys had complained that the Youngbloods were changing the ballots. And they had, on the direction of Bert Fuller, who spent the good part of the day casting votes for dead men and herding his whores up to the ballot box.

Ernest took a big swallow and then grinned a rotten row of upper teeth. He handed the bottle back to Reuben and Reuben turned it upside down, a single drop rolling out.

"Thanks," he said.

Johnnie handed out masks to Reuben, the brothers, and another one to Moon, before slipping one over his face. All identical, all rubber pullovers of the sad Emmett Kelly clown face. Big red nose, black shadowy beard, and droopy white mouth. The rain sounded muffled to Reuben with his ears covered.

He pulled the .38 from a clip on his belt. The others carried a variety of pistols.

"I seen him once," Johnnie said behind the Kelly mask. "Ringling Brothers in Atlanta. That rascal tried to smash a peanut with a sledge-hammer. My kind of guy."

JACK BLACK would often stop by that July on his midnight patrol, and I'd make him a cup of coffee and we'd usually sit outside on my back porch and talk in whispers and smoke cigarettes, and he'd tell me a little of what he was hearing out of the AG's office. About the only thing so far was that they were racking up a hell of a bill at the Ralston Hotel.

He told me a few good stories about the general in charge of the command, a millionaire in the steel business from Birmingham named Crack Hanna. Hanna had recently told a local minister to go piss up a tree after complaints that the troops frightened the towns-people.

I smiled. "We once had a minister here who decided to go all out against the Machine. He laid out a thick Easter Sunday sermon about the immorality of drinking and gambling and harlots and all that. I'm sure you've heard that kind of thing before. It wasn't but a few days later that some of the boys around here sent a prostitute to visit with the minister."

"She screw him?"

"No. She ripped off her clothes and yelled rape, and it wasn't but about thirty seconds later the doors busted down and in came Fuller and some deputies."

"Fuller is a piece of work."

"He's no fan of mine."

"I bet."

"You think he'll make a move?"

"Maybe." Black shrugged. "I'd watch my back if I were you. You hurt his pride, and for a guy like that that means everything."

"I don't know if I'd call it pride."

"He's pretty much a single-minded shithead."

"I bet you wish you were back in Birmingham right now."

"I'd be out on patrol, same as here."

"You like being a cop?"

"Sure." He shrugged. "Didn't figure myself on a desk job after I got out of the Army."

The rain had just started and it pinged on the metal roof, and Black looked above him and then out to his open jeep and shook his head. The phone started to ring.

Black flicked the cigarette under his foot and crushed it.

I caught the phone, and ten seconds later I was out the door with my rain slicker and ball cap.

Black ran alongside me, saying he would drive.

He knocked the jeep in gear and didn't even ask about the call till we were headed down Crawford. The jeep jostled and groaned as we took a hard turn up Summerville Road.

"Britton said he saw men creeping around his backyard."

"How many?"

"He couldn't tell. At least two."

"Let me guess, he didn't call the police."

I shook my head.

He reached for the radio.

THE YOUNGBLOODS TOOK THE FRONT DOOR WITH A CROW-
bar, and Johnnie picked the rear lock in seconds. Reuben followed,
shining a flashlight across the kitchen and a little refrigerator. He
heard the floor creak, and when he turned there was a huge boom and
a big hole appeared by his head. Johnnie rushed the old man and tackled him and the shotgun before he could reload, and Reuben turned on
the kitchen lights, his right ear deaf and buzzing. Hugh Britton was
dressed in blue pin-striped pajamas, his black-framed glasses crooked
on his head, and he was cussing up a storm.

The kitchen was a spotless, modern wonder of white appliances and
a light green tile counter. Reuben set his gun on the counter and
breathed.

No one said a word. Johnnie handed Reuben some rope, and he got
down to the floor and hog-tied Britton, the old man fighting and flail-
ing but quickly subdued. And then the Youngbloods, giggling and
laughing in those sad, white-lipped clown masks, pushed Britton's
wife through the door, a large woman—maybe twice the size of
Britton—in her nightshirt and hairnet.

She screamed and wailed and punched at the men with the flat of
her tiny fists.

The Youngbloods forced her down to the ground and tied her the
same way, before dragging the couple back to their bedroom and setting them in each of their single beds. One of the clowns, Reuben
couldn't tell who, leaned down and put a big, wadded-up panty in the
woman's mouth, and, as she screamed, kissed her on the head and told
her good-night.

The overhead light was turned off, and Benefield was in the living
room opening up his wood box and pulling out sticks of dynamite.

"You scared them," Reuben said. "Let's go."

"We ain't done."

"You didn't say we were keeping them here. Pull 'em out, goddamn you."

Benefield looked up at him with sad ole Emmett Kelly's face and pantomimed that he couldn't hear him, and then he gave a sad-clown shrug and went back to work setting out the slug bombs and attaching a long fuse.

But then all the boys heard the door creak and they turned their heads. Reuben ran back to the kitchen, and the door buffeted against the stiff, hot wind and rain, but he saw no one. He shook his head and closed the door and walked back to the TV room, where the three men played like three boys as they set the charge.

One of the Youngbloods held a flashlight over Johnnie's quick hands, and Reuben looked to each of them inside their rubber masks to see if their eyes showed anything. He took a breath and reached for his gun, but then there was a hard, booming shot and Benefield got kicked back to the floor.

Reuben dropped to the ground, only a night-light burning in the long hallway.

Benefield crawled on the floor, holding his bloodied shoulder and moving across the light blue carpet trailing a long red stain.

BLACK WENT ON IN THE HOUSE AHEAD OF ME AND I trailed back through the kitchen, hiding behind a door as the man in the mask walked inside and then turned away. I had Black's .45 cocked and locked, and I tried to control my breathing as I crept around Britton's linoleum floor, the room smelling of fresh biscuits and bacon, and made my way into a small dining room with all-new modern accessories from the Sears Roebuck catalog. Britton had covered the floor with the best and newest wall-to-wall carpet—baby blue—and I was damn glad now as it muffled my steps as I rounded the table, past the big buffet filled with his wife's china and a wall of sepia-toned photographs and new black and whites.

I moved into the living room, and it sat there empty and quiet, with a long green couch and little orange chairs and long bank of bay windows. On the floor was an open box, and I squatted down, seeing the dynamite sticks stuck down in a mud bucket. My mouth went dry as I stood and turned and faced a tall man in a clown mask holding a gun.

The light was narrow and dim from the back hallway, and he was just a shadow as he raised a pistol and I did the same.

REUBEN WAITED IN THE BEDROOM, WITH BRITTON AND HIS wife struggling in their beds. The Youngbloods looked to one another and then nodded, and then Ernest, the taller one, headed back into the short hallway, and Glenn, after checking his revolver again, followed. Reuben looked down at the two twin beds, the little round alarm clock between the couple and the big framed picture from a wedding back in the old days on the nightstand. Britton's glasses had been knocked away, and as he kicked and squirmed on the bed he squinted up at the dim light.

Reuben ran for a side window and pulled it open and pushed through a jagged holly bush, cutting his arm, and rounded his way on the lawn. Out in the little lawn in the wet green grass, the rain looking like silver pins in the streetlight, he saw a bloodied Johnnie Benefield lighting a stick of dynamite he held in his teeth.

I SLOWLY MOVED TO MY FEET, AND THE CLOWN STRETCHED the gun out in his hands, pulling back the hammer, and then there was a boom, and the clack of a reload, and the clown was down on his back, almost comical in falling, like a cartoon clown with the rug swept out from under him, but there was a hole in the middle of his chest that was large as a saucer. A big, ugly sucking wound, and his voice sounded moist and wet and cracked as I stepped down to pull off the mask.

Black called out behind me, and I quickly pulled up my .45. In the hallway was another one running for me and the downed figure on the baby blue carpet, and as he raised a pistol with his hand, rushing for me, coming hard, I shot him three times.

Black walked up beside me and pulled me with him, as I tried to kneel and check on the men, and he told me to go back through the back door and that he'd take the front. And then the whole outside bay window exploded in a lightning of sharp yellows and blues, and the concussive force knocked us both down to the ground, burying our heads in our hands.

"COME ON," REUBEN SCREAMED AS JOHNNIE LIT ANOTHER stick and pitched it toward the house with his good arm. Moon had fishtailed the Hornet on the slick street and barreled toward them, the big, round headlights looking like eyes as he zoomed down the road and fishtailed again, braking hard and throwing open the passenger's door.

Johnnie touched the fuse and it caught and zipped, and he launched it up on the shingled roof and it rolled into a gutter. "Hot damn!" he yelled.

They heard sirens, and Reuben reached for Johnnie's bloody yellow shirt and pulled, but Johnnie pointed a gun at him and told him to get to the car or he'd blow his fucking brains all over the street.

Reuben ran for the car, and, as he did, he saw a man coming around from the side of the house.

I MET ANOTHER CLOWN AT THE EDGE OF THE DRIVEWAY, but he had already seen me and had a gun drawn and pointed at my head, standing his ground, sirens in the distance. Then part of the roof exploded and cracked, and we were knocked off our feet, the house now catching on fire, and I couldn't see or think but scrambled for the man and the gun, but he was on his knees, looking at me, the pistol still out but shaking. I put my hands up, and we both steadied ourselves. A man by a black Hudson yelled for him to shoot the sonofabitch and come on.

And he pointed the gun at me, the silver rain falling sideways. I could not breathe, fear sweating through my skin and across my face. I closed my eyes, and when I didn't hear a thing I opened them and the figure was gone, piling into the Hudson and peeling away, dipping over the top of the hill, its red taillights shining and then disappearing over the ridge.

Black appeared from the front of the house, kicking down the front door and carrying Hugh's wife, which, in kind terms, was a hell of an effort, and Britton was alongside of him in his pajamas and without his glasses and looking up at his house all torn away and battered and on fire, and he stepped over to me, squinting into the rain and the black, and said, "Lamar?"

"It's me."

"There are two dead men in my house."

"I know."

"Major Black says he got another, but we can't find him."

"I only saw the two."

"You shoot them boys?"

"I shot one."

"Good going. You saved the others for me, right?"

"You know it," I said, and put my hand on the older man's shoulder and stood out there, watching his perfect little home burn, until the Guard showed up and the fire trucks and the neighbors and, ultimately, the newsmen, who would take pictures until five o'clock the next day.

I'D CLOSED UP the filling station for the night, locking the pumps, emptying out the dirty oil in the drums out back, and finally restocking some of the candy shelves, when John Patterson drove up underneath the overhang and honked his horn. I met him outside by a big Texaco oil display, and when I noticed his pressed blue suit and tie I knew he'd been to Montgomery to see Governor Persons. He walked with me into the garage as I put up some wrenches, and he told me about the meeting, talking in fast gestures, his face heated with summer sweat and excitement. As always, his black beard was beginning to show on his square jaw.

"Is Britton doing okay?" he asked.

"House is a mess, but he's fine."

"You?"

"Nothing happened to me," I said. "What'd the governor say?"

"How'd you know I'd been to see the governor?"

"You're wearing your good suit."

"Well, he used the same good words he'd had in the newspaper with us," John said. "General Hanna went with me. Told us how tragic the situation had gotten and the sorrow he felt for Britton and his family.

He even stood up from his desk and paced when I told him about Hugh's wife and how half their house was gone."

"You believe him?"

John shrugged. "I just keep thinking about that time when they blew up Bentley's house two years ago. Remember how Persons flew in on that little helicopter and surveyed the damage and shook hands and gave that pensive look he gives. You know the one, where he softens his baby face, makes his eyes like slits, and pouts his lips."

"He called off the investigation after a week."

"It was only a day."

I shook my head.

"Of course, we're talking about the same fella who fired the football coach at Auburn as his first act in office. Don't get me wrong, he listened, but he seemed more interested in showing off his gun collection. He was particularly excited about this big Nazi belt buckle he'd just bought. I guess he thought I'd be interested because I was in the Army."

"You're kidding."

"Apparently, it was a real rare find. Persons said they only made twelve. He let me hold it and then asked if I thought it was heavy. And I said yes, and then he opened up the cover on the damn thing and it was a .32 caliber pistol made for officers. I told him that was nice, and that just egged him on, and he went into another room to show us a Chinese hand cannon, making a point that it was a replica so we wouldn't think he'd spent the money on a real one."

"Did he talk about Phenix at all?"

"Well, I finally had enough as he was playing with that hand cannon. I just said, 'Governor, you've got to do something.'"

"What did he say?"

"He said, 'We have done something. I've sent troops and the best investigators in the state. A governor can't do much more.' And then he turned back to the damn belt buckle and played with it some more. 'Just genius,' he said. 'Isn't it? To think a country so violent and mean could produce a work of art like this. It's history. Just a piece of a culture that's been destroyed for good.' That's when I told him to put the town under martial law. I had to say it, because General Hanna was standing there right beside me, and I think if Persons had kept showing off his trinkets Hanna would've leapt over the desk and choked him. Did you ever hear why they call General Hanna 'Crack'?"

"I heard he was good with the pistol."

"He was also good with a baseball bat when he was a strikebreaker," John said. "He's who the Birmingham fat cats called when the union bosses came to town. And as Persons kept talking, General Hanna took a deep breath and stood, his face turning red as a beet. You know, in the war he commanded a Pacific jungle unit that inflicted so many casualties he set Army records."

"Persons will never go for martial law," I said, dropping a wrench into a toolbox and slamming down the hood of a '48 Ford truck.

John shook his head. "He said everything was going to be under control. He said you couldn't judge the situation by some bumps in the road, and said he had great faith in the state investigators."

"He can't be talking about ole Smelley."

"I told him what I suspected about Smelley. But he didn't buy it. He said Smelley was a good man and was doing a hell of a job."

We walked outside, and I closed the bay door of the garage, sealing it with a padlock. I found a spot on the edge of the platform of the gas pumps and sat down. My back ached; my feet ached. It was late, but there was still plenty of soft gold light. I lit a cigarette and stretched out my legs.

"So then he offered to send in more troops. But Hanna wasn't satisfied with that. He knew that was what Persons was going to offer when we drove over this afternoon and was prepared. He knew it was just a political move to keep the newspaper boys off his back. And Hanna told him that. Hanna said he wouldn't leave the governor's office till he had a green light to bust up the rackets."

"You want a Coca-Cola?" I asked John. But John said no. He looked more tired than me. His shirt was soaked through under the suit jacket, and despite his obvious exhaustion he paced underneath the overhang as he talked.

"So then Persons turned to me and ignored Hanna, as if I'd put Hanna up to this. He said, 'I don't understand what you want from me, John. I send you the National Guard, and the full cooperation of state investigators. Our acting attorney general is devoting his full time to the investigation into your father's murder. I can't do much more. You even went to Washington to ask for help. That move embarrassed our entire state. And, like they said, this is a state matter.' And that's when I knew this was going to be a big old pissing match. He was absolutely furious that I'd gone to Washington. He actually said I'd embarrassed the state of Alabama. Can you believe that?"

"And that's when Hanna let him have it."

"You bet," John said. "Hanna stood up as tall as that little fireplug could, those stars on his shoulders, shaven head, and leaned into the desk and said, and I quote, 'Governor, I mean no disrespect by this but you don't seem to hear a goddamn word of what's being said. The local crew of cops in this town is about the sorriest gathering of bastards I've ever seen in my life. They don't want us there, never wanted us there, and won't get off their fat asses to help. They want Phenix City back to its wicked ways. And that's fine if that's what you want, too. But don't go and blow smoke up our ass and tell Mr. Patterson here that everything is being done. Because, sir, it sure as shit is not. We're sitting around with our thumbs up our assholes while these hoods and gangsters ride past us every day, pointing and laughing at us like they're at the goddamn zoo.'"

"He said that?"

"He sure did. He told Persons, 'They intimidate witnesses and blow up people's homes. They aren't scared of us in the least 'cause they all know we're just there for the news boys to pose for some pictures. So, to the point, sir? Either use us to break this town apart or send us home. I don't mean to be so frank. But here it is, Gordon. Either shit or get off the pot.'"

"Glad Hanna didn't bring a baseball bat."

"Persons couldn't believe anyone would talk to him like that in the mansion."

I smiled, finished the cigarette, and squashed it under the sole of my work boot.

"Persons wasn't behind the desk; he was standing at the side, feeling around that Nazi belt buckle and the little buttons and springs. He said, 'Can you put this in a report?' and Hanna said, 'Goddamn, it's been five weeks since this man's father was gunned down. The local police haven't interviewed a single suspect.'"

I smiled at him, knowing what was about to come, knowing John had told me every detail because I knew where all this was headed.

"Britton gave you the Mr. X records, didn't he?" I asked.

"Well, Hugh let some of the newspaper boys take a listen this morning. But, for some reason, he wanted a couple of them held back. He wanted me to deliver them to the governor. I guess he thought Persons should be well versed on the entire situation."

"How long did it take for him to call you?"

John smiled. It was the first time I'd seen him smile since his father's death. "The governor left a message for me before I pulled into my driveway."

"And what did it say?"

"Apparently, that recorded conversation he had with Hoyt Shepherd about campaign contributions came through clear as a bell."

"Can I ask what happens next?"

"I guess he saw the big splash Mr. X made in the afternoon papers. Did you see Hugh was quoted with saying that there was more where that came from? Well, the governor said he had some phone calls to make."

"WHO THE FUCK IS MR. X?" HOYT SHEPHERD SAID, PULLING a big fat cigar from the side of his mouth as he spun in the chair of Cobb's Barber Shop and rattled the front page of the *Ledger*. Jimmie Matthews sat in a waiting chair, next to the coatrack and by the plate-glass window, and nodded. "Did you see this bullshit? Did you read it?"

Jimmie nodded. The barber, a relative of the former mayor, stepped away, added his scissors to the blue Barbicide, and walked over to grab some electric clippers.

"It says right here that this goddamn mysterious Mr. X turned over plastic recordings of crime kingpin Hoyt Shepherd having intimate phone conversations with known state and local politicians, including Big Jim Folsom, winner of the Democratic ticket for governor. Hell, they even say I had a talk with—get this—an unknown party about the killing of Fate Leburn. Hell, that damn bootlegger's been dead almost ten years. Who's digging up this shit on me? Let me tell you one damn thing. Jimmie, are you listening to me?"

Jimmie nodded, dressed in a crisp white shirt and tie, blue suit, and crossed his legs. He acknowledged his partner with a tip of his cigarette. His hair already nicely trimmed and slicked down with a good splash of Vitalis.

"You mark my words, they're gonna hang me for this. Right? These people, these National Guard Nazis and that green-as-grass prosecutor, Sykes, need a warm body and my fat ass is just the right size."

Hoyt's big face turned a hard shade of purple as Mr. Cobb trimmed the hair off the back of his neck and shaved off some black fuzz on his ears. Hoyt's big jowls flexed and twisted, and when the buzzing of the clippers stopped and Cobb reached for another pair of scissors for a few stray hairs, Hoyt continued: "Let me tell you something. There ain't no Santa Claus, there ain't no fucking Easter Bunny, and there ain't any goddamn Mr. X. It's the RBA trying to fry my ass for Pat getting himself killed, and they are gonna try every dirty trick in the book till I'm sitting in the hot seat at Kilby waiting for some old boy to flip the switch and grill me up like a side of bacon because it would make a hell of a picture."

Matthews shifted in his chair and recrossed his legs. He finished the cigarette and stubbed it out in a plastic tray on top of a big fan of *Field & Stream* and *Gent* magazines. He shrugged. His diamond cuff links twinkled.

Hoyt plugged the fat cigar back into his mouth and kept reading, Cobb snapping off the stray hairs and giving him a slick comb with some of that jug of Vitalis.

"Part it to the side," Hoyt said, not looking up from the newspaper. He grunted. "I look like a fucking country preacher."

The bell jingled above the old barbershop door and in walked Frog Jones and Red Cook, a couple clip joint owners. They walked inside, looking at the floor, no one to beat or shoot or rob, and they looked as dejected to Hoyt as little kids without their toys.

Hoyt looked back to the paper.

"What the hell is wrong with you two? I ain't seen y'all's names in the paper in a while."

The door opened again, and as Cobb removed the apron and Hoyt stood from the chair two guardsmen walked in and waited for Hoyt to turn. But Hoyt watched in the mirror as he counted out the change into the barber's hand and simply said: "Let me guess: Mr. X sent you."

One of the young boys held out a piece of paper to Hoyt Shepherd and said: "Sir, Mr. Bernard Sykes would like to see you at the Ralston Hotel immediately."

Hoyt nodded, walked to the coatrack, and grabbed his porkpie hat. "Well, that is just goddamn fantastic. I can't wait."

"THIS SURE IS A NICE SUITE. HOW MUCH ARE THE TAXPAY-ers shelling out for such comfort, Mr. Sykes?" Hoyt Shepherd asked.

Bernard Sykes opened his mouth and then closed it, looking to a couple of junior men at the attorney general's office and then back to Hoyt. In his pleated trousers and tailored shirt with painted tie, he nervously circled the dining room, where Hoyt sat at a long table. Sykes felt for the back of a chair, obvious to Hoyt that the man wanted to continue to stand to get a leg up, but Hoyt didn't care for games or this nervous kid.

"Why don't you sit down?" Hoyt asked. "All that walking and talking is getting on my nerves. When you're trying to gain some confidence, you need to sit down and be a regular guy. Don't stand over someone and act like a hard-on."

Sykes's face changed colors and he crossed his arms. He stood still and placed his hand over his jaw and mouth. He nodded and nodded as if unlocking some kind of secret about Hoyt Shepherd's character.

"Listen, unless you're gonna feed me lunch or buy me a drink I think I'll be on my way. There wasn't a damn thing on any of the mysterious Dr. X's recordings about Albert Patterson."

"Mr."

"What?"

"It's Mr. X, not Dr. X."

Hoyt nodded and pulled out a fresh cigar from his shirt pocket. He unwrapped it, the plastic making harsh, crinkling sounds, and stuck it into his mouth. "Since you're not from here and don't know much else besides what the newspapermen stink up in their print, I'll fill you in. Me and my partner, Jimmie Matthews, sold out our interests in every single club in Phenix City two years ago. You can verify that with anyone in town. And as far as Pat? Hell, Pat and I had some problems, and I never wanted to see him your boss. But there ain't a criminal in Phenix City with half a brain who'd kill a fella that way. I mean, give me a little credit. I know about fifty better places I could've had Pat plugged, if I wanted. But to shoot down the man in an alley on Fifth Avenue on a Friday night is as stupid as it is reckless. Just about dumber than shit, if you ask me."

Sykes grinned a bit and gave a nervous laugh. "So, you are telling me that you would've killed Mr. Patterson in another way?"

"Yes, sir. That is exactly what I said, and you wouldn't have found him for a long while either."

"You do that often? Make people disappear?"

"Goddamn. Can we get on with this bullshit? This is the deal, son. My boys and all the gamblers in Phenix City wouldn't touch killing Pat, because the odds were worth shit. And everyone knew that the house would come a-tumblin' down."

"What about the bombing last night? Did you know about that?"

"Read it in the papers same as you."

"But you'd have reason to want to quiet Mr. Britton."

"Thought we were talking about Pat."

"So who killed Mr. Patterson if it wasn't one of your hoods?"

"I'm gonna let that one slide, kid," Hoyt said, puffing the cigar up into the air and then right into Bernard Sykes's eyes and Hollywood hair and ski-slope nose.

"So?"

"Get them out of the room," Hoyt said, leaning into the table and helping himself to a pot of coffee. As he poured, Sykes cleared the room of all the prosecutors and the stenographer, who'd waited for the official interview to begin.

The table between Sykes and Shepherd was filled with empty boxes from a fried chicken joint and half-drunk cups of coffee and bottles of Coca-Cola. Ashtrays spilled out with ash, and mounds of newspapers and stacks of papers spilled over the table and onto the chairs.

Hoyt took a sip of coffee and then made a face. It was cold.

After some thought, he leaned in and started to talk, and Sykes couldn't hear so he leaned in, too. Close as lovers across an intimate table, he caught Hoyt's words: "Do you really need to look much further than Bert Fuller? Let me tell you something, he'd been ratfucking me for the last couple years, cutting the biggest, fattest piece of the Phenix City pie. Did you know someone broke into my goddamn home the night Pat got himself killed? They blew my safe with dynamite, nearly set my office on fire, and took fifty thousand dollars? With all this shit going on, I couldn't even get a sonofabitch at the sheriff's office to take down my name. Now, that's something to make a man a little pissed off."

Sykes looked up over his notebook. He tapped his pen.

"You got to know something, me and Pat had an understanding. We knew what teams we played for. You can't hold a grudge if a man's been straight with you all along. With Pat, he didn't make no secret of cleaning up this town. But to break into a man's home, and me knowin' it had to have been someone I hold close? Now, that is an insult. And let me be straight with you, Mr. Sykes. If I find out the sonofabitch who did that to me, he's as good as dead."

"You understand what you're saying to me?"

"Yes, sir. And I'll be damned to hell if me getting robbed wasn't Fuller's doing, too. If there is slop in the trough, he's gonna eat."

"Deputy Fuller?"

"Hell, you catch on fast, kid."

"Who else? Other policemen?"

"Policemen? Bert Fuller is a shakedown artist and a pimp, and since I've grown comfortable in my retirement he's about bled me dry on protection. But I don't know about other folks with the sheriff. If it were my guess, I'd say Fuller and Johnnie Benefield."

"Who?"

"Say, you are new to this town. As I told John Patterson, Johnnie Benefield is only the most coldhearted, sadistic sonofabitch I've ever met."

Sykes wrote down the name on a yellow legal pad and looked up.

"That's with one *n*."

Sykes nodded and made the correction.

"Jesus H. Christ," Hoyt Shepherd said, plugging the cigar in his mouth.

JOHNNIE BENEFIELD AWOKE IN A DARK ROOM, THE LIGHT-ning cracking outside the window. The bed sat in a metal frame, and in another flash of light he saw there were clothes folded for him on an old ladder-back chair. His boots clean and shined sitting right under them. He leaned back against the pillow, his head feeling as if it was about to rip from his skull, a knifing, hot pain in his shoulder. Reaching over, he felt for the bandages and found crusted blood on the tape. He moaned and closed his eyes. The room smelled like dried flowers and vinegar.

He heard footsteps down a long hallway. The steps were hard and clacked as they do against wood, and when the walking stopped he saw the slice of light from under the door go black for a moment and then the squeak of hinges.

A woman's shadow stood before him, carrying a bucket and a leather pouch.

She pulled up another chair and sat and held his cold, clammy hands.

Her face was darkened, and he only could see the outline of her hair. His eyes fluttered open and closed.

"You hurt?"

"Fannie?"

"It's me. You been out for some time."

"How long?"

"Two days."

"I'm hungry."

"Thirsty, too, I reckon."

"Can I get some whiskey?"

"You bet."

"I got the shakes, too."

"I know, baby."

Fannie opened the bag and pulled out a silver spoon and toyed with it a moment before clicking on a lighter and heating its contents. She grabbed a syringe and soon filled it and tapped the vein in his arm. She shot down the plunger, and he was filled with the most quiet, wonderful sensation, as if having sex to the point of climax and having it last and last. He closed his eyes and smiled.

"Where am I?" he asked.

"Hill Top."

"You keeping me in a whorehouse?"

"That I am."

"A dream come true."

"I need you well, Johnnie."

"You got me."

"Everyone is gone."

Johnnie opened his eyes and breathed through his nose. He closed his eyes again.

"The Guard. They got orders from the governor to bust up this town. I need you, Johnnie. Don't leave."

He reached up with his left hand and had a bit of trouble finding Fannie's heart-shaped face. She shifted his hand over to her left breast and said everything was going to be all right. "Don't you worry, baby."

A flame struck again in the dark little room, and he saw Fannie Belle's face and red lips and intent green eyes, and then it was clouded again in a puff of smoke. He heard her inhale, and then she passed the cigarette between his lips.

"I got the door locked," she said. "I turned the lights off and closed the gate. If they even think about busting down the door, I'll take a few of those bastards with me."

"I love you, baby."

"Johnnie, how 'bout you tell me more about this money you took from Hoyt. I sure like that story."

THE RAIDS STARTED that Thursday at exactly 4:30 with a proclamation from Governor Persons that Phenix City was under martial rule. That gave Hanna and the Guards the go-ahead to surround the Russell County Courthouse and relieve all law enforcement and city officials of their duties and make them surrender all weapons, squad cars, and badges. Just as General Hanna and Major Black burst into the sheriff's office, they found Sheriff Ralph Matthews sitting behind his desk, a big wad of chaw in his cheek, playing gin rummy with four deputies and a jailer. Another jailer was within earshot of the men, sitting on the office toilet and reading a copy of *Gent* magazine. As soon as the Guard leveled their shotguns and .45s at the boys, Matthews looked from deputy to deputy and then over to the jailer on the toilet.

He shook his head and threw the remainder of his cards into the pot.

The other deputies did the same and they all slowly stood, hitching up their gun belts on their uniforms.

"What can we do you for, General?"

"Not a goddamn thing," Hanna said, walking over to Matthews's desk and pulling a Hav-a-Tampa from a box. "Just leave your guns and badges on the way out."

"Sir?" Matthews laughed, the big plug in his cheek. His face turned a bright red.

"You heard me, you hick bastard," Hanna said. He lit a match against his thumbnail. "Now, take off those guns nice and slow."

Matthews shook his head again. He dramatically spit in a wastepaper basket and smiled with a lot of pity. He was a fat man with a big belly and a small mind, and he didn't quite catch on to what was happening. His fat cheeks looked like apples.

Just then there was a creak and the men turned, seeing the jailer stand from the little box bathroom and raise a pistol, his trousers at his ankles.

Jack Black fired off a round over the man's head. And although the shot missed him by a foot, the man ducked and landed back with a hard thud onto the commode and dropped the pistol into the water.

"Now," Hanna said.

Matthews went first, unhitching his belt and guns, laying them atop the big wooden desk. His deputies followed, and they all stood shoulder to shoulder as five-foot-five bulldog Hanna passed by them as in an inspection line, never once saying a word but eyeing the men as if they were the sorriest bunch of bastards he'd ever seen in his life.

It was raining, and the thunder belly-grumbled outside as the water pinged against the pane glass and slid down the windows. Hanna pulled his MacArthur hat off his head and held it out to Matthews, "I said badges, too."

"Murphy?" he called out to me. I entered the room.

Hanna handed me Ralph Matthews's badge and pinned it over my Texaco star. "I kind of like that one better. It suits you, Sheriff."

FOUR HOURS EARLIER, I'D SAT IN JOYCE'S BEAUTY SHOP drinking a cup of coffee and explaining to her the job I'd just been offered by the state. She was between appointments and cleaning out a sink full of brunette hair dye. The room smelled of burnt chemicals and sweet shampoos, and as I tried to make sense of the offer she just nodded and nodded, keeping her hands busy with the washing and some sweeping and some straightening of a couple of helmet dryers by a back wall under framed pictures from *Vogue*.

"Why you?"

"I have an honest face."

She nodded. She sat down in a stylist chair and faced me. I was still dressed in my coveralls, my Texaco baseball cap in my hands, as I looked down at the floor and waited for what was about to come.

But she didn't say a word for a long time, and when she spoke it was calm and confident. "Is this temporary?"

"It could be," I said. "It's just until the election."

"If the Guard is taking over, why do they even need you?"

"It was the best we could get. Something called limited martial rule. They have to have local police. The Guard can't make arrests on their own."

"You don't know a thing about being a sheriff."

"I tried to explain that to them."

"And what did they say?"

"They said John Patterson recommended me for the job. Jack Black, too."

"Can't they just find someone else?"

"Bernard Sykes already offered it to George Findletter."

"And what did he say?"

"His wife said there was no way in hell. She'd divorce him."

Joyce nodded. She inspected her painted nails and turned back and forth in her seat. There was a knock at the front of the little shotgun house, and she walked to the door and told a woman that she'd be right with her. She shut the door with a little click and walked back. You could only hear the air conditioner humming in a small window facing our yard.

"You already said yes, didn't you?"

I nodded.

She nodded back. Her hair was freshly done and curled, and she wore a powder of makeup on her face. Her cotton skirt hit her at the knees, and when she walked she sometimes put her hands in the pockets.

"I hope you know what you're doing."

"Me, too."

"You need this, don't you?"

"For a long time."

She looked at me. The woman outside walked back and forth on the little porch, impatient. I crunched the bill of my ball cap and then looked back at Joyce. She was looking right at me. Out of the corner of my eye, I could see our images in a bank of mirrors.

"I don't want our kids hurt."

"They won't be."

She shook her head and stood and reached down her long, lithe fingers to me. I looked up at her, confused, until I saw the way she held her hand. I took her hand and stood, and we shook on it.

AT MIDNIGHT, I WAS WITH THE GUARD DOWN ON DILLING-ham Street in the rain. I wore my civilian clothes under a yellow slicker but carried a standard-issue .45 Colt Jack Black had given me earlier. Black carried a pump shotgun in one hand and leaned against a jeep, while Hanna sat up in the driver's seat smoking a cigar and talking to someone on a field telephone. The street was dead and filled with rain and quiet and dark in the absence of all the neon. You could hear the roar of the Chattahoochee, filled with storm water and rolling and breaking over the dam, but Phenix City was still, not a car heading down the road besides Guard troops. In the silence, we heard a grunt, and Hanna climbed out holding an ax.

"Come on," he said. We headed over to the Bridge Grocery, and Hanna began to pound on the front door, about twenty uniformed men behind him. He banged some more, until I heard fat little Godwin Davis call out from behind the door that ain't nobody shown him a goddamn warrant.

"I got a warrant," Hanna said. He stood back and began to tear into the door with the ax, and when the splintering set in good he nodded to Black, who just stepped up to the door and kicked it in. I followed and walked into the dimly lit space, the lights with red bulbs looking onto a dirty concrete floor filled with one-armed bandits and horse-racing machines. Davis was shirtless, a portly little man with white chest hair, a fat, distended stomach, and breasts like a woman. He strutted around the room calling the troops names with a cigar between his teeth.

A tabletop projector showed a black-and-white stag film against the cracked plaster wall. A woman was having sex with a mule. Black shut off the projector and the reel stopped with a *click, click, click.*

When I got close to Davis, I could smell his peculiar barnyard odor and winced. He looked me over and saw the badge pinned to my slicker and shook his head, saying, "Well, I'll fuck a monkey."

"I bet," I said.

He grunted and turned away, wiping under his underarms with a rag and sitting down on a vinyl diner's chair and watching the troops carrying out the machines and tagging the equipment for evidence. Black nodded to me and handed me a piece of paper running down Davis's rights.

I read it to him. And he laughed the whole time and then spit right in my face.

I wiped it away while Jack spun him around and clamped cuffs on his wrists.

THREE HOURS LATER, WE STOOD NEAR THE UPPER BRIDGE, and for the first time in ten years I walked into one of the clip joints, a place called the Atomic Bomb Café. It took four men there to restrain old Clyde Yarborough, his jawless face worked into a howl, his long ape arms tearing and pounding against the soldiers' backs until they restrained him.

I turned on the house lights, and we walked behind the bar, finding three sawed-off shotguns, two .38s, and a .44 Magnum.

I pointed to the .38s and asked for a couple of the guardsmen to bag them as evidence.

"Not bad, chief," Black said.

"I watch *Dragnet* on occasion."

The guardsmen pushed Yarborough past me, and his misshapen flesh flexed like the skin on heated milk. His black eyes watched me, and then he grunted deep in his destroyed, toothless mouth with a bellowing laugh.

Black reached out and patted the man's ruined face. And while the guardsmen held him there, Black bent down and whispered something into the old man's ear. His black eyes grew wide, before he was pushed out the door.

"What was that?" I asked.

"Just saying hi."

"You know him."

Black shrugged.

"Clyde Yarborough. He's been here since the twenties. Taught Shepherd and Matthews everything they know."

"He looks like something out of *Dick Tracy*."

"But he's beautiful on the inside," I said.

"I bet," Black said.

We had to use a crowbar on a back storage room and then run flashlights over the endless rows of slots and card tables, roulette wheels, and soiled rollaway beds. There was a door off to the right of the room and a long row of blinds that a soldier opened to reveal a row of stalls. Soldiers appeared on the other side and tapped against the glass.

"Two-way mirror," Black said.

In each room, there were tools of the trade, boxes of jimmies and lubricant, some whips and handcuffs, long plastic devices shaped like a man's peter, and bottles of Lysol spray.

"God, it's awful in there," a soldier said. "It smells like rotten tuna."

A couple of the guardsmen showed off a long, socketlike device that could plug into a wall and they burst into laughter, holding it away from them with a handkerchief.

"What the hell is that?" Black asked.

"Do you really want to know?"

"Not really."

Boxes were brought in to gather the devices and the slots, and soldiers cataloged every single item, which were soon loaded onto trucks by hordes of other soldiers and driven back to the armory outside town. Several of the men explored the back rooms of the club, and one of them called over to Black about a door he found leading to a staircase. I followed and hit the beam of my flashlight, the steps running right into a tunnel of rock and dirt, a long, dirty hole that pinged in silence with the dripping of water.

The staircase stopped at a big metal door, and we had to use a pair of bolt cutters to free the lock to get into a huge storeroom. The room was filled with uncountable slots and roulette wheels, gaming tables, and box upon box of decks of cards and pairs of dice. Soon we found a large metal cabinet that held hundreds of canisters of eight-millimeter film.

I put a flashlight against one strip, and you could see the negative of two women having sex.

One of the boys found a junction box and hit the lights, each of them cutting on one by one in a domino lighting of the room. Against a back wall, a long case held an unlimited supply of sawed-off shotguns and pistols. Enough for a small army. There were boxes of dynamite and grenades, and even two Tommy guns.

All .38s were immediately tagged and bagged, and as the boys continued to go through the endless boxes and cases of guns, games, and whiskey Black and I found yet another corridor and we followed it. We figured it ran back under Fourteenth Street. At the end of maybe a hundred feet was a wooden door, rotten and falling from its hinges. We pushed our way through to a short row of blue-carpeted steps, stained and muddy, and up to a door that Black had to blast open with his shotgun.

He was smoking a cigar he'd bummed off General Hanna, and the smoke clouded the flashlight beam that crossed over the big room of Davis's Pawn, full of gold watches, engagement rings, government-issue pistols, and two full rows of paratrooper boots.

"They took their goddamn boots," Black said.

"You were in Airborne?"

He nodded, the smoke bleeding out of the corner of his mouth, the shotgun up in his arms. He used his own flashlight to cross over the endless pairs of gleaming black boots.

"You did basic at Benning," I said.

He nodded.

"So you've been here before?"

He spit on the floor just as we heard steps from the hidden staircase and a voice calling out. "Major, we have something you need to see."

REUBEN KNEW THEY WERE COMING AND HE OPENED THE door for them and even chilled the beer. But the Guard boys didn't want any of it and sat him right down in the corner and ripped through Club Lasso as his jukebox played out some of his favorite Luke the Drifter songs he'd loaded down with five dollars in dimes. He smoked and sat across from Billy, and Billy looked nervous as hell, and Reuben tried to comfort the boy by telling him dirty jokes and things he'd heard about the time they broke down ole Phenix in '21.

"Where's your girl?" he asked.

As the jukebox played, there were sounds of doors opening and closing in the little café and the clatter of liquor bottles—all those god-dang liquor bottles—being raked into boxes and carried out in jeeps.

"I don't know," Billy said, finally.

"You think she was picked up by the Guard?"

"I don't know," Billy said. His face looked as drawn as an old dog, and he smoked a few of his father's cigarettes as he talked. His little fingers shook against the pack.

Two guardsmen lifted the long oil portrait of a nude Mexican woman from above the bar and let it fall to the floor.

"Now, don't scratch that. Jesus Christ, boys. Have some fucking respect," he said, shaking his head, and turned back to his boy. "You know what a dog and pony show is?"

Billy nodded.

"Good, 'cause you're seein' one right now. It's all for the papers."

One of the troops heard him and yanked him up to his feet, and Reuben looked bored with it all as the man turned him against the brick wall and searched him, removing a little .22 from his boot.

"What's that?" the boy soldier said. Hell, he wasn't even twenty.

"I'm gonna guess it's a gun of some sort."

"Yeah?"

"Yep."

Reuben sat back down and drank down some more of his Budweiser and lit another cigarette and handed his boy the pack of Luckies. Billy looked dirty, grit up under his fingernails and his face shiny from oil and heat. He smoked and looked down at the table.

"Love is funny," he said.

Billy looked up from his hands.

"You ain't got a fucking thing to do with it."

Billy wouldn't look his father in the eye.

"Just like that whore. I know you say you didn't know she was a whore, and I don't mean any disrespect by calling her a whore. That's just the situation that little girl found herself in. Hell, we all got to eat."

The bar was empty of booze now, and the troops had even removed the kegs and taps. The walls were cleared of the old-time photos of the naked women, and soldiers walked back and forth from his storage room with boxes and boxes of stuff. Reuben didn't know what, probably just junk. Old guns and some 45s and all the slots.

They heard a diesel engine sound outside, and a large truck backed up to the door and the soldiers lifted up the boxes and some tables and chairs and even the neon beer signs that had hung in the window. Then the boys set to work on the old bar with crowbars and sledgehammers. And Reuben sat there and talked about love and women with his boy, smoking cigarettes and even sharing a beer, until they unplugged the jukebox and rolled it into the truck.

After the truck lumbered away, Hoyt Shepherd and Jimmie Matthews wandered into the old building and inspected the damage. Hoyt tipped his hat to the boy and Jimmie gave him a wink.

Hoyt wore a pair of overalls and an old straw hat, and Reuben figured that he didn't want any of the news boys recognizing him. Of course, Jimmie couldn't have cared less, dressed in gray pants, a dress shirt, and a thin knit tie.

"Took the jukebox, too."

"Yes, sir."

"And the booze?"

"I hid a bottle under the table."

"You got some glasses?"

"I do."

Hoyt sat down at the table, and Reuben sent Billy to fetch what he could for cups. The bottle was black label Jack Daniel's, and when Billy returned he laid down four cups. Reuben looked up at him, and as the boy sat back down he just shrugged.

He poured out a double in every glass.

Hoyt took a sip and made a face. "What do you cut this with?"

"Grain alcohol."

"Good God Almighty."

"How long is this mess gonna last, Mr. Shepherd?" Reuben asked.

Billy took a big sip and tried not to react, but Reuben saw that it had burned his throat something fierce.

"We're out," Hoyt said. "How 'bout you and your boy joining us down at Panama City Beach? I have a piece of a little putt-putt golf place that could use some new management."

Reuben took a sip. The whiskey tasted like gasoline.

"They're gonna put together a new jury pool. Get together something called a blue-ribbon grand jury, with some old-fart Bible-thumper to run it. You ever hear of Judge Jones? I heard last year he personally handed out five thousand Bibles. Now, I'm just guessing me and that man ain't gonna have a lot in common."

Reuben watched Jimmie look around at the brick walls and the destroyed bar, the empty place next to the stage where he'd painted up and around the heavy jukebox last year.

"Thank, you, Mr. Hoyt. But I'm gonna play things out here. I don't ever figure on leaving Phenix. They can arrest me if they want. Billy can run things till I'm out. Right, Billy?"

The boy nodded.

"Can we speak in private?"

"Whatever needs to be said can be said in front of my boy."

"I don't think so."

Reuben nodded to Billy and Billy walked toward the front door and hung out by Fourteenth Street, watching the raining gray dawn from underneath a tin canopy.

"Reuben, you stay away from Fannie Belle and Johnnie Benefield. You hear me? They will lead you down a path of blood and you're too smart for that. Only reason Johnnie hasn't wised up is because his mind is run by pussy, and that redheaded demon has the best pussy in the South."

Reuben nodded and shifted in his chair.

"They've been reckless," Hoyt said, smiling. "I don't know what they got to do with killin' Pat. But they sure as shit know who robbed me. There's some money in it if you can find out about Benefield. That old safe I had was solid. A sweet Wells Fargo number that cost me nearly a thousand dollars. Let's just say it took some real talent to bust her open."

Reuben nodded.

"I'm not asking for much. I just want to know if Benefield was in on the job. I can take it from there."

Reuben nodded again.

Hoyt watched him, studying his face, and then looked over at Jimmie.

Jimmie shrugged and finally tasted the whiskey, downing it without a wince. Hoyt slipped the beaten straw hat on his head and over his eyes and walked to the open glass doors. His voice sounded gruff and booming in the empty bar.

The rain had slowed to a patter, and Reuben could see the shape of his boy against the growing morning light.

"One more thing," Hoyt said, turning. "The Guard put up your old buddy, Lamar Murphy, for sheriff."

"He take it?"

"Don't know. If he did, I'd watch my step."

Reuben shook his head. "I don't think so. I've known Lamar since we were 'bout Billy's age."

Hoyt looked up and then around the empty room. "You ever seen that cartoon with the sheepdog and wolf where both of them are friends until they punch the morning clock?"

Reuben shook his head.

"See, when that clock is punched and they are at work, they try like hell to kill each other. But then when the sun goes down and they punch out, they are as gooda friends as you ever saw."

"Which one am I?"

"If you don't know, then you got more troubles than I thought," he said. "You let me know what you know about Benefield, you hear?"

Hoyt left with a tip of his hat. Reuben and his boy sat there in silence until dawn cleared and a soft, gray summer morning arrived at the last two chairs in Club Lasso. They could hear nothing but the soft patter of rain against Fourteenth Street and the running of rainwater down the gutters and along the soft slope of the street to the Chattahoochee.

"WHERE ARE YOU GOING TO GO?" JOHNNIE BENEFIELD asked, tucking in his cowboy shirt and slipping into his boots.

"Does it matter?" she said.

Fannie Belle sat in the salon of her empty whorehouse, chainsmoking cigarettes, a pearl-handled .32 on the plush velvet seat next to her. The furniture and lamps in the other room reminded Johnnie of something from the last century.

"They just better not lay a finger on my Hudson."

"You better worry about more than your car."

"Once I get Bert, we're blowin' this town."

"Cuba?"

"Does it matter?"

Fannie blew out some smoke and crossed her legs. Johnnie watched her, and walked back upstairs for his clothes and a suitcase he'd packed. She was at the landing when he returned, and she watched him as he slowed his walk and hit the first floor with his boots.

She kissed him hard on the mouth. And he pulled away.

"I got to get Bert."

"He's not going with you."

"The hell you say."

"He's got a platoon of soldiers up and around his house. They believe he's getting ready to split town, and they don't buy his religious act."

"Do you?"

Fannie just looked at him, cocking her head slightly to the side, and lit another long cigarette. She leaned her head back, pulling in the smoke, and drew a sweep of her red hair to one side.

"I want something from you before you leave," she said.

He turned at the front door, suitcase in hand. She whispered into his ear, and her breath was warm and sweet.

"You got to be kidding," Johnnie said. "You mention me and the Hoyt Shepherd job again and you gonna get me killed. Hoyt Shepherd will drop me in that ole river loaded down with logging chains just as easy as takin' a mornin' piss."

And, with that, he opened the front door and walked out on the old rotted porch and out to the Hornet hid back by some privet bush. He tucked the suitcase into the trunk and turned to the bush, where he started to take a leak.

He heard her walking behind him and he started to whistle.

"Listen, they may not even find you, Fannie," Johnnie said. "Hell, the Hill Top is two miles from the highway. You're the only goddang thing out here."

"Not far enough."

He zipped up and turned to her, jingling the keys in his hand. The old, rotten Victorian behind Fannie looking to him like a haunted house from a picture show.

"Why do you say that?"

She didn't say anything, only turned to the north and pointed to the dust buckling and rising from the dirt road. From the looks of things, a mess of cars was headed that way.

"Who else is in the house?"

"Few girls. Them twins. Some more from town that got scared."

"Get back inside."

"Why?"

"I said get the fuck back inside," he said, popping his trunk again and pulling out a Winchester Model 12. "Get your clothes off and put on a robe. Something sexy. Tell the girls to stay in their rooms. I said now."

Johnnie clenched his jaw, stocking extra shells in his pant pocket and down into the shaft of his pointed boots. He eyed a place up in the turret on the second floor, and looked to see the first flashes of the windshields of the approaching cars.

EVERY CLERK, PROSECUTOR, DEPUTY, AND JUDGE HAD BEEN cleared from the Russell County Courthouse. Only the Guard remained, with Bernard Sykes setting up command in Arch Ferrell's old office and Sykes's team from the state attorney's office already tearing through Ferrell's personal files and papers. General Hanna's stepson, Pete—an eighteen-year-old kid working as the general's personal driver—had taken us through the courthouse and out back to the brick sheriff's office, where Hanna ushered me down into a basement storage room filled with dozens of cardboard boxes. "These look familiar?" he asked.

I shook my head.

"Why don't you call your buddy Britton and John Patterson down here? It looks like a mess of uncounted votes going back to 1945."

"They kept them?" I asked.

"Sheriff Matthews may be everything else, but he'll never be accused of being a genius."

Thirty minutes later, we found more. In jail cells, we found car batteries hooked to head braces, horse whips, logging chains, and several fat leather belts fitted with silver dollars. Along the worn leather were traces of blood. Some of the cells had been fitted with iron shackles in the concrete, like something out of a medieval museum.

In another cell was a crude little motor that plugged into a wall with a needle and vial at the end. I thought it must be something for junkies and hopheads, but one of the Guard boys who'd been in the Navy said it was for giving tattoos. We wouldn't know for a while exactly why they'd be giving out tattoos in a jailhouse.

We'd been up all night, and everything seemed foggy and light. Jack Black set a coffeepot on a hot plate. General Hanna had upended Sheriff Matthews's desk onto the floor, where all his junk was being hustled into cardboard boxes and tagged.

He offered me a cigar like the ones he smoked with Jack Black. I thanked him and pulled out a Kool instead that I smoked with the first cup of coffee. I kneaded my temples with my thumb and forefinger and sat on top of Matthews's desk, something I'd still think of as Matthews's desk until weeks later when I had it taken out into the county landfill and burned.

A few minutes later, little Quinnie Kelley was hustled into the sheriff's office, and I stopped talking with Hanna and Black and introduced Kelley. He still wore his courthouse coveralls and clutched a thick, clothbound book in his arms.

He didn't shake hands with the men, only laid down the book on the table and said he'd taken it from Bert Fuller's office shortly after he'd been hurt. He kind of smiled and cut his eyes over to me when he said it.

"I didn't trust nobody, and I figured that someone might try to burn it up. But people should see it. See the shame of it."

I opened the book, and it revealed a pasted photo album, the kind you kept for the family, only these were black-and-white pictures of girls. Some of them nude, some clothed. Mostly just of their heads with a little pasted rundown on their measurements, color of eyes and hair, weight, height, any scars or deformities, quality of teeth, and special sexual skills. All of the women had been given numbers.

I looked up at him. "These were girls Fuller arrested."

Quinnie shook his head. "Y'all are slow. That's the registry, the goddang book, Lamar. That's Fuller's handwriting plain as day right there."

The familiarity of using my first name made me blush a bit, and I turned back to the book and studied the pages and noted the details about where they worked and what they did and various sexual perversions the women were willing to do. In the back pages was a ledger showing amounts owed and earned.

"He got twenty-five percent off every girl."

I nodded and set down the book.

"Thanks, Quinnie," I said, shaking his hand.

He reaffixed his Coke-bottle glasses and nodded, and then turned to Hanna and saluted him. Hanna just looked at the odd little man as he passed, and pulled the book over to him and flipped through the pages.

"Urination?" he said. "What in the hell? This is the filthiest, most vile town I've ever known. We should just burn it to the ground and let y'all start over."

"Make sure you skip over my house when you do," I said.

"How could you stand it?"

"You can't see what's hidden under the rocks."

Jack Black returned to the room and reached for his shotgun he'd left on the desk. "There is some kind of trouble in the county. You ever hear of a whorehouse called the Hill Top?"

I hadn't.

"There's been some shooting out there."

I looked to General Hanna. And he looked over to me and smiled. "You tell us, Sheriff."

WE PARKED DOWN the road from the old Victorian, the windshield wipers keeping our view clear, and watched the two lights from the upstairs windows. A dark figure appeared up in the turret and then was gone. The old house was unpainted, with a sagging porch and crooked columns; a red bulb light rocked in the light wind. A couple cars were parked down the road, but it was growing late and raining, and I could barely make them out where we'd parked. Major Black sat at the wheel, with me in the passenger's seat and Quinnie Kelley behind us. Since we'd left the sheriff's office, Kelley had talked non-stop, in between the occasional directions out to the Hill Top. His big bug glasses were fogged, but he hadn't seemed to notice.

"Now, don't be thinking that I know this place 'cause I'm a customer. I'm a married man."

"Wouldn't dream of it, Quinnie," I said.

"I mean, I knowed plenty of men who'd gone out here. But, see, the house used to be a place where this old woman lived when we was kids. We called it the Spook House, on account of it looking broken down and all. You know, like a haunted house?"

I nodded and looked over to Black. He wore no expression.

"When that old woman died, me and my brother used to play games outside there, and we'd bet each other that we couldn't last five minutes in that place. I took the bet one time, and I promise you it was the longest five minutes I ever spent in my life. I walked up to the stairway and, when I reached the bottom step, I felt a cold spot go through me. I'm not saying it was a ghost or nothin'. I'm just sayin' it scared the piss out of me."

"What do you say we ride down by the cars?" I asked.

Black cranked the jeep and we bumped along the dirt road, and hit the high beams on a Cadillac coupe and a brand-new Hudson. I'd seen the Hudson before.

"That the one from the other night?" Black asked.

I nodded.

Black killed the engine.

"You wait here," Black said.

"Hell with that," Quinnie said. "I ain't scared."

"It's not on account of those ghosts," Black said.

"I knowed what you meant. But I ain't scared, just the same."

Black told him to wait in the jeep, and, if he heard shots, to call it in on the radio. "It's important."

Kelley nodded, a serious expression on his face. "Yes, sir."

We mounted the old creaky steps and knocked on the front door. We heard movement inside and shuffling, and Black knocked again. His shotgun rested in his left hand while he knocked with his right.

There was a window in the top half of the door, but some yellowed lace obscured a good look inside. Black knocked some more and then finally stood back to kick it in.

I held up my hand, moved past him, and tried the knob.

The door opened.

Black grunted and moved inside, calling into the big, vacuous space and twisting his neck up to a wide staircase that stretched far and high along the right wall.

He called out again and then mounted the steps. He pointed me to the parlor and a long hallway that led to a swinging door.

THE WHORE HAD ABOUT BIT THROUGH JOHNNIE'S FINGERS, as he held her tight in the upstairs bedroom, listening to the boots on the wooden landing. She shuffled and cried in his hands but didn't make a sound, only bit down hard and tried to wriggle free.

There were two more whores down the hall and another downstairs with Fannie.

The door to the bedroom opened, and Johnnie waited there behind it. Through the crack between the door and frame, he saw a big man in a khaki uniform pass and then move out of sight.

As the man walked slow through the room, the young whore tried to twist free. But Johnnie held her there until the heavy boots passed and the rhythmic thumping was gone.

He let out his breath. The damn twisting and gyrating kicking up the pain in his shoulder something fierce. He twisted the whore's hair into his fingers and pulled out his wet fingers from her mouth.

Into her ear, he whispered: "You scream and I'll plug you a brand-new hole. You got me?"

The girl nodded.

And then he heard the shot downstairs.

The boots ran back down the landing and then hit the staircase.

"Goddamn," Johnnie said to the young whore. "That bitch is crazy."

The girl couldn't have been more than fifteen. She was doughy fat and white, with brown eyes the size of saucers. "Y'all got a back door here?"

The girl didn't speak.

Johnnie pointed the gun at her.

"I said, y'all got a back door?"

THE SALON LOOKED TO BE SOMETHING OUT OF THE OLD West. Red velvet couches and heavy oak furniture. Cut-glass whiskey decanters and boxes of cigarettes and cigars. Old-time paintings of fat naked women with red hair and red lips. I passed through the room and followed the long hallway, trying to keep quiet on the wood floors. The hallway seemed to elongate as I walked, hearing Black's boots overhead and then opening the swinging back door and hearing the crack of a shot.

I dropped to the floor and saw a woman pointing a pistol back down at my head. Before she could take aim, I tackled her to the ground and wrestled the gun free. Someone else in the room screamed, and I pointed the gun to her and she held her hands over her mouth and screamed and screamed, although she tried to stop.

She fell to her knees, and I pulled the woman to her feet and pushed her against the kitchen table.

"What are you doing here? This is my house."

"What's your name?"

"My name is Miss Fannie Belle, and if you don't leave my home immediately I will have you arrested."

Black ran into the room, his shotgun tucked into his shoulder, and pointed from corner to corner in the room. He held the gun on the red-headed woman.

"Ma'am, just whose Hudson is that parked outside?" I asked.

"It's not mine."

Just then, a car horn started honking and an engine started. I ran for the front door and out onto the porch, as the Hudson fishtailed and twisted in the mud and then broke free and shot right for the main highway.

Quinnie ran after the car for a long time, yelling for it to stop, until I lost sight of him.

I walked back into the house and held the women, while Black made a call on the radio for some help. Three girls he found upstairs waited in the hallway, toward the door.

"You want to tell me what you do, Miss Belle?" I asked.

I sat down across from her at the kitchen table and lit a cigarette while she and another girl, too old for the pigtails she wore, stared at the floor.

"I don't work."

"Then what do you do here?"

"Nothing."

"Who are these girls?"

"They are my nieces."

"Even the black one?"

Fannie turned her head and coughed, as if my cigarette smoke had invaded her space. I smoked it down a little more and squinted at her through the haze, reaching into my shirt pocket and pulling out the folded piece of paper Jack Black had given me.

I smiled, the cigarette clamped in my teeth. "You'll have to excuse me. I'm kind of new at this."

"What do you think you're doing?"

"Reading you your rights."

"I'm under arrest?"

"You did try to kill me, Miss Belle."

"You broke into my home."

"Sorry, I thought this was a cathouse."

She looked at me and snorted a bit, then reached down and squeezed my knee. I looked up at her and she smiled. "We can work something out, baby."

I didn't move, just started to read the paper in my hand.

"You goddamn sonofabitch," she said, as Black pushed the three girls into the kitchen. I started to finish reading but glanced up again, noticing something familiar about one of the girls.

She looked away as I stared. Black hair and blue eyes, china-white skin. I watched her cross her skinny white arms over a low-cut red velvet dress. She wore a lot of red lipstick, rouge, and she'd taken a heavy black pencil to her eyebrows like a Hollywood actress.

"Didn't I meet you on the Fourth of July?"

She didn't answer.

"You were with Billy Stokes," I said.

TWO HOURS LATER, I SAT WITH THE GIRL IN A BACK BOOTH of Choppy's Diner. The young girl looked as if she hadn't eaten for days, the way she scraped the eggs off her plate and cleaned the last bit of it with a piece of toast. I drank coffee and smoked cigarettes and asked her if she wanted another plate, and she looked up at me from where she'd leaned into the table and shook her head, her mouth full of food.

My arm rested on the back of the booth, a cigarette between my fingers. Jack Black had taken the others to the jail. This one, too scared to talk, didn't say a word to me, as I drove past the courthouse and took the upper bridge over into Columbus. I had to ask her three times to get out of the car.

"You work for Fannie Belle?" I asked.

She shook her head. Her hair hung down over a face that was so white it looked like it belonged on a porcelain doll.

"How old are you?"

She shrugged.

"You sure you don't want more to eat?"

She shook her head, her eyes still tilted toward the table but not chewing anymore.

I waited and didn't speak. The waitress came over and placed the bill on the table, and I put down a dollar and a fifty-cent piece.

"You the new sheriff?"

"That's what they're telling me."

Her hands shook so hard on top of the table that the salt shaker began to bounce and move. She started to cry but didn't move, even as I put my hand over hers. I gave her fingers a squeeze to reassure her.

She looked up at me and nodded and nodded. "I'm ready. I can do it. Let's go."

"Do what?"

Her chin tilted up and she looked at me, confused at what she saw, or didn't see, in my face. She shook her head and just watched me. The waitress came by once more and refilled my cup of coffee, and I lit another cigarette.

"Coffee and cigarettes are a fine thing," I said.

"That's all you want?"

"She speaks."

"Where's Bert Fuller?" she asked.

"Still lying in bed."

"He doesn't work for you?"

"You were there," I said. "We're not exactly good friends."

"So who's in charge?"

"The Guard. Town is under martial rule."

"What's that?"

"That means the town was so rotten that the governor replaced everybody. I'm the temporary sheriff till they can find someone better."

She nodded.

"You going to tell me how old you are?"

"Sixteen."

"Where's your family?"

She shrugged.

"Where are you from?"

She looked at me and excused herself from the table. I watched her leave for the bathroom, and she returned moments later. She'd washed her face of the makeup, and her hair had been tucked into a ponytail.

"Am I going to jail?"

I shook my head.

"Why not?"

"I could use some help."

"What?"

"Did you see a man inside the Hill Top tonight? The one that drove that Hudson parked out front?"

She nodded.

"You know his name?"

She nodded again.

"But you won't tell me."

"They'd kill me."

"They won't kill you. We arrested that Fannie Belle woman and we'll find him. If I could get some help understanding all this, maybe we could arrest a lot more."

She nodded.

"Did you ever go to school?"

She shook her head.

"How did you end up here?"

She shook her head and looked back down at her hands. I didn't say anything, just sat there smoking and watching it rain on Eighth Avenue and all the cars roaring by on the wet asphalt. I was thinking of home and getting some sleep when she spoke.

"I wasn't always a whore."

"You try to escape?"

"Can we get out of here, please? People are staring."

I looked around. There was no one in the diner but a fat trucker and his wife in curlers, and they seemed more interested in the chicken-fried steak than us. I shrugged and grabbed my hat.

Soon, we were on a back highway, just driving. The talking seemed to come easier the more we moved out of town, and she bummed some smokes from me and squinted into the hot wind as we rounded our way around Russell County.

"I tried a few times. To leave, I mean."

I just drove, listening and taking the curves as they came. I noticed a couple houses being built up on Sandfort, not far from where I kept my horses. Just a few years ago, it had been nothing but trees, most of the turnoffs unpaved.

"Aren't you going to ask me what it was like? How I could do those things?"

"Nope."

"How come?"

"You want to tell me?"

"Not much to tell."

"How often did you see Fuller at Fannie Belle's place?"

"Every night," she said. "That's when he came by to get his cut."

I drove some more and then found a good road, a paved road, and took it, and soon the lights down on Crawford were shining, and I passed the turnoff to my house and Slocumb's and kept on going to downtown. The service station looked oddly quiet closed up, with only some dim lights over the pumps. I wondered how my father-in-law was making out.

"I can find you a place to stay."

She shook her head and asked me to take her to the bus station.

"You have money?"

She didn't say anything.

At the bus station, I gave her a twenty-dollar bill and wrote out my home number. I told her to call anytime.

"I'm no snitch."

"Wonder who made that call from the Hill Top? Figured it came from inside. Nobody else lives around there."

She shrugged.

"Bert Fuller will get his due," I said.

"Did you know he had a pecker the size of a stickpin?"

"Nope."

"I figure that was why he was so mad."

I nodded. "It couldn't have helped."

IT WAS MIDNIGHT IN THE LIVING ROOM OF ARCH FERRELL'S house, and Madeline had finally gotten some sleep, the baby growing restless inside of her. When Arch knew she couldn't hear him, he slipped off to the sofa and dialed the number in Texas. He let it ring and ring, in that static connection, all the way over to Galveston. Finally, a man answered, and he sounded as if he'd just been roused from a dream.

"Si?" Arch said, whispering.

What?

"Si, listen—"

Arch?

"Hell, yes, this is Arch. Things are a mess. Governor Persons gone and did it. He finally did it. They shut down the whole town."

Everything?

"Every goddamn thing, you hear me? They're busting up slots and tables and arresting folks left and right. They got the goddamn jail so packed that the Guard's holding folks in pens like they were dogs. You got to get back."

I'm coming back.

"You mean it?"

I do.

"They even arrested Hoyt and Jimmie. Bernard Sykes questioned them up in the Ralston Hotel for nearly eight hours. This Sykes boy smells political blood, Si. And if you don't come back soon, I'm gonna be sitting in Kilby come Christmas. You left my ledger in your brief-case. Damn thing shows every penny I collected in Phenix City against Patterson."

Si coughed. He put down the phone, and Arch heard his echoed voice speaking to someone.

"Who was that?"

My nurse. She is the kindest colored woman I've ever met. She gave me a sponge bath yesterday and was so gentle.

"You know there is talk of putting you up on some kind of lunacy hearings if you come back. You understand that?"

I'm still the elected attorney general of the state of Alabama. I've read law since I was a child. When I'm well, I can resume my duties.

Arch crooked the telephone between his shoulder and ear. He lit a cigarette and poured himself a triple bourbon. A light flashed on in the bedroom, and he saw Madeline cross the threshold of the door in a nightgown, holding her big stomach and looking like a ghost.

She glowered at him from the door. He looked away.

"Well, you better get your goddamn head screwed on right quick or we're all gonna hang for this mess. You gave me your word you'd take care of this. You said you'd handle all of it."

I just needed some rest. I'll come back and everything will be fine. Just fine.

But Si's voice sounded sleepy and satisfied, the way an adult reads a storybook to a child with no sense. As Arch smoked down the cigarette and knocked down the rest of the drink, Madeline looking through the refrigerator for a nighttime craving, he wondered if Si Garrett wasn't gone forever.

"I'm coming to see you."

Not here. Not now.

"I'm coming to Texas. We need to talk. You gave me your goddamn word. What are you without your word?"

The phone line went dead, and Arch left it there buzzing in his lap for a long time, his face growing hot.

JOHN PATTERSON AND HUGH BRITTON MET ME AT THE sheriff's office the next morning. I opened some of the windows behind my desk to let in some air. It took some work, because the sills had been painted over and the windows didn't budge until I used a flathead screwdriver and a hammer. Finally, I got some air going and set a fan on top of the desk, where I sat on the edge and listened to Hugh Britton tell us both what he'd heard.

"Fuller is leaving town," he said. "I hear it's tonight. He's waiting till it gets dark and then he's gonna slip out past the roadblocks."

"You know where he's headed?"

"I don't."

"Can we hold him on anything?"

Patterson shook his head. "We could charge him with neglect of duty, but he'd be out within an hour. We'd need something that would stick, and let the judge set his bond high enough that he won't be able to leave."

"What about pimping?" I asked.

"You know anyone who'll testify to that?"

I thought of the girl and then shook my head.

"This whole town is still scared to death of that sonofabitch," Britton said. "But if y'all don't do something, Bert Fuller will be sitting on a beach in South America and we'll never see the bastard again."

I lit a cigarette and tried to open another window. It was only early morning but hot and muggy, and the office smelled of old tobacco and sweat.

I reached into a desk and found what I wanted and tossed it across the desk. "Found this in the files last night."

Patterson opened up little books of prints lifted from the Patterson Oldsmobile and handed them to Britton.

"I don't know if these are duplicates. Can we get these sent up to Washington to go with the prints on your daddy's car?"

Patterson nodded. He looked better than I'd seen him in a while. He was freshly shaven, wearing khakis and a light blue shirt. He stood up and helped himself to a mug of coffee from the pot we kept on the hot plate. His eyes clear and focused, black hair combed straight back. Not a single Democratic candidate had challenged him for the AG position, and he was already making plans to move to Montgomery come January.

Behind him, the gun rack sat empty. The only guns in the jail were on the Guard troops and the .45 Jack Black had given me. I had no uniforms. I had no deputies.

The file cabinet drawers were open and cleared, most of the contents being pored over by assistant state attorneys. One of the young boys—fresh out of University of Alabama law school—had brought the print book to me before I left my house.

"Where'd you hear this about Fuller?" I asked.

"A friend of his girlfriend," Britton said. "She thinks he's gonna skip out on her, too. She may be pregnant."

"You want to take a visit?"

"Sure thing," Britton said.

"I don't want to see Bert Fuller till he's in jail or sitting before a judge," Patterson said. "I don't trust myself with him."

I grabbed my hat.

"Aren't you gonna carry a gun?" Britton asked me.

I shrugged. "Not right now."

"You got your badge?" Britton asked.

"He knows who I am."

"I'd carry a badge."

"I think it's in my car," I said. "Hugh, how'd you like to be my deputy?"

"How much you pay?"

I told him.

"Think I'll stick to layin' carpet, if it's all the same," he said.

As we left, John Patterson sat in my office in a hard wooden chair, staring out my open window.

SOMETIME AFTER OUR RUN-IN ON THE FOURTH, FULLER had decided to move into the second floor of Homer C. Cobb Memorial. The hospital was named in honor of the former mayor, mostly known for allowing gambling to run wild during the Depression to keep Phenix from falling into receivership, and the two major donors to the building fund had been Hoyt and Jimmie. It was one of the finest hospitals in east Alabama.

Fuller was in bed reading a Zane Grey novel. He wore a pair of red-and-blue-striped pajamas and smoked a cigarette, and when we entered the room he smiled weakly and reached out his hand to me.

"Congratulations," he said. "I'm proud of you."

I looked over to Hugh Britton and he looked back to me.

"I'm glad you're here," Fuller said, crushing out the cigarette in an ashtray that rested on his belly and setting down the book on a nearby food tray. "I've been meaning to thank you."

"For what?"

"For helping me."

He put out his hand again, but I still didn't take it, and he smiled a little at that, fully understanding the situation.

"I was a sinner," he said. "But I'm not a sinner no more."

"That's nice for you, Bert," I said. "But I need to ask you some questions."

"Won't you pray with me?"

"Maybe later."

"I love you, Lamar. I love you for what you done."

I nodded and looked back to Hugh Britton. Britton was chewing a big wad of gum, and his jaw muscles flexed and worked as he eyed the big tub of guts in the bed. He just shook his steel gray head over what Bert Fuller had become.

"You want to tell me where you were when Mr. Patterson was shot?"

"Sure thing. It's no secret. I was at the jail with Sheriff Matthews. I've already told all this to Mr. Sykes."

"Well, tell me again."

"I'm ashamed to admit it, but we were playing cards. But let me tell you something, that's in my past. I don't gamble, and my lips won't touch a drop of whiskey. I am cleansed. Yes, sir. I just heard on the radio that Billy Graham wants to come to Phenix City for a revival. If that don't beat all."

"Bert, can you tell me how long you were at the jail?" I asked, pulling a little notebook from my shirt pocket. I clicked open a pen and took some notes.

"'Bout an hour," he said.

"What time did you get there?"

"'Bout eight, it was gettin' dark."

"And when did you leave?"

"When we got word what had happened to Mr. Patterson," he said. "I just grabbed my hat and ran out of the office."

"Did you leave your office any time before that?"

"No, sir. There were four other deputies with me there, and Sheriff Matthews, of course, and the jailer."

"I don't doubt those men will vouch for you."

"Mr. Murphy, you got to know I had nothing to do with this, and I'd give my right arm if I could find out who killed Mr. Patterson like that. I swear before my Lord Jesus Christ that I did not kill that man. Won't you pray with me?"

I looked down at him and then over at Hugh Britton. I shook my head.

"No, thanks, Bert. I don't think I will."

I turned to leave and Britton followed me, walking down the long hospital hall. "You believe that song and dance?"

"No, sir."

"What can you charge him with?"

I punched the button on the elevator.

"What about vote fraud?" Britton asked.

"Keep talkin'."

"What if someone was to file charges against Fuller for loading the ballot box?"

"You see that?"

"No, but I know someone who did."

"You think he'll testify before a judge?"

"Can't hurt to ask her."

"HOW MUCH YOU GET?"

"Two dollars."

"That's it?" Reuben asked. "Big old house and that's all they got to give to a poor orphan?"

"The woman didn't believe I was an orphan," Billy said. "She said my teeth were too good."

Reuben nodded and wheeled the car out from the oak shadows by the wide-porched, white-columned house in Columbus. He whistled while he drove in and out of the shadows and wheeled down by Broadway, and asked Billy to count out the change.

"How 'bout a hot dog?"

"I thought we were buying groceries," Billy said.

"Hot dogs are groceries. It's food, ain't it?"

They stopped up on the bluff and bought a couple hot dogs from a little brick stand and ate them in the car, the windows down, a nice little breeze coming down the street, working in the shadows. Billy watched his dad load them down with plenty of that free stuff, chopped onions and relish and the like, and part of it spilled down on his hands as he washed it down with a bottle of Coca-Cola.

"You think you could do a cripple?" Reuben asked.

"I guess," Billy said. "I can do a limp and make my eyes go kind of funny."

"If you could make yourself drool, we'd hit the jackpot."

Billy finished up his hot dog and watched the people come and go from the little stand. His father flicked on the radio, and they listened to reports about some A-bomb tests in the desert, and knowing all that was close kind of made him feel better about the day. Before everything was blown to hell.

"I know of a few more neighborhoods we can hit tomorrow."

"If you buy whiskey, I won't do this again."

"Goddamn it. I'm not going to buy whiskey. I told you that."

"You did last time."

"Well," Reuben said, starting the engine and twirling the car around. "Well, last time I needed it."

They drove over the bridge into Alabama and up the hill on Fourteenth Street, past all the jeeps and Guard troops. Billy saw a couple boys with rifles walking under the dead marquees smoking cigarettes. He turned back straight ahead, and soon they were headed up Summerville Road and home.

"I don't think they're going to leave till they find out who killed Mr. Patterson."

"Shit, they know who killed Mr. Patterson," Reuben said. He reached under the seat and pulled out a pint of Jack Daniel's, taking a hit. "They just are doing this for the newspapers. Soon as Governor Folsom comes in, these people will be gone, and me and you can start making some money again."

"Who was it?"

"Bert Fuller."

"I guess everybody knows that," Billy said. "Problem is that nobody saw him."

Reuben took a hit of the whiskey and wheeled onto the long dirt road that would take them home. The sun had started to dip to the west, and everything was nice and gold and warm on a hot August day.

"Someone saw him," Reuben said.

Billy looked over at his dad and pulled a cigarette from his pack of Luckies. He fiddled with the lighter in the dash.

"I seen that sonofabitch standing in that alley beside the Elite not two minutes before Mr. Patterson was shot. He was crouched down behind a car. I wasn't the only one either. I seen two more people walk right by that sonofabitch and look him right in the face."

Billy stared over at his father and couldn't breathe for a moment. His father shook his head and put an index finger to his lips. "You think I'm messin' with that clusterfuck and get myself killed? Hell, no, son."

He parked the car in front of the farmhouse but only got halfway there when the screen door of the porch creaked open and out walked Johnnie Benefield with a sling on his arm and a smile on his face.

WE FOUND HILDA COULTER IN TOWN AT THE LITTLE flower shop she ran right next door to Hoyt Shepherd's pool hall. In back, she arranged some spindly white flowers at a table with what seemed to be some kind of fern. Hilda was in her late twenties or early thirties, and wore a blue dress with a tiny belt at the waist. She was a brunette, with big, perfectly done hair, and looked downright annoyed when we walked in and she had to turn down a small radio that played Rosemary Clooney.

We all knew each other. Hilda had started the RBA's women's auxiliary in '52. She was a firecracker. A female version of Hugh Britton who would run with any assignment that old Albert Patterson had given her, from campaigning to visiting officers at Fort Benning. She didn't think anything of talking down to some generals in the most genteel language about what services were offered for the soldiers.

She kept on with the arrangement, adding in some long-stemmed roses, measuring the stem and then cutting a bit back.

"Hey there, Hilda," Britton said.

"What do you boys want?"

"We need some help."

"Lamar, can you tell Joyce to call me? I've been trying to get an appointment all week. I need to get my roots done."

"She's been a little busy."

"'Spec so, with you playing sheriff."

"I'm not playing sheriff, Hilda. I am the sheriff."

"Appointed, Lamar. Don't let it go to your head," she said. "So what's the favor?"

Britton ran a hand over the back of his neck and remembered to take off his hat. "We want you to swear out a warrant on Bert Fuller."

She kept on arranging. No expression on her face as she pulled out the ferns and then added some sprigs of little white flowers. She poured some water on a green sponge and set it back in a vase.

"Can you believe the cost of roses these days?"

"Will you do it?" Britton asked.

"We can offer you protection," I said. "The Guard."

"I don't want those boys hanging out at my shop. It'd be hell on business."

She gave a little laugh and stepped back from the arrangement, her hands in the pockets of her dress. She smiled at what she'd done and then looked back at us. "Of course I'll do it. What's the charge?"

"You remember when Fuller was taking ballots out of voters' hands a couple years back?" Britton asked.

"Sure, I filed charges then. But Sheriff Matthews just laughed at me."

"File 'em again," I said.

"Don't you all have bigger things to charge that boy with?"

"It's coming," I said. "We just want to hold him here awhile. We just need some time to find some witnesses. We can get you before the judge later today. But I warn you, Hilda. You gonna have to stand up there in court, and Fuller may be there. The newspapermen will hound you, too."

"I understand. I understand. You want me to do it or you want to sit there and try to scare me out of it?"

"So?" Britton asked.

"Don't you boys want to bring something nice home for your wives? I mean, they put up with all your mess. We are having a sale on the most gorgeous little summer mix."

"Sounds nice, Hilda," I said. "Maybe later."

"Lamar Murphy, I do believe you are the cheapest man I have ever met."

"I AIN'T EVER BEEN A FAN OF RED PUSSY, BUT I'LL BE GOD-damned if it ain't sweet as hell," Big Jim Folsom told Fannie Belle in the bed they shared at the Capitol Motel in Montgomery. The light barely broke through the shades, and due to the headache Folsom had from the fifth he'd drunk last night he couldn't tell the time.

"Glad you like it, Governor."

He leaned over the bed and looked at the watch on the nightstand.

"Baby, you mind turning on the television? I believe it's time for Gene Autry."

"You like cowboys?"

"I like his horse, Champion. I believe that's the smartest damn horse I ever seen."

Fannie Belle got up in all her white-fleshed nude glory, her sizable but shapely butt swishing to and fro, pulling the knob on the TV on just in time for the theme song "I'm Back in the Saddle Again" to start playing.

Fannie walked to the curtains on the second floor of the motel and moved them out of the way to look at the little horseshoe shape of the two-level units and down into a soft green swimming pool filled with kids splashing around and giving their parents hell.

Over at the little dresser, she poured out a little more Jack Daniel's, handing Big Jim the glass. He took it but didn't thank her, and watched as Gene and Pat Buttram found their way into another western town and more adventure. This one having to do with a hidden gold mine and some mean desperadoes beating up an old man.

Fannie, still as nude as a jaybird, lifted her arms up in the weak light of the Capitol Motel neon sign and played with and straightened her red hair, still stiff with spray. She cocked a hip and smoked a cigarette, looking down at the huge man watching a kids' show, a glass of Jack Daniel's in his hand.

"What do you say, Governor? You gonna give Phenix a break?"

"Sure thing, baby. Whatever you want."

She moved over to the TV and pushed in the knob. The shooting and yelling stopped and the screen went dark.

"Now, why'd you do that, baby?"

She kept the cigarette in her mouth, hands on her hips, and stuck her big chest out. "Figured we need to talk a little."

"I told you not to worry. Them boys will be out of Phenix City before I even take my oath."

"Your friend Bert Fuller is gonna fall hard."

"He didn't kill Patterson."

"I want your word you'll get those troops out of Phenix."

"Let them make their arrests and give a little show."

"What about Fuller?"

"There is no one in their right mind who would testify against Bert.

I have it on rock-solid authority that Bernard Sykes will never make a case for the Patterson killing. Hell, he has about fifty investigators who can't even turn up a witness. What are the chances of them finding one now?"

"You think you can talk to Mr. Sykes? Get him thinking about his future in politics?"

"I better leave that one alone, sweetie."

"You wanna bet?"

Fannie opened up the bedspread and crawled inside, laying her body across Big Jim and moving herself against him. She smiled at him and he smiled back.

"You don't tire much, do you?" she asked.

"No, ma'am. I guess I never get tired of bourbon and pussy."

"That's why you'll always have my vote, Governor."

Big Jim leaned back and Fannie straddled him, as he hummed the opening notes to Gene Autry's theme song.

QUINNIE KELLEY STOPPED BY AFTER SUPPER, MAYBE A week after those first raids. He was sweating and hatless, and it was one of those hot summer nights where the temperature only seemed to grow in the darkness. I invited him in, but he shook his head and wanted to talk outside. So I walked him around back, near the shed and Joyce's beauty shop, and we sat at a little picnic bench right near my canvas heavy bag.

Quinnie took off his glasses and cleaned them on the lip of his light green shirt and put them back on his face. He put his hands in the little pockets of his pants and rocked back on his heels, looking down into the dirt.

"You got something to tell me, Quinnie?"

The night air was filled with night sounds, and among the crickets and cicadas, head still down, Quinnie told me that he was sorry. He said he'd lied.

"I did see someone that night Mr. Patterson was killed."

I waited.

"I seen a man come around the back of the post office and cross Fourteenth. I was standing right on the stoop of the courthouse, on account of making sure they was done with that Boy Scouts meeting. But I don't think he saw me 'cause I'd just cut off the lights. He passed right in front of my face, right on the courthouse lawn, and ran around back behind to the jail."

I rubbed my face and massaged my wrist, which had grown sore from a loose punch on the heavy bag. I walked over to it and let it rock on its chain, and it groaned and squeaked with its weight and gently pushed back on me.

"You see his face?"

He nodded, staring up at me. His face filmed with a light, sweaty sheen. "I haven't been able to sleep. I prayed about this. I talked to my wife and my minister. Don't get me wrong, I never met a fella more evil in my life than Bert Fuller. But when I heard y'all was about to charge him with murder, well—"

"Who was it, Quinnie?"

"Ferrell."

Quinnie stood before me and shook, his glasses fogged from the humidity. But he held his ground and returned my stare.

"You can't be sure of that. Can you, Quinnie?"

"I heard them shots. I thought they was kids playing with firecrackers, but not ten seconds later did I see Mr. Ferrell in an all-out run pass right in front of my face."

"You sure it was Arch Ferrell?"

He nodded.

"Will you testify to that?"

Quinnie looked away for a moment. In the little back window of my house, I could see Joyce and Anne doing the dishes. One of my neighbors played a ball game on the radio.

"If they let me live," Quinnie said. "What are the chances of that?"

"I want you to do me a favor."

"Anything," Quinnie said, hitching up his pants and standing as tall as Quinnie Kelley could ever stand.

"I don't want you to tell a soul what you told me tonight."

His face dropped.

"You're not hearing me," I said. "Just keep it to yourself until the time is right. And when it is, I'll protect you."

"How you gonna do that, Mr. Murphy?"

I looked away. I shrugged and put my hand down on his shoulder. "I guess I'll figure it out."

BERT FULLER HAD TOLD EVERYONE THAT HE WAS INNO-cent, but not a damn person would listen. He knew what people had been sayin' about Arch Ferrell protecting him, but that was the biggest dang lie that had ever been told. Arch Ferrell thought just because he was a college boy, a war hero, and his daddy was a judge, that he couldn't be soiled. But Judgment Day would be comin' on that man's soul, and all the stones he'd been throwin' wouldn't protect him a lick. When Phenix came a-tumblin' down, every finger came pointing at the sheriff and his right-hand man, because that was easy. Those newspapermen couldn't know what it was like to keep order in a town like Phenix. Sure, he'd kept a little nut away for himself, but he'd deserved it, trying to keep those Machine boys in line. It would take a powerful man to try and walk a mile in his boots.

Fuller finished up adding some clean shirts, blue jeans, and underwear to his old leather suitcase, and tossed in his pearl-handled .357s
and his family's King James Bible. On last thought, he grabbed the
framed picture of him with Lash LaRue and buckled it closed. He buttoned his shirt, put on his boots, and tried on his Stetson hat.

It was midnight and time to get the hell out of Dodge. He wasn't
taking the rap for this mess.

Since they'd taken away his squad car, he had his girlfriend from
church pick him up at the curb, and just as he got to the door he heard
the motor running.

The air was thick with heat and crickets, and he tossed the suitcase
into the backseat and sat down. He clutched a silver cross that had
belonged to his mother in his gun hand.

"Where to?"

"Atlanta. Get me out of Alabama."

She turned the car around, the headlights catching the shrubs and
dense magnolias around his garage apartment, and she headed north,
far away from the two bridges that would be watched by the National
Guardsmen. Fuller took off his cowboy hat and rested it on his knee.
His girlfriend, Georgia, turned on the radio to a gospel station out of
LaGrange, and the good ole-time church music made Bert Fuller
know that he'd found a new path.

He figured he'd catch a bus or a plane in Atlanta. When he pulled
out the whore money he'd been squirrelin' away, he figured he could
pretty much go where he liked.

"Did you tell anyone?" Georgia asked.

"No. This is between us."

"Take me with you, Bert."

"I'll send for you. I promise. I must go where the Lord takes me."

"You remember when I told you that I was pregnant?"

"I do."

"I wasn't. I just had gas. I'd eaten some bad chicken."

"Well, that's good, baby."

"I'm glad you've changed, Bert. You sure aren't the man I used to know."

"Thank the Lord," Bert said and gave a drowsy smile, as they rounded their way by the airport and headed fast up Park Hill, up to Summerville and to Lee County, where they'd head east again. "We have the rest of our life together. I know a little spot just on the other side of the Rio Grande where a white man can live like a king for pennies a day."

"Mexico?"

"You said it, baby."

"Are those people Christians?"

"They got more churches in Mexico than in Alabama."

"That a fact? But they speak Mexican."

"They speak Spanish."

"When will you send for me?"

"Just as soon as I get my land," Bert said and placed his mother's cross in Georgia's palm.

"Oh, Bert."

He affixed the cowboy hat on his head and had a big smile on his face, almost feeling that county line coming up. He tapped the dashboard in time with "I'll Fly Away" and grinned and grinned. That was until the light grew bright on the highway ahead, and he soon saw the red lights and white lights mix and the squad cars and the jeeps and men holding rifles up in their arms.

Georgia slowed the car, and a guardsman asked her for her license. She reached across Bert into the glove compartment, and Bert looked away even as the deputy crossed a flashlight over his profile.

"Good evenin', Mr. Fuller," the young boy said. "We been looking for you."

Fuller squinted into the flashlight's beam.

"We got a warrant for your arrest."

He shook his head and rolled down the window, spitting out on the ground. He breathed some more and then simply said: "Well, I'll be goddamned."

REUBEN AND JOHNNIE BENEFIELD sat on the farmhouse porch and watched the sun go down through a row of diseased pecans planted before both of them had been born. They drank moonshine from a jelly jar and smoked Chesterfields, Johnnie telling him about what had happened out at the Hill Top and how he'd nearly gotten taken by the Guard. Reuben stood and flicked his cigarette out into the bushes and then sat back down in a rusted porch chair. He looked over at Johnnie, who was leaned back with his old boots on the ledge.

"You sure it was Lamar?"

"Sure," he said. "I know Lamar Murphy."

"I'm broke, Johnnie," Reuben said. "I don't care much for studying on politics right now."

"Broke?" Johnnie said, cracking a grin and polishing off a good bit of that old 'shine. "You got to be kiddin' me."

"I said I wasn't gonna touch that money and I ain't."

"Well, aren't you the Boy Scout. A gold star for you, Reuben."

"We dig it up when it settles."

"So you got it buried out here?"

"Check all you want. You ain't gonna find it."

Johnnie laughed some more. He grinned, smashing a cigarette against the sole of his boot. "Listen, I want you to set up a meeting with Lamar."

"Who wants to talk?"

"Fannie. Some of the boys."

"What boys?"

"Mr. Davis and his brother. Red. Papa Clark. Maybe Frog Jones."

"They ain't gonna change his mind."

"You know how much he could get paid for just playin' stupid?"

"I sparred with that man for nearly five years. That man's got the hardest head ever put on this God's earth."

"You know I had to get rid of the Hudson? Them boys had seen it over at Fannie's and they know I was there over at Britton's house. I sold it off to some niggerman over in Loachapoka. He was gonna paint it and cut it down a bit. Said he was gonna sell the engine and paint it gold. Ain't that just like a nigger? Makes me sad to think about that engine in another body. Rips the heart out of her. But I'll get another. But, man, oh man, I sure loved my little Hornet."

"Where'd you get this 'shine?" Reuben asked.

"Moon," he said. "They still ain't found his still."

"They ain't found a lot of stuff. They rootin' around all around the county. I heard yesterday they busted in at Papa Clark's farm and found all those brand-new horse-racing games. I also heard when they come for him, he nearly had a heart attack."

Johnnie nodded and stood, combing the five long black hairs over his head. He cupped his hand and lit another cigarette. He wore a crisp pink cowboy shirt with a bolo tie.

"When did men start wearing pink shirts?" Reuben asked.

"I seen a magazine where Tony Curtis wears pink."

"You ain't exactly Tony Curtis, Johnnie."

He shrugged and picked his nose, snorting a bit as he did. "You want some more 'shine?"

"No."

"Listen, don't get all pissy on me. I told you I'd come through for you and I did. Didn't I tell you that ole Hoyt and Jimmie didn't trust banks? Hell, Hoyt made his first dollar in the damn Depression. And I was the one who knowed people who used to work for Mr. Hoyt. That's how I knew about the kind of safe he'd got and just how to blow that baby open."

Reuben smoked down the cigarette and lit another Chesterfield, liking the design on the pack because he'd seen a picture of Gregory Peck smoking them while filming *Twelve O'Clock High*. Johnnie had brought a carton with him, and it was the first decent cigarettes he'd had in a week. The sun almost gone, just a thin little hot slit through the pecans and down at the dead peach trees. The trees died while he was getting shot at in the Philippines, but if the old man were still alive he'd be blaming him for their loss.

"What's the split?" Reuben asked. He poured out the last of the 'shine, only a mushy peach left at the bottom, just as ripe as the day it was picked and soaked in corn liquor. "Figured that's what we're beatin' around the bush about. Let's figure it out."

"Three ways."

"Three ways?"

"Cut between some inside folks."

"I think that's horseshit."

"I told you I got an inside man."

"Who?"

"You wouldn't believe me if I told you."

"Why don't you try."

Johnnie shrugged and snuffed some smoke out of his nose. "All right, hell. Clyde Yarborough."

"Bullshit."

"Bullshit back on you."

"Clyde trained Hoyt and Jimmie. He's the one who taught them the whole game."

"Let's just say, Hoyt ain't rememberin' that in his Christmas list."

"Well, I'll be goddamned," Reuben said. "I still say we need to keep that money hidden for a while. Wait till the time is right."

"The time is now. You got other options of feeding that moody-ass boy of yours?"

"Say, why doesn't he like you?" Reuben asked. "He hasn't said one word since you showed up. I ain't seen him all day."

"You think I give a shit," Johnnie said, unzipping his fly and urinating right off the porch into what used to be his wife's flower bed. He grinned, a cigarette clamped in those tombstone choppers of his. "I just got that effect on some people."

Reuben waited, finished the cigarette, and stood. "You know Hoyt wouldn't think nothin' 'bout killin' both of us."

"Life ain't nothin' but a spin of the wheel."

THAT SATURDAY, I SPENT THE MORNING ON MY LAND UP ON Sandfort Road. I brought Anne with me, and together we fed and watered the horses, cleaned out their stalls, and went for a short ride through some cleared trails in and around the pines and oaks, the kudzu beaten to the trail's edge around our small pond. By the time we returned to the little barn, the horses were calm and gentle, the restlessness and nervousness gone, and Anne brushed them while I hung up their saddles and tack. I nailed up some shoes that the blacksmith had left by the gate and I tightened a loose nut on the water pump. I checked the mineral levels in their tank. I checked the fencing up by the front gate.

I was hammering up some barbed wire that hung loose when I heard the unmistakable high-pitched gears on an Army jeep and saw Jack Black behind the wheel, with his buzz cut and gold aviator shades, stop short of my gate.

"We got him," he said.

I leaned into the fence and looked back at Anne, who fed Joe Louis an apple. Joe shook his head back and showed her his teeth when he was done.

"The FBI matched the prints taken off Mr. Patterson's car with the prints we took off Fuller."

"They sure?"

"They said it looked as if someone had tried to smudge the prints on the door frame, but they got part of a finger and his thumb."

"That was Ferrell. I have two people who saw him rubbing his arm over the roof of that car. Guess he missed a spot."

"Guess so."

"So we can charge him?"

Black shook his head. "Sykes wants to wait. He doesn't want this getting out too soon."

"What else does he need?"

"He's trying to be careful. He says he wants more and doesn't want to spook Fuller."

"What about the guns?"

"Nothing yet," Black said, squinting into the sun behind my back. "They're testing the bullets they took at the autopsy with those .38s we got at Fuller's place. There's also talk about exhuming a couple bodies from men Fuller killed a few years back to compare bullets."

"You don't look optimistic."

"Fuller is stupid."

"But not that stupid," I said.

"You never know."

"I'm 'bout finished up around here."

"That's a nice-looking horse."

"His name is Joe Louis."

"And the other?"

"Rocky."

Black smiled. "Of course he is."

Anne walked up to us, skinny and lean in a pair of crisp blue overalls and little cowboy boots. She climbed up on the swinging gate and said hello to Black.

"You gonna make him work?" Anne asked.

"Just a little," Black said.

"I liked him better when he pumped gas," she said.

"Don't you like that car with a siren?" I asked.

"You don't even have uniforms," she said.

I looked over to Black. "I hate wearing those duds they left at the office."

"No rule you got to."

"You know when you're headed back to Birmingham?"

Black chewed some gum and leaned back a bit. "Thought I might stay around here. You know, if there's a job."

"You know it doesn't pay much."

"My other job ain't exactly making me rich. Besides, General Hanna thinks it wouldn't be a bad idea for you to have an adviser."

"Advise away, Major."

We shook hands, and Black walked back to the jeep. Before he crawled back under the wheel, he yelled: "You ever hear of a place called the Rabbit Farm?"

I shook my head.

"A girl called the office this morning and said her friend was being held at the Rabbit Farm. When I told her I didn't know what she was talking about, she acted like I was crazy. Said she wanted to talk to the sheriff, that he would know."

"You ask Fuller about it?"

"Of course."

"Play dumb?"

"Well, he's so damn good at it. You know that sonofabitch is giving sermons to the inmates? He wrapped a bedsheet around him like it was a robe."

"I think the only soul he's thinking about saving is his own."

"You coming in?"

"Let me drop off Anne. The woman leave a number?"

"She said she would call back."

"HER NAME IS SHEILA," THE GIRL, LORELEI, SAID. "I haven't heard from her since Mr. Patterson was shot."

"Where was she working?"

"Last I heard was a place called the Rabbit Farm."

"You know where that is?"

"No, sir. I don't know the way back. They'd blindfold you when they'd take you there. That's why I came here. I thought you would know."

The girl looked down at her hands. She looked like a girl today, not like when I'd seen her at the Hill Top. She wore a flowered shirt that showed off her long teenage arms and blue jeans and saddle oxford shoes. Her hair was in a ponytail, and she didn't wear a trace of makeup. It was hard to think this was the same girl that I'd talked to at Choppy's.

"You doin' all right?"

She looked to the floor in the office. I sat next to her in another hard wooden chair but not behind the desk. It seemed to go easier that way.

"I'm fine."

"How'd she get into this mess?"

"She was doing some B-girl work with her mother," Lorelei said. She chewed gum while we talked and then dropped the gum into her hand and then into the wastebasket.

"Where?"

"Bamboo Club. The Silver Slipper. She worked for a while at Ma Beachie's."

I nodded. Beachie's was a high-end place, mostly stage shows, with the best girls in Phenix City. The clientele was high-dollar, with fraternity boys from Auburn and businessmen from Atlanta. The girls would work out backroom deals only if they liked the offer.

"But she met up with some fella and she fell in love, but it turned out he wasn't doing nothin' but tryin' to turn her out. I heard he worked her out of some motels over on Crawford Road, and when he'd gotten what he wanted he cut her loose, sold her off to this Rabbit Farm, and then left town."

I put up a hand.

"What do you mean 'sold'?"

Lorelei didn't change expression, just looked at me level with her clear blue eyes and said, "Sold. Just like I said."

"Who was the man?"

"That fella who was in the papers. The one who got killed, Ernest Youngblood."

I looked over to Jack Black and he adjusted the blinds, letting in a sliver of light and causing Lorelei to put a hand up over her eyes with the flat of her hand.

"Deputy Fuller knowed the place," she said. "Sheila should be sixteen now."

Black was smoking, and his exhaling breath and the light behind him obscured his face.

JACK BLACK DROVE AND FULLER SAT IN BACK, TALKING about what he'd learned in his years of police work and how it all had brought him to God. He said he'd been offered five hundred dollars to tell his story to the *Saturday Evening Post,* but when he turned in his handwritten notes they never called him back. He said they only wanted sensational details about sex in a modern-day Sodom and nothing about his conversion.

"I told them I seen a blue light that day in church. You were there, Lamar. You know it."

"You mind turning up the radio?" I asked Jack.

Black turned on a Montgomery station and I hung my arm out the window. We drove a brand-new Chevy, flat black, with no official markings. That's the way I wanted it, and figured on keeping it that way for some time.

Still not out on bond—we heard Papa Clark and Godwin Davis were out collecting signatures and cash—Fuller was dressed in pajamas and a bathrobe. He smoked cigarettes and talked a little about his aching back and shifted in his seat, looking to find some comfort. He said he had broken two vertebrae.

I pointed out a country crossroads store and Jack slowed down and stopped while I asked a man about a place called the Rabbit Farm. He looked at us and then Fuller in the backseat. The man took a breath, nervous, and shook his head.

"Who would know?" I asked.

He shrugged, from where he sat atop of an old bucket. He scratched his neck and spit.

I got out and showed him my badge. It was the first time I'd done it.

Black drove the car out of earshot, and I spoke to the man a little about the weather and the heat and how we expected a bad cotton harvest. I then looked over at the car and back at the man and told him that Fuller didn't work for me and didn't have a clue what we were talking about.

The man muttered the name Clanton and wandered off. I got back in the car and told Black to keep driving.

Jack rolled on, the countryside dry, yellow, and harsh. It hadn't rained in weeks, not since the night the Guard took over. As we drove, the radio station broadcasted the latest news: *The president of Brazil commits suicide. The* Lone Ranger *broadcasts final radio episode after twenty-one years.*

"Gosh dang," Fuller said. "I love the *Lone Ranger.* They ain't a thing on radio no more. No heroes."

We bought a Coca-Cola at another filling station down the road, and the woman who worked there knew me and she told me that she knew Clanton. She said he had a farm five miles down the road we just crossed. I thanked her, and brought Coca-Colas out to Jack and Fuller, and Jack doubled back.

"Your memory coming back to you, Bert?"

"No, sir."

But as I pointed out the turn and Black hit a straightaway bordered by a long barbed-wire fence on cedar posts, Fuller looked as if he'd swallowed his tongue. We passed loose groups of cows lying in shallow, drying mud pits and under large, lone pecan and oak trees, swatting flies with their tails and trying to escape the heat.

Down the road, a little single-story white frame house came into view, and Black turned in to the dirt drive. He had to slow down at the mailbox, on account of a group of guineas that wouldn't move out of the road, and a skinny hound bayed and wailed as we circled to the front porch and killed the engine.

I knocked on the screen door, the door open into a shallow little hall. Junk spilled from the front door out onto the porch and into the front yard and driveway. Old washboards and bed frames, engine parts, rocking chairs, and piles of garbage.

I heard the chugging of a tractor nearby but didn't see one. Black walked around the building and came back to the front porch, a man appearing from the far side of the property in overalls, no shirt, and work boots. He had dark circles under his eyes and didn't look like he'd bathed in some time.

Black leaned against the spotless black Chevy and smoked. He nodded to me and I walked over to the man, not offering my hand but slow and confident.

"Mr. Clanton?"

He nodded. He was a hard country man, with brown parched skin and gold teeth. He wore an oversized straw hat and black-framed glasses. One of his eyes seemed a little crossed, or it could have been because of the light magnifying in the lens. Either way, it was damn hard to figure out which one to look at while you spoke.

I introduced myself, deciding to go with the left, and Black asked him what he did out here.

"Farm."

"You do any other business, doc?"

"No, sir."

"You ever rent your place out?"

He tilted his head at me, his stubble beard a stark white, and made a face like something stank. Then he looked to the backseat at Bert Fuller and his face changed, and he smiled and said, "Hey, Bert. I ain't seen you in a coon's age."

Fuller didn't say a word, just turned to look across the road at the fields and pretended not to hear.

CLANTON STAYED ON THE ROTTED JUNK PORCH AND SPOKE
to Fuller, who we kept chained to a D ring in the backseat. The window was down, and after Clanton talked to him about what the
drought did to his watermelons he asked Fuller to join him on the
porch but Fuller said he was doing A-OK in the car. There was a chat-
tering up in a chinaberry tree, and a small monkey skittered out from
the branches, scratching himself and twirling a rock in his hands
before dropping it hard.

"That little sonofabitch is Wilbur," Clanton said. "Bought him off
an Army sergeant who got him overseas."

Clanton moved over to the tree, and, despite the chain, the monkey
jumped up onto his back and took a spot on the old man's shoulder. As
Clanton spoke to the monkey, the monkey seemed to take on the exact
same facial expressions as the old man.

I traded looks with Black, and the monkey noticed and stuck out his
tongue.

"I think he wants you to give him a penny," Clanton said.

"I don't have any change," I said.

The monkey ran off Clanton's back and toward me, and Clanton
yanked him back to the ground. "You got to be careful—you don't
give him a penny, and he'll piss on your head."

Clanton let the monkey go and went back to his failing front porch,
sitting down on the steps and rolling a forearm across his brow. As we
walked around the house, I heard Bert Fuller start a conversation with
the old man.

"Mr. Clanton, may I ask you a personal question?"

"Sure, Bert."

"How is your relationship with Jesus Christ?"

Almost out of earshot and around the bend, we heard Clanton respond, "I don't know, Bert. 'Spec same as yours."

We found a small shed out back where Clanton kept his tractor and feed, some spare parts, and a couple of discs that looked like they'd last been pulled by mules. He had some tanks of gasoline and little drums of oil. There was a workbench and a vise, and some files laid out from where he'd been sharpening a scythe.

I headed into a thick, wooded area that bordered a few acres of cleared farmland. Clanton was with us again and staring up at Black.

"You sure are a big sonofabitch."

"Where's that path lead?" Black asked him.

"That's a hog trail. You must not be from the country."

"I was raised on a farm," Black said.

The man craned his neck at him and grinned a stupid smile.

"Never seen a hog who could drive a car," Black said, and motioned down at the twin rutted tracks going over weeds and into the privet bush.

We walked into the woods and Clanton followed, asking if we'd like to sit down and have a discussion. And I asked him what about, still looking down into the mouth of the leafy tunnel, but he just said he'd just butchered a chicken and could fry it up. He said his wife could cook up some field peas, too, if we liked.

"You got family out here?" I asked.

"Just me and my boys."

"How many boys?"

"Three. They all in town working in the mills. All of them at work, yes, sir."

The path seemed to be maybe a fire road, and it ran up a slight hill and then disappeared up over the ridge. It was cool and dark in the thickness, a stifled heat, branches underfoot, dead leaves covering the tire tracks. Squirrels up in their nests and birds fluttering from branch to branch under the thick canopy of pecans, oaks, and tall, skinny pines. A few small leaves flitted down high from the ceiling.

I saw a movement up on a little hill, but it was quickly gone.

I stopped and held up my hand to Black. He stopped, too. He readjusted the shotgun in his hands.

"Ain't no whores in them trees," Clanton said, smiling to himself and thinking he'd said something really smart.

We crested the hill, and Black motioned his head to farther down the path.

"Is that a barn, Mr. Clanton?" I asked.

He stopped cold and looked to me and then looked deep into the woods. There was another flutter of movement, and I reached for the gun on my hip just as the old man's lip curled above his gold teeth.

BERNARD SYKES MET BIG JIM FOLSOM AT A CATFISH HOUSE overlooking Lake Martin as the sun set through the pines and a dinner party brought laughter and shrill squeals along the shore of the lake. A band dressed in western duds took a stage decked out in Christmas lights, tuning their guitars and fiddles. Folsom waited alone, downhill on a small weathered dock, wearing a tent-sized seersucker suit. He rattled ice in a bourbon glass as he waved to a couple girls on a speedboat.

"Thought we were going fishing," Sykes said.

"Come on up," Folsom said. "I have some folks I'd like you to meet."

"I'm fine right here, Governor."

One of the girls on the boat dropped a pair of skis into the water and jumped in after them with the towline. Big Jim lit a cigarette and watched as the other girl in a black bathing suit drove the boat slowly away, making the line tight.

"You want a cigarette?"

"No, sir. Thank you."

"Don't call me sir. Call me Jim."

"I'd rather call you Governor."

"Call me whatever the hell you like. You want a drink?"

"Little early."

"It's never too early for whiskey," Big Jim said, winking in a con-spiratorial way. "You married?"

"Yes, sir."

"Kids?"

"A couple."

"I have six."

"I know."

"You do?"

"You were in the papers this weekend with your kids."

"Guess I was," Big Jim said. "How'd I look?"

"Like you do now."

Big Jim nodded, pleased with that, and smoked, watching the speedboat zip away, yanking the girl up on skis, taking her for a quick turn in front of the dock for the governor's appraisal, and then dis-appearing around a bend in the lake.

"Pussy is gonna kill me."

"Sir?"

They didn't talk for a long while, and Sykes tried to look at his watch without the governor seeing him. He'd grown comfortable with the sunset and the gaiety of the dinner party, and that made him more nerv-ous. When Folsom's driver, Drinkard, came over to the Russell County Courthouse with the invitation, he should have turned it down flat.

"I bet your wife is looking forward to living in the mansion," Sykes said. The question came out of nowhere, just something to say. "Lot of history. That's where Jefferson Davis lived right before the war."

"Let's skip the bullshit, Bernard," Big Jim said. Up on the hill, Sykes heard the country band finally strike up, with some women's cackling excitement. "A man like you needs to think about his future. And I don't take you for a stupid man. I think you've worked long and hard to get where you've gotten so fast. What are you, thirty-six? I'm sure you know you probably ain't on any short list to be on Patterson's team when he takes office. No matter what you do, he still is going to see you as Si Garrett's man."

Sykes recognized the band's song as "Jambalaya." And as the music played on, you could see the people dancing on the deck overlooking Lake Martin. The sweet good-time song poured down the hill and spread out and echoed across the water and the soft coves of light and shadow.

"How's that investigation coming?"

"It's gonna take time."

Folsom seemed to grow impatient, standing there on the dock with the two girls in the speedboat gone. He kept on staring around the bend for their return but soon crushed his cigarette under his gleaming shoe.

Folsom rattled the ice in his glass and looked down to Sykes: "You sure you don't want to loosen that tie a bit, son?"

BLACK SAW CLANTON'S HAND REACH INTO HIS OVERALLS and he coldcocked him with the butt of the shotgun without paying much attention. He reached down into the heap of old man and picked up the little rusted pistol and put it in his pant pocket. I followed along, my .45 out now, and he motioned me to head over to the left and up the ridge. He would circle in the other way. I nodded and crept along the path, feeling my hands sweat on the butt of the gun and hearing every damn sound in the woods, waiting for a crack of a limb or the crunch of boots on the molded leaves.

I crested the hill and saw the barn in the opening. The barn was one of the biggest I'd ever seen, the kind they built before the turn of the century, not just for livestock but to run a business. I skirted the edge of the woods, the sun bright and hard on the tin roof and loading dock built out back. There was another road from the east that we'd missed because it hadn't been on any map.

I couldn't see Black but headed that way anyway.

Just as I reached the big door, Black was behind me. I pulled on the lock and chains keeping the barn shut up. The lock was old, tooled for an old-fashioned key.

"You want me to go back?"

He shook his head and suddenly pushed me to the ground and fired off his shotgun twice. Two more shots, pistol shots, pinged over us against the door. Black reached into his shirt pocket for some more shells.

I fired into the tree line three times.

The summer air fell hot and quiet for a minute or two.

Then there were voices and the sound of feet. I started to stand, but Black pushed me back down to the landing just as a shot fired over my head. It was then we heard the pounding from the other side of the door, the sounds of screams and yells and dozens of hands slapping the old, sun-bleached wood, crying out for help.

BLACK YELLED FOR EVERYONE to step back because he was about
to shoot off the lock. And when the screams and yells died down, he
counted down one, two, three and hit the dead bolt and chain with the
.44 from his belt and they fell to the loading dock with a clank. We
didn't move from our hands and knees, opening the big barn doors, a
hot, rank smell coming from within like a rotted mouth, and crawled
inside, shutting the doors closed. We felt hands on us, on our arms and
chests, faces and fingers over our mouths, and I could barely make a
thing out as I yelled for everyone to move back, my eyes adjusting to
light coming in slats. It all was like a fun house, with partial faces of
skinny girls with dark circles under their eyes and bony arms sticking
through feed sacks and torn clothes. A few were naked. Others wore
satin dresses covered in hay and red dirt, the women bone thin and
with mouths parched, begging us for water and something to eat.

Black pushed them away, and I craned my neck up to the cathedral
ceiling, streaks of light crisscrossing over the dirt floor and hay. As I
moved back from the women and the wailing, I realized I was in the
floor of an arena, wooden bleachers all around me. There were rooster
cages filled with chicken shit at the edge of the wire arena, maybe fifty

shiny new slot machines stacked in the center ring, and Black had already mounted the steps up into the loft, which squared the upstairs like the balcony in a theater.

I looked back over toward the door and in the beams of light, I saw twenty girls. Maybe thirty. They'd sat back down on hay bales or on their backsides, and they covered their eyes with their forearms. Some cried. The nude ones were covered in sweat and dirt and moved in and out of shadow with no more shame than an animal. They were so skinny, I could see all their ribs. Many of them looked to be children.

I walked back to the door and found a one-by-six to fit into a pair of brackets and keep anyone out. The barn was hot, a sweatbox down in the pit and even worse upstairs, where I found Black walking with hard thumps in his Army boots looking into little boxes that surrounded the arena.

Each one had a hutch door and was enclosed in chicken wire.

"Rabbit Farm," he said.

"How long they been keeping those girls here?"

"Maybe since the Guard got here," Black said. "I saw some tins on the floor and some empty buckets. They would be feeding them some."

"I saw a girl down there that couldn't be any more than twelve."

Black's face turned into shadow, not replying, as he walked from stall to stall. Each floor covered in a filthy mattress, smelling putrid and rotten, piss buckets on the floor and pie tins covered in mold.

In one, there was a woman in a fetal position. The smell was worse here. She wore a cotton print dress, a dress that reminded me of the ones my mother had made from catalog material she'd bought at a country store. Black turned over the woman with his boot, and she was gray in the face with a purple tongue.

We checked other stalls, and then Black bounded down the loft steps and walked into the center of the arena. He called all the girls to the center with him and they emerged into the brighter light, the criss-cross patterns that made them look like pieces of a jigsaw puzzle.

"I know none of you have had anything to drink or eat in some time. But you hold on, we're getting you out of here."

I asked if any of them were named Sheila.

A girl walked toward us. She was a child, but not the child I'd seen earlier. She wore a filthy man's shirt and clogged along in a pair of men's wingtips that were three times larger than her feet. Her hair was matted with straw and her face was devoid of any expression. She just craned her neck at me and said: "They said you were coming."

"Who?"

"The Clanton boys."

"When did they say that?"

"Yesterday. They said they brought you here to kill you."

AFTER MURPHY AND THAT GUARDSMAN WALKED INTO THE woods, an old woman with the face of a shriveled apple tried to use a mattock to pry Fuller loose from the D ring. The woman said her husband kept some bolt cutters and a hacksaw in his shed. And after giving up on the bolt cutters, she sawed right through the cuffs. Fuller worked circulation back into his wrists and hands and fingers, and asked the old woman for a gun. She went into the house and came back with a pistol, a six-shooter that looked like a Jesse James special, and Fuller checked the cylinder for ammo and realized he was loaded and ready.

"Where're your boys?" Fuller asked.

"In the woods. They probably got them in the barn by now. Their paw-paw told 'em you wanted to be the one killed Murphy. He's the bald fella, right?"

Fuller nodded and stripped out of his bathrobe, but kept on the pajamas and bedroom shoes, and moved through the woods on the path. The woman called it the hog path, and before he ducked into the woods Fuller asked what happened to the swine.

"We ate 'em."

"Y'all do some good barbecue."

"I could barbecue an ole dog and make her taste good."

Fuller looked down at the mangy hound trotting alongside him and its skin-and-bones coat, some mange around the face and ears.

He soon came out of the path and into the clearing and saw the Clanton boys waiting up by a loading dock to the barn where Fuller had spent many a night watching the best roosters in Alabama tear each other a new asshole.

Both of the boys were short and so painfully white that they seemed to glow. One chewed tobacco and offered him his pouch. The other smoked a cigarette and leaned on a rifle. The whites of their eyes were yellow and the lids almost pink.

Fuller knew they never left the woods during the day, keeping the fire around those stills stoked and ready for the runners to move that 'shine all over the state and into Georgia.

Fuller pushed onto the door. It held.

He pushed again.

And then the two boys joined him, heaving and pushing, with fat and sinew and muscle, until they heard a pop and the great doors opened, flooding the dark, hot barn with a light that almost seemed biblical to Bert.

He pointed the gun into the arena, seeing nothing but the girls, and moved slowly under the loft rafters, where he heard a short click, almost sounding like a cricket. As he turned the corner, he felt a pop to his jaw so hard and quick he blacked out before losing his feet, his mouth bleeding, and realizing he'd just been smacked in the jaw by the stock of a gun, the big guardsman boot on his chest.

Those hillbilly Clanton boys now opened up to shoot with rebel yells.

I WAITED IN ONE OF THE STALLS, RIGHT BEHIND THE COOP door, and listened as two sets of feet bounded up the landing, the men speaking together in some kind of garbled countryspeak, seeming to divide and take each side, squaring the arena. The footsteps moved in closer to me on the slatted-wood floor. The sound was unmistakable, each step telegraphed before the next. Holding the gun, I found it tough to breathe but tried to keep my breath silent in the hot air.

There was the sound of opening and closing doors. They were checking each hutch, looking for me.

I relaxed my muscles and took in a breath. They were getting close.

FULLER GOT TO HIS FEET AND FELT HIS MOUTH, FEELING the swelling, and tasting the blood as he spit out two teeth. He wavered on his feet and moved through a group of girls, who screamed and seemed horrified by his presence and his looks, but he had no time for them as he walked to the center of the ring, circling the mass of silver slots, and called out for Murphy. "You goddamn coward, come out. Quit hiding. You gonna sneak up on me now?"

Behind him, the women retreated back into a dark corner, and Fuller smiled at that. He didn't know who they were, but even in pajamas they sure as shit knew him and, for a moment, he felt good.

He spit on the red-dirt ground, covered in chicken shit and cigarette butts, and called out for Murphy again.

But he heard no answer from the coward.

ANOTHER HUTCH BANGED OPEN AND THEN SLAMMED SHUT,
and I waited until he came into mine, my breath slow and even and
controlled. A skinny boy, just a teen with glowing skin and recessed
eyes, moved into the dark coop and turned to me.

I simply yanked the gun from his hand and knocked him on his ass
with the back of my hand. The youth scrambled back onto a piss-
stained mattress and screamed out, his mouth open with rotten teeth,
and I grabbed the kid's dirty white T-shirt and hauled him out of the
coop, holding on to his neck.

I pulled the boy along, the .45 loose in my hand, my finger not even
on the trigger.

As I turned the corner, there was the same boy—a mirror—this one
in overalls and a slight bit older, with a rifle up to his shoulder and his
eye, smiling a dirty, rotten smile, no shoes and no shirt.

He spit and leveled the gun before half his head misted with a loud
boom.

As he slumped to the ground, Black was there behind him.

The boy I held caterwauled and fell to his knees, crawling to his
brother, the old twin, yelling, "Paw-paw. Paw-paw. He's gone. He's
gone, Paw-paw."

The boy screamed and held the dead boy's head against his chest,
covering his dirt-stained shirt in fresh blood.

Black looked down at them and shrugged, reaching down for the
dead boy's rifle and holding it just as the old man scrambled up the
landing, a gun in his left hand but not raised. Caught by the sight of his
two boys, he didn't even try.

"Drop it, old man," Black said. "Or I'll drop your hillbilly ass where
you stand."

Bert Fuller screamed nonsense from the floor of the cockfighting arena. Girls screamed and yelled from down below, the doors full open now, and the mass of them yelling for the outside and the light.

I looked down from the loft at Bert, defenseless in his pajamas and bedroom slippers. Him calling out my manhood.

"Bert, you are a true surprise."

"Come on, Murphy. Let's go, you sonofabitch."

"I'm tired," I said and threw down a pair of handcuffs I kept in my pocket. "You want me to come down there and do it myself?"

"I do, Murphy. I got you now."

"Yep, Bert," I said. "You got me right where you want me."

I looked over at Black. He'd cuffed the old man and the son behind their backs and tossed them into the same coop as the dead girl.

"You really hate these guys," I said.

"Got a good reason."

"Wanna tell me about it?"

"In time."

It didn't take much to restrain Fuller, and as I pushed him through the barn door and into daylight I saw the girls all standing by a hand pump and drinking with their hands as the water overflowed from buckets.

I asked the little girl in the man's shirt her age and she told me she was twelve.

"We have help coming."

I touched her shoulder and she jumped, running for the woods, moving so fast she lost the shoes on her bare feet.

WHEN LORELEI FINALLY CALLED, IT DIDN'T TAKE TWO SEC-onds for Billy to steal his father's car and drive over the river to find her. She said she'd been staying with a friend, and Billy soon found the friend was a six-foot-tall she-male named Chesty LaRue. They sat in the front yard of Chesty's little bungalow in a run-down section of old Victorians and beaten houses not far from the river in the old district and watched the children Chesty babysat on her off days. According to Chesty, the off days had been plenty. Billy would never have guessed that Chesty was a man unless Lorelei had whispered it to him, but the more Chesty talked, drinking a cup of coffee and smoking cigarettes in a Japanese robe, Billy could tell he had a mighty strong chin and a heavier brow that most ladies.

"Did I tell you about this one fella who liked me to sit in the corner with a lampshade on my head and say goo-goo?"

"Why he do that?" Billy asked.

"You never really want to know," Chesty said. "Take this one fella, he liked to be treated like a baby."

"Maybe he was just feelin' low," Billy said. And he looked over to Lorelei and smiled.

"You don't get it," Chesty said, adjusting the scarf he wore over his wigless head. "He liked to wear diapers and suck on a pacifier."

"Good God Almighty."

"I got some more stories."

"That's okay, Chesty," Lorelei said. "Thanks."

"You kids want some Coca-Cola?" she asked, just like any other mother on a hot summer day looking out for the neighborhood kids.

They said no thanks. Chesty clutched her robe tight against her chest as she walked, like she had something that would pop out.

"Do her fellas know she's a boy?" Billy asked.

"Some."

"Don't they go crazy?"

"Some like it."

"Get out of here."

"I think they don't feel as bad about bein' with a man if that man is dressed as a woman. You see what I mean?"

"Not really. I think I'd about fall out if I was with some girl and a big old wiener hopped out of her pants."

Lorelei laughed and put her finger to her lips, trying to quiet him down. "Chesty has been good to me. Lets me sleep on her couch. She's fed me and that means a lot, because I know she hasn't worked in weeks. She's thinking about moving to Cuba. Apparently, they like boys to be strippers down there, because they're more reliable than women, and they do all kind of freak shows, too."

Billy sat back on the steps and watched the dirty children playing in the yard. One big husky boy, maybe four, led three others in some kind of military drill, and when he stopped marching they all tumbled to a stop, about running into each other, and he turned and gave a salute, pulling out a plastic gun and making *bang-bang* noises.

"Let's get the hell out of here," Lorelei said. "Chesty's husband is coming back from Korea next week and that doesn't leave me with much time. You said something about California and that's fine by me. I think I can get enough up for gas money, and, if you already got your daddy's car, we can hit the road. Come on, say you will. I can be packed in a New York minute."

"How long is that?"

"Sure as hell faster than one in Alabama."

Billy gave her a weak smile. He leaned up from where he sat and watched the kids who had broken up into two different teams and were hiding behind scraggly little trees and pointing plastic guns, some of them in Indian feathers and cowboy hats, and the husky boy in a real military helmet. They made those *bang-bang* noises for a long time, and Billy was glad for them because they sure as hell filled in those long silences.

Lorelei pulled the black hair from her clear eyes and smiled.

BY THE END OF AUGUST, the blue-ribbon grand jury had handed down more than five hundred indictments against more than fifty crooks in Phenix City. The latest being Clanton, his common-law wife, and their surviving son, who looked at a stretch at Kilby for the rest of their lives or maybe the chair. Jack Black said they wouldn't know what to do in jail on account of it being so clean.

"Do you think they bathed?"

"I think if they'd seen a bar of soap," he said, "they would've eaten it."

We made daily trips out to the county dump where the Guard troops would haul roulette wheels and card tables and one-armed bandits and horse-racing machines. They'd back up heavy-duty flatbed trucks and dump the shiny chrome equipment into massive heaps before pouring on diesel and setting fire to them all.

I was always curious about why Black took so much enjoyment in this. It became almost some kind of ceremony for him as he'd light a cigar—usually from a box taken from some hood—and he'd smoke for a moment while the sun went down, before dropping it on the fuel, the whole thing going up in a blue woosh.

He'd stay long after I left home for supper, sitting at a good distance and watching the smoke trail high into the clouds and burn away, a big smile on his face and the ever-present bottle of Jack Daniel's waiting within easy reach.

WE LOADED DOWN THE EMPTY WOODEN GUN RACK OF THE sheriff's office a few weeks later. All the guns were new and oiled, their barrels and stocks gleaming in the early-morning light. We had a dozen shotguns, already cut down to eighteen inches for close work, and two Thompson machine guns that I'd bought from the Army surplus store across the river. I'd outfitted the men, for the most part, with long-barrel .38s, but Jack Black preferred having a .44 in hand just in case he had to shoot through an engine block to stop a getaway car. And although the big, hard violence had stopped for the meantime, we were pretty damn aware the fire could kick back up at any moment.

I moved over to the main desk, and deputies Jack Black and little Quinnie Kelley—in his Coke-bottle glasses and awkward new suit—checked out a couple of 12-gauges and then loaded their pistols. I refilled the cup of coffee I'd started at five a.m., right after my jog and some heavy-bag work. The police radio clicked and chattered at the front of the office.

"Drinking a pot of coffee ain't gonna make this much easier," Jack Black said.

"Thanks, Jack," I said. "I was kind of hoping it would."

Quinnie looked down at the ground and hoisted the pistol up on his right hip. I smiled, biting my lip. He still reminded me of a kid at Christmastime trying out a new toy.

Books on detective work and Alabama state law cluttered my desk, with empty coffee mugs, two full ashtrays, and a stack of green 45 records marked MR. x that I'd been logging into evidence. A Chamber of Commerce calendar for September 1954 hung on the wall, along with a certificate for me being the regional owner of the year for the Texaco Oil Corporation. Beside the certificate hung an autographed photo of Joe Louis.

I was much more proud of the Joe Louis picture.

"Well, hell," I said, "let's go."

I unhinged a long wooden bar and felt for a Winchester 12, feeling more ceremonial than useful, and closed the latch and slipped the padlock back on with a click.

I'd worn a new gray suit that morning—tailored at Chancellor's Men's Shop on Broadway—a pressed white shirt and striped tie. I'd even shined my Florsheim wingtips, and they clacked on the concrete floors with a steady confidence that I didn't feel as we made our way out back to an unmarked Chevy sedan and all climbed inside.

Quinnie and Jack were dressed in a similar way. We'd burned the old sheriff's office uniforms, dropping them right on top of the slots and card tables.

I closed the doors and waited till everyone climbed inside. I looked down at the wide, shiny console and the dangling car keys. Jack Black reached for them and said: "Why don't I drive, Sheriff?"

WE FOUND REUBEN AT HIS FARMHOUSE, ASLEEP IN THE driver's seat of his old Buick with the radio and headlights on. He didn't notice us until I tapped on the side window and he smiled, his eyes still closed, and smacked his lips, turning his head. I tapped again, and he opened his eyes and looked back and just stared at me, before yawning and mouthing, "'Mornin'."

I tapped on the glass, and he made a big show of stretching and dialing down the radio and rolling down the window. "Was I speedin', Officer?"

"You missed your court date."

"I was held up by unforeseeable circumstances."

"You were drunk."

He shook his head. "Last night? That ain't drunk."

"You have charges against you for running a gambling establishment with no liquor license."

Quinnie and Jack waited by the patrol car, Jack smoking a cigar and Quinnie standing with feet wide apart, his eyes narrowed, watching me and the car.

"How 'bout you come with us?"

He turned around in his seat and saw my deputies and started to laugh. He laughed so hard he started a short, hacking cough. "You made Quinnie Kelley a deputy? Lamar, you ought to be ashamed of yourself."

"He's a good man."

"For a munchkin. Only place he should be a deputy is in Oz."

"Open the door."

"Oh, for Christ's sake."

Reuben let out a breath, jimmied the handle, and used the big weight of the Buick's door to try to stand. His hair had gone dry without oil, and he wavered on his skinny legs. On the dashboard, I saw a pair of purple women's panties.

He saw me notice the panties and smiled.

"The car sure is spacious. Just like a living room."

Jack met me between the cars, and he didn't say much but turned Reuben and fit a pair of cuffs on him. I heard the thwap of the front screen door and saw Billy standing there watching us, and I saw Reuben look up at his boy and then back to me.

He just shook his head.

"You sure have changed, Red Irish."

I'd fought under the name the Red Irish Kid. He hadn't called me that in years.

"I miss you down at the filling station," Reuben said. "Can you talk to your father-in-law about keeping the cooler a little colder? I bought a Coca-Cola the other day and it was as warm as piss."

"Sure thing. I'll see what I can do."

"You know, bein' appointed sheriff ain't like being elected."

"I don't have your vote?" I asked.

"You really think the people want that?" Reuben said. "How are they supposed to work? Feed their kids? We just going to be a bunch of slaves on those mills over there. You know what that's like. Don't y'all see that?"

"I never knew you were such a moralist."

"You didn't need to come here and do this in front of my boy."

"It's my job," I said.

He looked at me and then back at Billy on the porch before Jack led him to the back of the car. "Well, open up the door, Quinnie," Reuben said. "You goddamn little munchkin."

THE PHONE ALWAYS RANG ABOUT DINNERTIME, AND THE calls came as expected as Joyce's pot roast with potatoes and carrots on a Wednesday night. I was halfway into my plate, a half-eaten white roll in my hand, complimenting the dinner, when the ringing started. I took a breath and pushed back my plate, even though Joyce had asked me to just unplug the damn thing from the wall. But I said I'd be right back and reached for the phone, the one with the listed number, not the personal one that we had installed in our bedroom, and answered with a pleasant hello.

Quit now and we won't kill you. Remember what happened to Hugh Britton? That's child's play.

"Well, hello," I said. "What's up, doc?"

You idiot. I said I'm gonna have your blood.

"I heard you. Everything going well with you?"

You goddamn moron. You turn in that fake badge of yours and step back.

"I sure appreciate your concern, mister. Do you know where I live?"

You're goddamn right.

I repeated the address.

"Come on by anytime, I'm not big on phone visits. We can talk, chat a bit, catch up on life. I'd love to meet in person."

You're one dead, crazy sonofabitch. You just a fillin' station grease monkey.

"Bye-bye, now. Have a good evening."

I walked back to the dinette table and started back into the roast.

Joyce flashed her eyes up at me and I smiled back at her and winked. She looked down.

Anne clattered on about her day at school and wondered when I'd be taking her out to the barn again to feed the horses.

"Maybe tomorrow," I said.

"Can we go to a movie on Saturday?"

"Sure."

Thomas sat next to me, working his fork awkwardly with his little fist and taking bites in the same motions and timing as I would. When Anne noticed what he was doing, she started to giggle, and Thomas grew embarrassed, looking down at his food, before looking back up and sticking out his tongue.

The phone rang again, this time in the bedroom, and Joyce stood and told me to sit down and finish my dinner. When she left the room, I poured out a cup of coffee from the silver pot.

By the time I sat back down, she was back. "It was Quinnie. He's headed on over."

I looked up.

"Some kind of trouble out at a place called King's Row. You know it?"

I shook my head. "Good thing about this work is you see places you never knew existed."

Joyce raised her eyebrows and went back to the kitchen to start the suds in the big sink.

QUINNIE DROVE THE NEW CHEVY WITH THE WINDOWS down, and we could smell burning leaves and trash fires coming off the hills, the first fallen leaves scattered like jigsaw pieces in the blowing wakes of cars passing them on the road to Seale. He drove close to the wheel and, despite the huge glasses he wore, squinted into the night. The headlights cut like blades into the black, wide-open country.

"What'd she say?"

"Two neighbors heard a couple gunshots and a woman screaming. One of them knocked on the door and the man there threatened to kill them, too."

"You got a name?"

Quinnie shook his head. "No, sir. Woman who called just told me and hung up."

We soon turned off the paved two-lane and drove down a winding gravel road bordered by dead cotton fields and a handful of clapboard shotguns. Quinnie took another nameless road, twisting back to the north, and we found a stretch of six shotgun shacks, not even six or eight feet between them despite endless fields and forests around them.

"My dad said the most comforting sound to a country man is to hear his neighbor's toilet flush," I said.

"Except for these people don't have flushing toilets."

Quinnie kept the patrol car, a flat black '54 Chevy, running and the headlights aimed at a group of fifteen or so people standing in a little mass and staring into the bright light. White, hardscrabble folks in overalls and housecoats, clutching babies and plates of food. Some of the men wandered around in the open with jelly jars full of clear liquid.

"You want me to stay here?" Quinnie asked.

"Why?"

"You know," Quinnie said, "on account I'm not a real deputy."

"Says who?"

"Ever'one knows the only reason you took me on was so I could carry a gun."

I nodded and opened the door. I looked over at the much smaller man with the big Coke-bottle glasses at the wheel. "I took you on as a witness. But you're doing a fine job."

"Really?"

"Come on."

"Yes, sir."

We walked into the swath of the headlights, the click and squawking sounds coming from the radio under the dash. A woman in curlers and a housecoat marched right up to me and pointed to the third house from the left and said there was a man inside who'd shot his wife and aimed to kill everyone on King's Row.

"That's what they call this place?"

"That's the name of the road," she said, a cigarette bobbing in her mouth. She held her housecoat closed, her slippers caked in orange mud, and then shuffled back to the background and clutched a young boy to her side.

I walked back to Quinnie and Quinnie stood like a gunfighter, hand on the butt of his .38, his jaw clamped.

"Call Jack and have him send a couple more deputies this way," I said. "I'm gonna try and talk to this fella."

"You want to wait for Jack?"

I shook my head and walked through a narrow walkway piled high with broken toys, produce boxes, and rusted car parts. An engine block rested on bricks on the front porch.

No light shone from the house.

I knocked on the screen door. And heard nothing.

I knocked again, harder.

"If you don't stop that, I'm going to blow a hole through that god-damn door."

"This is Sheriff Murphy," I said. "Just checking up to make sure y'all are all right."

"Mr. Murphy?" There was the sound of a heavy fist against a wall, and I heard the man begin to cry, not a sniffling kind of cry but a deep broken wail that almost rattled the house. "It's me, Phil."

"May I come in?"

The wail only grew louder, and I tried the doorknob.

A mammoth blast blew out two front windows by the door, and I dropped to the beaten porch, covering my head with my hands. Two more deputy cars arrived and shone their lights up onto the shotgun house while I crawled back behind the safety of the patrol cars. I stood and ran my hands over my filthy suit.

"Doesn't want to talk?" Jack Black asked.

"How'd you get that idea?"

Black nodded. "Want to flush him out?"

"Guess we have to."

Two other deputies I'd taken on rolled behind the house with scoped hunting rifles, and Black and Quinnie stayed behind the doors of the car. I took out a 16-gauge Browning, a Sweet Sixteen, from the trunk of the Chevy and closed the trunk with a hard clack.

An hour later, the man yelled for one of you sonsabitches to come on in and work out his terms of freedom.

"Terms of freedom?" Black asked.

"Sounds reasonable to me," I said.

"I wouldn't do that."

"Oh, hell," I said, handing the shotgun to Jack.

I walked up the broken steps again to the porch, unarmed and with my hands in the air. I stepped to the open door that let out a hot, filthy smell like a mouth of a human and called out the man.

I moved inside, where the air seemed superheated and dimly lit with a kerosene lantern. Something moved to my left, in the corner of my eye, and I turned and saw a big man with no shirt and dirty brown trousers holding another lantern to his face. A large red welt covered half of his face, dropping it into red shadow, a partial mask.

"She threw hot mush on me."

I nodded.

"I beat her for it. I cain't let something like that go."

"Where's she?"

"She in with the kids, got a butcher knife in her hands as long as my arm."

"You shoot her?"

"I tried, but the dang bitch moves too fast."

"She stab you?"

He shined the light onto his side, showing a bloodied shirt. "Sort of," he said. "Mr. Murphy, you don't remember me, do you?"

I looked at him.

"I used to come in the filling station all the time. Had that '49 Hudson with all them brake problems. You set me up that time when I couldn't pay for gas. I brung it back to you."

"Sure, partner," I said.

The man smiled and nodded.

And I began to walk through the hall of the shotgun, noting holes in the wall and blood smears. I pulled a flashlight from my pocket.

"Mr. Murphy?" I turned back, facing the front door. "Cain't let her go. You understand. She said she's going back to Atlanta to be with her folks and I cain't understand that. You know what I mean. A woman cain't just decide something like that."

I kept walking. I heard a cylinder click into a gun.

I turned back to look at the man and the man saw something in my eyes that made him lower the hammer.

I flashed the light into a small room with wooden walls and floor. Three small iron beds running side to side. Against the wall, and in the narrow scope of light, I twisted my head to see a small woman with a bloodied face, nose broken and bent, crying into the shoulder of a child not even two years old.

She had welt marks on her neck and cigarette burns across her forearms. Her face looked like a piece of rotten fruit.

"Come on, ma'am."

"Where?" She snuffled and coughed.

"Out of here."

I turned to the hall, and the man stood with the kerosene lantern in his left hand and the .38 to his head.

"They cut the power Tuesday before last. I ain't had work since all you shut down the town."

"Where'd you work?"

"Atomic Bomb Café, for Mr. Yarborough," he said. "Worked for Mr. Yarborough for fifteen years."

I kept the flashlight low, and across a table I saw a milk bottle half empty and an open bag of white bread. Three bowls sat on the table with a mush that looked like gray paste.

"You try the mills?"

He nodded. "They ain't ate in three days. I brung all this and all that woman did was cuss me out."

He screwed the gun into his ear, ramrod straight, and shut his eyes. "Phil."

Jack Black moved through the open front door, a hulking, silent shadow, a shotgun perched in his shoulder, the barrel stretched out before him. A floorboard creaked, and the man closed his eyes.

The man took a breath, not making a sound, tears running down his scalded face. He opened his eyes, as if coming wide awake, and dropped the gun, it falling with a clack to the floor.

"This town is a goddamn mess," he said. "Why'd you do that, Mr. Murphy? Why'd y'all go and do that?"

JOHNNIE AND MOON SLIPPED BACK OVER THE COUNTY LINE sometime that night. Johnnie had stolen one of those new Dodges, a Custom Royal Lancer convertible with a big ole V-8. He'd seen it on the commercial where they called it having "Flair Fashion," and with a personality as new as tomorrow's headlines. The damn dashboard looked like something in an airplane, quick and round, right there before him. Nice two-tone paint job in pink and black, with fat white-walls, and tight-nubbed fins in back. He popped on the lighter in the dash and told Moon to get his fat fucking feet off the dash 'cause he was acting just like a durn nigger.

Moon grunted and shifted, a shotgun between his legs. Johnnie didn't think he'd ever seen Moon without the shotgun, almost an extension of his hand as he walked around his still, checking the corn liquor coming out and stoking that fire. That fat sonofabitch was stupid as hell but kept his mouth shut. He wasn't too sure about Reuben these days. On account of the way he acted when he'd offered up rob-bing Hoyt Shepherd. He didn't figure Reuben had gone straight, but maybe he'd gone soft, like he was thinking of getting a job for a living.

That man had been crooked since before the war. Johnnie remembered seeing him take a five-hundred-dollar payday, right there in the back of Hoyt's Southern Manor, to take a dive on some no-talent wop from Philadelphia who he could've pounded into the canvas with one hand.

"You with me?"

Moon grunted.

"If they stop us," he said, "we just huntin'."

Moon nodded.

"Listen, you know Veto's Trailer Park? Right down the road from the Skyline Club and the El Dorado Motel?"

Moon nodded.

"We get in there, get the work done, and we'll be on our way. We can get rid of the mess somewhere downriver."

Johnnie's eyes caught the intermittent flash of streetlights up on telephone poles as he turned down Crawford Road. He looked at a group of soldiers standing and talking in the parking lot of Sam's Motel and shook his head.

"They make me sick," he said. "They act like they own the goddamn town. If they didn't have all those tanks and guns, I'd personally ace them off the goddamn planet."

The fall air felt good from the open top of the convertible and he took a hit from the pint between his legs. He rolled slow and easy, not caring if they spotted the car because they'd ditch the car sometime later tonight and steal another.

He listened to the radio and turned down the road to Opelika and passed by Kemp's Drive-In and the Hillbilly Club and turned in to Veto's Trailer Park, the white lights in the crooked arrow calling them on in.

Moon spit out of the window and broke apart the shotgun, thumbing in a couple shells from the bib of his overalls. He wiped his mouth with his forearm and hoisted his fat ass up out of the Dodge. The whole car flattened down for a moment as he balanced on the door, and then he waddled toward the Airstream, a perfect little stainless steel egg of a trailer, walking with no gun, only a good ten feet of rope in his hand.

"YOU WANT TO SEE YOUR DAD?"

"No," Billy said. "I came to see you."

"Go ahead."

"Not with them," he said. "Can we go to the office?"

We'd just come back from King's Row, Billy coming up from the back door to the sheriff's office and meeting us inside the chain-link parking lot. He was cold and his teeth chattered, standing in a white T-shirt, jeans, and sneakers.

He seemed glad we went back to my office, and I closed the door behind us.

"Can I have a cup of coffee?"

"Sure," I said, and I got him one from a pot Jack had made that morning, smelling bitter and burnt.

The kid didn't seem to notice and drank it down anyway.

"Your dad is getting out tomorrow."

"You think he killed Mr. Patterson?"

I looked to him, the question coming out of nowhere.

I shook my head. "Why do you say that?"

"I just figured that's why you brought him in."

"We brought him in on two counts of running a gambling establishment and a bunch of other charges on violating the liquor laws and having slots."

"Is he going to jail?"

I shrugged. "He may. How bad is that coffee?"

"Tastes fine to me."

I sat on the edge of my desk. Billy's right leg jumped up and down with nerves, reminding me of the way I felt before a fight, wanting to go ahead and get to it.

"What'd you come to see me about?"

He looked out the open window, where you could see down the hill and just make out the lights over the river to Georgia. The night air smelled of rain.

"I need you to do me a favor."

"Sure, bud."

"You remember that girl I was with back in the summer? The one that Fuller tried to beat on."

"Lorelei?"

"Yes, sir."

I waited.

"She's gone. I can't find her anywhere and I've been looking everywhere. I think somethin' bad's happenin'. I don't know what. But I think they got her."

"Who?"

"The people she told you about. She was real scared after what happened at the Rabbit Farm."

"Who else knows she talked to me?"

He shrugged.

ARCH FOUND HIMSELF AWAKE at three a.m., walking the woods near his house with a whiskey bottle, wandering around the endless acres of pine trees with deep thoughts of Bastogne and those holes that would explode and swell like an open wound and bullets that would whiz by your ear but miss you, as if you were protected by the hand of God. His men buried deep in foxholes, their feet frozen black and purple, the snow mixed with the ash from the broken forest. As Arch weaved in and out of the maze, the fall moon hanging low, full and bright, he lost himself for a moment, half expecting to see his breath crystallize before him. Instead, he stopped, his heart jackhammering in his chest, and took another drink. He decided to walk back to his house for his keys and shaving kit. He stopped for only a moment, Madeline awake now, and kissed her on the cheek and told her he'd be right back.

"Arch?" she asked. "Where are you going?"

But he had already started his car, a new-model Pontiac, and he turned quickly from the gravel and the new boxed ranch with big modern glass windows that let in plenty of light and out onto the open road, the moon a traveling friend as he headed back to the soft glow of

Phenix, soon finding the turn to Highway 80 and Montgomery. He lit endless cigarettes and finished the last of the Jack Daniel's, both hands on the wheel and sweating, hearing only the purr of the big motor and the warm morning air coming in through the windows as he got to Montgomery, quickly cutting south and soon finding daybreak just around Fort Deposit. But it was a false dawn, just purple and black, and in the darkness he watched the Alabama city signs flash by, in minutes and hours or seconds, coming right after one another. GREENVILLE, CHAPMAN, EVERGREEN, CASTLEBERRY, POLLARD, FLOMATON, ATMORE. And soon it was midmorning, and he looked at the scruffy, unshaven face in the rearview mirror before crossing the bridge over Mobile Bay and through the little town of Grand Bay—where he stopped for two cups of coffee, gas, and to use the bathroom—and then over the Mississippi line, hugging the green shore of the Gulf of Mexico, and the little beach towns mixed with the big ones, taking him to places he hadn't been in years, not since becoming county solicitor in '47, and he crossed through Pascagoula, Biloxi, Gulfport, Pass Christian, and over the St. Louis Bay. It was late summer, and children played on wide green lawns and people sat on wide stately porches built sometime around the Civil War, living in their own world covered in a canopy of ancient oaks disguised in those sloppy beards of moss.

Before he knew it, he was in Louisiana, with New Orleans seeming like a dream. In the roughneck town of Morgan City, he stopped for a piss again and found himself in a vile, filthy bathroom puking in a dirty toilet, and when he washed his face in the lavatory he had no idea why his nerves had acted up.

He bought a Coca-Cola and a piece of fried chicken to settle himself, pumping gas, and moving on over the bayou in New Iberia and Lafayette. It all was a storybook down there, with the wildness of it all and all the little waterways and clapboard shacks and sunburned people with sharp eyes who seemed to see something in the man with the Alabama plates that made them stare. Hell, he wasn't even tired by the time he hit the Texas line and Port Arthur by Sabine Lake and hugged the lapping green waves of the Gulf, feeling stifled and hot and sweaty even though the windows were down, the Gulf and Texas bringing him nothing but humidity and hellfire gospels and twangy country music on the radio.

He knew that if he was caught, they'd revoke his bond, but he was sick of just sitting on the couch smoking cigarettes and drinking Jim Beam and watching *The Lone Ranger* and the *Adventures of Superman* on television with his daughter. And Madeline not talking to him, lying next to him at night, wide awake with worry because she just knew he'd killed Mr. Patterson even though he'd sworn he had nothing to do with it.

When he got near Galveston, he found a city park to change into a seersucker suit and black shoes. He mopped his face with a fresh handkerchief the whole ride out onto Galveston Island, listening to a sermon about the dangers of vanity and how even the slightest bit could invite the devil for dinner in your very home. The man said it as if the devil was a little red man in a red satin suit who could pass you the peas.

Arch found a circular drive winding its way to a grand old Victorian with a big wide porch where people in white spoke to each other from rocking chairs and played chess and cards. It looked like a postcard of heaven.

There was a nurse and then a doctor and then another nurse, and then finally they brought him out back to a soft little garden under two big oaks, a fine view facing the Gulf. A group of five or six people played croquet, and they laughed and cheered with each other, in their short pants and knit shirts, and, to Arch, they didn't seem to be all that crazy.

He took off his coat and sat by the fountain under the canopy of oak arms with curtains of Spanish moss. He unbuttoned his tie and lit a cigarette, the aftereffects of the booze from a day ago floating through his head. He took a long breath as if it was his first since first starting his car early that morning.

Then he heard the squeak and turned to see Si Garrett being pushed along in a wheelchair, one arm and one leg in a cast, his neck in a high brace, looking like a curious turtle, his eyes magnified by those great circular glasses.

The nurse in the little white hat left them. Si didn't say anything, and Arch just sat on the edge of the fountain, it trickling down in a soothing way along the rocks, mixing in a nice way with the Gulf surf.

"They don't keep score," Si said, finally.

Arch looked to him.

"Every one of them is crazy but doesn't know it," he said. Arch could tell it was hard for him to enunciate with the brace on his neck. "I told them I could keep score, you know. I can write with my left hand, and since I don't seem to have much else to do I thought they would appreciate it."

"When are you coming back?"

"That's up to Dr. Edwards."

"Who's that?"

"My physician."

"I didn't figure he was your barber."

"It's in God's hands now," Garrett said. "I tried to come back. You know that. But it wasn't meant to be."

"You think God made you crash that car?"

"I felt the strangest sensation in my fingers before I veered off the road, as if someone had pulled my hands from the controls, to show me the way."

"They showed you into a fucking tree."

"Perhaps."

"That's funny," Arch said, squinting into the smoke and watching the surf, feeling like Seale, Alabama, was on the other side of the earth. But he was ready to take that drive back just the same because it wasn't a place he wanted to leave. It was a place where he wanted to make a stand. "I just kind of wanted to hear you say it."

"Say what?"

"That you are a coward in hiding."

"Are you angry?"

"Hell, no. I'm not angry. Why in God's name would I be angry? My life has just been flushed down the toilet."

"Would you push me to the ramp over there? The sunset looks so beautiful out in the ocean. The water looks like emeralds and gold."

Arch stood behind Si Garrett and pushed his heavy mass around the garden and the croquet court and up onto a wooden landing and a small boardwalk. They were in full sun now, but every few moments the sun would dip back into a stray cloud or two.

The two men watched the surf. They watched the sun drop near the lip of the ocean. They didn't speak for a long time.

"Just what happened in that alley, Arch? Where did all this go so very wrong?"

"Nothing went wrong," Arch said. "Everything went according to your plan. You said what we did was for the state of Alabama and that you'd protect us all. But where did you go, Si? Are you hiding in there?"

Si just looked out at the water.

"I never hurt a soul," Arch said. "I dare any man to say that what I did was wrong."

A COUPLE OF GUARDSMEN FOUND HER LATER THAT NIGHT. She must've been there for at least a day, they said, broken and bleeding on a big gray slab of rock on the banks of the Chattahoochee. Her dress had been torn away, and the hard rains from the night before had left her shriveled and pale, her body curled and white on top of the rock dimpled with pocks of green mossy water. The men had been walking patrols and had heard her animal cries, until the swath of their flashlights found her body. She was naked and bloody and resembled something out of an old mariner's book. Her breathing came in ragged gasps of air and muddy water.

They'd figured her ribs were broken, from the redness and black bruises. She'd lost a lot of blood.

I figured she probably had been dumped upriver, and kept alive in the current until she hit that big rock, somehow climbing to the top, finding a foothold in the night. It took the guardsmen an hour to make it out to her and pull her into the boat, covering her with a standard-issue Army blanket.

She was nearly dead by the time she got to the hospital, in shock and vomiting buckets. They gave her a shot and pumped her stomach.

The doctors told me she'd been junked full of heroin and raped. Her face had been beaten bloody by fists, not the rocks, and both arms were broken and a leg. They told me how many ribs were broken, but I don't recall.

I didn't even recognize her, the only identifying mark came from Billy, who had told me about the number tattooed on her bottom lip.

"Will she live?" he asked me later that night. He sat in the front seat of the black Chevy. The only illumination came from the panel's dash and the red light on my radio.

The radio clicked on, and our dispatcher said an old woman needed help starting her car. I turned it off.

"I don't know," I said.

He just looked ahead through the big, broad front windshield. We didn't talk for a long time. It was night and no light came from his house. I asked him if he needed any money.

"No, sir."

"Would you like to come home with me? Just for a few days."

"No, sir."

"You can talk to your daddy, if you like."

He shook his head. He started to cry, but his voice was firm as he spoke. He told me about his daddy being a worthless drunk and having friends who were mean and violent, his father too stupid to know he was being led around by his nose.

"When are y'all gonna arrest the man who killed Mr. Patterson?"

"That's a question I get about every day. It's real complicated."

"But you know who killed him."

I nodded. I leaned my head back and took a deep breath. "Listen, let me buy you dinner over at Kemp's."

"What if someone saw what happened? Could you get them?"

"Yes, we could," I said.

Billy nodded, agreeing with a decision he'd already made.

LATER ON, I STOPPED BY THE SHERIFF'S OFFICE AND WENT down into Reuben's cell to give him a cup of coffee and a pack of cigarettes. He was up off his bunk and pacing, and when I walked in he knocked the coffee out of my hand, telling me that I was no better than Bert Fuller.

It was past midnight and hot as hell down in the jail basement. Most of the cells were full of prostitutes and some negro Bug writers we'd picked up. They groaned and insulted me as they saw me, calling me "mister" and "boss." Reuben should have been gone, but I went ahead and kept him an extra couple days to see if he'd open up a bit.

I was glad now.

"I seen the judge. He set a court date. I know my bond is paid."

"How do you know that?"

"'Cause my dang lawyer was just here and he told me. He said you're hiding behind this martial-rule thing and don't have a lick of sense when it comes to the law."

"He's probably right."

"Don't you smile at me, you goddamn sonofabitch."

"Take it easy, Reuben."

"Take it easy? You ain't been kept in this hellhole for four days. I need a shower and shave. Do you know I got to shit in that toilet over there that doesn't have a seat? About every time I get close to using it, they bring in some whores down this row and they look in on me like I was a monkey in a cage."

"You'll be out tomorrow."

"I want out tonight."

"You sure you don't want that cup of coffee?"

He snorted and sat back down on the bunk. He ran his hands through his hair like he thought about tearing it out. The oil had dried on his pompadour and it stuck up wild. He wore a pair of beige slacks and a men's undershirt that was stained with sweat, dust, and dirt.

His shoes sat near the bunk without laces.

"Look at you, with that fifty-dollar suit on with that ruby pin and slick tie. Don't give me no pity, Lamar. That just about turns my stomach."

I tossed him the pack of Lucky Strikes. He shook his head and tore open the pack, tucking a dry one in the corner of his mouth and continuing to talk. "You didn't have to do me like that. Arrest me in front of my boy. You have a son. You didn't have to do that."

He looked straight at the brick wall, away from me, and stared.

"A while back, we found a whole barn full of girls, most of them children," I said. "They'd been locked up without food or water. One of them died. Another one of them was twelve. Tonight, we fished your boy's girlfriend out of the Chattahoochee. She'd been beaten to the point Billy couldn't recognize her. She'd been stomped and her ribs went into her lungs."

He nodded. "Did I have anything to do with that? I run a beer joint. I got some slots. How in God's name can a man make money in Phenix any other way? This town has always been like that. You know it was an Indian outpost before the war, that this was the last place to get a woman and a drink before sliding into redman's land?"

I shook my head. "You don't get it. She was a friend of Billy's."

"That girl knew what she was into."

"That's pretty rough."

He lit the cigarette and shrugged. "Don't you drag me into your morality play."

"I need your help," I said.

"If that don't beat all."

"I can get you a deal with the judge. He can get you in and out of Kilby in less than six months."

"That's mighty white of you, Lamar."

"You were there when Mr. Patterson was gunned down. You were parked across from the Elite."

Reuben stood, just inches away from my nose. His face had turned a shade, his breathing quick, that sly, perpetual cockiness melted away. "Where did you hear such a god-awful lie?"

"I didn't say you killed him. I said you were there. You saw something important. On that street."

"I didn't see a thing."

"You're a liar."

"You wouldn't even been on half the title cards if it wasn't for me. You rode my coattails for five fucking years. You know the Kid didn't even want to train you till I begged him. You remember when he'd be gone for the night and I'd stay and I'd teach you to keep your feet, keep your head in a fight. You remember how you were all arms and elbows, tripping over your legs? Who stayed with you in that shithole gym till somethin' clicked in your head and you could move your goddamn feet?"

"You didn't correct me."

"'Bout what?"

"Bein' a liar."

He stepped back.

"You don't know half the things I done for you since Mr. Patterson gone and got himself killed. If I hadn't stepped in, we wouldn't be talking."

I waited. I watched him.

He paced.

"You hear me?"

"Billy needs a daddy," I said. "Make a deal, serve your time, and get out. It's over."

He pushed me with the flat of his hand and spun to face me, jabbing me hard in the eye with the left and knocking me back. I lost my feet for a moment and then caught myself against the row of bars.

I used the bars to right myself.

Jack Black appeared on the other side, his hand on his gun.

"It's okay, Jack," I said. "Let him out."

"Sir?"

I felt the egg forming under my eye. I looked at Reuben and shook my head. "Go ahead and let him go. I'm done with him."

Reuben spit on the ground between us, his fists hanging ready at his side.

"Just one question," I said. "Just how long did it take y'all to blow Hoyt's safe and get back to town?"

A FEW DAYS LATER, JOHN PATTERSON INVITED ME TO GO fishing with him on Lake Harding. It was a brisk fall day, and we stood on the shoreline of some cleared land and cast our Zebcos out into the dammed-up Chattahoochee. We sat in easy chairs, talking about our children and the weather, and some about his mother, Agnes, and some man from Hollywood named Diamond who wanted to come to Phenix City and make a picture about what happened to his father.

"He has a script," Patterson said. "I've seen it. He has me in a slugfest with some kingpin named Red. I'm pretty sure he got the idea for this Red fella from Hoyt Shepherd. He's a fat good-ole-boy type who pretty much runs the town."

"Maybe he's based on Red Cook."

"No, this guy is more likable. He's the kind of guy quick with a joke and a wink but will kill you all the same. And then there is an honest girl who deals cards in a casino. She's smart and beautiful but can't find her way out."

"Who else is in it?"

"He's made me into some kind of hero. He liked the idea of me taking over the martyred father's nomination. But he said it wasn't dramatic enough, so he has me calling the governor at the end of the film and has everyone in Phenix City yelling into the phone for justice."

"How are they all on the phone?"

"It's some kind of crowd scene. Who knows?" John stood and cast his hook again, and let the bobber stay, and then sat back in the chair and offered me a beer, which I declined.

"You never drink, do you?"

"Not for a long time."

"There a story behind that?"

"Not a good one."

John nodded. "Anyway, I don't have much to do with this. But this Diamond fella, I think he's from New York, wants to film it here. He said it's the kind of story that has to be shot in the South. It can't be some Hollywood back lot."

"Seems like a story without an ending."

"He thinks it's over."

"What do you think?"

"Not by a mile."

"Have you spoken with Sykes?"

John shifted in his chair and pulled a ball cap down in his eyes. He shifted the rod and took a sip of beer. "I have."

"You don't seem too happy about it."

"I don't know what he's up to. He must have two dozen prosecutors and investigators interviewing every soul who was even close to Fifth Avenue on June eighteenth. They have maps, building blueprints, models, and photos of every angle of my dad's Rocket 88. Hundred interviews with people who heard shots, saw someone parking a car, saw anyone walk close to that alley. In my opinion, it's a calculated mess. An equation that everything implied means absolutely zero."

"No one who saw anything."

"Besides Quinnie. But Sykes believes Quinnie will be cut to pieces on the witness stand because he changes his story. At first he saw a man he didn't know and then later says it was Arch Ferrell."

"He was scared."

"Sure he was. But think what they'll make of those big glasses he wears. You don't think they'll call his eyesight into question?"

"And no one else saw a thing."

"People saw a car. They heard the shots. They saw a man leaving that alley. A group of teenagers moving some office equipment out of the Coulter Building saw my dad dying on that sidewalk. So did Hugh

Bentley's mother, at her grocery, after hearing those shots. They've been keeping it real quiet about Fuller's prints on the car."

I nodded. "But those can be explained away."

"Of course they can. Fuller can say he was talking to my dad the day before the killing or accidentally touched the car after the murder. Hell, he was the lead investigator on the case."

"Now we have Fuller or Ferrell."

"Or both," John said.

"Or both," I said.

John finished the beer and placed the empty bottle back in the cooler. I lit a cigarette and settled back, feeling a little tug on my line and seeing the bobber disappear and then pop back up. I didn't jerk the rod because I wanted the damn fish to swallow the hook whole and that quick move always lost me the fish.

"Hilda Coulter is getting some threats," I said. "Someone has been following her, tried to run her off the road."

"Fuller's buddies."

"You know about what happened to that girl?"

"The prostitute?"

"Yes."

"These are evil people, Lamar. Sodom doesn't have a thing on Phenix City."

"Hilda didn't want Jack in the flower shop, said he'd make a spectacle of himself," I said. "So he's just keeping an eye out for her. At night, he has a couple boys keeping watch outside her house."

"I get those phone calls, too. So many, I don't even answer the phone. Mostly, they say, 'Do you want to end up like your daddy?,' or they threaten my kids. I had a few of them checked out. But they always go back to pay phones. Not a lot you can do. Oh, that was the other thing."

"What?"

"The picture. In the script, some of the gangsters drive by my house and drop a dead colored girl in the front yard."

"Why?"

"I think the colored girl has a note pinned to her saying this could happen to my child."

"That's pretty rough."

"Diamond says you have action every five minutes in a picture or else people will fall asleep. How 'bout you? How you like being sheriff now?"

"I make less than half what I made running the filling station."

"But you are running."

"You bet."

"So there must be something you like."

"I think I look good in a suit."

"That shiner looks pretty good, too. You mind me asking where you got it?"

I touched the place under my eye that had already turned purple, the swelling almost gone. "Had a little fight with a friend."

I told him about it.

"So that was the last time you saw Stokes?" John asked, hooking another worm, squinting into the early-afternoon light.

I nodded.

"Did he leave town?"

"I'm not sure."

"And he knows what happened to my dad?"

"You bet."

REUBEN DROVE DOWN to Panama City Beach, Florida, one morning in late October, turned in to the Flamingo Motel just around two and parked right in the vacant lot, knowing the beach was a hell of a place when summer died. He killed the Buick's engine and combed his hair in the rearview, knocking on the door that Johnnie had told him to, right next to the ice machine. The whole motel built of cinder blocks and painted a bright pink, with a big old sign outside with a flamingo in front of a palm tree. Reuben knocked again and heard some movement inside, and the door gave. He stepped back a little.

The door creaked wide open to the cooling breeze off the ocean in the dead motel and the hum of the ice machine.

Reuben pulled out the .38 from the flat of his back and toed the door, opening it wider, and saw a flame kick up in the darkness. Johnnie Benefield, with no shirt and a pair of swim trunks, fanned out the match and showed the palms of his hands, "No tricks, okay?"

"Stand up," Reuben said.

Johnnie did and he turned around like a little girl in a recital.

"Who's in the toilet?"

"Nobody."

"Where's Fannie?"

"Working on her tan."

"A little cold for that."

"Fannie's a brave woman. Now close the door and let's talk."

There was a little table by the plateglass window; big, heavy plastic curtains shut tight. Reuben walked inside and then past Johnnie—but still watching Johnnie—and checked the crapper and behind the shower curtain.

"You are a riddle."

"Don't you trust me?" Johnnie said.

"I drove all morning, didn't I?"

Reuben took a seat. Johnnie plunked down a bottle of Jack Daniel's and two of those little motel glasses. He cracked open the fresh bottle, still in the sack, and pushed an ice bucket forward.

"You want some ice?"

Reuben shook his head.

"Go get my fucking money," Johnnie said.

"I didn't bring it."

"I don't believe you."

Reuben took a sip and tossed him the keys to the Buick. "Check for yourself."

He shook his head. "You dumb sonofabitch. Where is it?"

"I haven't touched it since the night we robbed Hoyt. Scouts' honor."

Johnnie stubbed out his cigarette and took a seat across from Reuben at the tiny motel table. "Did you know that Fannie sunbathes with no top on? She doesn't care who sees her, and if some maid or someone says something to her she'll tell them to eat shit. You don't believe me, look outside and you can see her big titties from here."

"I didn't get the money 'cause I can't get to it. Every damn move, I'm bein' watched. I've been in jail for four days. Lamar Murphy is riding my ass."

Johnnie smiled, those big teeth showing like a hick car salesman's. "I don't believe a goddamn word you say. I'll ask you again, where is my fucking money?"

Reuben poured himself some more Jack Daniel's. "Can you really see her titties from here?"

"Sure thing, boss."

Reuben stood and walked to the back of the motel unit, looked out a little square window and saw a redheaded woman in white sunglasses. She was slick with sweat, red lipstick on, and, as advertised, big titties pointing toward the sky. "Well, I'll be."

Reuben turned with the glass in hand, and when he fell into a sliver of light from those big plastic drapes Johnnie had a gun on him. It was a .38 just like Reuben's. Everybody seemed to have .38s.

"What if I decided to paint the fucking wall with your head?"

Reuben walked in front of the mirror and checked his hair again, watching his face, those droopy Mitchum eyes.

"Then you are dumber than I thought. You'll never be able to cash out."

The .38 clicked and fell onto a void space in the gun, and Johnnie showed those big old choppers again and said: *"Pow!"*

THEY TOOK THE BOTTLE AND WANDERED OUT BY THE swimming pool facing the beach, seeing Florida's Gulf Coast "Famous Sugary Sand," just like on the billboards. Reuben had also heard it called the "Redneck Riviera," but it was early fall and the rednecks had all gone, leaving the miniature golf courses, shell shops, and oyster houses empty. And even though Fannie had decided to tan her boobs in the cool air, there was no one around but him and Johnnie to see them.

Reuben walked ahead and Johnnie hung back, finding a place to sit on the diving board. He had the motel glass in his hand and pulled on a pair of black plastic sunglasses, Reuben knowing that Johnnie must've thought he looked like a movie star in his head.

Reuben looked down at Fannie, who lay on a pink beach towel protected by a cardboard windscreen, the inside shiny metallic to pull in the sun. With her white sunglasses on, he couldn't tell if she'd heard him walk up or not until he heard her say, "You're blocking the sun."

Reuben looked behind him, squinting, and stepped back.

"You got it?"

"No, ma'am."

The inside of the silver walls looked like a little nest, with the clear bottle of Johnson's baby oil and two more pink towels and some copies of movie-star magazines showing off Star of the Year Audrey Hepburn.

"Pull up a seat."

"You want to put something on?"

"Reuben, how many times have you seen my titties?"

"I don't reckon I recall."

"Exactly."

Fannie's white skin had grown reddish, her face flushed. She was a curvy woman, with ample hips and just the slightest hint of a belly. She turned to drink a cocktail from the straw, and Reuben noticed her backside was big but nicely shaped. When she finished with the drink, she looked over her shoulder and caught him staring.

"We heard you threw in with Lamar Murphy."

Reuben laughed. "You lost your mind."

"Aren't you two big buddies?"

"Not anymore."

She nodded and turned back over. "Don't you hate it when the summer is over and you know everything is going to get all brown and ugly? I try to keep it going for as long as I can. I can tan in this little hotbox all through January. I saw the advertisement in the back of *Vogue* magazine. It's all the rage in France."

"You don't say."

"You know Johnnie will kill you if you don't bring him the money."

He nodded.

"I heard Clyde Yarborough's in with you, too."

"Johnnie sure likes to run his mouth."

"He talks in his sleep."

Reuben pulled up a plastic chair and watched as Fannie flipped through the pages of *Vogue* and then tossed it away and then shielded her face with a copy of *Look*. Cover story on Deborah Kerr, another crazy redhead.

Reuben just waited.

"What's it gonna take?"

"Jesus H. Christ. Would you two let things cool off? I just got out of jail."

"For what?"

"I slept in my court date."

"Murphy arrest you?"

He nodded.

"He sure has a hard-on for you. What the hell did you ever do to him?"

"Not a damn thing. He just thinks he's a big man 'cause of the badge. He came out to arrest me at my farm, right in front of my boy. And he kept me there longer than the law said."

"Why'd he do that."

"To play with my head. I 'bout knocked him out cold, too."

"You hit him?"

"Sure did. That's when he asked me how long it took to rob Hoyt. But I could tell he didn't know a thing. He just threw it out at me, waiting to see how I'd react, but I didn't say nothin'."

Fannie turned back over, sitting on her butt and pulling her knees up to her titties. She tucked her sunglasses up on her head and squinted at Reuben. "Did boxing really mess your brain up that bad, sweetie?"

"What?"

"Murphy has someone who tipped him off, and if you don't tell the sonofabitch what you saw in that alley he's gonna let you deal with Hoyt."

"He didn't mean it. He'd never do that. He was fishing."

"How'd you like to make a friendly wager?"

THE COFFEE WAS ON AND THE KIDS IN BED JUST AS I SAW the big headlights flash into my driveway and cross over the television and shine on the knotty-pine wall. It was election night, and I'd just returned from the sheriff's office, taking phone calls and later meeting with Hugh Britton and some folks from the RBA. I met Jack out back on my porch as Joyce finished up putting up the leftovers. I'd taken off the suit and wore a gray sweatshirt and workout pants from hitting the heavy bag in four rounds counted off by Thomas on my Bulova after supper. He liked to keep the time on me.

Just as he stepped inside, I handed Jack the mug of coffee and could tell by his whiskey breath he needed it. He sat on a folding chair at the edge of the deck.

He shook my hand, "Congratulations, Sheriff."

"I was the only one running."

"But now it's official."

You could smell the smoldering of burning leaves from my neighbor.

"I let out those two drunks from the other night," Black said. "That car was a real mess. I don't think they're even gonna have it towed."

I drank the coffee. I lit a cigarette.

There was a harvest moon tonight, and, in the black sky, it looked absolutely huge. One of those times that the moon felt as large as the earth and you could reach out and touch it.

"I need to tell you something, Lamar."

"You're not leaving, are you?"

He shook his head. Jack had let his hair grow back like a civilian, and his sideburns had gotten long and dark. He still wore his gray suit and jacket, black tie and shoes, a badge clipped to his belt.

"You know by the time I jumped at Normandy, I wasn't scared. We'd been in Italy, and those combat nerves were gone. It's kind of like getting sex—the first time you do it, you worry about not making a mess."

"I bet it's a little different."

"But there was one night in France when the Germans were trapped on each side by some hedgerows. They had to either run through them and get shot down in a big open field or go right for these two big Sherman tanks. Some ran right for the tanks, and, as we followed, we had to step over their bodies. Can you imagine running for a tank? Some of them were dead, flattened like pancakes by the tracks, some of them half dead, crying out in German for their mamas or Hitler or their souls."

I drank some coffee.

"I spent my twentieth birthday at the Bulge," he said, not touching his coffee yet. The steam rose off the top, the cup still in his hands. His eyes unfocused and clouded. "I guess what I'm saying is, I'm not the sensitive type."

"Never figured that, Jack."

"Did you know my real name is Rudolph?"

"I think I saw that somewhere."

He kept staring down past Joyce's little beauty shop toward the creek.

"My buddies call me Jack 'cause of Black Jack whiskey. As you can tell, I like to drink."

"No."

"Quit kiddin' around, boss. You know I was here at Benning? That's something I never told you. Before the war and when we processed out."

"You okay?"

"Yeah, I'm fine."

I waited. Joyce walked out the back door and asked us if we wanted some more coffee, and we both thanked her as she walked back inside, drying her hands on a dish towel.

"Me and this boy from Erie, Pennsylvania, named Wurst, were good buddies. Been through battle and blood and all that bullshit. About the same age. Too stupid to know what we'd gotten ourselves into but now wanting to live it up. Every day feeling like a goddamn gift."

He stood up, his feet unsteady.

"We were horny as goats and took our pay on a Friday night over to Phenix City."

He lit a cigar, one that had already been smoked halfway, and told me the story. They'd come over the river in '46 and met some girl at Clyde Yarborough's Café, before he'd opened the Atomic Bomb.

"But this girl, they called her Barbara LeMay, wasn't a girl at all. Turned out her name was really Ed, and he had a pecker bigger than a horse. My buddy started to raise some hell with Yarborough and Yarborough threatened him. When I stepped up, that mush-mouthed freak about split my skull with the butt of a 12-gauge. It all ended up in a slugfest with Yarborough and this other hood. This boy had a hell of a punch, but we just about had 'em when Yarborough shot Wurst in the head and me in the chest."

Black loosened his tie and pulled down the collar of his dress shirt, showing a patchwork of skin grafts and scars across his upper chest.

"What about Wurst?"

Black shook his head. "They tossed us both into the river." He paused a moment. "I made it out."

"And Ferrell never prosecuted, of course."

"He called it abnormal behavior to solicit a man. You know the Army came over and did an investigation? They never did find Wurst's body. I was in the hospital for about six months."

I could see only the glowing red tip of the cigar, smelling the tobacco mix with the fall leaves smoldering up into the white of the moon.

"You know the other man with Yarborough?"

He nodded.

"It was your friend Reuben."

"You sure?"

"You don't forget a night like that, boss. You watch out for him. He's the same as the rest of 'em."

REUBEN SAT AT THE BEATEN KITCHEN TABLE CLEANING A gun with a dirty red rag, the potbellied stove giving off a dull, warm heat. And it felt good, as he sat in his union suit, unshaven, cleaning and working the cylinders in a little .22 pistol that he hadn't owned but two hours. He had some of Moon's fresh 'shine in a jelly jar, and he'd already smoked the last of the cigarettes he'd gotten in jail. He felt hollow, and his hands shook as he loaded in the little skinny bullets, and he took another drink just as Billy walked in and saw two T-bone steaks thawing on the counter, a couple of baked potatoes already in the stove.

"You all right?" he asked.

"I'm fine."

"I'm goin' out."

"Ain't you got school?"

"What's that got to do with anything?"

"What you seein'?"

"Hmm?"

"What you seein'? I figured you goin' to see a movie."

"I'm goin' to shoot some pool."

"You need to stay out of those pool halls. Ain't nothin' in them but trouble. They'll pick your pocket dry."

Reuben stood and wavered for a moment, and he thought about the stories he'd heard about Moon's special 'shine and how he'd used formaldehyde and embalming fluid to give that corn liquor a special kick. A few years ago, a damn raccoon had been tempted by that sweet mash and crawled in the still, only to become part of the 'shine himself.

"You can't even stand up."

"Hell you say. I'm just hungry. Go ahead and put them steaks on the skillet. I got some sauce, too. Some of that A1 you like from over at Mr. Hoyt's place."

Billy just stood there staring at him, his skinny arms crossed over his body. And there was something different about him, a little shadow above his lip, some grease in his hair.

"You look like a damn punk," Reuben said.

"I learn from the best."

"I didn't have a thing to do with that whore. Don't you go blaming me on that."

"Those are your people, aren't they? Johnnie and Bert Fuller. That fat-ass moonshiner. They're all your buddies."

"They didn't have anything to do with it either."

Reuben breathed, tried to catch an air of dignity, righting his shoulders, and then crossing over to set the black iron skillet he got from his mama on the stove, putting those T-bones on in with a hiss. He didn't say anything, just tried to keep his eyes open, that 'shine filling his veins and making him feel hot. When the steaks got nice and pink, not frozen but good and bloody, he cracked some eggs next to them and the whole thing smelled so good he almost forgot about Billy.

But Billy was still there, the little Emerson radio in the kitchen catching "Louisiana Hayride" with Hank Snow, and Reuben's mind coming back to having that pride of driving ole Hank Williams around and how, even though he wasn't a hero, just being a part of the show made him feel alive and important.

Before he knew it, old Snow was playing that "Long Gone Lonesome Blues." And Reuben sang along with it, his mind back on Shreveport on a hot summer night where girls in white cotton dresses and suntans smelled like flowers just picked off a thorny bush.

"Why'd he fire you?"

"Who?"

"Hank Williams."

"He didn't fire me. Hell, he died."

Reuben stuck a fork in the steak and flipped it and a hard-fried egg—more hard than he liked it—up on a plate and set it before Billy, asking him if he wanted some of those Mexican beans that his mama liked.

"No, sir."

"No, sir? A steak dinner sure can get some respect in this house."

"Whose gun is that?"

"Mine."

"Not one I ever seen."

"I got a lot of guns."

"Thought the Guard took most of them."

"The ones they could find."

"What're you gonna do with that one?"

"Would you just eat your supper and go on?"

They ate, and the damn silence was so intense you could hear every scrape of the fork and grunted chew and labored breath. But then Reuben had to stop, and he walked over to the big farm sink and stuck his head under the pump, dousing his face with the cold water.

He took a good portion of the liquor inside of him and then walked back to his bedroom, his steak left half-eaten. The eggs not touched.

When he came back, he was dressed in blue jeans and red-and-green boots, the ones with a cactus on the shaft. He'd shaved and he'd combed his hair back with some pomade, and, with his sleepy eyes, he looked down at Billy, scooping up the gun and tucking it inside his front pocket.

"You do me a favor?"

His boy looked at him.

"Get out of this place. Get as far as you can from this farm because it will spoil your soul."

"I like it here."

"You ain't too bright. And you stay away from Lamar Murphy. I know what you told him."

Billy pushed the steak dinner away and looked up at his father and shook his head. "You are one sorry, worthless bastard."

Reuben took a breath, wavered on his feet, and walked, every step of those big boots making his boy flinch just a little bit more. He breathed hard, keeping it in like you would a lungful from a Lucky, and he raised the back of his hand, but he shook and held it there, watching the boy duck, placing his hands over his head, waiting for it and, some-how in a strange way, seeming to want it. He wanted Reuben to beat the hell out of him.

Reuben leaned down and kissed the boy on his head, tasting the pomade and smelling the strange odor of the kid, a man's sweat. It was all so damn unfamiliar.

Before he left, he told the boy what to do if he didn't come back by daybreak. Get away from Phenix City and Russell County and the ghosts of dead men who would wake you in your sleep, second-guessing your every move.

REUBEN PARKED BEHIND A USED-CAR LOT ON CRAWFORD, close enough to Slocumb's filling station that he could hear the sound of the air-hose bell every time a new customer drove in. His Buick looked fine among the other cars for sale, sitting there on the main commercial drag of PC, under the streetlights and colored flags that beat in the fall wind. He hadn't noticed how his hands stuck to the wheel, even with the ignition off, till he tried to light a cigarette, his hands unsteady and sloppy, and his eyes dead and straight when he looked back at himself, the sleepy-eyed Mitchum in the mirror.

He left his hat on the backseat and made his way to the little woods behind the filling station, taking a worn trail whose meaning wasn't lost on him, rounding a little powdery curl, hearing the tinkling of some wind chimes from the brick house in the clearing.

He squatted there and waited, trying to steady himself. Calm, or maybe forgive himself for what he was about to do. He kept thinking about Billy, wanting to walk away from this hell-soaked fire of a life after the war with something for him instead of some rotten barns and dead fruit trees.

Lamar's heavy bag rocked back and forth on thick chains.

JOYCE AND I SWITCHED BETWEEN *PABST BLUE RIBBON Bouts,* watching a replay of a Pete Rademacher fight, and *Down You Go,* with Phil Rizzuto and Boris Karloff trying to guess a secret word or phrase some housewife had sent in to make five dollars. Of course, if you stumped the panel, you got twenty-five bucks. I was beating Joyce, recognizing damn near every one—of course it wasn't hard to get ahead of Frankenstein himself—and repeating as she would say the wrong word, "Down you go." I was feeling pretty good and cocky as I walked back to check on the children, the night routine going like clockwork, Thomas already in bed pretending he was asleep and Anne taking a bath.

When I knocked on the bathroom door, I heard her splash around and ask to please give her some privacy. "Yes, ma'am," I said.

I went back to the kitchen to make another pot of coffee, looking up at the clock, knowing Jack should be over anytime. I landed back in the easy chair watching the nightly news out of Atlanta, Phenix City finally not being featured every night as a "Sin Den" and just plain "wicked." I caught the weather, colder nights ahead, and leaned back into my chair, dozing a bit, smelling the coffee, Joyce coming in once before I fell asleep, saying "Down he goes" back to me and me hearing it and smiling with closed eyes . . . never hearing the back door click open.

SINCE HE'D BEEN BACK FROM PANAMA CITY, REUBEN HAD gotten to know Lamar's routine, watching it and studying on it. Lamar hadn't changed a damn bit, always getting to the gym at the same time, always folding his trunks the same way, and the same religious wrapping of his knuckles through the center of his hands. Reuben looked down at his watch, knowing that big gorilla deputy wouldn't be over for another twenty minutes and that the children would be in bed. He couldn't and wouldn't harm a child or a woman—that was a line he would never cross—and he waited there, watching Joyce turn out the light in the bedroom and the gray-white flicker of the television box in their family room. And he took a breath and moved forward, his gait strong and controlled, moving across the backyard and by Joyce's beauty shop, trying to think of Lamar as an opponent or the way he felt about a Jap—nothing at all—and he knew it would be over in minutes and Phenix would be gone and in his rearview.

Billy could have something. Reuben wouldn't need forgiveness. His goddamn scorecard was already so punched full of holes that even Jesus Christ himself wouldn't cut a loser like him a break. Lamar had taken the first shot and it had been a sucker punch, and when you sucker punched a man the comeback would be tenfold. Reuben told himself things like that, trying to think about the killing as a strategy. He lifted up the lock on the screen door with a pocketknife and turned the knob in the kitchen, smelling coffee, hearing the slurp of it perking, and as he turned he saw Lamar sprawled out and repeated the word *palooka* in his mind. Lamar being a big, bald, laid-out palooka, looking like he'd just hit the canvas and gone to bed.

It would be easier like this. He'd never even have to look him in the eye.

Reuben moved for him, the moonshine making his skin glow, his face sweat, smelling the way you only did when you were fearful, like a skunk. His own odor making him catch some bile in his throat. Some reason, thinking about that crazy old Kid Weisz and what he would think about this final bout between his two boys, but telling himself the Kid would understand. He'd understand what it meant to be neutered by someone, to be cheated, to be lied to. Lamar Murphy was a coward, and if it wasn't Reuben it would be Johnnie Benefield. And Johnnie didn't have the goddamn right.

He had the right to take the lights of the big palooka, snoring it up in the chair. So comfortable in the chair, with the knitted armrests and the little silver picture frames and the china settings hung on a wall. He moved into the family room and nearly tripped over his feet, Lamar grumbling and shuffling. The television talking about the Auburn

University Tigers taking on Georgia Tech this weekend and hearing Coach Jordan's voice sounding like that of God, saying that "the boys needed to take apart the offensive machine" and that "they'd shown some real spunk in drills and to expect a real contest in Atlanta."

Reuben froze. He staggered again and moved backward, no longer thinking but moving backward, feeling his stomach lock up and feeling that steak and eggs and ole Moon's formaldehyde whiskey. It was the thought of the formaldehyde and stiff dead people and blood that made him rush for the closest door and bust on in through it and stick his head right in the commode and puke his ever-living guts out.

He heard a girl scream and scream and he looked over at Anne—a girl he'd first seen at no more than knee-high when he got back from the Pacific, about a million years ago—and she screamed and kicked herself back into the corner of the tub, Reuben ignoring her until the big shadow appeared in the doorway, looking down on him—without fear or pity—but Lamar with that curious look on his face as he pointed an Army-issue .45 down at the man in the toilet.

Reuben fell back to his ass and wiped his lips with his shirt. He didn't know if he was crying or not, just saying the first thing that came to his mind: "You think that coffee is ready yet?"

"SO WHAT DID YOU DO?" Hugh Britton asked, sitting across from me in a booth at Kemp's Drive-In.

"I poured him a cup of coffee."

"When did you know he had a gun?"

"He told me," I said. "We sat down and didn't talk for a long time. He left the gun in the kitchen, and we watched the *Tonight Show*. Steve Allen can really play the piano. He played that song before Gene Rayburn did the news, 'This Could Be the Start of Something,' and that kind of made Reuben loosen up."

"The man came to your home to kill you," Britton said.

"No, he didn't," I said. "He wanted an excuse. He was drunk, wasn't thinking straight."

"You sure are making a hell of an excuse for him."

"Do you know what he asked me?"

Britton shook his head. It was morning, a couple days after finding Reuben in my bathroom, and the light was still gray, a cold mist outside, what the Irish call a soft day.

"He wanted to know why Joyce and I never invited him to dinner."

"What did you say?"

"I told him that I didn't think he'd come. I said our life was pretty boring. About the only excitement came on Wednesday night, when we have pot roast and mashed potatoes. I told him we don't drink, just watch television, sometimes the kids get to eat off these TV trays. Funny how someone can be offended by the smallest thing."

"I don't think it was not having him over that ticked him off."

I took a sip of coffee and looked out at the soft day, the brown leaves fluttering and spinning down from the trees. A couple of guardsmen laughing and coming into the diner, taking their hats off and putting them on a rack by the door.

"He stayed for breakfast," I said. "Joyce cooked up some bacon and eggs with grits, and then he rode on with me right to the jail."

"And he's been there ever since."

"He'll stay there until he goes before the grand jury."

"Who knows about him?"

"Only John Patterson and Sykes. We're keeping it under wraps even from Sykes's team right now. We don't want any of those newspapermen to get hold of it. The only thing they're good at is turning the world into a circus."

"So what exactly did he see?"

I lit a cigarette, keeping it burning in one hand, and rubbed my bald head with the other, getting comfortable in the booth.

"He was going to the Elite to have dinner, and when he passed by the alley to park he saw Arch Ferrell and Bert Fuller talking to Mr. Patterson. He said he parked on the other side of the street and was listening to the end of a radio show out of Montgomery, some kind of gospel hour, and because it was June he had the windows down."

"He heard the shots?"

"*One, two, three.* He said he knew right off, didn't think there were damn firecrackers or any of that mess. Reuben knows the sound of a gun."

"I bet."

"He see any other witnesses?"

"He mentioned that big ole black car Ross Gibson saw. He thinks it was a Lincoln. Said a man and a woman were in the front seat, parked right at the mouth of the alley."

The waitress came over and set down our plates and heated up our coffee. I smiled and thanked her. Britton craned his neck over the table and waited for me to finish, not even noticing her or the food.

"Did he see them run away?"

"He said he saw Fuller. Ferrell must've ducked back through the alley."

"Where Quinnie saw him."

"It fits."

"Did he see them arguing?"

"He said it looked like they were just talking and didn't think nothing of it until he heard the shots."

"And so what does this mean?"

"John says it will be enough for Sykes. He knows he's gonna have a battle with Reuben's record. He said the defense will shred his character on the stand. But I'm just glad he wasn't caught for half the things he's done. Can you pass the ketchup?"

I lifted my hand out.

"But he was there."

"Yes, sir."

He handed me the bottle.

"When does he go before the grand jury?"

"Today."

"And that's when all hell will break loose."

"He won't remain out of my sight. He's moved in the jail perma-nent. I got his boy to bring over some fresh clothes. I got him some cigarettes and magazines. He's already got to be real friendly with some of the women down there."

"The prostitutes?"

I nodded.

"He's always had a way with them."

SINCE BERT FULLER'S BOND HAD BEEN REVOKED, HE'D spent the weeks at the Russell County Jail reading Zane Grey, *True West* magazine, *Amazing Stories,* and the Bible. Sometimes, when he read them all together, he'd forget if he'd read about the word of God with David and Goliath or about Wyatt Earp against the Clantons. He read one story in *True West* that seemed right out of the Bible, about a man named Moses Jones who'd led a wagon train through the paths of hell out to Utah or somewhere, a place they called the Holy Land. Fuller was pretty sure that the story was cribbed from the Bible, and he thought maybe that was some kind of sin, later realizing the whole Bible was nothing but a western.

The Jews were nothing but homesteaders with redmen all around them, trying to take what was promised to them by the Lord Almighty. Today, he read a book Georgia had brought him called *Code of the West.* It was a modern western, set out in a place called Tonto Basin in Arizona with this woman Mary Stockwell, a frontier school-teacher. Fuller had just gotten to the part about Mary's sister, Georgiana, coming west to cure her tuberculosis, and the woman thought, *If Georgiana could stand the rugged, virile, wild Tonto Basin, she would not only regain her health, but she would grow away from the falseness and over-sophistication that followed the war.*

All Fuller wanted to know is if Georgiana had big tits like his Georgia. Zane was really letting him down with this one. He introduced two women, and Fuller still didn't know what they looked like. He thumbed through the pages, waiting for the gunslinger or bounty hunter or sheriff to enter the picture and give those two Yankee spinsters what they'd been needin'.

He put the book down and walked to the corner of his brick cell to take a leak and then went back and lay down on his bunk. The light was hard coming through the cell window, and he laid a forearm across his eyes. Some men were talking down the way, and he recognized one of their voices, wasn't unusual for some bootlegger or clip joint operator to finally get picked up on warrant, and Fuller would call down to them and ask them how was business, as some kind of joke.

Frog Jones had just spent last week two cells down, and they'd shared some good stories about the days during the Border Wars and some of the women they'd known out at Cliff's and where everybody had all been scattered about.

About two hours later, he saw an old nigger card dealer he knew push a mop bucket down the hall. He'd been there since Fuller had first been arrested on that vote-fraud joke charge, and sometimes the boy would smuggle him in some fresh biscuits and candy bars.

"What you got for me today, boy?" he asked.

"What you want?"

"Who's that down the hall? I know that voice."

"That's Mr. Reuben."

"They picked up every club owner in town."

"He ain't in here for that. He's a witness. They figured he better be kept in a cage."

"Who's he testifying against?"

The old card dealer leaned against the mop handle and smiled big at him, a big old Amos-and-Andy smile, and said: "He's testifyin' 'gainst you and Mr. Arch. Ain't you heard nothin'?"

Fuller jumped from the bunk and reached his hands around the bars, grabbing the old man by the throat, and shook him, rattling the entire cage. The old nigger on the other side of the bars didn't do nothing but laugh and laugh.

"Go ahead and grin it up, nigger," Fuller said. "Judgment Day will come soon enough."

"I ain't scareda you no more," the man said.

"But you'll still work for that dollar."

"Bet your ass."

Fuller let go of the man and walked back to the bunk, where he tore the title page out from *Man of the West,* with a simple black illustration of two cowboys riding along on their horses, a sketch of mountains in the background. He wrote beneath them a simple note and handed it back to the old man.

"You call this number here and you repeat what you just told me. There's twenty dollars in it for you."

"Sez who?"

"It's an honest bet on just a goddamn dime."

I LOANED REUBEN AN OLD SUNDAY SUIT BEFORE HE GAVE his testimony to the grand jury that afternoon, with Bernard Sykes leading him—no kind of cross-examination—and with me waiting for him in the courthouse hall when he got done. The suit was brown with wide lapels, and his shirtsleeves cuffed well into the palm of his hand. He nodded to me, and we walked together down the hallway.

"This the best you could do?"

"I didn't have time to get you a tailor."

"I look like a corpse."

"You did real good today," I said.

"I bet your daddy is finally proud of you now," Reuben said. "I remember how much he hated you bein' a fighter."

"Proud for what?" I asked.

"Being sheriff."

"Are you kidding?"

Reuben looked at me.

"The first thing he said to me was, 'How low can you go?' "

"What's his problem?"

"He thinks it's a redneck job."

"Well." Reuben smiled and shrugged. "You got anything more to eat?"

"Joyce dropped off some leftovers. You can have them if you want them."

"No, that's all right. She didn't mean them for me."

"I'm not all that hungry."

"No, I couldn't."

"Would you please shut up, Reuben. I'll get Quinnie to bring it in."

"Lamar, please excuse me for being ungrateful. I mean the food is really good, please thank Joyce for that, she's always been good to me, but I really can't stand to be in this shithole anymore. I haven't talked to my boy in a week. I don't know what's going on out at my place."

Ten minutes later, I drove slow out into the country, turning off the paved road, the unpainted farmhouse growing in the windshield. I wheeled around and parked along a gully, and he wandered out ahead of me, dead leaves from a big shade oak twisting and scattering in the light breeze.

I watched him walk and heard the hard thwap of the screen door close. I waited there in the car and looked at the unpainted house with its rusted tin roof, the lean-to nearby that Reuben's father used as a smokehouse. There was an outhouse, a burned-out shed, and a rotten barn. An old skinny tire, like they used to use on Model Ts, hung from a knotted rope from a pecan tree.

I didn't see Billy and heard no sounds coming from the house.

I knew of the boy's mother, a woman Reuben had met in California before the war, and had heard how she had left in '48, tired of Alabama, or perhaps tired of this new man who had returned with a limp from the Philippines. A man she'd heard had been dead for two years.

But she'd left with little else but a suitcase, the boy thinking his mother would return and perhaps still believing it.

I stared at the unpainted house again and the antique tire swinging in the wind. Reuben came back with a few things wrapped up in some fresh shirts, and I started the car and drove back to Phenix City.

"How long am I gonna have to keep this up?"

"Till the trial."

"When will that be?"

"Couple months."

"Could they at least get me a hotel or a damn television? You ever watch the *Red Buttons Show*? That sonofabitch sure makes me laugh. You ever see that dumb boxer he does? Rocky Buttons? I never wanted to end up like that with half your brains left out there on the canvas. Maybe it was a good thing the war happened."

"You don't mean that."

"Sure I do. Listen, what about the German? What's his name, Keeglefarven? That one makes me laugh, too. You know, on Red Buttons's show."

"I'll see what I can do."

"This is funny, ain't it?" he asked. "Us ending up this way. You ever see that cartoon with the sheepdog and the wolf?"

REUBEN COULDN'T STAND THE CELL. EVEN THOUGH THAT big Jack Black kept the door unlocked and he could use the real bathroom and shower and shave in the same room as the deputies and could even get free Coca-Colas from the courthouse, the damn place made him itch. After a few weeks, just about Christmastime, Quinnie or Jack and even sometimes Lamar would let him walk downtown and have lunch at the Elite or Smitty's and just kind of stretch his legs. He wasn't a prisoner, and they knew it was his own decision to live at the jail. An old B-girl he used to see stopped by every day and brought him cigarettes and sometimes a jar of peanut butter and Hershey's bars. He got letters in the mail from some of the women who'd worked for him, one card was even postmarked from Havana.

But he never could get dry, not even inside, and would drink himself to sleep every night, the deputies knowing he kept the hooch under the bunk but not really caring. It was on a cold day, sky dark as hell, that he'd just about run out and walked to the sheriff's desk to have Lamar drive him to the liquor store. But Lamar was out.

He asked some new fat boy to call him on the radio. But the boy said Lamar was in Montgomery.

Reuben headed out the back door and walked out the chain-link gates, out and around the jail and the courthouse and up to Fourteenth to Chad's Rose Room, a clip joint that had gone legit. Reuben sat there at the bar and drank down a couple Budweisers and ate a bowl of chili. He punched up some Ernest Tubb on the jukebox, listening to "Slippin' Around," "Filipino Baby," and "Merry Texas Christmas, You All!" He liked the last one so much, he played it again.

He had another couple beers and tried to call Billy. He hadn't seen him since he'd been in jail. There was silver tinsel all along the bar, with Christmas lights that winked.

He drank another beer and called the jail, asking for Lamar, who was still out.

He played "Merry Texas Christmas, You All!" twice more. And then the cook asked him to leave, and Reuben said that was fine 'cause he wouldn't pay for chili that tasted like dog shit.

He walked down to the river, past all the old joints boarded up. The front door to Club Lasso boarded up with a CLOSURE notice, compliments of the Guard. He didn't have a jacket, and his teeth chattered as he looked over the Chattahoochee churn for a while and then turned back up the hill, the street pretty much closed up and dead, making leaning shadows, trash piled up in big bunches along the road, and then wandered down Fifth Avenue, where some sonofabitch had hung candy canes from streetlamps, and the pharmacy, fake snow sprayed on the window, not fooling a soul.

His teeth chattered more as he walked by the Palace Theater, noting there was a new movie on called *Atomic Man,* along with *White Christmas.* He stepped inside to get warm and asked the usher if he'd seen a boy that looked like Billy. The teenager looked at Reuben like he was just some crazy drunk, and Reuben told the usher that he looked like a monkey in that bow tie, and that he bet *White Christmas* was a crock a shit, that Bing Crosby had never been no GI.

As he walked, it almost startled him that it had grown dark, seeming to close Phenix City in a little curtain. The taillights on the Hudsons, Nashes, Fords, and Chevys glowing bright red up and down Fourteenth.

He kept moving past the courthouse, not feeling like stepping back in that cell, and gave a two-finger salute to some of the Guard boys, stepping around them, down by a bus stop by the railroad tracks and Niggertown, thinking that maybe someone would have some 'shine down there.

That's when he was greeted by something that struck him downright funny. A troop of Boy Scouts standing across from the courthouse, all duded up in their green uniforms, yellow bandannas around their necks. They marched behind a man who was dressed just like those kids, and the sight of him made Reuben really giggle. A grown man dressed up like a Boy Scout, having to march right by them Guard troops.

He stood as they passed by and he kept the salute to all of them, laughing a little bit, before turning toward the railroad tracks that cut Phenix City in half and down under a little trestle, where he found a couple of old negro men sitting on their old rotten porch eyeing him like he was about to steal one of the bald tires they had out in their yard.

"Excuse me, preacher," Reuben said, "could I ask you a question?"

With a jelly jar full of hooch and it coming up on night, Reuben was ready to go back to the cell and maybe play a game of cards with Quinnie. How he loved playing cards with Quinnie. If the boy had any more tells on him, he'd be a damn dictionary.

The car came out of nowhere, skidding to a stop, the door popping open and a man jumping out, Reuben's eyes having to focus and shift on the man's face.

He saw those big choppers first as the man smiled. "Howdy."

Reuben searched for something to say, but that was right when Johnnie reached into his coat pocket, popped open the switchblade, and gouged it into his throat.

REUBEN LAY THERE on that street corner, holding his throat, his face turning pale as a bleached sheet, as the Boy Scouts ran to him, circling him, the troop master pressing his bandanna to Reuben's bloodied neck. Some of the boys ran for the courthouse, yelling, and Reuben lay there looking up at the sky, not moving his eyes or blinking and twice trying to talk but his voice unable to work right. He finally gathered it in a sputtering, bloody gag, and he asked for the sheriff. He asked for me twice more, before a woman walking down the road, a stripper who had worked for him at Club Lasso, spotted his cowboy boots hanging off the curb. And she ran to him, wobbling on the big red high heels that matched her tight red dress, and she dropped to her knees, taking Reuben's head in her lap and calling out for help, and being told the boys were finding it.

And she cried and held him there on the street corner, more people gathering around, circling Reuben, the curious sight of him and the buxom woman holding him in her lap and crying. His face grown whiter now, still calling out for me, and another boy running off when they knew he'd meant Sheriff Murphy. A short man in a suit said the man on the ground had just testified in the Patterson murder, and the crowd all started talking and whispering while Reuben spit up more blood, hearing a siren in the distance.

Reuben's eyes shifted for a moment, his body shook, and he smiled up at the girl, recognizing her face, and croaked, "Howdy, Birmingham."

She smoothed back the hair from his forehead and cried, screaming for everyone to clear away, and then a path opened, Jack Black pushing his way through and kneeling down to see Reuben and yelling for more room so they could all breathe.

Reuben waited, his arms splayed out open, Texas show boots crossed at the ankle and a smile on his bloody lips. "I bet I sure look like shit."

The stripper held the Boy Scout bandanna, not gold now but soaked in blood, and men rushed from an ambulance and spoke to Jack Black and then hoisted Reuben onto a gurney, taking him to Homer C. Cobb.

I didn't learn what had happened until I drove back into Phenix City and was met at my house by Quinnie Kelley, who drove me to the hospital. Reuben had already had a blood transfusion by that time, and I sent Quinnie out to look for Billy, but, by midnight, Quinnie had returned alone.

It was about that time a nurse told me that Reuben had called for me, and I left the waiting room where I was staying with Joyce and walked back to his room. Reuben was there, his neck bandaged, two nurses working on him, and I half expected him to sit up and make a joke about ladies in white. But he just lay there, eyes closed, shirt off, but still wearing blue jeans and muddy boots.

He opened his eyes, asking for Billy, and I had to kneel down and tell him that he was on his way. And Reuben nodded and closed his eyes and jerked a bit like you do nodding off while trying to stay awake. The nurse pushed me out of the room and wheeled him fast around the corner.

I followed, a door with a circular window slamming in my face.

Not five minutes later, the door swung back open, and a doctor gripped my upper arm, a man I knew from church, and he told me he wanted me in surgery.

"I'm fine right here."

"You don't understand," he said. "I know who this man is and what he did today. If something happens, I want you to watch as a witness."

I was hustled into a bleached smock and told to stand back from the operating table, up on a wooden apple crate. I watched them fill Reuben's pale chest and throat with tubes, opening up the gash below his chin, more fresh blood being pumped into his body.

He lay there, out cold, with his slicked hair and closed, droopy eyes and what looked like a smile. An honest-to-God smile. I watched his face, trying to figure out the smile, the last joke on all of this, just as the sound of cracking startled me, the doctor sawing into Reuben's chest. My head jerked back, as if hearing the report of a rifle, and I watched as the doctor held Reuben's heart in his simple human hands and tried to massage him back to life, only to give up minutes later and check the watch on his wrist.

"HOW MANY MORE OF US HAVE TO GET KILLED BEFORE someone will make a damn decision?"

John Patterson was outside by the hospital fountain, yelling at Bernard Sykes, who just stood there taking it but shaking his head in disagreement. I joined them, listening, John telling Sykes to present the grand jury with everything, don't hold a piece back on Fuller or Ferrell or they'd never indict. But Sykes shook his head, saying they'd have to wait for the grand jury.

"It's a slow process," Sykes said. "We have to build the case."

"This case is going to be taken away from you. Don't you know that?"

"They're going to indict."

"Not a word of his testimony can be used in court," Patterson said. "The defense can't cross-examine a dead man."

Patterson rubbed his neck, exhausted, and looked at Sykes and then back at me. He shook his head in defeat, before walking back out into the shadows.

IT WAS TWO A.M. WHEN BILLY ARRIVED AT THE HOSPITAL, walked in by Jack Black and Quinnie. He moved slow through the lobby, the older people there watching him, seeing if he knew, how he would react, would he fall or keep upright.

I put my arm around him, not saying a word.

He'd been told.

In a back hospital room, Reuben lay on the gurney, covered up to the chin by a white sheet, the stripper sitting near him, as if guarding his body. In a chair, she shined his boots with a cloth and mug of soapy water.

"Who are you?" Billy asked.

"Just a friend," she said.

She stopped while wiping down the cactus on the shaft, smoothing her black hair over the soft leather and crying, and watched as Billy moved to the body, standing there and looking down at his father.

"This is yours," the woman said, handing the boy an envelope with his name scrawled on it in Reuben's hand.

He just wavered there for a few moments, and, without a word, turned and ran out the door, leaving the room and leaving the hospital.

BILLY WOULD HIT THE ALABAMA-MISSISSIPPI LINE EARLY the next morning at seventy miles per hour, feeling the air rush from his lungs as he left the state. He felt for the first time that he could catch his breath, even though he couldn't tell a damn bit of difference from one state to another. The moon shone on the same clapboard houses, the same tired laundry lines with flags of dresses and overalls blowing in the cold wind, and the same winding, muddy roads leading off that main highway for hardscrabble folks to follow. He lit a cigarette early that morning and turned the dial on that old blue Buick's radio, searching for a station in range. He'd gotten only a few miles into Mississippi when he got a solid signal out of Memphis and leaned back into his seat, cracked the window, and felt the cool air slice across his face.

He could breathe better, without a doubt.

And, in the rearview mirror, he peered at the two faces, the tired boy and the girl who slept on his shoulder. Her face still scarred, nose broken, but no less beautiful to him. He could feel a warmth spread in his chest as she shifted herself toward him, making him feel that solid, firm weight anchoring them together.

The envelope lay unopened on the dash, fluttering in the wind.

A WEEK LATER, WORD SPREAD THAT THE GRAND JURY HAD made a decision. Outside the courtroom doors, the Russell County Courthouse became choked with reporters and attorneys and normal folks off the street who waited to hear the news. I saw Arch Ferrell in the middle of it all, dressed in a gray suit and shaking hands, smiling, knowing he was going to beat it all. He stayed for a while, but by three p.m. he drove off in his Pontiac. Not two minutes later, the courthouse doors opened, newspapermen running out to their typewriters and telephones, saying Ferrell and Fuller had been indicted for the murder of Albert L. Patterson.

There were gasps and yells. A few people clapped.

John was there, and we shook hands and hugged. Soon, Sykes

moved out of the courtroom, trailed by dozens of newspapermen, and he led them all out to the courthouse steps where he confidently answered their questions. Afterward, he followed me back to my office, reached into his briefcase, and handed me three neatly typed and folded arrest warrants.

Si Garrett had been indicted as an accessory, and, under Alabama law, Sykes explained to me, that was the same as pulling the trigger.

We wasted no time. Jack Black drove, I sat in the passenger's seat, and Quinnie in the rear, as we made our way to Bert Fuller's garage apartment. His lawyer had finally finagled him a house arrest for the vote fraud because of an injured back from a "fall from a horse." And he'd been there for weeks, with boys from the Guard taking turns watching him lie in bed in his pajamas, reading the Bible and watching television, only leaving the bed to relieve himself.

A shapely blonde met us at the door, chewing gum, hands on hips. And I reached into my pocket for the warrant, but she just let the door swing open and waved us in with the flat of her hand, saying, "We've been expecting you."

Bert Fuller woke, as if being gently woken from a dream. He smiled up at me and Jack Black and said, "Blessings."

"Get your fat ass up, Fuller," Black said. "You're hereby under arrest for the murder of Albert Patterson."

He tilted his head, still not moving it from a pillow. "Boys, I am not fit to move from this bed. I'm under bed-rest orders from an Atlanta physician, and any move from my bed could paralyze me."

Black nodded and looked to me.

"Quite a place you got here," Black said. "I like those lassos and hats on the wall. Just how many pairs of boots do you have?"

"Twenty-seven."

"Well, I'll be," Black said. "You ready?"

"I said I can't move."

"Sure thing, hoss."

Black called in four negro trusties from the jail who'd been brought over with the Guard. They took their posts on each corner of Fuller's bed and, with the word from Black, lifted him up like a fat sultan and whisked him out the door.

"Load him in the truck," Black said, following.

THE PARADE OF CARS CONTINUED OUT OF PHENIX CITY AND down along the curving country road to Seale and Arch Ferrell's big ranch house. His wife, Madeline, met us in the front drive, holding her newborn daughter, and she shielded her eyes in the bright sunshine, looking out at the hordes crawling out of their automobiles. I asked her to please get Arch.

She said he wasn't there. She said she thought he was at the court-house.

So we all waited about an hour, leaning against the cars, the deputies and prosecutors and photographers and newspapermen, until we saw Arch's familiar Pontiac drive slow, a funeral pace, down the long road to his brand-new house, and kill the engine.

He climbed out of the car with a smile on his face and removed his hat. "Madeline, you mind waiting inside for me?"

The baby had started to cry, and Madeline mounted the steps and path to the house, closing the door behind her.

"Did you hear?" Arch asked.

I waited.

"Governor Persons has just suffered a massive heart attack. They've rushed him to the hospital."

I shook my head.

"This town is killing everyone," Arch said.

I didn't say anything.

"Now, just what is this about?" he asked.

I looked at him, giving a slight shake of my head, and told him he was under arrest for the killing of Mr. Patterson.

He nodded and asked if we had a warrant, and I slipped a piece of paper from my new gray suit jacket and handed it to him. He stood there, a bit shorter than me, and read through the simple document as if judging its legal validity, showing he was still very much a man of the court.

And then he nodded again and looked up.

Black was at my elbow, his hand on the butt of a .45, waiting for Arch to take off or explode. Quinnie waited at the black Chevy with a 12-gauge in his little arms.

"Can I talk to my wife?" he asked. "I'd like to be the one to tell her."

I looked to Jack and then over at Quinnie. There were twenty-odd cars parked out at crazy angles, maybe forty newspapermen and photographers circling us.

"Sure thing, Arch."

As he walked up the steps and to the front door, everyone fell silent. He met Madeline there and he leaned in to kiss her but missed her cheek, whispering something. She put her hand to her mouth and began to cry as he leaned in to kiss his newborn on the forehead. His older daughter, Anne's friend, held back in the black void of the open door with a dull expression on her face, numb to it all.

THE NEXT DAY, JOHN PATTERSON AND I FLEW OUT OF Montgomery to Houston, where the local sheriff drove us over to Galveston and Si Garrett's sanitarium. We were met in the lobby of this big white antebellum building by a doctor and a lawyer, one with a clipboard and one with a briefcase, fully ready to fight us. I presented the lawyer with the warrant and extradition papers while the doctor rattled on about all the delicate and frail sensibilities of a very ill man.

"Can we see him?" John asked.

The doctor looked to the lawyer. The lawyer shrugged.

They led us out the east wing of the building, following a well-worn brick walkway through colonnades and past large twisted oaks that grew only in this part of the country. The doctor used a key from his pocket to open a side door and walked ahead down a long gray linoleum hall dimly lit with artificial light. He spoke to a nurse sitting at a desk at the end of the hall, and we all followed to a small metal door, where he used another key from his other pocket.

He unlocked and opened the door, light following the sharp edge, opening like a weak dawn into a small square room where a skinny man lay huddled in the corner squinting up at us.

"Mr. Garrett?" I asked.

The room smelled of antiseptic and urine.

"I am Silas Garrett."

"I'm Sheriff Lamar Murphy of Russell County, Alabama," I said. "I've been sent to take you back to face charges of killing Albert Patterson."

From the corner, Garrett palmed his way up on the two walls and stood. He wore a white smock. He looked much smaller than I remembered him, without the crisp white suit and big clean Stetson. His brown eyes looked confused, his hair thin, skin pale with the scruff of a black-and-gray beard that made him seem dirty.

"Are you well, sir?" I asked.

He shook his head. But he wasn't looking at me. He was looking at John Patterson. He began to tremble.

Patterson looked across at Garrett, the man fumbling with his hands and looking away. John's jaw clenched. I waited to hold him back.

"I'd really like you to explain to my mother why you killed her husband over a political pissing match."

He shook his head. He looked down. A scolded child.

He looked eighty years old.

"It doesn't take much to keep you quiet. It took three bullets for my father."

"As you can see—" the doctor started.

"He looks fine to me," I said.

"Under no circumstances," the doctor said, already walking out of the room. "Rest, Mr. Garrett. Please, just rest."

He turned off the lights, arguing with us out in the long, endless linoleum hall. As he spoke, I watched the door close, the narrowing of artificial light, that swath cut down to just a sliver, and I saw Si Garrett fall back into that far corner, bracing his back and sliding down to his haunches. Doing nothing but staring into the dark as the door closed with a click.

IT WAS THREE DAYS BEFORE CHRISTMAS, AND I WAS DOWN at Slocumb's checking up on how my father-in-law was making out with his other son-in-law who'd taken my place. Anne and Thomas rode over with me and were raiding the ice-cream freezer, to the great aggravation of their grandfather, who had always been known to be stingy with the cones. I talked to my brother-in-law a little about the dozens of fugitives we were looking for, including Fannie Belle and Johnnie Benefield, and gave him a wanted poster to tack on the wall by the cigarettes.

He commented that Benefield's picture was enough to scare off customers.

We were going to swing by and pick up Joyce and then head down to Columbus and Broadway to spend the rest of the day Christmas shopping. Thomas and I talked about maybe catching a movie after paying a visit to Santa Claus.

I excused myself, as Thomas was trying to climb into the cooler with his grandfather pulling him back by his sneakers, and walked around out back to smoke a cigarette. From around the garage, Arthur joined me and I gave him a cigarette, and we stood there looking across at the muddy creek and the path that had led to my house, now tangling up in weeds.

Arthur wore grease-stained denim overalls and a wide smile on his worn negro face.

"You miss me?" I asked.

"Not at all."

"You ready for Christmas?"

"You know it, Sheriff."

"You know you can just call me Lamar. I'm no different."

"No different, except you can put my ass in jail."

"You do have a point."

He smoked the cigarette fast and crushed it under his work boot. He looked around, just to make sure no one was in earshot, and said, "I was listenin' to the radio in the shop the other day. You know, like I always do. And, anyway, Mr. Patterson come on and started talking about Phenix. He was talking about the way the sheriff and the police didn't let no one have any rights. He said livin' in Phenix City was like livin' over there in Russia."

I nodded.

"He said a man's vote didn't mean a thing here. He said there hadn't been an honest election in a hundred years."

"That's probably true," I said. "So what's the point?"

Arthur shook his head. "No point, just something I found mighty interesting."

"You're talking about the negro situation."

He caught my eye. I smiled at him, my cigarette burning down to a nub, singeing my fingers.

"Fella came by to see you the other day. I told him to find you at the jail, but he left a number. Wanted to talk about that reward you put up."

I shook my head. "People been calling for two weeks about that reward money."

"I figured," Arthur said. "That's why I didn't think much of it. Hell of a car, though."

"What's that?"

"That fella that stopped by. Had the longest goddamn car I ever seen. A '39 Lincoln, black, and about a mile long. That's what I call an automobile."

"Where is that number?"

"By the register."

He followed me back into Slocumb's, where I shuffled through some receipts and deposit slips and found a phone number for a man named Padgett. I showed it to Arthur and he nodded.

I had the phone in my hand and started to dial.

"I've been prayin' y'all catch the fella that did that to Mr. Patterson," Arthur said, wiping the sweat off the back of his neck with an oil-stained rag. "I prayed for it since it happened. Figured it's my town, too. Ain't that right?"

"I'M NOT GOING TO LIE TO YOU, MR. PADGETT," I SAID. "IT'S not a position I'd want to be in."

Cecil Padgett was in his late twenties. A slender, handsome man with intense blue eyes and that kind of tanned skin that comes from hard outdoor labor. He smoked and listened to me, sitting on a sofa in the center of an Airstream trailer he shared with his wife. He nodded with everything I said, grounding out his cigarette in a tin can on the coffee table.

His wife hovered around in their tiny kitchen, pretending to be rearranging dishes but exchanging glances with him until he stopped looking to her.

"So they might try and kill me."

"Yes, sir."

"I read about that other fella. Not a good way to go."

"He was connected with the rackets. The man who we think killed him probably did it because he switched sides."

"Those gangsters probably wouldn't be pleased with me either."

"We would ask that you and your wife stay in a hotel with protection until the trials."

He nodded.

His wife dropped a tea cup and it shattered on the floor. She put her hand to her mouth. I looked to Padgett and he stood, asking if we could get some fresh air. It was night, and we stood out by our cars, the fat ceramic Christmas lights hung over the little canopies set up from all the Airstreams at Tropical Paradise Court in Columbus.

"Why were you downtown?"

"We wanted to see a movie," he said. "I was checking the times."

"Did you stay?"

"No, sir," he said. "It was a western, and those things always leave me feeling kind of low."

"How's that?"

"Too many people have to die."

I nodded, and reached out to shake his hand and said, "Merry Christmas."

He looked past me. From one of the trailers, a fat woman in a big red sweater walked outside, waiting for her little dog to squat and go to the bathroom. Another trailer door opened, and a man threw out a bucket of dirty water, heat steamed up off the gravel. Nearby, Padgett's '39 Lincoln sat with the hood open, its engine in pieces.

"So when do I have to let you know?"

"When you can."

"How 'bout now?"

"Now is good."

"This ain't about the reward."

I nodded.

"When I read about that fella dying and me not standing up. . . . It's hard to put into words."

"I understand, Mr. Padgett. You're standin' up now."

"Guess I am."

"Feels good, doesn't it?"

ON CHRISTMAS DAY, Thomas got duded up in his brand-new Roy
Rogers gear, complete with vest, hand-tooled belt with R.R. written in
studs, and a deluxe holster filled with a pair of toy six-shooters loaded
with caps. He'd already shot at Anne's cat four times, and that caused a
minor break in the peace. But she'd forgiven him and gone on outside
after breakfast to try out a pair of white J. C. Higgins roller skates and
say hello to a schoolmate who lived two doors down. Santa had also
brought Thomas a junior boxing set, and Joyce, as a joke, had bought
him a Happi Time service station set that came complete with plastic
figures of the attendants who worked the grease rack, platform, and
pumps. All this coming as a joke, because he liked to see me work at
the station more than sit behind a desk at the sheriff's office.

Joyce picked up one of the figures, eyed it, and looked back to me
and said, "The fella wears a hat. How come you didn't wear a matching hat?"

I'd given her a fourteen-karat watch I'd seen her eyeing at Kirven's,
and she'd bought me a Craftsman electric razor kit. While Anne
zipped around in our driveway on new skates and Thomas raised hell

in the backyard, I picked apart the kit and placed the contents on the coffee table.

"You see the mirror plugs in, too," Joyce said. "It has a small light."

I reached behind the chair where I sat, still in my robe, and plugged it in. "Well, I'll be." I studied my face in the reflection, seeing Joyce's chin resting on my shoulder, and she gave me a solid smile.

"How'd you ever land such a handsome man?" I asked.

"Lord knows, it was tough," she said. "So do you like what you see?"

LORELEI SHOWED UP JUST AFTER WE'D FINISHED UP A BIG Christmas dinner—Jack Black joining us while taking a break from the night patrol—and, as I opened the door, I realized I hadn't seen her since she'd been found half dead on the rocks. I'd heard she'd left town with Billy but never expected to see the girl in PC again. The surprise must've shown on my face, because she stepped back off the landing to the walkway and looked down at the ground, unable to speak.

The first thing I thought about after I invited her in, her declining and standing there shivering, her breath like smoke, was that her nose and under her eyes reminded me of a fighter with all that scar tissue. There was also a long scar that ran down half of her face that looked as if it had come from a knife but maybe from the sharp rocks.

"Come on in."

She wrapped herself with her arms, wearing nothing but a man's long dress shirt and pegged blue jeans. "I cain't," she said. "Billy's got trouble."

Jack was beside me now. After two more sentences from Lorelei, I nodded, and Jack moved for the car. I took the girl's arm and drew her inside.

Just then, Thomas popped up—still dressed as Roy—and aimed his gun at her. She jumped, holding her chest, and I grabbed the end of the barrel and pulled it down.

"Watch it there, partner."

With her head down and under my arm, she moved into the kitchen. "Joyce, this is Lorelei. How 'bout some supper?"

Joyce smiled, her arms elbow deep in suds, and looked back at me. She knew all about the girl. "Please join us," my wife said.

Not a minute later, we were in Jack's car, and I radioed into the office to Quinnie to call in some of the Guard boys.

"It's Casa Grande," I said. "Right off Opelika Road. That place that looks like the Alamo."

AN HOUR EARLIER, BILLY HAD DRESSED IN THE MIRROR AND combed his hair back with pomade he'd found in Reuben's medicine cabinet. He studied his eyes and steadied his hand as he'd practice going for the gun tucked in the small of his back. He'd imagine the skinny figure before him wasn't him at all but Johnnie Benefield, and he'd wait till Johnnie would ask him about his daddy's money, *Did you bring it?*, and Billy would say, *Sure*, and he'd empty his gun into Johnnie and drop the bastard in the dirt, right in the very place where he'd soiled Lorelei, Billy still seeing that hairy back and slabbed teeth in a jack-o'-lantern's grin.

Billy reached for a pack of Luckies and pulled on his daddy's two-tone leisure coat, covering up the gun at his back, and slipped in some bullets in the pocket. He studied himself again and practiced three times more to make sure the oversized coat wouldn't be a burden. But it wasn't a burden at all, and, each time, he saw the image of Johnnie dropping in the reflection behind him.

They'd come back for the money. He'd known about it for a couple weeks after finally reading his daddy's letter just outside Memphis. And Lorelei begged for them to never come back, but it didn't take long before they couldn't pay for breakfast one morning and that wrinkled letter in his pocket was already feeling like a hundred-dollar bill.

When they got to the farm, they found every piece of furniture upside down, his grandmother's pie safe turned to sticks, dresser drawers turned inside out, and before Billy could get to a hiding place Benefield was there. Benefield put a gun in Lorelei's mouth and gave Billy a phone number to call when he, as he said, "got his head straight."

That Christmas morning, after he'd watched Johnnie Benefield's taillights fade away down the dirt road, Billy had gone to the outhouse and pulled that knotted rope from the dark hole, six burlap bags tied hard, but pissed and shit on so many times that they'd turned black.

Lorelei begged him to leave.

They got as far as Notasulga, and he turned his daddy's Buick back. *He'll find us,* Billy had said. *Wherever we would go.*

Billy liked what he saw in the mirror, liked the way the coat made him feel bigger, liked the image of the cigarette in the corner of his mouth, and, before he walked away, he looked at himself a final time, trying to make his eyes grow slack and sleepy, trying to settle down that jackhammering in his chest.

THE GANG WAS ALL THERE. JOHNNIE BENEFIELD AND Moon, Clyde Yarborough—just two days out of Kilby on the only charges the grand jury could make—and two nigger boys they'd paid forty bucks apiece to join them. Six shotguns and a pint of Canadian blended sat on the bed. A deck of playing cards and a couple of nudie magazines.

"Let's drink to Bert Fuller," Johnnie said. "May he fuck the jury up the ass!"

Yarborough garbled out a no, or maybe a hell no, lifted up the bandanna on his face, and spit on the floor.

"No?" Johnnie asked. "You still blaming him? Well, he still deserves a drink. Everybody deserves a drink on Christmas. And to Phenix City, too! May that beaten old whore rise from the ashes."

"I got to take a shit," Moon said in that high-pitched, little-girl voice.

Johnnie thumbed back at the toilet in the back. "Moon will make this whole place smell like the elephant house at the zoo."

The phone rang and Johnnie answered it, smiling and nodding and cupping the receiver between his shoulder and his ear. "Yes, yes." He smiled some more. "Billy, I'm so damn glad we've come to a fucking civil agreement. You're a fine young man."

Johnnie lay down the receiver and looked over to the two niggers for hire. "You two boys get back to where I need you. Don't drink, don't piss, don't breathe. If the boy comes alone, we don't need you. But we all know he ain't got the goddamn sense. If a soul comes along with him, you wait till I raise my hands like this."

He raised his hands up in surrender.

"And you kill every sonofabitch that ain't me, Moon, or Mr. Clyde here. Understand?"

Mr. Clyde chortled out a laugh, his black eyes narrow, his breath smelling of dirty ashtrays and onions.

WE PARKED DOWN THE ROAD, BETWEEN THE OLD HILLBILLY Club and Veto's Trailer Park, and Jack opened the trunk and tossed me a 12-gauge, lifted another shotgun for himself, and then pulled out the Thompson and fitted on the round clip. He smiled and took a moment to relight a dead cigar in his mouth before slamming the trunk of the new Chevy.

About that time, another black Chevy drove up behind us and Quinnie got out, dressed in the same lightweight suit I'd bought him in September, with a star proudly pinned to his jacket. "You sure Benefield is in there?"

"That's the rumor," Jack said.

"Kill the lights, Quinnie," I said. He'd been so excited that he'd hopped out with the motor running and the headlights on. Pretty soon, two Army jeeps pulled up, four men in each, and I quickly updated them on the situation and what we expected to find.

"Wait till we see if the boy's in there," I said.

The guardsmen nodded and fanned out back of the stucco-and-tile units behind the big Casa Grande façade. The old motel probably seeing better days when car travel was a novelty, a place where Model Ts huddled up for the night and folks ate chicken dinners Mamma had packed herself. The road sign was missing several white bulbs, had been ever since I'd known the place, no one giving a damn to replace them.

In the parking lot, we'd spotted three cars. No one on desk duty, the motel closed down during the raids for running whores.

"Jack, would I hurt your feelings if I told you I hated guns?" I asked. "I never even liked to hunt."

"No kidding."

"No kidding."

"That .45 on your belt loaded?"

"Oh, yes."

BILLY DROVE RIGHT THROUGH THE CASA GRANDE PORTICO and parked right in the middle of the center lot, the stucco-and-tile units fanning out in a U shape. He shifted in his coat, feeling the gun on his spine, and outside let out a deep breath, clouding his eyes. When he popped the trunk, the money still let off an awful reek—even after being repacked—of being deep down in that shitter for months, and the smell about made him want to puke.

He grabbed the burlap bag, PURINA FEEDS printed on the side, and walked toward the only unit with the lights on in the entire place. He heard the sound of foot stomps and laughter.

Billy gritted his teeth and speeded up his walk, but, as he did, he tripped and the gun loosened from his back, slipping down his butt and down the leg of his saggy jeans. He stopped, looked around to see if anyone noticed, feeling the gun come to rest on the top of his shoe.

But as he bent down, the door opened and out walked Johnnie Benefield in a man's tank top and plaid pants and boots. He was eating an apple and ambled down to meet Billy, who stood up, not moving, that gun sliding over his shoe and down onto the gravel.

Johnnie just kept chomping on the apple, working it like a wheel in his mouth and then tossing it in the bushes, before shaking his head and reaching down to get Reuben's pistol.

"Well, I'll be goddamned," he said. "You brought me a Christmas present."

And then he yanked Billy by the neck, slapped the boy hard across the mouth, and tugged him to the door and then threw him in the room, the big bag of money in his right hand. "Man, it's colder than a Minnesota well-digger's ass."

Billy fell to the floor of the efficiency, looking up into the face of that fat bootlegger Moon. The fat man ate at an orange from a giant fruit basket set in the center of the room. He didn't say a word, just ate, and then took a drink from a whiskey bottle, warming himself by a gas heater.

Johnnie turned over the burlap bag and let the money snow out on the bed. He smiled and smiled as Billy wavered to his feet, inching backward to the door, before Johnnie said, "Where in the name of baby Jesus is the rest? This ain't all of it. It ain't all by a mile."

Moon got off the bed and set the orange on the nightstand with a thud. He unlatched his big overall and let the straps drop, pulling up his flannel shirt and mammoth stomach, telling Johnnie to bring the boy to him. He licked his lips as he used the flat of his hand to test the bed springs.

"It's all there was." Billy's voice shook.

"You know, Moon 'bout split your girlfriend in two. He's hung like a goddamn donkey. But I guess you'll figure that out."

He threw down an apple at Billy's feet. "Just bite down when it hurts," he said.

FROM THE OTHER SIDE, I WATCHED AS TWO NEGRO MEN moved from the shadows on top of two motel units with pistols in their hands and whispered back and forth to each other. We had four of the Guard boys right behind them, two more at the far end of the motor court and two with me and Jack. We told Quinnie to wait by the radio for when all hell broke loose, and the little man's face turned red with frustration, but he said, "Yes, sir."

The guardsmen had the pair of negroes in the sights of their rifles and could drop them in a second. They stood ready.

But then another door opened at the bottom of the motel's U and out walked Clyde Yarborough with a big .44 in his hand, looking around the empty motor court. He passed the blue Buick and circled around, eyes darting up to the negros and then back over to us. Not seeing us in shadows, he tilted his head like an animal.

That bandit bandanna covered his face as he moved forward, his feet crunching on the gravel lot. It started to sleet, and in the streetlight it looked like sharp little silver pins.

Yarborough got within maybe ten yards from us when we heard the scream of a child and his head quickly turned. He tucked the .44 back in his belt and yelled and pointed to the negroes on the roof, making noises with his destroyed mouth.

MOON WAS ON HIM, CRUSHING OUT ALL THE BREATH FROM Billy's lungs, the last sound being that of a scream, and Billy felt the sick flesh against his leg and the whispering weird voice in his ear, so high-pitched and sugar sweet it sounded like that of a little girl. Moon's breath was hot and old and smelled dead and cancerous, whispering to Billy, as he was pushed facedown, and calling him his little baby. All Billy could see was Johnnie Benefield laughing at him, sitting across from the iron bed in a chair and smoking a cigarette, coolly taking a sip of whiskey from a bottle. Billy's face felt as if it was about to explode from blood, unable to breathe or scream but just eyeing Johnnie, wanting to kill him so badly that he ignored Moon grunting on top of him, trying to motivate his weak flesh.

Johnnie pulled the cigarette from his mouth and said, smelling a pack of hundreds, "Why does this cash smell like assholes?"

WHEN YARBOROUGH POINTED, THE TWO NEGROES TURNED and spotted us, raising their pistols and squeezing out several shots before the guardsmen opened fire, hitting one direct, the back of his head bursting in the harsh white lights before he twirled and fell from the roof, and clipping the other, who scrambled and tried to crawl back in the shadows, his feet losing the roof tile under him like the shuffling of cards.

Jack hoisted up the Thompson in his arms and walked dead center into the motor court, calling out for Clyde Yarborough to drop his gun, but Yarborough didn't hesitate when he saw him, drawing and leveling the .44. The chatter of bullets from Jack's Thompson raked across him and kept him up in the air, in a marionette's dance, until Jack let go of the trigger, letting the man twirl and fall in a heap.

I kicked in the front door and found a fat bootlegger named Moon, his pants around his ankles, his tiny penis flaccid and stuck to his leg as he reached for a shotgun on the bed. As Billy crawled into a corner, he reached for the gun, too. As the fat man struggled for it, I blasted him three times with the sawed-off, splattering his grease and blood against the far wall. When Moon fell, Billy yelled, seeing Johnnie Benefield coming from behind the front door, a pistol pointed at me, smiling in the bright light as he crossed the door's threshold and jerked Billy off the bed, my gun on him and his on me.

He held us both there.

And I didn't breathe for half a minute, as he plucked Billy from that room, the barrel of his gun shifting from my face and onto the boy's neck, and he walked backward, me coming into the light, the sleet stinging my face, those small, sharp needles pinging me, as I moved slow down out of the motel unit and onto the gravel. The guardsmen out now, all guns on Johnnie, who crept back with the kid and moved to Reuben's baby blue Buick, smiling, holding the gun with one hand and saluting the guardsmen with the other.

He held Billy so tight that the boy's face had turned a bright bloody red.

I kept my gun on him and looked over to Jack, who did the same.

BILLY FELT FOR HIS CASE FOLDING KNIFE DEEP IN HIS pocket as he was tugged along on the gravel with the gun barrel up in his face. He reached for the knife, making a fist around it, Johnnie too caught up to see him or feel his movements. And with his thumbnail, Billy pried open that old pocketknife made of bone and steel, which had rested in his grandfather's pocket since before the turn of the century and in his father's pocket deep in the jungles of the Philippines, and now the old bone seemed to burn in his hand like a fire poker, steady, solid, warm.

He moved the knife to the side of his leg.

And just as Johnnie pulled open the door to the Buick and tried to push him inside, Billy Stokes jabbed that four-inch blade deep into Johnnie's cheek and the hands freed from around him and went for that sharp pain just as the blasts of shotguns and pistols and the short chatter of a machine gun rattled off like the final, deafening notes of those final sparks that light up the Fourth of July night.

I HELPED BILLY TO HIS FEET. HE WAS STILL TRYING TO breathe, and my ears rang as we moved from the car and Benefield, who was facedown in a puddle. The silence seeming electric and strange, with only the soft, subtle taps of sleet off the motel roof and the hood of the Buick.

"You okay?" I asked.

"Yeah, sure."

We walked over to Black and stood around Clyde Yarborough, who looked more natural in death than he had in life, curled into a C shape in the gravel. Jack knelt down and drew hard on his cigar. After he got a good burn, he reached over and tapped the ash into the giant O of what had been Yarborough's mouth.

He leaned in, whispered something in the dead man's ear, and stood up.

I felt as if I'd intruded on something and led Billy back to my squad car. We were soon met by an excited Quinnie who wanted to know about every shot.

"Ask Billy."

But Billy shook me off as I touched his shoulder. "Why didn't you let me kill Benefield? You had no right. You had no damn right."

WE DROVE WITH THE SUNSET behind us in that last leg from Birmingham, where we'd just watched Arch Ferrell be acquitted of murder. I can't say it wasn't expected. He'd already been acquitted in his vote fraud case, and, if he'd been acquitted in that, the motive fell flat. Fuller had been quickly tried before Arch and quickly convicted in the killing and sentenced to life in prison. And that spring of 1955, as we were headed home from Ferrell's trial, me and Joyce, and Quinnie in the backseat, Si Garrett was still institutionalized, with little hope of him returning to the state of Alabama anytime soon.

"I just don't get it," Quinnie said, behind us.

Joyce was driving. My window was down, and I smoked a cigarette while watching the ribbon of road cut through the countryside.

"It just don't make no sense," Quinnie said.

A mile later, he said: "If it don't beat all."

When he started to speak again, just as we hit the county line, the sun dropping like a big orange ball behind us in the rearview, I held up my hand. "Quinnie, we get the point. But that man won't ever hold office or practice law in the state of Alabama. I don't know what will happen to him. I guess the best we can do to Arch Ferrell is ignore him."

We rounded the corner into Phenix City, and I flicked my cigarette out the window.

"I just can't believe it," Quinnie said.

THAT SUMMER, I FOUND MYSELF IN PANAMA CITY BEACH, Florida, with two local deputies following up on a lead on Fannie Belle. She'd skipped town with charges against her, one of dozens who'd fled Phenix. I wore a light suit, crisp blue, with a white shirt, and I remember all the stares I got from the sunburned people as we rounded the pool with our guns and badges past the tiki bar and raft rentals and found the unit and knocked on the door.

When we didn't get an answer, the manager knocked again.

A hot wind blew off the beach, around the cool shadows of the first floor facing the parking lot.

The manager knocked again and then tried the key.

The room was empty. A sliding door facing the Gulf was open, the curtains fluttering in the breeze. I opened the bathroom and searched inside, only to find a used razor and some wet towels. On the night-stand, I saw an empty gin bottle and a dirty ashtray. Hearing the kids outside splashing around in the pool, that hot putter of wind in the curtains, there was no mistaking she'd been there only moments ago.

You could smell her perfume just as if she stood behind you, waiting to whisper in your ear.

I knew I'd always wonder where she went and what new name she'd taken. I wondered if the new men in her life would ever know anything about her.

The Gulf stretched out green and endless across the summer horizon.

I'D ALWAYS FOUND COMFORT BEING AROUND HORSES. I even liked working with plow mares on my father's farm, and there was a strong feeling of peace just watching them graze, standing around them and hearing their massive teeth reach into the ground and pull a clump of grass right out of the earth. The farm had been, and continued to be, for the years I remained sheriff, a sacred ground, a place where I could retreat and work. Even when Anne grew older and went off to college and Thomas had discovered cars and girls, I'd go out there alone and feed the geldings their sweet feed and hay, clean out their water tanks and talk to them. They liked to be talked to. It soothed them. It soothed me.

I needed it sometimes. Quinnie was right. Some things you couldn't wrap your head around.

Bert Fuller didn't spend life in prison.

He only spent ten years for good behavior and well-placed friends.

In 1965, he'd already been out two days when I heard he planned to return to Phenix City. That was also when I learned of our star witness, Cecil Padgett, and his fate out in Texas—killed when he fell from the open door of a train, not far from the town where the newspapermen said he'd become a drunk.

After the trial, Cecil and I had become friends. I even recommended him for a few jobs, and, later, when John Patterson became governor, replacing Jim Folsom, Cecil became Patterson's driver.

I didn't see him falling. I couldn't imagine it.

I saw Bert Fuller behind him, pushing him from an open door, destroying the man who had destroyed him, and riding the rails, the big locomotive chugging and turning on those hot steel rails, hammering like blood in those veins, all the way back to Alabama.

No one had to warn me that Fuller was coming for me.

I'd dreamed about it for ten years.

AFTER EVERY ELECTION, THE JOB BECAME EASIER. JOYCE
helped me run the books and keep the prison kitchen going. Quinnie
stayed with me for a short time, but Jack didn't last a year, trading the
slow pace of the new Phenix City for Atlanta, where he worked as a
detective for several years. Most of my deputies worked traffic stops
and stolen bicycles. We had some real excitement one time when someone was stealing tractors and hauling them away on flatbed trucks.
Most of the old racketeers had left for Biloxi or southern Tennessee,
where they'd become the foundation of what people later called the
Dixie Mafia.

Hoyt Shepherd stayed until he died an old man.

I'd see him every so often at the barbershop.

I broke in new deputies, studied the law all I could, and tried to
keep that slow-going pace.

We were in a heat wave when Fuller came back.

I stopped by a halfway house close to the railroad tracks and found
him sitting on the floor of the room listening to a Gene Autry 45. He
stood, embarrassed, but greeted me with a warm handshake like an
old friend.

I told him I didn't want any trouble.

And he spent the next forty minutes witnessing to me, quoting para-
bles from the Bible, casting himself as Phenix City's Prodigal Son.
When he'd finished, I asked him again about what had happened to
Mr. Patterson, telling him he didn't have a thing to lose now that he'd
served his time. I told him how much it would mean to the Pattersons
to know how their father died.

But his face was filled with ignorance and questions, and in a
soft child's voice he said, "I don't know any more 'an you what hap-

pened in that alley. I guess that's something we're all going to have to live with."

"You know I'm going to keep asking?"

Fuller nodded. "Say, you know what's showing at the Palace?"

"Bert, they tore that place down two years ago."

He looked sad but pumped my hand again as I left, and I drove away, heading out to the farm.

Two nights later, he made his move.

RAIN HIT THE TIN ROOF OF THE BARN, AND I HAD BOTH MY horses in. Old Braddock was still hanging on, his back sloped and teeth worn, and I had a new one, a sweet filly I'd bought from a man in Auburn. The zap of the electric storm in the bright blue daylight made them skittish and they shook their heads, their eyes wide. I soothed them with talk.

I put up some rope, coiling it in my hands, and went to close a back gate after letting them in. A long row of tiny white bulbs lit the interior of the barn but flickered and sputtered out with a harsh boom, lightning hitting not a mile from where I stood.

The ground shook. The horses raised up on their hind legs.

Without their bridles, I smoothed their rumps, and they turned and turned, wide-eyed, until they slowed in the cooling darkness of the storm.

He appeared as a shadow to me at the mouth of the barn. The storm moving away now, the thunder retreating and cracking from far away. Wind rocked the flypaper that hung from the rafters of the loft, and I didn't move, I just stood there, seeing the shadow man, and simply said, "Come on in, Bert."

But he didn't say anything, the dark shape shifting, studying me in the wide box of light. His hand disappeared for a moment and then reappeared with a pistol. He aimed the pistol at me without threats or words and drew a close bead down the sights.

The gun fired and fired again.

The shadow tilted and then fell back, trying to stand his ground, but losing a grip on the barn door and falling into the light, half man, half shadow.

One of my young deputies climbed down the loft ladder and walked toward Fuller, slowing as he grew close, making sure it was really him, and then he fired again. Twice more. Fuller in the mud, rain streaking across him, blood coming from his mouth. He fired twice more into the mud and blood.

I was outside with the deputy.

"I think he's dead now, Billy," I said.

He looked over at me, shaken awake from the dream.

"I want to be sure."

I looked down in the mud, Fuller's head sinking into the places that my horses had made soft with their hooves.

NOT LONG AFTER, BILLY AND I RODE THE TRAILS ON MY land, hearing the sounds of the bulldozers and earthmovers cutting Phenix City in half with a highway bypass to Columbus. We found a spot at my small pond to let the horses drink, calm and sweaty from the ride, and they felt gentle and tired as they filled themselves with cool water and we made our way back up that well-worn path to the barn.

"Did I tell you my wife was pregnant?"

"Must've slipped your mind," I said. "Her folks okay with y'all living here? Or they still want you in Atlanta?"

He shook his head. "They didn't know things had changed."

We were silent for a moment, just the sounds of hooves on earth, as we crested the hill.

"You like being a father?" Billy asked.

"Very much," I said.

I dismounted and walked back to my patrol car, pulling out a beaten cloth book that'd I'd found deep in our evidence locker and carried the great weight of it back to the barn, chaining the gate behind me.

"What's that?" Billy asked. He dismounted and tied the horse to a post.

I handed him the book and he flipped through all the pages, all the black-and-white photographs of all the girls and all their statistics and numbers that corresponded with the tattoos in their mouths.

He flipped through a few times and then stopped on one picture. He stared at it and then closed the book with a thump.

"Thinking about burning some of that old hay," I said. "Want to join me?"

Billy grinned, a tall, skinny man in his deputy uniform.

He helped me toss some of the old bales into a heap and I put my Zippo to the edge of them, the dry grass quickly catching and igniting in a rush of fire. Billy picked up the book and tossed it into the dead center of the bales. We stood there for a long while and watched it catch and burn, seeing some of the faces of all those lost girls from long ago curl and smolder and turn to nothing.

As we walked back to the horses, taking off their bridles and slipping the saddles from their backs, I asked, "Did you ever hear from Lorelei after she left?"

"A few times. I got postcards from North Carolina, and even one from New York. She never left an address. After a couple years, they just stopped."

"You ever get your daddy's Buick back?"

He shook his head.

"Or the money you cut from the Hoyt Shepherd job?"

"Wasn't much."

"Enough to start over."

"I guess."

From the damp earth, you could smell the last bits of the fire, dying and smoldering, and leaving the smell of fall on the wind.

ACKNOWLEDGMENTS

Background information provided by: Ed Strickland and Gene Wortsman, *Phenix City: The Wickedest City in America*; Margaret Anne Barnes, *The Tragedy and the Triumph of Phenix City, Alabama*; Alan Grady, *When Good Men Do Nothing: The Assassination of Albert Patterson*; the film and newsreel *The Phenix City Story*; the Albert Patterson murder trial transcripts; and files of the *Columbus Ledger*.

Nuria Chaparro, your constant friendship, support, and tireless replies to my questions were the foundation of this book. Thank you for introducing me to your father, the heroic Lamar Murphy. I'm better for knowing him.

Thanks to the entire Fussell family for the round of introductions in Phenix City and Columbus, Georgia. And to the Carson McCullers Center, for shelter while I researched this novel, and to Tim Chitwood at the *Ledger*, who went above and beyond to get me the Phenix City files.

For my two important friends in New York: Neil, wasn't that easy? You're a tough, demanding trainer. And I'm grateful for it. Esther, what can I say? You are the greatest agent of all time. I'm honored to know you.

A special thanks to two great writers: Elmore, the knock-out artist, for his continued wisdom, humbling example, and great work, and Bob Crais for a much-needed pep talk and brainstorming session.

Thanks to John Patterson, a man who lived this story, for giving me his valuable time and patient answers that meant so much. And to Joe Atkins, my great friend and brother in noir, who brought me back to Phenix City and showed me a story that lived in my family's backyard.

For all of those who provided support or took me back to the wickedest days of Phenix City, thank you: Jim Cannon, Charley Frank Bass, Jan Shepherd, Rankin Sherling, Ray Jenkins, Billy Winn, John Lupold, Pete Hanna, Jere Hoar, and my boxing trainer, Larry Greene.

Norwood Kerr and Rickie Brunner at the Alabama Department of Archives and History opened their doors and made me feel right at home. And Jake Reiss, who has been pushing me to write about my home state for some time—Jake, here's that Alabama book!

For my family: Mom, Charlie, Paige, boys, and all manner of in-laws. And to my grandfather, Bogue Reuben Miller, who knew most everyone in this book but died too early to tell his secrets.

As always, thank you, my brother, Tim Green, for your never-ending loyalty and friendship and pushing me in the last round. And to Angela, my beautiful, brilliant, wonderful wife, the best friend a man could have.

BEHIND THE STORY

When *White Shadow* was released two years ago, I received several letters from family members connected to that true story. Sons and daughters of old detectives. Relatives of long-deceased hit men and mafia bosses. One such letter came from the son of a Florida tough by the name of Johnny "Scarface" Rivera, who was upset I'd put some of his dad's exploits back in print.

He offered the taunt: "I see you're from Alabama. Why don't you go back there and write something about your own family? The Deep South has no shortage of crooks."

Okay, Mr. Rivera. Not a bad idea.

Sometimes the best stories live in your own backyard. With the novel you now hold in your hands, that's definitely the case. My sixth novel is, surprisingly, the first about my home state of Alabama (although Birmingham bookseller Jake Reiss has been bugging me to write an Alabama book for years).

I was born in Alabama, with deep ties to the state. My mother's father was an engineer for the highway department. My dad's father was a farmer. And Phenix City, Alabama, was just another town.

That was the story, anyway. In typical Southern fashion, unpleasant subjects were not discussed.

I first learned about Phenix City while in high school, about twenty miles away, in neighboring Lee County. We cut through the small town on the banks of the Chattahoochee River on the way to shop in Columbus, Georgia. The small town's Central High School was a regular on our football schedule.

As a cinema-obsessed teen, I ran across a listing for *The Phenix City Story* in a guidebook to old movies and laughed at the entry on a film noir about "The Wickedest City in America." Sleepy Phenix City, with its strip malls and dead downtown, had little wicked about it. Surely, this couldn't have been the same place. But it was.

Years later, when I turned to Phenix City as the setting for my next book, I wanted to learn every detail of the place. I waded through thousands of pages of court records, old newspapers, and historic photographs, and interviewed the surviving players of the true drama. One of those interviews was with John Patterson, whose father was gunned down after being elected the state's attorney general on an anti-vice ticket.

I read every book. I watched old newsreels. I visited Phenix City a lot. Beneath the modern, sleepy veneer, I saw Phenix City as it once was—populated with whores, bootleggers, gamblers, con men, safecrackers, and pornographers. Servicemen from nearby Fort Benning were routinely shot or stabbed and dumped into the Chattahoochee River. Babies of prostitutes were put up for sale to the highest bidder.

Any honest citizen of the town—of which there were plenty—who complained against the Machine was threatened or killed. One man who protested the rigged elections had his home dynamited.

This was a foreign world to me, a world far more dangerous and violent than even Tampa in the 1950s. This was not the Alabama I knew in the 1980s and '90s. But I soon learned it was an Alabama that wasn't foreign to my family. Both of my grandfathers had ties to illegal business in the state.

During the 1940s and '50s, my mother's father raised his family in Alexander City, Alabama, and worked for the state highway department. I only knew him as an old man with a great sense of humor. I heard stories that he'd often drunk Jack Daniel's with Hank Williams when the famous singer would visit a next-door neighbor who worked as a disc jockey.

But according to my family, his job went far beyond just designing the highway system. His territory included Phenix City, and for many years he worked as a go-between for Governor "Big Jim" Folsom, the flawed demagogue of Southern politics who features heavily in this story.

On a fishing trip with her father as a child, my mother remembers a car pulling up to the secluded fishing hole. She watched large satchels of what she'd later realized was cash being piled into their car.

The highway system was big money—knowing where new roads were being built could make a property owner very rich. In the early 1950s, my grandfather's business often took him to the epicenter of the action—Phenix City—where he surely crossed paths with some of the biggest players in state politics at the fish camps, where back deals were famously done among heaps of fried catfish and hush puppies.

He perhaps even stumbled upon a recipe created by Dad's father.

For many years, I was told he had been a simple farmer who'd spent his life raising cotton and corn. Later, I learned it was mostly corn—the main ingredient in moonshine.

This grandfather ran a large still in a small town in western Alabama, not far from the Mississippi line. His sons worked as drivers, running to every corner of Alabama—from Tuscaloosa to Mobile and across to Phenix City—in souped-up cars with special shocks to hide the heavy load in the trunk.

They ran with their lights off on back highways, evading cops and rival bootleggers. At ten years old, even my aunt drove a sedan as a scout while my grandfather moved the still with his tractor. My father was the only child who refused to work the 'shine trade, instead focusing on sports, leaving his small town on a football scholarship that would later lead him to the NFL.

The tarnished, illegal family history was something always discussed in whispers. But for a crime novelist? It's a point of pride. For years, I stayed away from my home state in my storytelling, but this novel—*Wicked City*—brings it all back into focus.

Corruption is timeless. For me, the story of the rise and fall of Phenix City is the ultimate Alabama story. Fifty years have passed since Phenix City came tumbling down, but the legacy of that age continues to haunt the state in other ways.

One recent governor was found guilty of pocketing $200,000 during his term. Another is serving time in a federal prison for racketeering and taking bribes. My own university's academic integrity has been damaged by political abuse.

There is the natural tendency to dismiss the past as an unpleasant memory. But storytelling often brings out those timeless truths about where we all come from, whether it's connected to our family or not.

With *Wicked City*, I'm laying out the plain, unvarnished truth of my home state and family history. Many of the characters are real. One of the leads is a composite based on both of my grandfathers. The sordid, violent details of the major events are all too true.

For all of you who steered me back to Alabama, both with hope and taunts, my thanks. As a teenager, I never imagined that one of the best crime stories of the twentieth century happened just a few miles down the road.

Turn the page for a preview
of Ace Atkins' new novel

DEVIL'S GARDEN

Available in hardcover from G. P. Putnam's Sons!

San Francisco
September 1921

WITH HIS TWO BEST BUDDIES and his movie star dog, Roscoe Arbuckle drove north in a twenty-five-thousand-dollar Pierce-Arrow that came equipped with a cocktail bar and a backseat toilet. Roscoe was a big man, not as fat as he appeared in those two-reel comedies that had made him famous in which he wore pants twice his size, but portly nonetheless. His eyes were a pale light blue, the transparent color of a newborn, and his soft, hairless face often reminded moviegoers of a child. A two-hundred-and-sixty-pound child stuck in all kinds of bad situations where "Fatty" Arbuckle, as he was known to America, would dress up like a woman, nearly drown, or sometimes get shot in the ass.

As they hugged the rocky, sunny coast of northern California, Roscoe had sweet thoughts of his new three-million-dollar Paramount contract and a weekend with ever-flowing Scotch and endless warm pussy.

His dog, Luke, who now earned three hundred a week, hung his head out the window and soon sniffed the fetid air off San Francisco Bay, while in back, Roscoe's buddies Lowell and Freddie smoked cigars, played cards, and poured more whiskey for the chauffeur, who hadn't touched the wheel since Los Angeles. And soon that big Pierce-Arrow glided down Market Street, passing cable cars on the way up the hill, and toward the Ferry Building, before curving with a light touch of the brakes into Union Square and the St. Francis Hotel.

Roscoe pulled up under a portico, honking the horn and tossing the keys to the doorman, and heard whispers of "Fatty" and "Fatty Arbuckle," and he smiled and winked and took a few pictures with Luke for the newspapers before doffing his chauffeur's cap and checking into the twelfth floor.

"Luke's hungry," Roscoe said, relaxing with a plop into a red velvet sofa. "Order up a steak."

"For a dog?" Fred asked.

"For me and the dog. Make it two."

"What about gin?"

"Use the telephone, have 'em send up whatever you like. And a Victrola. We got to have a Victrola."

Crates and crates of bootleg gin and Scotch whiskey appeared in the suite as if by magic, carried in on the strong backs of bellhops, and Roscoe peeled off great gobs of money and placed it into their palms. The men ordered ice and table fans and opened up the windows as pitchers of fresh-squeezed orange juice arrived for gin blossoms. The Victrola was wheeled in on a dolly with a crate of 78s and Fatty selected James Reese Europe and the 369th U.S. Infantry "Hell Fighters" Band playing "St. Louis Blues." And the music came out tinny and loud and patriotic and festive at the same time and Roscoe sweated a bit as he moved with it. He cracked open another window looking down upon Union Square, feeling a breeze off the San Francisco Bay, hearing the sounds of the cable cars clanging, and spotting a crowd gathered down on Geary.

They were looking up at the perfect blue sky, hands shielding their eyes from the sun, and for a moment Roscoe thought the word must've spread he'd come to town. But he heard a noise from a roof, a motor, and one of the bellhops, now wheeling in a cart filled with silver platters of steaks—Luke licking his chops as he sat in a velvet chair—said there was a circus man about to ride his motorcycle over a tightrope.

Roscoe smiled and took his drink up to the roof just as the man, dressed in leather, with helmet and goggles, a woman beside him in a sidecar, revved off on a line of ridiculously narrow wire crossing over the people on the street, the paper hawkers and the newsboys and the dishwashers and the cooks, and the crowd whistled and clapped and yelled, their hearts about to explode from the excitement.

And Roscoe took a big swig of Scotch and clapped and applauded and yelled down to the crowd, the newsboys taking a shot of the famous film star cheering on the acrobat.

Roscoe walked to the hotel's ledge and peered down, pretending to test the line and pantomiming a test walk, and then waved his hands off from the wire, and everyone yelled. All the dishwashers and maids and raggedy kids on the street. And that made Roscoe Arbuckle feel good, as he returned to room 1220 and asked his friend Fred to fetch up some women.

He twisted himself into a pair of striped pajamas and put on a silk robe and knew this was going to be a fine vacation, not planning on leaving the room till they carried him out. He cranked up the Victrola as far as it would go, playing his new favorite, Marion Harris singing "A Good Man Is Hard to Find."

As he waited for the party to come to him, Roscoe cut up Luke's steak and placed the silver tray on the floor, rubbing the nubbed ears of his old friend.

SAM HAMMETT HAD CASED THE OLD SLUMP-BACKED ROAD-house for two nights, following up on a forty-dollar payoff to a San

Quentin snitch named Pinto about the whereabouts of "Gloomy" Gus Schaefer. A few weeks back, Schaefer's boys had knocked off a jewelry store in St. Paul, and the Old Man had sent him out to this beaten, nowhere crossroads just outside Vallejo to make sure the information they got was good. It was night, a full moon, and from the protective shadow of a eucalyptus tree Sam watched the sequined girls with painted lips and their rich daddies in double-breasted suits. They stumbled out onto the old porch and to their Model Ts and Cadillacs, while poor men in overalls would wander back down the crooked road.

Two of the Schaefers' black Fords sat close to the rear porch, his gang upstairs laughing and playing cards, their images wobbly through the glass panes. Schaefer himself had appeared twenty minutes ago, Sam knowing instantly it was him, with the hangdog face and droopy eyes, leaning out an upstairs window, checking out the moon and stars, before taking off his jacket and resuming his place at the card table.

Sam craned his head up to the window and shook his head.

He found a foothold under the second-story porch and climbed, careful not to rip a suit he couldn't afford in a month's pay, and shimmied up a drainpipe, finding purchase on the rail, and hoisted himself over the banister with a thud.

He breathed slow, trying to catch his breath and feeling that wet cough deep in his throat. He tried to silence the hacking with a bloodied handkerchief.

Lying close to the windowsill, he could see the figures and hear them now, every word, as they talked about everything but the heist. Mainly about a batch of hooch loaded up in one of the Fords for a delivery to a tong in Chinatown named Mickey Wu.

One of the boys had a girl in a short skirt on his knee and bounced her up and down like a child. She clapped and laughed as the boy wiggled a poker chip over his knuckles.

Sam coughed again and bit into the handkerchief to silence himself. His hands shook as he righted himself on the railing, sitting there for ages, maybe an hour, before the conversation turned to another meeting, somewhere in Oakland, and a trade with Gloomy Gus's wife.

Sam leaned in and listened, thinking about who the hell would've married a fella like Gloomy Gus, and then there was a small crack. The slightest splitting of wood that sounded like warming ice.

Sam held his breath, unsure what had happened, and reached for the railing.

Then he heard a larger crack, and within seconds the entire porch fell away from the roadhouse. Sam tried to hold on to the drainpipe, keeping the entire rickety affair up in the air for a few moments, enough that he steadied himself and got some air back in his lungs, but then the porch leaned far away and crumbled like a tired fighter into a solid, violent mess.

The Schaefer gang was on him before he could get to his feet. They extended their revolvers down as he lay on his back. The air had gone out of him like a burst balloon.

Four of them, including Gus, stared down at him. He tried to catch a breath.

"Hello, Gus."

"Shut up," Gus said.

"Sure thing."

"You the cops?"

"I have some business."

"What business?"

"Diamonds," Sam said, two men pulling him to his feet as he dusted off the pin-striped suit. He tried to look annoyed at the dirt on his elbows while two of the boys poked guns into his ribs, another frisking him and finding the little .32.

Someone had hit the headlights on a Model T and Sam turned his head and squinted. Schaefer nodded thoughtfully, checking out Sam, with the shock of white hair and the young face and the wiry, rail-thin frame.

"In times like these," Sam said, coughing, "a man can't be too careful."

Schaefer's droopy eyes lightened. He smiled.

Sam smiled back. A crowd started to form on the roadhouse's porch. The tinny sounds of the piano player started again.

"Somebody shoot this bastard," Schaefer said.

"Now, Gus."

"Don't make a mess," Schaefer said. "Put down a blanket or something first. We'll dump him in the bay."

They brought Sam upstairs, tied him to a ladder-back chair, stuck a handkerchief in his mouth, and locked him in a broom closet. He heard the men walk away and waited until he heard laughter and poker chips again to try to work his hands from the knots.

HER NAME WAS BAMBINA DEL MONTE.

Her name was Maude Delmont.

Her name was Bambina Maude Delmont Montgomery. Hopper-Woods, if you count the last two.

Her last husband, Cassius Clay Woods, was a real screw. He hadn't known she was still married to the Hopper fella and was still sending her sap letters about eternal love and even little poems he'd written, really horrible ones about her eyes being like the sky and her skin the color of milk. Her eyes were black, her hair was black, and she had her father's dark Italian skin. Who was this guy trying to fool? But that's what happened to a man who'd slipped a vise on your finger and still didn't get into your drawers.

It was after hours at Tait's Café, a speakeasy on O'Farrell, and as usual Al was late. Paddle fans worked away the smoke that rose from marble-topped tables where couples sat in little wiry chairs. There was a big stage, but the stage was bare except for a placard announcing A SPRIGHTLY AND DIVERTING ENTERTAINMENT INTERSPERSED WITH GUEST DANCING.

She ate ice cream and drank bourbon, mixing the two a bit, and hadn't a clue on how she was going to be paying if Al didn't show up with some cash. He was the one who drove her from Los Angeles along with the girl, the whole way bragging how they'd soon be dining in Paris on a king's budget.

But Al Semnacher didn't look much like a king when he walked through the alley door of the speakeasy. He looked more like a god-damn rube, with his graying hair, low hairline, and horn-rimmed glasses. A guy who'd stutter if his hand touched your tit.

"Anyone ever tell you that you look like a rube?" she asked. "Why don't you clean your glasses now and again?"

"He's here."

"Who?"

"The mark."

Maude rolled her eyes. "Just pay the tab and let's fly. 'The mark'? You never worked a con in your life."

"What's that?"

"Bourbon and ice cream."

He wrinkled his nose, making him look like a spoiled-rotten kid smelling something he didn't like.

"It's good. Want some?"

"It's gone."

"So it is," said Maude. "Say, your girl doesn't exactly look like her pictures."

"The nightie shots or the one from *Punch of the Irish*?"

"Both," Maude said. "She's gotten fat."

Al Semnacher leaned back into the chair and drummed his little fingers. He readjusted his thick, dirty glasses and leaned in, speaking in his little voice: "She needs money and we need her."

"And she'll stick with the script?"

"A variation on the Engineer's Daughter. But it's a long con."

"I'm glad you listen," Maude said, thumping her fist on the table. "But, Al?"

"Yeah."

"Let me do the thinkin' in this relationship."

Al fiddled with the long spoon, dabbing out just a teaspoon of the melted ice cream. He winked before he slipped the spoon into his mouth and said, "I like your hair."

"Do you, now? You don't think I look like a boy?"

"With those knockers that'd be kind of tough."

Maude reached down and hefted those big boobs on her skinny frame and asked, "She'll get us in?"

"She's been knowin' ole Fatty for years now. His pecker will get hard just hearin' her name. Trust me."

Maude met Al's eyes and she smiled, keeping the contact.

"You have balls, Al. No brains. But a big set of 'em."

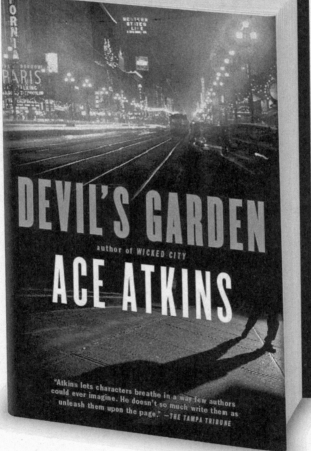

Coming Soon in Trade Paperback

WHITE SHADOW

by

Ace Atkins

Tampa, Florida, 1955: a city pulsing with Sicilian and Cuban gangsters, cigar factories, sweet rum, and violence. The bludgeoning death of a retired kingpin known as White Shadow sends the city into a tailspin, with cops, reporters, and his former associates all scrambling to discover the truth behind his death.

For Charlie Wall, the White Shadow, had his secrets—and those secrets could destroy a criminal empire and ignite a revolution.

"[Ace Atkins] can write rings around most
of the names in the crime field."

—Elmore Leonard

"Classic Florida noir…Atkins has done a
superb job of re-creating old Tampa, a place
whose underworld was as dangerous and
debauchedas Chicago's in its prime."

—Carl Hiaasen

penguin.com